W9-BNN-409

Burning Shadows

By Chelsea Quinn Yarbro from Tom Doherty Associates

BURNING SHADOWS

A NOVEL OF THE COUNT SAINT-GERMAIN

Chelsea Quinn Yarbro

A TOM DOHERTY ASSOCIATES BOOK

NEW YORK

This is a work of fiction. All of the characters, organizations, and events portrayed in this novel are either products of the author's imagination or are used fictitiously.

BURNING SHADOWS: A NOVEL OF THE COUNT SAINT-GERMAIN

Copyright © 2009 by Chelsea Quinn Yarbro

All rights reserved.

A Tor Book
Published by Tom Doherty Associates, LLC
175 Fifth Avenue
New York, NY 10010

www.tor-forge.com

Tor® is a registered trademark of Tom Doherty Associates, LLC.

Library of Congress Cataloging-in-Publication Data

Yarbro, Chelsea Quinn, 1942–
    Burning shadows : a novel of the Count Saint-Germain / Chelsea Quinn Yarbro. — 1st ed.
        p. cm.
    "A Tom Doherty Associates book."
    ISBN 978-0-7653-1982-1
    1. Saint-Germain, comte de, d. 1784—Fiction.   2. Vampires—Fiction.   I. Title.
PS3575.A7B87 2009
813'.54—dc22

                                                                            2009034661

First Edition: December 2009

Printed in the United States of America

0 9 8 7 6 5 4 3 2 1

For
Christine Sullivan

with additional nods and catnip to

Crumpet,
Butterscotch,
and
Ekaterina the Great,
who helped whether I needed it or not

The Huns set all the huts and barns outside the walls afire shortly before sunset, then rode around the town walls, firing arrows, many of them deep-barbed, some of them aflame, into the town.

In spite of our attempts to strike them down from the top of our walls, we had little success against them, for the firelight and smoke turned the mounted warriors into burning shadows, and we could not see them clearly for long enough to take good aim at them.

> Gregorius Mirandus, *Secondary Praetor of Mursella,*
> Report on an attack near Aquincum, May 441

Author's Note

Until the rise of Attila (pronounced, despite all you have heard to the contrary, AH-teel-lah), the Huns had been just another one of the many groups of barbarians moving toward Europe through what are now the Crimea, Ukraine, Romania, Bulgaria, Hungary, the Carpathian and the Balkan Mountains. They were known as raiders and looters, no better and no worse than many others but for their persistence. Although the stirrup had not yet been invented, the Huns had superior saddlery that gave them a significant advantage against the divided Roman Empire in combat. The Huns who did not ride traveled by tall carts, and those who did, did so on sturdy steppe ponies, bringing their flocks of goats and sheep and their herds of ponies with them, looking for undisputed pastureland. To support their westward expansion, they hired out as mercenaries to the newly flourishing Byzantine (Eastern Roman) Empire, particularly in its remoter outposts where many ambitious Constantinopolians preferred not to serve; in general they were well regarded by their Byzantine employers, and often achieved high rank as well as a generous portion of any spoils they gained while in Byzantine service. Compared to what the Vandals were doing in Spain, North Africa, and Italy, the Huns before Attila had been hardly more than an annoyance, worth the inconvenience of occasional raids so long as they continued to fill the distant Byzantine ranks as mercenaries.

Recent discoveries have revealed that the Huns were more ethnically mixed than originally thought; some had blue or gray eyes, and many of them had brown or reddish hair, not unlike the mysterious mummies found in western China. Apparently they began as nomadic herders in the Asian Steppes; certainly their early style of fighting was based on their herding, rounding up their opponents with cavalry and picking them off with arrows.

Attila changed all that, taking on the conquest-intentions of the Romans, with the purpose of establishing an empire that would reach from the North Sea to the Middle East. Following in the footsteps of his uncle, who had sought to gain political and economic control of the Carpathian region as well as permanent military conquests there, Attila intended to gain dominance of as much of Europe as he could. In the nearly twenty years from the time he murdered his brother Bleda (around 433–34) and assumed total leadership of his people until his death (453), Attila was the absolute authority for the Huns; under him they became a formidable army, preying on the remnants of the Roman Empire. Rome itself was still recovering from the sacking given to the city by Alaric the Goth in 410, and had lost a great many of the Legions as a result of Alaric's conquest.

The high mobility of the mounted Huns gave them an advantage against the better-trained but less flexible and largely infantry Roman Legions, which were already stretched thin fighting the Vandals, the Longobards, and the Goths, as well as being less willing to undertake protracted campaigns due to reduced wages and limited arms and matériel. At the height of his power (447–452), Attila had taken military control from central Gaul to Persia, from Serbia to Poland. Once he died, it took less than two years for the Hunnic Empire to fall apart.

Huns were only one of the many problems confronting the Roman Empire, East and West. In the three centuries since its maximum expansion, the Roman Empire had been losing ground steadily to various barbarian peoples; even parts of the Empire that were still nominally Roman were in actuality fiefdoms of barbarian groups who encouraged the Roman presence because Romans improved trade, maintained financial continuity, and honored standards of exchange, weights, and measures. The Byzantine Emperor continued the Roman practice of appointing non-Roman regional guardians for borderland territories to continue Western Roman policies after the Romans and Byzantines were officially gone from the edges of the Empire. Much of what had been the Province of Dacia in what are now Hungary and Romania had been lost to the Germanic Gepidae, the Ostro (Eastern) Goths, and Visi (Western) Goths, who in turn were being pushed west by Avars, Alans, and Huns coming in from Central Asia.

As I have mentioned before, in *Blood Games*, at the suggestion of my editor, I set up the names of the fictional characters along present-day name order—personal name, family name, clan name (Atta Olivia Clemens), instead of the Roman order: personal name, clan name, family name (Atta Clemens Olivia)—but by the time of this novel there had been considerable shifts in Roman nomenclature traditions, and only the oldest aristocratic families in the Western Roman Empire kept to the old personal-clan-family order.

By 400 CE, while Rome itself was being hard-pressed by the Goths, the Hungarian plains and most of the Carpathian Mountains had fallen under the control of the Gepidae, one of the Germanic tribes driven down from the north toward the Black Sea, and the might of the Roman Empire in the East, which was increasingly separate from the Roman Empire in the West, despite continuing high-flown rhetoric about unity. During most of the fifth century CE, exact boundaries and territorial borders in the region were far from fixed. The Gepidae seized most of the Roman towns and camps in the former Province of Dacia, but left a few larger installations and strongholds to the remaining Romans as a means of bolstering the region's defenses and to ensure ongoing trade with major commercial centers from Hispania (Spain) to Gaul (France, Belgium, and western Germany) to Carthago (northern Africa). Most of the Germanic tribes were structured along kinship-and-clan alliances as well as complex obligations arising from issues of honor and vengeance. These Germanic societies lacked the infrastructure of Roman governance, with its emphasis on civil order, standardizations, and laws, which made early Germanic society far more difficult to preserve over time than the Roman was, and which is why over time much of what was Roman was absorbed into the various Germanic societies.

By 435, much of both parts of the Roman Empire were officially Christian—sufficiently so that conflicts had arisen within the Christian communities about issues of Christian dogma and the nature of heresies. Most liturgy was not yet fixed, and the titles and structures of the Churches, Roman and Greek, were still in flux. Yet paganism of various kinds, and other religions, hung on throughout the two portions of the Empire. Mithraism was popular with soldiers; so popular, in fact, that many of the hero stories of Mithras were taken over by the Christians and told about Jesus, such as being born at the Winter Solstice of a virgin mother, persecuted by corrupt officials, killed for the benefit of all mankind, and resurrected at the Vernal Equinox. Islam was still two centuries in the future, yet in addition to Mithraism, Zoroastrianism flourished in the Middle East, especially in Persia. Coptic Christians in northern Africa were increasingly forced away from Mediterranean ports by the Christianized Vandals, and down into what is now southern Egypt and Ethiopia, where they remain to this day. Mediterranean Christianity, in theory cohesive, was in fact fiercely divided between the Orthodox (Byzantine Rite) and the Catholic (Roman Rite) Churches. And within the Orthodox Church, there was an increasing dispute as to whether the nature of Jesus was more divine or more human, arguments that led to riots, slaughter, and persecution by each sect of the other.

As the Roman Empire continued to break apart, those territories near the fracture-points tended to be left to fend for themselves against invaders, since the intense political rivalry between East and West inclined the military to avoid actions in areas where Empire divisions were most acute, and where they might be at risk from the very folk they were supposed to protect from harm. The Eastern and Western Roman response to the early campaigns of Attila tended to be relegated to local military garrisons, often composed of barbarian mercenaries, who often as not defected to the Huns; by the time the Western Roman Empire awoke to the danger Attila represented, he was raging through central Europe and northern Italy. The reputation of the Huns was so frightful that many towns and cities in Europe bankrupted themselves to prepare to defend against Hunnic armies that never arrived.

In the first century BCE, Julius Caesar had reformed the Roman calendar, but by the 430s, it was already running a little slow again, and there was a degree of discrepancy between the Western and Eastern calendars. For the sake of this book, the calendar is solidly based on the modern calendar, the seasons and dates balanced with a leap year that makes a more regularized progression of years. Whenever possible, the dates are given in terms of proximity to solstices and equinoxes, which was a common practice at that time.

For those non-Roman guardians appointed in former Roman provinces, there was more responsibility than authority in their offices, but without such men, the Roman Empire erosion would have been more catastrophic, and barbarian conquests more total. By setting up a system that allowed the advancement of responsible foreigners, the Eastern and Western Romans were able to avoid the burdens of dealing with disputed regions, and provided a wonderful scapegoat for any corrosion of already reduced Roman authority in areas that were no longer actual provinces. In addition, the Christianization of the various barbarian groups would have been markedly less than it was had the Roman Empire not become officially Christian under Constantine. The eventual development of Europe as a specific entity would probably have taken much longer to occur without the cohesion of Christianity. It can also be argued that when the Church became a political/military power in the West, it opened the door to widespread corruption and influence-peddling, even while it extended its authority into all aspects of European life, which proved both disastrous and beneficial through the Dark Ages and the Medieval Era. Personal rights and property rights that were the hallmark of Imperial Rome (especially as regards

the rights of women and slaves, and the upward mobility of freed-
men and freemen) gave way to Christian dogma and a policy of re-
pression and fixedness that defined and supported the religious status
quo. One of the Roman Church's earliest political/military acts was
the bribe Pope Leo I paid to Attila to take his typhus-stricken army
and leave Rome; that act set the Roman Church firmly on the path
that led to the politicization of the institution; it is a path that many
sects of Christianity follow to this day.

Thanks are due to a number of people who supplied needed information for this book: to Thomas Byrne for his material on the split
of the Eastern and Western Roman Empires; to Emily Cummins
for the loan of two texts on the barbarian invasions, and for filling in
some regional gaps for me; to Paul Gonsalves, S.J., for sharing his
vast knowledge of early Christianity, including liturgies and Church
hierarchical structures; to George Hope for access to a raft of fasci-
nating, if spotty, records of the deurbanization of the Roman Empire, the decline of the Roman courts, and the development of
protofeudalism in border regions of the Empire; to Eric Hunter for
providing much insight into the rise of Byzantium; to Perry and
Genevieve Ognissanti for wonderful references on language drift
and regional dialects of the fifth century, which combined elements
of Byzantine Greek, vulgate Latin, and Germanic dialects, as well as
coming up with Rotlandus Bernardius' occasional garbling of Imperial Latin; to Diane V. Razelton for the loan of her thesis on the
development and collapse of Attila's armies; to Beatrice Tully for
providing her translations of Greek documents of the period; and to
Hal Wainwright for delineating conflicting versions of fluctuating
borders from eastern Europe into the Balkans. Errors in the text are
my own and should not be attributed to these most helpful people.

On the publishing side of the ledger, thanks are due to my
agent, Irene Kraas, for her staunch support of this series; to Tor and
my longtime editor, Melissa Singer; to the incomparable Wiley
Saichek, who handles so much of my online promotion; to Paula

Guran, the designer and webmaster for ChelseaQuinnYarbro.net; to Lindig Harris (lindig17@gmail.com) for her newsletter *Yclept Yarbro*; to the Lord Ruthven Assembly and the ICFA for their continuing enthusiasm; to Elizabeth Miller of the Canadian chapter of the Transylvanian Society of Dracula and *Dracula* expert; to Sharon, Stephanie, Libba, Brian, Steve, and Maureen for their sharp eyes for errors of all sorts; to Delilah Crosby, Jim Estrander, and Corrie Nahum, the recreational readers for this book; to Alice, Megan, Peggy, Charlie, Gaye, Lori, and Marc for useful feedback; to Peter and David in England; to RC for being RC; to my redoubtable and doughty attorney, Robin A. Dubner, who watches over Saint-Germain's legal welfare; to the book-dealers who have done so much to sustain the series for three decades; and to Saint-Germain's faithful readers, without whom the tales would not continue. On to #24.

CHELSEA QUINN YARBRO
Berkeley, California
9 January, 2008

PART I

ATTA OLIVIA CLEMENS

*T*ext of a letter from Demetrios Maius, merchant of the Porolis-ensis region of the old Province of Dacia, to Gnaccus Tortulla, Praetor Custodis of Viminacium in the Province of Moesia, written in Latin vulgate with fixed ink on parchment and carried by Es-ephanos Stobi, private courier for Dom Feranescus Rakoczy Sanctu-Germainios, regional guardian of Apulum Inferior, in the company of Maius' fleeing family members; delivered in ten days.

Ave, Praetor Custodis Gnaccus Tortulla: may God and the old gods hold you in their favor. On your recommendation, we have appealed to the Goths who now rule in the southeastern quarter of the old Da-cian region, seeking protection for those of us who are Romans still living here, from the increasing ferocity of the Huns; the small raiding parties of three decades past are still growing in numbers, and in-creasingly they are forming more extensive fighting companies. More than continuing their search for grazing lands, they are determined to hold the land they have over-run as their conquest rather than passing on to broader pastures as they have done before, unless this is a ploy to drive the last of the Roman settlements away from these mountains so that they will only have to fight the Gepidae and Goths. We have lost the good-will of the region, for it's said that the Huns follow the old roads to settlements and towns, as merchant-travelers do, and these are all Roman.

If you will not provide us some relief from these Huns, and main-tain some level of military presence around us, we must flee or die. Al-ready one in five of our people is gone, and those numbers are steadily

increasing as the Huns become a stronger force. The Gepidae are occupied with protecting their own clans, drawing in to their territories,
setting up patrols and guards, and are in no position to offer us any
protection. There are more than thirty merchants in this region, and
all of us have the same risks, so it will be wise if we bring our causes
together and through bargaining as a group, ensure our protection
and the preservation of our stock-in-trade. We may also enlist other
Romans remaining in this region in building up fortresses and
strengthening towns.

Roma is far away, to be sure, and Constantinople's Generals are
unwilling to risk their fighting men by taking action against the Huns
while they have employed so many companies of Huns to reinforce
their border garrisons. We must find support through other means
than Byzantine fighting men, or we will be killed and our lands over-
run by Huns, who will strike westward and south from this place, farther into Christian lands. We are not a garrison-town but a trading
center, and we are not in any position to become a regional fortress,
for we have lost so much of the goods in which we trade that we cannot cover all the costs of constructing a proper stockade for all Porolissum, at least not as quickly as we are likely to need it. Surely there are
devout men in Moesia who would be willing to fight for their salvation, and would come north to join with us in our battles. I beseech
you to tell your soldiers of our plight and to appeal to them to help
us. I have carts and mules I can provide for those who wish to help us.
You have only to send word and I will dispatch muleteers to bring
fighting men to us. If the men serve well, at the end of our fight they
may keep their mules if they had them from me.

It has been a hard year so far; half our crops have been ruined
by marauding Huns, and what has not been trampled or burned has
been seized; when the harvest is made, we will have very little to lay
in against the hardships of winter, and what little we do bring in we
have small hope of keeping. Our herds and flocks have also been
raided. More than a third of my stores have been looted, and most
of the merchants here have suffered a similar fate. The tiered mills
have been burned and the grain within them taken. Shepherds and

goatherds have been killed in their summer grazing up the mountains, their animals confiscated by the Huns; the few remaining flocks have been moved to the enclosed fields of two local monasteries in exchange for twenty percent of the numbers of the animals to feed the monks.

As we are about to enter the month of Julius, we will have to look to our defenses, and attend to them before autumn arrives. Once the weather turns, our prospects for saving all of us from our enemies will be diminished to a dangerous degree. Already nine of our local merchants have announced their intention to shift their center of operations westward. If you will not provide those of us who seek to remain here some soldiers, we will find ourselves more in danger than we are now, with no prospect of relief. If you cannot spare men, then I implore you to send us weapons at least, or prepare to open your gates to your Roman brothers, for we will have to abandon our Porolissensis towns, either for Viminacium or the old fortress near Apulum Inferior, assuming we can restore its walls in time, or even to the monastery in the high valley between Ulpia Traiana and Apulum Inferior where we will have to retreat when the Huns return if no other fortification is made available to us. I pray you will grant us aid in this desperate time, for without some help we are all dead.

A Roman widow whose horse-farm to the south of the town has guaranteed us fifty horses for our defenders when they arrive. She has also provided silver and gold to help us pay for the strengthening of our walls, and arranged to move many barrels of food to wherever we Romans are to winter this year. This generous woman is the noble widow Atta Olivia Clemens, a blood relative of the foreigner Feranescus Rakoczy Sanctu-Germainios, serving as the regional guardian for Apulum Inferior, and he has pledged to see that her wishes are carried out. After this summer, Bondama Clemens will remain at Lux Perpetua Chapel, inside the northern gate of the monastery, where women stay. When she leaves the protection there, she will carry letters for us.

The monastery of Sanctu-Eustachios the Hermit, nearer the old Roman garrison-town of Ulpia Traiana than Apulum Inferior, may *provide us shelter through the winter if we receive no help from other Romans, but it is unlikely that the monks would allow us to stay on past the thaw if our presence would serve to attract more Huns without also gathering more Roman soldiers to protect us from Attila's forces. The monks will fight to defend the monastery and their faith, but as I have said already, they are unlikely to do anything more than that if the barbarians follow us to their door. Yet we have an obligation to see that the monks are spared the risk of death that must be the destiny of soldiers. In this, Priam Corydon agrees, and as head of the monastery, his cooperation is essential to our purpose.*

To secure the protection of more than Christ, I will leave a sacrifice for Mithras, and one for the old Greek Ares, whose temple is on the eastern side of the city. We have two churches here in Porolissum, and three private chapels. This is not so minor a place that everyone beyond Roma has no reason to pay attention to our plight, for it is towns like this one that will hold back the Huns if they are given aid now. The Church sends its priests here, and allows monks to man their monasteries, so it is not so remote that all the Christian world has no cause to be concerned for us. Seharic the Goth has allowed the region to support Christians, so long as the men will defend their lands, to which the Bishops of Porolissensis have consented. The priest who is assigned to our garrison will say his Masses for our fighting men—and tup our wives for us, if the rumors are right. There will be a home for us beyond the setting sun, as is always the end of men who fight.

There has been notice sent to us from Thracia that reports on another series of fearsome raids and the information that the Huns are stealing horses and food. Virginius Brolanor, a merchant from Odessus who had just left Serdica when the attack began, claims he would not be surprised to see more raids in winter than the Huns had ever made before. His house in Odessus was burned to the ground, and most of his family has vanished. Brolanor has declared that he will walk every road in the old Empire if it means he will have his family back. His father-in-law has promised Brolanor a new house so long as Brolanor brings back one of his grandsons; he has sworn an oath here that whether he lives to see that goodly day or not, the sum for the house will be settled in the Church of the Evangeloi, to be held against the restoration of Brolanor's family. We are encouraging those with land or gold to put them in trust to the Christian Church so that there will be a chance to salvage some of the valuables and treasures that supported our way of life before the Huns arrived.

This is being carried by seventeen members of my family: my two younger brothers and their wives, six children of theirs, four children of mine, my widowed sister, my wife, and my half-brother, whose mother died last winter; he is very young. With them are such servants as are required for this journey. I ask you to receive them well. Furthermore, I hope that you will allocate housing for them, and see that they make a place for themselves in Viminacium, unless the region becomes over-run, in which case, pray send my family south to Narona or Aquileia. The Church has funds in trust for such travels.

I will soon depart for Illyricum and Macedonia, and plan to stop and visit with you in about a year. Whatever remarkable pieces I have found I will offer you at minimal profit for me, to show my appreciation for the kindness my family has enjoyed, thanks to you. In such uncertain times as these, it is a great relief to know that the old standards of Roma can still be found in such a man as you.

> Demetrios Maius
> merchant of Dacia
> region of Porolissensis
> town of Porolissum

four days after the Summer Solstice in the 438th year of the Christ

1

"Why should I leave if you refuse to?" Atta Olivia Clemens stood with her arms folded as she faced Feranescus Rakoczy Sanctu-Germainios across her withdrawing room, her features set with determination, her hazel eyes snapping; she knew she was being unreasonable, but she also did not care: she would not admit to fear or misgivings, not even to her oldest, most trusted friend. "This place is as much my home as it is yours."

"We might say that of a dozen towns," he remarked. "You have a good number of holdings where you may go."

"You know what I mean," she said in an uncompromising tone. "But look out there. Summer is glorious here, in spite of everything. If I can't be on my native earth, this is a very pleasant second choice—the more so for you." The Latin they spoke had a heavy admixture of Greek, and a sprinkling of words borrowed from the local Germanic tribes, as well as a little Dacian.

He gave a single, sad laugh. "To reach my native earth, you must travel east along the Danuvius toward the bend in the mountains and then turn north at Durostorum Minor: it is a good deal closer than Roma, but it is still distant."

"How literal you are," she said, tweaking his sleeve.

"You are not safe here, Olivia," he said somberly.

"Probably not," she conceded. "But I still think it would be best to remain." She brushed her fingers together as if to rid them of dust; she was staring directly at him, daring him to contradict her. "Think, Sanctu-Germainios, what would be the point of leaving Porolissum? The roads are dangerous and we would not be welcome

in many Roman towns, not with so many people trying to find protection."

"The point would be that you would not have to fight the
Huns," he said bluntly. "I cannot believe that you would want to engage them in battle, not with so much to lose to them."

"You needn't remind me of my risks, but leaving Porolissum is
no certainty that I won't have to fight the Huns," she said, and then,
in an attempt to shift the subject, she looked at his silver-and-black
paragaudion and his diamond-patterned Persian femoralia of the
same colors. "Very handsome. Elegant without gaudiness, and not
so elaborate that everyone must point you out. Gravitas, beyond
question. Has anyone tried to rob you of the silver?"

He smiled and reached out to brush her cheek with his hand.
"You will be safer in Aquileia, Olivia. Ask Niklos, if you doubt me; he
still has ties in Thracia and Moesia, and he knows where the Huns are
active, and what they have done," said Sanctu-Germainios, annoying
her by refusing to fight with her. "Better to leave now, in accordance
with your own plans; that way you won't be cast adrift in a crum-
bling world. Since you have another horse-farm on the west side
of Aquileia where you can continue as you do here, with the advantage of being in Roman-Gothic territory, and therefore protected."

She gave him a wide, insincere smile. "You make it sound as if
this move is a step up in every way."

"It is better than trying to reinforce your fences with stone
high enough to keep the Huns out—assuming you have time enough
and masons to build the walls before winter."

"So you think I may have to lose my estate if I remain here; it is
much more certain that it will be lost to me if I leave, isn't it?" she
challenged him. "You don't believe there will be enough reinforce-
ments provided for these towns and fortresses to stop the attacks.
Why are you so convinced of it?"

He still would not be lured into open argument. "This is more
than a simple matter of fighting off a band of marauders. Where your
land here is concerned, you may have to make swift arrangements to

keep your herds from being decimated by neighbors as well as Huns; the Huns are stealing more horses, and yours will be much sought-after by them. If it becomes necessary to leave hurriedly from Aquileia, you can take to the sea. The Huns are not known to be sailors." He made a minimal bow and then smoothed out the small tablion on the front of his paragaudion.

"I don't like the sea any more than you do," she said brusquely. "Running water and tides." She shuddered to make her point.

"Do you prefer the Lux Perpetua Chapel and monks around you day and night?" He asked it lightly enough; he knew she found the Christians stultifying and that it was the only part of the local monastery where women were allowed to shelter.

"Certainly not—I want to stay here, in my house, on my land. I like Porolissum. I don't mind the Gepidae, or the Goths, nor do they mind me." She started to walk away from him, then relented and came back to his side. "If I could remain here without danger . . ."

He did not quite smile even though he felt relieved. "But for the sake of your household, you will go to Aquileia, out of harm's way. Please do it, Olivia. Your servants will appreciate your concern on their behalf. They have no wish to stay here to be taken as slaves or killed by the Huns, and who can blame them. You have the option of returning to Roma, whether the Goths are there or not. Since you are a Roman, you cannot be denied the right to return to Sine Pari."

"How am I to travel with so many? Won't that make us all the more vulnerable to attack by robbers, if not Huns?" It was a genuine concern, for she had lost a fair amount of money to robbers in the last six months, and the need to carry large sums on the road made her uneasy.

He took a pouch of coins from his belt, extending it to her. "Something more that may make your present circumstances less straitened: if you want to pay your household's wages before you leave, you may return me the sum when you like, or use it for lodging and food. I would not like to have you become a mendicant, not with so many in your care. Use as much as you need and when you have harvests and herds, then requite what I tender." He knew her well enough to know she would only agree to use his money if he were willing to have her return the sum.

Olivia accepted the pouch, saying as she did, "Thank you. This will be most useful. I have to admit that I'm much obliged to you for your kindness. It would be awkward, after my courier was taken by the Huns and my semi-annual payments from Lago Comus along with him, to have to compensate the entire household as well as the drayers and muleteers from my strongbox, thin of gold as it is. This will make my situation a bit easier, and provide a modicum of sus-tentation during our travels." She sighed in exasperation. "But since you continue to insist that I leave, I suppose it's fitting that you help me arrange it."

"Yes, it is," he agreed, knowing that her overbearing manner hid her increasing anxiety; his blue-black eyes were shining with relief.

"I imagine that Niklos worries almost as much as you do on my be half. It's kind of you to be concerned for me, even though you insist on my departing." She said this as if by rote while she fussed with the ma niakis where it fanned out over her shoulders. "It's the very devil being a widow this last century. No entertainments. No bright clothes. No jewels beyond pearl mourning-rings, and moonstones for earrings And a dark ricinium over my hair, so that I will not be thought a loose woman." She turned her palms up in a show of helplessness. "How long for red and ruby and amethyst and luminous greens, or brilliant yellow and gold. But no, being a widow, I must perpetually mourn; the Bishops require it. That I should mourn for Justus!" She made an em phatic gesture at the mention of her depraved husband, executed dur ing the reign of Vespasianus. That his name could still distress her after nearly four hundred years!—she turned toward the upholstered bench under the window, thinking as she did that her long, loose sleeved tunica was much the same color as the clouding sky beyond the opening. Over the tunica she had wrapped a trabea of dull-blue Antioch silk, darker than the maniakis, and secured it with a pearl encrusted pin. "We'll have thunder and lightning before day's end."

"Very likely," he said, and waited for her to go on, letting her persuade herself.

She pursed her lips in thought. "How am I to watch after my estates if the Bishops keep limiting what I am allowed to do? I am mandated, as the owner of the land, to ensure it is in good heart, but that means going against the Bishops' strictures, inspecting the herds and the flocks and the fields, but that means being seen about my land without the escort the Bishops compel widows to have. It is most inconvenient to have to accommodate the demands of the Church. You may be guardian of this region, but you are also a successful merchant, and the Bishops do not impose upon you as they do me."

"I would be as disheartened as you are, were I in your position," he said with genuine sympathy.

"I'm not disheartened, I'm furious," she said calmly. "The Bishops are martinets, to a man."

"That they are," said Sanctu-Germainios, who had spent much of the previous day trying to persuade the Bishops of Porolissum to allow the farmers of the region to be permitted to use some of the more remote monasteries as look-out posts; two of the Bishops refused absolutely, for it would turn a religious building into a military one.

"None of them will be party to lessening the restraints they impose on women," she said, unable to keep the disgust out of her tone.

"Surely you can appeal to the local officials to modify your constraints," he said, but found himself doubting that Olivia would be made an exception to the rules the Bishops had instituted. "If you were in Apulum Inferior, I would lift all your restrictions, since you are a land-owner, but my authority does not extend to Porolissum."

"And our Praetor here is a Bishop as well as our district administrator. It's useless to appeal to him." Her stern gaze softened and she said conciliatingly, "I know, my oldest, dearest friend. I am expecting trouble and that makes me contentious. I have to arrange to do what I can to see my horse-farm remains intact, whether I am here or not. Those of us here in Porolissensis who intend to preserve our lands, one way or—"

"Most of the people here are Gepidae, not Roman," Sanctu-
Germainios reminded her. "They are dependable enough in their
way, but they will be preferential to kin."

"That is the way of the Goths, as well," she said dismissingly.
"All barbarians are like that."

"For no Roman ever showed preferment for his clan," Sanctu-
Germainios said, making no excuse for his sardonic tone.

"Of course we did, and do. But we value the Empire as much as
we value our families. Or we did."

Sanctu-Germainios smiled enough to show he was not deceived. "You learned your conduct in another time."

"So did you," she said back to him; she glanced toward the door.
"Niklos," she called, "will you ask the household to meet with me in
an hour?"

A tall, athletically lean, gloriously handsome man in a dark-
orange Persian kandys, femoralia of deep-brown knit goat-hair, and
wooden-soled peri, who appeared to be about twenty-five, came and
stood in the door; a slight glint of amusement in his eyes made
clear that he had been listening to their wrangling. "Where would
you want us to gather?"

"In the old courtyard. It won't rain for a while yet; we might as
well enjoy the afternoon while we make our arrangements." She accepted his salute, watching him stride off to alert the household.
"You were good to provide me a bondsman, since you and I cannot
remain together. He has come to be more worthwhile than my family: with all the new limitations put upon women, I have needed him
very much."

"I am pleased you have him, then."

She paused, then continued, "I can't think how I managed without him for so long. But then, even a century ago, I had fewer hin-
drances to deal with."

Sanctu-Germainios regarded her levelly. "It is a great misfortune
that you have to deal with so many . . ." He faltered, going on in a
slightly more wry tone, "With such depredations as have been imposed on you. It is unjust."

"And it will lead to worse: I know it will."

He stood beside her, not quite touching her. "I hope you prove wrong," he said, although he seconded her fears.

"So do I," she murmured. Then she stretched a little. "So. I conede you are right: it is probably imprudent for me to stay here with he Huns becoming so very aggressive. I will have to arrange for my leparture." She moved a little distance away from him. "Since you re the instigator of my coming journey, increase your usefulness by >ffering your suggestions for my travels."

Sanctu-Germainios had been expecting something of this sort, nd so he said, "How much of your household are you planning to ake with you, and how many will you release?"

"I don't know; there are forty-two of them, not counting the grooms, the shepherds, and swineherds. A handful of servants come rom the town and will remain here, but for those in the household self—" she said, and pondered again. "It depends on what they vant. I imagine at least four of them will want to remain here with heir families." She paused, thinking. "Unless they want their families to leave here with the household, which would increase the numbers coming with me."

"Is that a possibility, do you think."

"It could be." She began to pace the room, studying the murals f the reign of Marcus Aurelius on the walls as if she had never >oked at them before. "I'll have to wait until I know what the ousehold wants before I make actual plans."

"It seems a worthwhile idea."

"You're indulging me," she accused.

"I am encouraging you to talk," he said.

She shook her head slowly twice. "What am I going to do with ou?" she asked him without looking at him.

"You are going to keep in mind that it would pain me beyond all eckoning to lose you to the True Death because you wanted to rove a point. When you became one of my blood, the Blood Bond nsured that you will always have my—my piety, in the old Roman ense of enduring, affectionate dedication; I will devote myself to you as I do to any who love me knowingly, as you did when you were still alive." He laid his hand on her shoulder. "I know you have courage. I know you are purposeful. You need not take on the Hun to convince me of either."

"Sanctu-Germainios," she responded in a uncertain voice, shaking her head in puzzlement. "I can't think what I'm supposed to say to you."

"Anything you like," he told her, and kissed her forehead. "So long as you do what you can to stay out of immediate danger."

"I could say the same to you." She reached out and took his hand in both of hers. "I sometimes find it inconvenient that your protection and devotion is all that we share now. Not that I am not pleased and nourished by the lovers I have had of late, but they were not like you."

"Now that you and I are of the same blood, it is all we are able to share, or need I remind you about what we seek from our lovers?" He saw her disappointment, and recalled how keenly he had felt it himself, a thousand years ago.

"I would be willing to hear you out on anything but that," she said, reverting to her teasing manner. "You are going to tell me what you think of our present circumstances, in any case, aren't you?"

"Unless you forbid it." He gave her a quick smile. "Indulge me, Olivia. I might have some useful kernels among all the chaff."

She studied his face for a long moment. "Very well, then," she said, a genial note in her voice and a mordant arch to her eyebrow as modifier. "I'll be glad of the benefit of your long experience."

"Most gracious," he murmured, and indicated the two couches and three chairs at the east end of the room. "Shall we be comfortable?"

"If you would like," she said, and chose the more elaborate couch for herself. "Are you going to be here tomorrow?"

"Probably only in the morning. I must return to Apulum Inferior shortly. I have a meeting of landholders scheduled in four days." He chose the Byzantine-style chair, and adjusted the cushions before he sat. "Do you intend to come through Apulum Inferior on your way south?"

"I haven't decided," she told him. "It depends on where the bridges are still open. I've been told that it's best to cross at Viminacium. From there, it's straight west to Aquileia."

"Or you can bribe the Gepidae and cross the Danuvius to Aquincum and Pannonia Inferior," he suggested, watching her attentively. "From Aquincum, the road goes to Poetovio, Emona, and Aquileia. There are fortresses along the way which would provide you protection. You would be in Roman-Gothic territory sooner by that route."

"More Gothic than Roman, these days," she said, not excusing her irritation at his suggestion. "The garrisons are manned by barbarians, and they aren't completely reliable. They do not honor my titles to the lands I've purchased in those old provinces, saying that when the Legions left, the deeds were no longer legitimate, and no claim could be made based on them."

"A problem not limited to the Romans and barbarians," he observed, thinking of the many, many holdings he had lost over the centuries to the claims of conquerors. "The Goths are pressing to claim all the Italian Peninsula."

"And I fear they will succeed." She looked toward the window.

"The Gepidae are restoring some of Legionaries' Dacian forts," Sanctu-Germainios observed. "In time that will help protect these mountains."

"If the Gepidae do not go to be mercenaries for the Byzantines, or hire out as road-guards for the Goths," said Olivia in a welling of world-weariness.

"Alaric prefers Goths in his fortresses," said Sanctu-Germainios.

"Not like the Byzantines, with their Hun-soldiers on the borders."

"The Byzantines do not want to send their hired soldiers so far from Constantinople as these high plains; I doubt they would send Hun-companies while the raids continue to worsen."

"So they won't send any companies of soldiers to help us," said Olivia, her voice flat with certainty.

"The Emperor in Constantinople might be persuaded to engage mercenaries from Roman territory to protect the region; a thousand mercenaries could be here by the end of autumn if they were to be dispatched now."

Olivia shook her head slowly. "The roads aren't better-maintained in much of Moesia than they here. I would expect some disrepair in this region, since the Romans have lost most of it, but Moesia is another matter, and in the last thirty years, you know as well as I that the roads have been neglected. Neither Roma nor Byzantium is prepared to maintain the roads in this portion of the old Empire, especially here, where the Gepidae rule, for fear the other portion of the Empire would use them to their advantage. So we languish between them, disputed by both and claimed by neither, except in regard to taxes." She glared at Sanctu-Germainios. "I am being candid with you, not to offend you, but to—"

"But to express your own misgivings and perturbation," he said levelly, meeting her gaze with his own. "I do understand, and I share many of your apprehensions. The reason I suggested leaving westward rather than south is that it will move you out of this disputed expanse of former provinces more quickly, and bring you into provinces that retain their links to Roma."

"Oh." She stared at the window again. "I'll have the shutters put up shortly, to keep the rain out."

"An excellent notion." He studied her, and when he spoke again, it was in the Latin of her youth. "It may be some time before you reach the point where you can reclaim all you have lost, and while I think it most advisable that you try to keep as much of what is yours as you can, I would hope that you do not make yourself an object of scrutiny. Your true nature is more dangerous to you than Hunnic raiders are, for the Church would condemn you for it. If you are revealed for what you are, that could prove troublesome whether the fighting worsens or not."

"I gather you think it will—get worse, that is." She spoke Imperial Latin with a kind of nostalgia that troubled her, but not enough to use the modern version of the tongue.

"I fear the circumstances will encourage more deterioration," he said a bit distantly. "I must shortly decide how to guard the Romans of Apulum Inferior not only from Huns, but from Gepidae."

"Then you suppose that the Gepidae might turn on the Roman settlements?"

"If we are left to fight these Huns alone, yes, I do. I have seen such things happen before."

"There isn't reason enough for the Romans or the Byzantines to come to our assistance as matters now stand; less so if the Gepidae want to be rid of us," she said. "That much is plain, and I think you're right in your vexations. But if circumstances should change, what then?"

"Change in what way?" he asked, aware that this matter could prove crucial if the changes were abrupt.

"If we could provide soldiers to defend the places we live, then the Gepidae may decide that we are worthy allies."

"Do you have knowledge of any companies of soldiers you would be willing to hire for such a purpose?"

Olivia shook her head, ordering her rushing thoughts and making herself speak more slowly than she wanted to. "But there is a Legionaries' camp near Apulum, not more than two leagues from Apulum Inferior. It hasn't fallen to ruin completely, and it could be reinforced effectively. As the guardian of the region, you could order all those whose claims are from the Roman times to contribute to securing the town and the villages around it. If the men of the region could be persuaded to help in the restoration, then the chance of engaging Roman free-soldiers would increase."

"It would depend upon how you and those like you decide to respond to threats from raiders. You are not the only Roman still in Dacia who would rather not leave these towns, but you have the good sense to accept the reality of the invasions; you will take your household and go, and that will allow you to retain more of your goods and servants than trying to defeat the Huns in battle. It may not be possible to unite the remaining Roman allies against the Huns, with or without soldiers to man the fortresses." He swung around toward the open window. "That was lightning. There will be thunder in . . ." He held up his hand and counted to sixteen; thunder trundled through the air. "It is distant, but it will soon be closer."

Olivia sat up on her couch. "Niklos!" she called. "Call the household—go into the dining room, not the courtyard; that will keep us dry. And have Esculus and Spargens put up the shutters."

"Yes, Bondama," Niklos replied from the depths of the house.

Sanctu-Germainios rose. "Come; so your servants may secure the windows in here," he said, holding out his hand to her.

She took it and stood up. "The storm is moving faster than I thought it would," she said.

"The wind is picking up. This is going to be a real storm by nightfall," Sanctu-Germainios said, escorting her through the small atrium toward her book-room.

As if to confirm this, a long rumble of thunder rolled along the southern sky, far enough behind the lightning still that there was a noticeable gap between them. Four of the household servants rushed toward the side-door, shouting about shutters as they went.

"You may have to remain here through tomorrow," said Olivia as she and Sanctu-Germainios slipped into the antechamber to the book-room, one of three rooms in her villa that had glass in the windows.

Sanctu-Germainios achieved a single laugh. "You are right: I may have waited half a day too long."

Olivia took a moment to compose her thoughts. "I'm sorry to have been the cause for—"

"It was my decision, and a shift in the weather, nothing you did," he said with a fond chuckle. "You are not responsible for either of those things."

She shrugged. "Still," she said as she led him into the book-room, accompanied by a louder report of thunder that shook the house. "Still."

Text of a note from Rotlandus Bernardius, Tribune of Ulpia Traiana, to Priam Corydon, leader of the monastery of Sanctu-Eustachios the

Hermit, four thousand paces from the town gates, carried by local messenger.

Ave to the most esteemed Priam of the Sanctu-Eustachios the Hermit monastery; this is to inform you that there has been a flood on the road to Viminacium, and the crossing is much damaged as the result of the unusually heavy rainstorms that have marked this summer. In my capacity of Tribune, I have assigned men from the small garrison of Ulpia Traiana to participate in rebuilding the wooden portions of the bridge. We will need many more hands to make the repairs in a timely way, and for that reason I approach you, most reverend Priam, and ask you to consider sending us some of your workmen to join in our efforts to restore this important crossing on the Danuvius. All of us need to be able to reach Roman territory without having to cover mountains without roads and then to boat across the river. Deus salva!

I would also hope that we may discuss plans for securing the region from attack before snowfall this year. It has been a troubling summer, and all of us living in this region would do well to maintain contact with one another for the purpose of defense and shared dangers. We have more alarming reports of the Huns coming into the mountains and seizing camps for the winter, and this does not augur well for the year to come. Preparations must be made to protect our people. Volens preparatus.

Inform my messenger of your thoughts on these matters, or entrust a note to him. He is utterly reliable in regard to such communications, since he cannot read. His memory is excellent, and anything entrusted to him will be reported accurately.

May the God you adore show you favor and preserve you, body and soul, from peril.

> *Rotlandus Bernardius*
> *Tribune of the garrison of Ulpia Traiana*
> *In Dacia Superior*

On the fourth day of the month of Augustus

2

Sergios of Drobetae was drunk. His eyes were shiny with it, and his thoughts roamed about in a way that made him pleased to be at the estate of Verus Flautens, three leagues from his guard-camp at the town of his birth, for there were inspectors coming from Constantinople to Moesia and the former Dacian border-towns to assess how well the old Roman treaties were being enforced now that Roman rule was diminishing; Sergios, who had no wish to be reported for insobriety—such an account of him would damage his chance of advancement to Praetor—had accepted with unseemly haste Flautens' invitation to spend three days at his country estate.

He had arrived at mid-morning, accompanied by four Gothic soldiers and six personal slaves, and now, a short time after mid-day, he was enjoying wine and appetizers in the reception-room, Verus Flautens showing him generous hospitality while Sergios did his best to concentrate through the wine-fumes on the problems that were burgeoning throughout old Dacia, and how many of those problems were being foisted on what was left of the courts. He was twenty-six, turning stout, with large, deceptively soulful eyes and a twice-broken nose. "Half the officers operate on bribes, and many of the remaining Praetors are as corrupt as tax collectors. An honest man is not safe, even from his staff and slaves." At this remark, his thoughts wandered to the men who had come with him and were now in the staff's dining room, having porridge and chopped vegetables.

"Have you received any direct threats, then?" Flautens inquired, clapping his hands to summon his slave. He resembled his Roman father—rangy, even-hewn featured, but with fair, wavy hair

rom his Ostrogothic mother—and kept to Roman manners when
ntertaining.

"Not from the Huns, but by implications from the Ostrogoths—
o disrespect intended. There have been reports all along the Danu-
ius, both on the Moesian and the Dacian side of the river. The
)strogoths are determined to hold on to their territory. You must be
ware of this." Sergios nodded several times. "The Roman settlements
re all up in arms, or would like to be. For now they lack the soldiers
nd fortresses to be sure of their prevailing. The Gepidae are—"

"I've been told that there will be battles before winter," Flaut-
ns said, determined to direct their conversation in order to learn as
nuch as possible before Sergios became incoherent.

"Who has told you that? Is our predicament so bad as that?"
ergios asked, the words not coming out quite right. As one of
lautens' slaves refilled his cup, he muttered a thanks and sat back
o listen to all that his host was telling him, his linen lacerna hanging
pen over his cotton tunica, both garments feeling too heavy and
ot for this sultry afternoon.

"It is bad enough. The reports from the north are growing trou-
lesome, what with the Huns raiding well into Gothic territory,"
lautens said, not quite as bibulous as Sergios was, but no longer as
ucid as he had been when they sat down together, "and yet we have
o continue to pay off the Gepidae in order to keep the lands left to
s by our parents and their parents, or lose all. Yet it is far from clear
hat the Gepidae are in any position to preserve our holdings for us.
And now the remaining Romans are demanding that we all con-
ribute to building and reinforcing defenses throughout the region,
earing the expense of our own protection. Yet there is no assurance
f those defenses being extended to our lands, which is a dreadful
mposition, what with paying taxes to Constantinople as well as the
Gepidae."

"True enough," Sergios rumbled, reaching for a wedge of cheese
et out upon the central table on a tray with flat-breads. He had a
ittle difficulty putting the wedge on a slice of bread, and leaned to-
vard the table to keep from spilling his food.

"Have you been in contact with Gnaccus Tortulla?" Flautens asked with little sign of interest.

Sergios chewed energetically, gulped the cheese and bread down with more wine, then said, his face turning ruddy from the wine and the heat, "The Praetor Custodis of Viminacium? I am awaiting an answer from him in regard to our worsening predicament. I've received a brief note from Rotlandus Bernardius, the Tribune of Ulpia Traiana who's as worried about our situation as I am. He has been attempting to gain support from all the towns in his region, but he is having little success."

"Do you suppose the Roman garrison will be allowed to remain in Ulpia Traiana? Will the Gepidae permit them to remain with the garrison?" Flautens asked. "Half the troops are barbarian of one stripe or another: can they be counted upon to remain faithful?"

"I don't know," said Sergios, abashed that he did not have such vital information. "If they're Dacians, I think they might."

"Sarmizegutusa, that's the Dacian name for Ulpia Traiana, isn't it?" Flautens said a bit absently, finishing the wine in his cup and signaling for more.

"Yes, it is. There're standing stones there, and some other religious structures. The Christians don't like it," said Sergios. "Impressive stoneworks, quite ancient." He had more wine. "This is very good. Local, is it?"

"From Drobetae, truly." Flautens drank less eagerly than Sergios. "One of the heartier grapes."

"Not from your land, though—according to the records, you don't have vineyards." Sergios felt a rush of pride that he was alert enough to recollect this. "You grow oats and barley, and some wheat and beans and lentils." He was a bit surprised that, given his state of mind, he could remember something so specific. Perhaps he was beginning to lose the undercurrent of dread that inspired his coming to Flautens' villa. "You raise hogs, sheep, horses, and donkeys. And mules, of course."

Flautens nodded. "Also timber: oak, larch, and pine. In addition the hogs eat the acorns, and we get nuts from the pine. And I have two stands of hives." He drank again. "All in all, this land produces well for me. I would not like to lose it."

"Are you making any plans to defend it on your own?" He reached for more cheese. "Do you think you might hire fighting men to guard your stock and crops?"

"It may come to that, I fear." He snorted in dissatisfaction and drank more deeply. "I am sending my wife and children to Aquileia with a Roman noblewoman bound there from Porolissum. I met with her two days ago, at the Triceum Fortress, to make our arrangements. No doubt you will enjoy meeting her. She has a company of forty-seven servants and household with her, including armed men, and in exchange for six mules, she has agreed to include my family in her company." He smiled lopsidedly. "I will be pleased to know they're safe."

"Aquileia," said Sergios. "A fine place. I hope your family will be happy there."

"They will be gone for some months, I fear."

"But they won't be alone, will they?" Sergios asked.

"I have a cousin whom I am asking to receive them," said Flautens. "He has dealt with many of our relatives and we are all grateful to him. He can arrange for my family to establish themselves in a villa until I can join them."

"Very good," said Sergios, and signaled for more wine. "I will do my utmost to keep you informed of anything having to do with Aquileia."

"I will appreciate that," said Flautens, and leaned back on his couch. "How long do you think the Constantinopolitans will be in Drobetae?"

"Three or four days—that's as long as they've stayed in the past."

"Do you intend to meet with them at all?" Flautens watched his slave fill Sergios' cup again.

"On the last day, so I may offer them a report that will be useful to them; I will be able to say that I have been gathering more immediate information for them." He made a gesture that might have been intended to show how clever his intention was. "If I had more rank, I would have a clerk present the report. Since I'm a freeman, I need to be as accommodating as possible, and to put myself at the service of the Byzantines in the most obvious way possible."

"So you'll stay out of the town while the Byzantines are gathering their information, will you?"

"Until the last day." He drank again, his manner more at ease. "They will have less opportunity to judge me, and that is a wise precaution for me to take, given how much we have to contend with. I want to give them little occasion to find fault with what I have done. For all I know, they'll want to put one of their own in my place. It has happened in other towns."

"Do you know the inspectors?" Flautens did not change his posture or his demeanor, but his eyes grew brighter as he slipped a small plate from under his couch and felt for what it held.

"Possibly," said Sergios. "They usually send one man who has made the journey before, so that there will be someone who can compare the present circumstances to past conditions."

"Do you think this person will remember you?" He took a preserved fruit, popped it into his mouth, then held out a shallow bowl of the delicacies to Sergios. "Have some. They're preserved in honey." To emphasize how tasty the fruit was, he smacked his lips as he finished eating one of the dark fruits.

"Thank you," said Sergios, helping himself to two of the fruits and drinking more wine. "Very good—more tart than sweet." His face flushed to a mottled red, and he gave a little flurry of dry, hacking coughs. "Very good. In fact, delicious."

Flautens watched Sergios with mild concern. "Are you all right?"

"Just a touch of the heat and dust, nothing to bother about," Sergios said, and coughed again a bit more energetically.

"You are quite roseate," said Flautens with a suggestion of a laugh. "Shall I have my slave fetch you some cheesed-cream? We keep it quite cool."

Sergios shook his head even as he whooped out more strained

coughs, his face growing livid. He tried to speak, but managed only a wheeze, then doubled over and vomited suddenly, his face and neck empurpling.

"Are you ill?" Flautens asked.

For an answer, Sergios jerked off the couch onto the floor, where he thrashed and convulsed, his body voiding spasmodically; the room began to reek. His eyes grew huge and seemed to start out of his head. For an instant he went rigid, then Sergios gave a short, ragged howl and lay still.

Flautens rose from his couch and clapped for his slave. "See this is disposed of without notice. No one is to know he's dead. Say only that after the afternoon nap, he wanted the tepidarium so he could be relieved from the heat." He was wiping his hands on the linen cloth the slave handed him. "Take his freeman's ring from his finger, so I have something to show to Gnaccus Tortulla's messenger. He will want proof that Sergios is dead."

"That I will," said the slave, who was the custodian of the house. He bent to work the ring off the first finger of his right hand.

"And tell the household slaves, when they clean this room, that Sergios suffered a violent attack of indigestion and has gone to lie down."

"They might not believe it," the slave warned as he gave the ring to Flautens. "Slaves sometimes gossip."

"No matter; they will not learn of his misfortune," said Flautens, moving away from the body. "And get rid of the honied fruit. Make sure none of the livestock or poultry can get to it. There's enough poison in that bowl to bring down a horse." He handed a small dish to the slave. "And wash this yourself, so that no one will suspect that I didn't share everything he ate. Use one of the troughs."

"I'll seal the remaining fruit in a jar and put it in the back of the wood-room behind the bath."

"A very good notion. All it can poison there is rats." Flautens sighed. "You'll have to hide him for now."

"I know. I can't dispose of him permanently until after dark," said the slave. "But he has to be hidden until nightfall."

"Where can we conceal him?" Flautens asked furtively.

"In the rear of the creamery, in the drainage ditch," the slave reminded him. "But he'll have to be moved soon—the heat will add to the stink, and even if I wrapped him in a hide, he could be discovered."

Flautens nodded. "True enough. And his escort will want to know what has become of him, come evening."

The slave went and closed the door leading into the atrium, putting the brace into position so that it could not be opened. "Yes, I will say he has been feeling unwell. By morning he will have vanished."

"Is there any way to put him into the midden?" Flautens asked suddenly, the idea only now occurring to him. "No one will notice the smell, not with the two dead pigs in it. And they won't want to poke into it."

"It might be more difficult than the original plan, at least until nightfall. The barnyard is active all day."

"If you can arrange it, that would be a good solution," said Flautens. "Better than the potters' kiln, which I had thought of before."

"The potters are keeping near the kiln, and they might notice the odor of burning flesh," the slave reminded him. "But the midden will be unattended after the convivium. I will double him over in the ditch so that when he stiffens, he will fit into the midden when I move him into it." He went to the far corner of the room and pulled a rolled blanket from under the serving-ware chest, and brought it back to Sergios' corpse, where he laid it down clear of the effluvia.

"Hredus," Flautens said as he watched the slave maneuver the body onto the blanket, "when this venture is finished, you will have your freedom. You have my word on that."

"Then what can I do but thank you?" He touched his iron slave's collar in a kind of acknowledgment, then lowered his head and did his best not to look at Sergios' body as he folded the blanket around it, then tugged the blanket away from the center of the room, sliding it into the small hallway that connected to the vomitorium and led out into the farm. He was back in a short while, his face impassive.

"No one saw you?" Flautens asked. He had spent the time wiping down the floor, and now he held two filthy cloths away from his linen pallium.

"The goose-boy saw me rinsing the plate in the sheeps' trough, but he's simple," Hredus said. "He was carrying a basket of eggs toward the kitchen."

"A basket of eggs?" Flautens wondered aloud.

"For the cooks," said Hredus. "A very good sign. It means he won't be looking for eggs again until tomorrow morning, and won't stumble on the remains before I move them into the midden."

"Oh. Yes." Flautens reached for the wine and drank the last of what was in his cup. "Have Chrodi come to my records-room after we dine tonight; he is to leave for Viminacium before dawn."

"I will." He took the two cloths from Flautens. "Let me dispose of these for you."

"Fine. Then send in a pair of house-slaves to wash the floor." He shook his hand as if to rid it of any lingering taint. "I will go bathe and then repair to my records-room to compose a report for Gnaccus Tortulla." He went toward the small door that led out to the vomitorium, adding over his shoulder, "And a writ of manumission for you. You may claim it after the convivium."

"I will ask the local priest to say a month of Vespers for your kindness," said Hredus.

"The smith will strike your collar off tonight," Flautens added, then left the reception-room.

Hredus looked around the reception-room, trying to see if any tell-tale sign remained of Sergios' death, but there was only a patch of slimy moisture, which would not cause any suspicions once he explained that Sergios had been unwell and was resting. He went and opened the door to the atrium, looking to see if the footman were at his post. Satisfied that Ayard was dozing, Hredus went down the corridor in the direction of the slaves'-room, where he found nine of them working at small tasks while the heat of the day passed.

Nomrid, Hredus' older sister, who was the webster for the household, was setting up the loom in the corner, her long fingers moving with rapid ease. She stopped as she saw her brother coming toward her. "What brings you to this room?"

"Thaeta and Urius are needed to wash the floor in the reception-room. The guest became sick and has gone to rest. He has asked not to be disturbed. If he is still unwell, he'll remain in his room until morning."

Thaeta and Urius rose from their places at the long table where they had been sorting mushrooms and bundling herbs for drying. They said nothing as they trudged off toward the kitchen to get pails of water and brushes.

Had they been alone, Hredus might have told his sister about his coming freedom, but with others of the household still tending to their chores, he said nothing but, "I will see you at dinner, after the convivium is served." As the household custodian, he would supervise the serving of the meal.

"Certainly," she said, and went back to stringing the loom.

"Have you seen Chrodi?" he asked as he made for the door.

"He said he was going to the stable. The roan foal cut his pastern, and he is going to treat it with honey and pepper." It was Vache who answered while he continued to braid a new driving-whip.

"I'll find him," Hredus said, and left, continuing on toward the barnyard and across it to the stable, calling for Chrodi as he went.

Flautens' courier answered from the stall. "What is it?"

Hredus made his way down the broad aisle toward the sound of Chrodi's voice. "Dom Flautens wants to see you in his records-room when he has finished the convivium. He has a message for you."

Chrodi came out of the stall, frowning. "The colt-foal is in a bad way. I don't like leaving while he's doing so poorly. He's going to need constant care for several days, or we may lose him."

"Have your apprentice care for him. The message you are to carry is an important one."

"The colt-foal is well-bred. The Dom would not like to lose him." Chrodi lifted his jaw stubbornly.

"Ask him about that when you report to him tonight," said Hredus.

Chrodi shrugged, but said nothing more; he went back into the stall and knelt down on the hay next to the miserable four-month-old.

Hredus remained in the barn for a short while, looking out into the large paddocks where most of the horses stood in the shade of trees, their tails moving constantly to keep off the flies. Finally he said, "You'll have to depart at first light, for Viminacium," and left the barn without expecting anything more from Chrodi. Crossing the stable-yard, he noticed that Patras Eldom's mule was tied to the hitching-rail, meaning the priest had come early for the convivium so that he could hear the confessions of the household. He whispered an ironic prayer of thanks that the priest had not arrived while he and Flautens were disposing of Sergios of Drobetae. As he went into the house again, he resisted the urge to seek out his master, going instead to the solarium, where he assumed Flautens' wife, Maryas, had gone to sew pearls on her new tablion.

"Hredus," she said as he called through the door. "What news?"

"Patras Eldom has come. Shall I send him up to you?"

"Would you please?" She waited a moment, then asked, "Has he seen my husband yet?"

"I don't know," Hredus answered, certain that Flautens would delay his confession as long as possible. "He may wait until tomorrow, so that he can fast."

There was another brief hesitation. "He may want that," she said in a troubled voice. "I will ask him."

"Will you join the convivium or would you prefer to eat alone?"

"Since there are no other women to attend, Patras Eldom would not approve of having me among the company. I will dine in my withdrawing room. Tell Lysianna to arrange this for me."

"Yes, Dama," he said, trying to decide how best to inform Flautens of his wife's intention.

"Be good enough to remind my husband that I have packing to supervise tonight and tomorrow, so I will have little time for entertainment were it appropriate. My husband will understand that, at least."

"The Roman noblewoman is expected to come here tomorrow afternoon, isn't she?" Hredus asked.

"She is staying at a travelers' fortress two leagues from here. No doubt she will be here by sundown tomorrow."

"Very good," said Hredus, admitting to himself that he would miss Flautens' soft-spoken, beautiful Byzantine wife; as soon as he realized this, he forced the knowledge from his mind. "God give you a good evening, Dama."

"And you, Hredus."

As he turned away from the solarium door, Hredus tried to decide how to avoid confessing, for Patras Eldom would condemn him not only for helping to kill Sergios of Drobetae, but for daring to hold his master's wife in affection, and for betraying Flautens if he should admit to either sin.

Text of a letter from Dorus Teodoricos, garrison commander at Durostorum in Moesia Inferior, to Nestor Phinees, Praetor Custodis of Serdica, Moesia Superior, carried by garrison courier, delivered in nine days.

Ave to Nestor Phinees, Praetor Custodis of Serdica, Moesia Superior: may God and the saints show you favor, grant you long life, robust health, and good fortune, that will in some way recompense you for the pain I must impart to you now.

It is my unfortunate duty to inform you that your son Kosmos has succumbed to the wounds he received in battle twenty-four days since, thirty-three days before the Autumnal Equinox. He had conducted himself with bravery, keeping his men on the main wall of the fortress at Troesmis from which point he held off the Huns, who attacked in great numbers. Unfortunately, our losses were high, your son being one of three hundred seventy-eight; there may yet be more who will not recover from their wounds.

Our hired soldiers acquitted themselves well, and our forces' withdrawal to Durostorum was conducted in good form, and the men did all that they could to keep the Huns from harrying our retreat. We received them five days ago, and have added the soldiers of Troesmis to our own men, and we have every hope that our numbers are sufficient to hold off any renewed assault. If we do beat back the Huns, it will be to the credit of officers like your son, who remained steadfast and made his men proud to face so ruthless an enemy.

With prayers and thanksgiving to your family, who have had so admirable a son.

> Dorus Teodoricos
>   garrison commander at Durostorum
>   Moesia Inferior

3

Rhea Penthekrassi was frowning as she watched Feranescus Rakoczy Sanctu-Germainios remove an elaborate wooden box from his iron-banded chest; she tugged at the ornamented and pleated sleeve of her palla of gauzy, violet silk; over this she had draped a trabea of gold-shot linen, both of which complemented her olive skin and russet-colored hair. "What is that?" she asked uneasily. Now that her time with him was coming to an end, she felt more and more separated from him; she glanced toward the glass-covered window, and beyond, the harvesters in the fields teased by a fainéant wind.

"It is for you, so that you can fend for yourself if it comes to that," he said as he gave it to her. "Look inside, if you like." In his black pallium with the collar of silver links, he was unusually impos-ing, and that made her uncertain about the box, since it appeared to be part of his farewell to her.

She took hold of it, surprised at how heavy it was. Reluctantly she slid back the lid, and very nearly dropped it as she caught sight of the large variety of jewels it contained; her hold tightened and she stared at him in astonishment. "This is all for me?"

"Yes."

"How many are there?" She wanted to count them herself, but knew it would be unacceptably rude to do so where he could see.

"Thirty-six; that should be enough to take care of you for many years, and they may provide you a dowry if you decide to marry. If you would prefer not to marry, you will not be reduced to beggary, but will be able to keep yourself in good comfort, unless the Em-peror will not permit you to secure property." His voice was even and reassuring; for the first time that afternoon she felt safe in his company.

"I believe you're right; it will keep me a long time," she said, thinking she could purchase a husband for half of what the box con-tained. "Unless I am reckless."

"But you will not be," he said with a kind of warning that left her determined to be worthy of his trust in her.

"No, I will not," she confirmed. "You are incredibly generous."

"You will find a deed of gift on folded parchment in the lid. Keep it in case you have to prove your right to the jewels." It had not been so long ago—less than three centuries—that such a pre-caution would not have been necessary, but as matters currently stood in the Byzantine half of the Roman Empire, without such a deed, Rhea was not entitled to control the jewels, nor benefit from their value.

She went a bit pale. "I will. I will keep them concealed and pro-tected. No one will know that I have them, or who gave them to me."

"An excellent plan," he approved. "I know from my trading company that Constantinople is a costly place, with high standards for those who live there. Unless you want a life of hardship, you will need some things from me beyond these jewels to make your situation tolerable. Your clothes and household goods will go with you. You may keep the horses I will provide for your journey, and the wagons they will draw, all of them. Your escort will take only those animals they need to ride back here. But the horses you will keep need food and shelter; with these stones you can secure a house and stable so that you may live satisfactorily for some time to come."

She closed the box carefully. "Why such wonderful gems?"

"They are easily concealed and their value should remain constant no matter who is Emperor, or what the Patriarch declares. Any sea captain will accept them for passage, if your life there goes awry." He had taken the last ten days to make the jewels in his athanor, along with fifty-eight more. "You deserve to live well, wherever you live."

"I will thank you every day," she said, remembering how she had left Constantinople. In a distant tone, she spoke her thoughts aloud. "We lived well until my father had fallen from favor with the Imperial Censor. Then, when he was dead, my uncle removed me from the hovel that had become our home. I never thought I could return to the city of my birth, except as a concubine, or a lesser wife of some barbarian or other. Now—" Now she would be able to live as well as she had for all but the last year of her father's life. To her surprise, she felt tears on her face.

Sanctu-Germainios went to her side. "You have no cause to weep," he said as he put his arm around her shoulder, more consolingly than seductive.

"Except that I will miss you, no, I don't; for me that is reason enough," she agreed, wiping her eyes with her free hand; she made herself disengage from him, afraid that she would behave in an unseemly fashion if she remained with him any longer. "I had best go secure these in my traveling chest. I should do it myself, so they will be completely concealed." She slipped out of his arm and went to the door. "Perhaps you will join me later?"

"Perhaps I will," he said with a smile that lit his dark eyes with promise.

"I'll look forward to it," she almost purred.

As he watched her pull the door closed behind her, he found himself thinking of Melidulci, who also enjoyed him as a lover but wanted no part of his life after death. "By all the forgotten gods," he murmured, trying to keep from despondency. He paced the length of the room, distracting himself with reading the titles over the vast array of pigeon-holes, aware that the book-room of his villa felt too quiet with Rhea gone, as he knew the whole villa would seem after the coming morning; for a short time, Sanctu-Germainios stared at the shelves and pigeon-holes with extreme blankness of expression, then he selected the ancient papyrus he had been given when he was High Priest of Imhotep, laid it out on the table, and unfolded it. He read over the recommended treatment for sprained ankles and the course of herbs and infusions for inflamed intestines, and was about to review the formula for relieving hives when he heard a soft tap on the door. "Who is it?"

"Rugierus," said his manservant.

"Come," said Sanctu-Germainios in Alexandrian Latin.

Rugierus stepped into the room and closed the door behind him. In his cotton pallium of dusky gold, he seemed to be made up in shades of tan and beige, except for his faded-blue eyes; he, too, spoke Latin in the Alexandrian idiom. "I have chosen a closed wagon and two carts for our travel, horses for the wagon, mules for the carts," he said in the same dialect. "I'll ride and take a remount, and an extra mule in case there is any trouble. One of the serving-women will attend Dama Rhea, and four drivers—three to drive and one extra as a precaution. We'll carry four additional wheels for each vehicle, and a complete harness, with two extra sets of reins for the wagon and carts, and one for the horses, along with three replacement bits."

"Very prudent. Let us hope that you will need none of them." Sanctu-Germainios folded the papyrus closed and returned it to its pigeon-hole. "Be sure to carry food and water, and grain for the animals."

"Certainly, and gold coins hidden, in case we must pay high passage fees," said Rugierus. "Too many of the towns and regions ally themselves to whomever provides the most: loyalties change from barbarians to Greeks to Romans on little more than a whim, and are abandoned in abrupt pretermission."

"Have we received any news of shifted alliance or territorial changes in fealty, or alignments? Has any region become the land of newcomers?" He waved his hand. "Not to pelt you with questions: as the regional guardian, such information is essential to this task." He relied on Rugierus and his two couriers to sort out rumors from truth through his communications with various clerks and messengers.

"Nothing that can be confirmed," said Rugierus.

"And that is unlikely to change soon," said Sanctu-Germainios. "Not with these regions in such disarray."

"If the Huns keep on the attack, the loyalties and private agreements may not matter much."

"Truly, old friend," said Sanctu-Germainios, then abandoned the fruitless speculation. "Have you worked out the length of your journey yet?"

"All things being equal, we will strive to travel at least four leagues in a day, five if the weather is good and we have no misfortune. We will rest our horses and mules every five days, and purchase food at every town boasting a market. Assuming we leave tomorrow, we should have good weather most of the way. Once the rain and snow come, then we will not travel as quickly."

Sanctu-Germainios considered this. "That is not unreasonable; you are not on a military campaign," he said. "I can hope that the roads you will use are not in complete disrepair."

Rugierus' austere features were touched with amusement. "They were not in good condition when you left Salonae for Apulum Inferior twelve years ago; no report since then has said much about improvement. And you informed me that the road to Porolissum was in poor condition when you returned from your visit to Bondama Olivia."

"Because no one is willing to provide the men or the supplies to repair them." Sanctu-Germainios shook his head once.

"You could pay to restore the roads," Rugierus said.

"I could, but at present, I am providing builders and lumber to strengthen the walls of this town, and for other towns in the region, as I am duty-bound to do. If I paid for anything more, the Emperor Theodosios in Constantinople would order me to leave the region, and no one in Roma would dispute his order, neither Roman nor Ostrogoth. Doubtless my departure taxes would be very high and the mercenaries at the garrison might seize my holdings and demand money for their return before I was out of the territory; they might resort to torture to get what they want. Remember what happened to Kyros Esaias? And after all they did to him, they never found his fortune—if he actually had one."

Rugierus pressed his thin lips tightly. "Is he still alive?"

"He is, but his mind is gone; the monks care for him," said Sanctu-Germainios; he was silent for a long moment. When he spoke again, it was in a steady tone. "Take money enough to pay for a courier in case you should have to send me word of any significant development. Keep it in the hidden pocket under your saddle, so that no one will know you have it."

"Are you expecting trouble for us along the way?" Rugierus inquired with no indication of worry.

"It is possible. Raiders of all descriptions are everywhere, and many people are seeking a haven from the raids. Either way, you might find yourself having to defend Rhea and all you carry." He folded his hands. "If you run into conflict, search out a monastery or a church. Rhea is likelier to be safe there than in a fortress, soldiers—especially mercenary soldiers—being what they are."

"Not that monks are much better," Rugierus said.

"They are more easily stopped, and more readily shamed," Sanctu-Germainios remarked.

"And less likely to be armed. Most monks have only farm-tools for weapons." Rugierus nodded, continuing in a matter-of-fact manner, "If we encounter no delays, we should be in Constantinople in twenty-five days or so. I and the drivers will leave the horses with

Dama Rhea and ride back on the mules. The serving-woman is to remain with her, as well."

"Send me word when you cross the Danuvius, and when you have covered half the distance from here to Constantinople; if there is any news you believe I can find advantageous, spend the money and send it along to me, as well," Sanctu-Germainios said. "Use hired couriers, not merchants or travelers bound this way, for they may not act promptly in delivering your message. If anything has gone wrong here, I will send a courier to the place where you crossed the Danuvius with information where I am going."

"Drobetae or Oescus, one or the other is where we'll cross," Rugierus said.

"Very good. They have ferries as well as bridges," Sanctu-Germainios said in agreement.

"Then over the mountain to Philippopolis, and from there to Constantinople," Rugierus recited.

"A fine choice of route," said Sanctu-Germainios. "Be careful in the mountains."

"Robbers and landslides: yes, I've thought about both of them. I'll provide the drivers and guards with spears and Hunnic bows, and some shovels," said Rugierus. "I think one of the drivers should be Rouaric's assistant Bainiu; we may need a smith and a farrier on the road."

"Bainiu is a good choice. Take an anvil with you as well, and hammers. I only wish you could include a forge."

At this Rugierus actually smiled. "We will find forges at estates and towns and garrisons as we go. No doubt we will be able to pay for the use of a forge, in coin or in labor. You and I have done such in the past, my master."

"You're thinking of our journey beyond the Stone Tower, fifty years ago, or perhaps our leaving Shiraz, after Srau—"

Rugierus held up his hands. "It came to mind."

"A trek neither of us likes to remember," said Sanctu-Germainios.

"It has its useful lessons," said Rugierus. "I will bear them in mind." He ducked his head. "Shall I order the bath warmed for you?"

"If you would," said Sanctu-Germainios. "An hour or so after sundown."

"As you wish," said Rugierus.

"I am going now to spend some time with Rhea."

"I'll tell the staff not to disturb you." Rugierus took a step toward the door. "When would you like to have her cases loaded?"

"Later tonight. Keep the wagon and carts locked in the stable."

"Shall we load them while you're bathing, perhaps?"

Sanctu-Germainios considered this. "If Rhea agrees."

Rugierus held the door open for Sanctu-Germainios. "Is there anything more you would like me to attend to?"

"Whatever you think needs your attention; I have implicit trust in you," said Sanctu-Germainios, nodding once before striding across the atrium toward the stairs that led to the private quarters of the villa. He passed the door to his own rooms and continued on to Rhea's, stepping inside her small withdrawing room, where he found two housemaids working to pack Rhea's garments in one of three large chests; both women stopped and ducked their heads to their employer. "Will you tell me where Dama Rhea is?"

"The inner room," said the older of the two.

"Thank you," said Sanctu-Germainios, and passed on into the inner room where Rhea slept and tended to her appearance; she was sitting on the end of her bed, braiding a trio of ribbons into a circlet for her hair. "Rhea, are you willing to—"

Before he could finish, she hurried up to him and put her fingers against his lips. "Don't say anything. I've just stopped crying," she whispered; her eyes were reddened and swollen.

"Is anything wrong?" he asked as he gently wiped away her tears.

"I'm . . . I'm sorry to be going," she said plaintively. "I know I must, and I understand that it must be now. I realize that you have been very kind to me, so I feel at odds with myself, for I can't help but wonder if what lies ahead is as pleasant as this has been."

"This may not be pleasant much longer," he said with kindness.

"You will not want to be here if there is fighting. Your uncle would agree."

She stamped her foot. "If I hadn't committed myself to a brief stay, I might have been able to remain through the winter, but the Praetor Custodis requires that I leave, or permit my uncle to disown me."

"Then the situation is out of your hands, and mine," said Sanctu-Germainios, leading her toward the narrow couch near the window rather than toward her wide bed. "Here. I don't want you to feel you are being pressed."

"I didn't understand about you." She stared into his eyes, weighing her doubts against his steady acceptance. "I still don't."

"I am a foreigner; that is what I ask you to recollect when you are conjectural," he said, offering his arm for her support as she sat down.

"More foreign, it turns out, than I was told," she said, trying to keep from giving way again.

"All the more reason for you to leave," he said with an element of regret. "If you stay here, things will change between us; you and I will no longer be able to lie together safely."

"But it's only been four times," she wailed quietly.

"Six times and you will risk transforming to one of my blood when you die, and you have said you have no wish to do that. You recall what that would mean for you, do you not?" He spoke much more calmly than he would have done five centuries ago, and made no attempt to dissuade her.

"No. If what you told me is true, I wouldn't want to become like you." She touched the small, golden fish hanging from a hook on the wall. "The Bishop would condemn me if I should rise after death: it would be blasphemous."

"And burning brings the True Death," he said sympathetically.

"So you explained to me," she responded, reaching from the fish to his hand. "But we have this one last chance, don't we?"

"If it is what you want." His nearly black eyes glowed blue in their depths. "You have only to tell me."

"Oh, yes, it is what I want. We can say good-bye in the morning, but now, I want a farewell that will last for years to come." She eased her hand into his and tugged to pull him down beside her, taking advantage of the confined space to embrace him. "Let this be something I will remember for all my life."

"I will do all I can of what I can," he pledged, and drew her close to him, kissing her lightly but persuasively, letting her warm to him, sensing passion rising in her.

She moved away from him as the kiss ended. "Wait. Wait while I send my serving-women away; I don't want to be interrupted," she said, breathing somewhat more quickly than she had before the kiss; she got to her feet and went to the door, half-opened it, and ordered the two women to tend to choosing the bedding for the wagon. "Make sure it is soft," she said, and watched them depart before closing the door and coming back toward Sanctu-Germainios, untying her trabea and letting it fall to the floor as she approached her bed. "This will be more comfortable, Feranescus. There is more room and the mattress is softer."

"As you like," he said, rising from the couch and going to the bed, standing to face her at its foot.

She stretched up her arms. "Remove my palla, if you would." The challenge in her mien was a mixture of desire and sadness.

Sanctu-Germainios unfastened the elaborately braided belt under her breasts, slipped his fingers under the pleated shoulders of the palla, and whisked it upward, swinging it to let it fall on the couch behind him. "What about your mani and fascae? Shall I—"

She was already loosening her underclothes. "I'll tend to them," she said, and stepped out of her mani, leaving the fascae for last. "You can help me with this, if you want to."

He stepped behind her and untied the flat knot between her shoulder-blades, sliding the Egyptian linen slowly free of her breasts. He felt a faint quiver go through her, and he put one knee on the bed. "Would you like to recline?"

"No. I'd like to make love," she said, turned a little, and fell back landing with arms spread on the lower half of the bed. She wriggled up to the array of pillows at the head, holding out her arms to him as she settled among them. "Work your way up from where you are. Begin with the soles of my feet."

"The soles of your feet? Very well." He sat down on the side of the bed, leaning as if reclining for a feast; taking her left foot in his hand, he bent and playfully kissed the sole, then lightly ran his tongue along her toes.

She gave a sharp laugh; she was ticklish. "That's . . . fine."

He rolled a little nearer to her and repeated his ministrations to her right foot; this time her toes curled in pleasure, and she gave a long, luxurious sigh. With a feather-light touch, he slowly moved his fingers up to her knee, shifting himself so that he could glide between her legs.

The disparate urgency that had been taut within her began to give way to an exhilarated repose. Her flesh seemed bathed in a warm tide of increasing passion, her skin growing more and more sensitive to his most minuscule attention. Because Sanctu-Germainios did not demand an intense reception from her, she began to feel one build within her; his gently coaxing kisses summoned an ardor from her that was greater than her sorrow at their parting. Her senses heightened, she all but held her breath as he continued up her body, finding centers of pleasure as he went, lingering where she responded most, anticipating his caresses to the soft folds at the joining of her thighs. She shivered as his fingers awakened the nub of pleasure between her legs, and as his fingers probed more deeply, she shuddered in anticipatory rapture while his tongue took the place of his fingers.

Continuing to arouse her with his hand, Sanctu-Germainios moved up her body, meeting her lips with his own, touching her breasts as she hovered on the edge of release. Answering her ecstasy with his own, Sanctu-Germainios nuzzled her throat as her first cries of fulfillment, hushed with awe, and her glorious spasms enveloped him in the gratification that exceeded all she had longed for.

"God and the Archangels," she whispered as she came back to herself. She felt him slip off her, lying close beside her while her heartbeat and breathing slowed, and she succumbed to sweet languor, drifting at the edge of sleep. "Stay with me a while?"

"Yes; a while," he told her, leaning to kiss her forehead. "Lie quietly."

She pulled his arm across her body, smiling muzzily. "And you didn't take off your clothes," she said. "You never do," she breathed, letting her attention float with her into delicious sleep.

By the time Sanctu-Germainios left Rhea's bed, the room was deep in shadow and the air was cool. As he rose, he wrapped her blanket over her, then went and lit the single oil-lamp at the door before he left to bathe—his mind still full of her—and then to make the last arrangements for her departure.

Text of a letter from Priam Corydon of Sanctu-Eustachios the Hermit monastery between Ulpia Traiana and Apulum Inferior to Gnaccus Tortulla, Praetor Custodis of Viminacium, Moesia, written on vellum, carried by a Roma-bound band of pilgrims and delivered sixteen days after being dispatched.

To the most esteemed Praetor Custodis, Gnaccus Tortulla, the respectful greetings and faithful prayers of the Priam Corydon of the Sanctu-Eustachios the Hermit monastery in former Dacian territory, Ave, on this, the Autumnal Equinox.

I am grateful to you for your offer of a company of slaves to assist us in fortifying our walls, but I fear what is needed here are soldiers not slaves. We have more than enough monks to attend to the necessary labor, but most of our Brothers are not trained in fighting, and if we must feed and house fifty men, we must require that they be capable of mounting a true defense of the monastery. We have good reason to think that we may have to sustain against an attack before long.

You, of course, must face similar problems, and I sympathize with your predicament, since if you are to supply us with soldiers, it means that you must reduce your garrison, and that cannot be a welcome notion. But without some kind of reinforcement from

ained fighters with weapons of their own, we may face complete
estruction.

   I have asked my brother, who commands a fort in Novae, if he is
a a position to dispatch soldiers to us, but I have yet to receive an
nswer from him. I doubt that he will be able to aid us, which leaves
e to cast about for help from good Christians to come to the aid of
eir fellows and to uphold the Church. If you refuse, then I will
ave to look farther afield for soldiers, all of which means more de-
y during which time we will be wholly vulnerable to attack.

   There are those within the monastery who claim that if God
oes not provide the fighting men we need, then it is His Will that
e be destroyed, and that if we mount any defense, we defy him at
e peril of our souls. They may be right, and if they are, I will an-
ver for it on the Day of Judgment. But to my mind, since I have the
ardianship of the monks, it is fitting that I do all that I can in this
orld to preserve the Brothers and this monastery for Our Lord, for
hom I hold it in trust.

   I adjure you to consider our plight and to offer as much help as
u deem fitting, and to that end I and my Brothers will offer up
ayers.

Priam Corydon
Sanctu-Eustachios the Hermit monastery
Gepidae territory, formerly Dacia Superior

4

hen the courier from Porolissum reached Apulum Inferior at mid-
y the town was already in an uproar: goatherds from their vantage-
oints on the mountain had seen the horsemen coming along the old
ad little more than a day's fast ride away and had brought their
imals back down the mountains, penning them inside the stout,

wooden walls of the town, then had informed the leader of the Watch and the regional guardian of the approaching danger. They had barely completed their report when an official courier arrived on lathered horse and hurried into the central villa, and was directed to the reception-room by the footman at the door.

"There are more than fifty mounted men heading this way; if they continue at their present pace, they may get here by midnight, and they could still attack; if they arrive after that hour, they won't attack until morning," the courier reported as he stood before the guardian and the captain of the Watch in the reception-room; he was tired, thirsty, and dusty, his buckskin paragaudion and femoralia were stained and torn; his temper was short. "The rest of their men have occupied Porolissum and apparently plan to hold it for their leader, possibly as a regional headquarters for him."

"Would he be Attila?" Mangueinic asked, speaking the language of the Gepidae; unlike the courier, it was not his native tongue. He was of Gothic and Dacian heritage, a common blend in this part of the Carpathians, and he had made a place for himself in Apulum Inferior that marked him as a man to be trusted by all parties: as captain of the Watch, he was responsible for the security of the town until soldiers arrived to take over the task of protection. Short, blocky, and strong, he was open-faced and wore his red hair and beard trimmed close to his head.

"That is what they claimed," said the courier. "I left hours before the Huns arrived, not long after the scouts brought their report from Ebussa, which was afire when Attila broke off their assault. Another six couriers were dispatched when I was, shortly after the attack began. Those of us sent out were given this mission because we can understand some of the Hunnic speech, and enough Gothic and Greek and other languages to comprehend most of what we hear when we stop to remount, or to deliver our messages." He patted the satchel secured to his belt. "This is where I have the dispatch for you. It tells you much the same things that I have, but it has details and information I did not have the time to learn, since

peed has been essential. You may have to fight as soon as tomorrow,
o I have traveled as fast as my horse would let me."

"You have done well," said Sanctu-Germainios, and was about
o go on when the courier interrupted.

"Coming here, I passed a group of foreigners," the courier an-
ounced. "About thirty of them, with a flock of goats and a dozen
arts coming, they said, from the north side of the Pontus Euxi-
us . . . I believe is what they said. Their language was unknown to
ne and only two had any command of Byzantine speech; they may
ave said the south side, but their location would make little sense
f . . . Their village was destroyed by Huns and they are hoping to
ind a haven near Constantinople, where they might be safe, or so
heir leader claimed, and if I understood him correctly. They might
ave been Sarmatae, but I can't be certain. There will be more of
hem coming this way."

"This is a strange direction to take to get to Constantinople.
Vhy should they climb the Carpathians when they might as readily
ave continued along the shore of the Pontus Euxinus." said Sanctu-
Germainios. In his black-silk pallium, black femoralia, and short,
lack Gothic boots, he was like a shadow in the room, which his
eserved manner emphasized.

"They admitted as much; they were not on the road they planned
o follow. They hadn't wanted to scale the mountains. But there has
een fighting along the edge of the sea, and they are not prepared to
ndure pitched battles, so they have gone around the combat and—"
he courier fussed with his red, identifying shoulder-sash. "They may
e bound for this town, or some other settlement in this region; they
idn't appear to have a specific destination in mind. It would be un-
ortunate if they should lead the Huns here. If the Huns come upon
nem before this town is in sight, that may delay their arrival here."

"At the cost of those foreigners," said Sanctu-Germainios soberly.

"That's useful of the foreigners," Mangueinic remarked with a
vial cynicism. "It's better that they cause the Huns distraction
nan that we have to decide if we can offer any shelter to them."

Sanctu-Germainios felt disheartened to hear such a callous re
mark, but stopped himself from making the outburst that sparked
within him, knowing that it was as much fear as indifference speak
ing in Mangueinic; he addressed the courier. "If you will give u
your dispatch, you may go to the kitchen; my cooks will give you a
meal and wine. When you have eaten, you may go to the bath-house
or to bed, as you think best. Unless you are to ride on, in which case
I will provide you a fresh horse." He nodded to Mangueinic while
the courier pulled out the parchment, its author's name, location
and office written in a cobbled version of Latin and Greek; he offered
it to the master of the Watch.

"I thank you for the horse and the meal, but I will have to con
tinue on until sunset." He slapped at his paragaudion, coughing a
little as dust sprayed from it. "Anything would be better than wha
I've been eating."

"Then I will have a new horse saddled for you; it will be waiting
when you finish your meal." He turned to Mangueinic. "Is there
anything you want to ask this brave man before he restores him
self?"

"No; I will want to talk with him before he departs," said
Mangueinic, taking the parchment from the courier. "I want to fine
out more about those foreigners. I'll catch him at the gates."

Sanctu-Germainios rubbed his jaw. "We will have to summor
all the men in the town before the day is over. We will call them t
the forum, at the third quarter of the afternoon."

"And not only from the town, but outlying holdings." Mangueini
scrutinized the parchment, frowning. "You were wise not to remain a
your estate, but to come to your villa at the middle of the town."

"As regional foreign guardian, it is my duty to do so. As you an
I must together organize our men for defense." Noticing tha
Mangueinic was having difficulty making out the scrawl on the parch
ment, and was holding it upside-down, he said, "Would you like me t
have a try at it?"

Discomfited at being recognized as unable to read, Mangueini
gave the sheet to Sanctu-Germainios, saying as he did, "You me

hants are always better at reading than we builders are. You have lerks and we have laborers and slaves."

"Skills follow necessity," said Sanctu-Germainios, using the old phorism learned on his first visit to Roma, almost five centuries before. Perusing the hasty writing, he said, "This informs us that the Huns were coming from east-by-north, in three groups of mounted oldiers, the smallest of the groups numbered more than one hundred twenty men, the largest was more than three hundred. The middle group took up the attack on Porolissum, shouting that it belonged to Attila now, and would become his city, and for that reason hey would not raze it. The smallest group turned south, the largest continued west-by-south so long as the shepherds and goatherds ould see them. The writer is Bishop Perrus, and he fears that these Huns are truly bent on occupying the land they over-run. He says his people are terrified of what may become of them."

"Nonsense," Mangueinic scoffed, scratching the edge of his beard. "Everyone knows those eastern barbarians are raiders, after plunder, not conquerors, bent on claiming land for their people. We Dacians and Gepidae and Goths do that—we take land—but such barbarians as the Huns do not."

"This says this new leader, Attila, isn't like the others. He wants to keep the lands he occupies, not graze them and move on, as the Hunic people have done for . . . for uncounted years." Sanctu-Germainios let Mangueinic have a little time to think about the implication of such intelligence, then added, "The Huns have raided in the past, but not like this. They always moved on after taking what they wanted. Now they remain and expand." He began to fold the parchment.

"The Huns are mercenaries for Constantinople," said Mangueinic sulkily. "They have been for more than fifty years. Whole Byzantine garrisons are manned by Huns. Let the Emperor in Constantinople give them land."

"But Attila was not their leader when those men were hired, and they will not be easily appeased," said Sanctu-Germainios. "Attila has taken a lesson from the Romans, and that is why we find ourselves having to defend our lands and our towns."

Mangueinic scowled. "Do you believe that this is true? Or could it be that these barbarians aren't Huns at all, but some other band from the east? What about the company of foreigners the courier saw?"

"They were fleeing the Huns, at least the courier seems convinced of that. And thirty people with flocks of goats and carts are not fifty mounted warriors." He hesitated, musing. "Attila is splitting his men into smaller companies: he is trying to conquer a large area quickly."

"Those foreigners: do you think they could be scouts, or spies?"

"Too many and too obvious to be spies, too slow to be scouts," said Sanctu-Germainios. "For now, I will suppose they are what they claim to be."

After taking a moment to mull this over, Mangueinic said, "I'll tell my Watch to be on the lookout for them. They could help us defend the town in exchange for our protection. Or, if they seem treacherous, we can keep them outside Apulum Inferior, to draw away the Huns."

"Whatever the case where these foreigners are concerned, we will have to do our utmost to be ready to face the Huns," Sanctu-Germainios said, concealing his dislike of Mangueinic's insensibility toward the unknown travelers; this was no time to argue with him about the fate of strangers—not when his town was in peril. "I will arm my servants and send them to you for posting. As captain of the Watch, it is for you to arrange our defense; I will not interfere with your task. I will do what I can to organize the town, and warn the outlying farms and villages, which is my province." He gave a fleeting smile as he thrust the fan-folded parchment through his belt and looked around the reception-room. "I will want to call all my servants together by mid-afternoon, and will assign to you such of them as come under your purview. Then I will want to speak to the clergy and the foreign merchants in the town."

"If you decide to close the gates before sundown, inform me. I think we had best keep the gates open for the outlying villagers and farmers, and to find out about the foreigners on the road. Otherwise

they're apt to be killed, and that will not help us fight the Huns."
Mangueinic looked out at the blustery brightness. "Are you going to
send your messengers—"

"Shortly," said Sanctu-Germainios. "I'll use my personal courier
to go to the chapels, churches, and monasteries, and the town's messengers for the rest. They should be gone from here before mid-
afternoon, and not return until tomorrow morning, if then. I am
going to instruct them to stay away from here if there is fighting. I'll
make sure they have bows and arrows as well as smoked pork, in
case they may encounter trouble on the way. If all goes well, half
of them should return by midnight." He clapped his hands, wishing
that Rugierus were with him and not on the road to Constantinople;
he reminded himself that wishing was not useful, and gave his full
attention to his approaching crisis.

"Funny," said Mangueinic, "we've had a lot of warning since
spring, but I never thought it would really happen—that the Huns
would actually attack Apulum Inferior. I was sure they'd be stopped
before . . . But then, I thought we would have more soldiers here if
there were any real threat, I always supposed they'd head for Apulum, and we would have time to make a retreat."

"That could still happen," said Sanctu-Germainios, more to reassure Mangueinic than because he was convinced of it.

As the house-keeper appeared at the inner door he ducked his
head to the guardian. "Dom Sanctu-Germainios." His conduct was
completely contained, but there was a wildness in his tawny eyes
that revealed his fear.

"Urridien," Sanctu-Germainios said. "Summon the household to
this room at mid-afternoon, and send Estaphanos Stobi, and Samnor
of Porolissum, Polynices Ridion, and Vilca Troed to me as soon as
possible. I will see the messengers in my office as soon as they can
get there. Then send word to the stable to have Atlas saddled."

Urridien ducked his head. "Yes, Dom Sanctu-Germainios," he
said, and hurried away, grateful to have something to do.

As soon as he was gone, Mangueinic asked, "How many men
will you be able to provide me?"

"I will know in little more than an hour, and will send the men to you with my report; I reckon between twenty-five and thirty." He paused, then added, "My clerk will give you the report."

Mangueinic gave a single, curt nod, raised his hand in a gesture that was not quite a salute but more than a simple wave of farewell. "I'll send a messenger if there are any changes."

"Thank you," Sanctu-Germainios acknowledged this, then strode off toward the room designated as his office, where he spent a short while writing out his dispatches on leather squares with an Egyptian stylus and fixed ink. When that was done, he made a list of his servants. By the time he had dispatched his courier and the town messengers, the afternoon was half-gone, and the town was filled with barely contained panic; as Sanctu-Germainios went out to issue his orders to his household servants, he was keenly aware of the terror that was welling as lava rose in the mouths of volcanoes. Everyone was afraid, and that fear was feeding on itself.

Urridien stood at the head of the household servants in the reception hall. Fifty-three men and women and six youngsters waited silently, apprehension in every aspect of their presence. "I brought the gardeners as well as the rest, and the grooms from the stable," the house-keeper announced, his voice cracking from his increasing edginess.

"Very good. We will need their help, too," said Sanctu-Germainios, and turned to address the gathering. "No doubt you have heard that there is a possibility that a mounted company of Huns is coming this way. Whether it is true or not, we must be prepared for that eventuality." He paused to give the servants a little time to think about this. "I will ask all able-bodied men—no matter what your function in the household—to report to the captain of the town Watch for assignment to a fighting post. Glamode, that does not include you. I want you to go into the cellars and make sure our foodstuffs, water, wine, and cloth are kept safe. And Bacoem, you will have tasks to do here."

Glamode, who was almost forty and leaned on a stick to walk

ınd who guarded the kitchen pantry at night, ducked his head. "Very kind, Dom Sanctu-Germainios."

"And what will I do?" Bacoem, the poultry-keeper, asked; he ıad lost his lower left arm in a construction accident, and though ;trong and capable, could not wield a weapon.

"In a moment, Bacoem. The youths will go to the Watch barracks, ınd help the Watchmen to arm themselves. The girls will remain here, ın the weavery, where they can make bandages from the selvage on :he looms." For the first time he was relieved that he had taken the ıme to provide brass-and-leather loricae for the men of the town; nost of the townsmen could not afford to buy armor for themselves. "While you are there, you are to assist the monks in tending to any vounded," Sanctu-Germainios said, and saw the assuagement in all of the servants. "If you have to leave the barracks, go to the town :hapel, and remain in the crypts under the sanctuary until it is safe to ∍merge." He considered adding another place of retreat, then :hanged his mind; if the chapel crypt was unsafe, the whole town .vould be lost. "The women will remain here. Set up an infirmary for ınyone wounded. Bacoem will help you arrange the beds. Make sure ∕ou have sufficient blankets; if you believe you need more, let me <now and I will have them brought in from my estate." He could sense :hat having something to do was reassuring to most of the servants, ınd that served to restore him as well. "Tonight when the household lines, I will ask the cooks to make extra cauldrons of stew and set :hem in the root-cellar, covered, and ready to be warmed tomorrow. The same with bread. And bring in four large wheels of white cheese ·rom the creamery. If there is fighting tomorrow it might not be pos- ;ible to stop long enough for a meal. This way the cooks need only ight a fire to heat the stew, and it can be served in a bowl."

Urridien clapped his hands twice. "There. The Dom is provid- ng for us. We would do well to follow his orders." He was about to lisperse the servants when a single question stopped him. He looked ıt Sanctu-Germainios. "Have you made any provision for those of us vho die?"

"I have asked Patras Anso to place himself at the town's service," said Sanctu-Germainios. "You will have his help and consolation until the fighting is over, and beyond if need be."

The senior footman who had asked now took a deep breath. "Will he be sufficient?"

"We must trust he will be. Patras Nestor and Patras Iob will have to attend to the chapel." Sanctu-Germainios held up his hand to command full attention again. "Do your duties in order of importance: the most important first, then those less necessary, and the last, those that may be left undone without undue hazard." He paused. "If the Huns do not arrive until tomorrow, use the night to sleep when you are not on Watch. You will need all the rest you can accumulate."

"And how will we keep guard in the house?" Urridien asked nervously. "Where shall we be safe?"

"We have women here, and they have eyes and ears. They will sleep in three shifts, and then, if there is a battle, they will divide their guard duties with caring for any wounded brought here, and so will do one third of the full day asleep, one third on guard, and one nursing."

"Women?" Hovas, the master gardener, asked in disbelief. "Keep guard?"

"And why not?" Sanctu-Germainios asked. "Keeping guard is easier than cleaning wounds. Surely if they can tend your hurts they can guard the villa."

There was an uneasy silence, and then Urridien said, "Be about your work."

The servants left the reception-room uncomfortably; only Sanctu-Germainios and Urridien remained behind. When they were quite alone, the house-keeper asked, "Can this town stand against the Huns, do you think?"

"I wish I knew," said Sanctu-Germainios quietly. "I fear we may find out."

"What will happen—if we can drive them off? Will they come back again?"

Sanctu-Germainios considered this question for some little while, then said, his dark eyes fixed on the middle-distance, watching a memory from Panticapaeum more than sixty years ago, when he and Rugierus returned with Kirit Honsilat ud-Kof from the lands north of China. "From what I have seen of the Huns over the years, they fight in the manner they herd: they do not form in lines and squares on foot as the Romans have done for centuries; they fan out on their horses as if to gather their herds together. They surround their foes on their horses and drive them as they would drive wild horses, and when they have them in a pen, or a town, they attack by circling them. When I saw them, they were in a band of around two hundred, including women and children. They had tall carts and their flocks and herds, and they skirmished with a company of Byzantine soldiers, raided, and moved on. Now they leave their families at base camps, or so the reports indicate." He thought a bit more. "Mountains will slow them a little, and forests will, also; bows are not very useful in forests and herding is awkward among close-growing trees. If we drive them away, we should expect them to return."

"Shouldn't we leave the town?" He was doing his best to remain calm, but his voice shook. He started to pace the length of the room, as if moving would lessen his dread.

"If we leave, we are likely to be herded into a trap, or be ridden down like game." Sanctu-Germainios sighed. "No. Dangerous as it may be, it is best to stay here, since the number of Huns seen heading this way is small. There are farmsteads to raid before they attack the town, which will tire their horses, if not the men riding them. If the walls are not set alight, we should be able to hold them off long enough for soldiers from Apulum and Ulpia Traiana to get here. If there were three times fifty, then we might have to abandon the town, and at once."

"And go where?" Urridien asked bluntly.

"That is what I hope to arrange." He took a long, slow breath. "Because if we hold them off this time, they will return, in greater numbers and angry; we should use that time between to get away."

"Could we . . . pay them? Would they leave us alone if we gave them money or horses and goats—or slaves?" He coughed once, aware that Sanctu-Germainios had no slaves, only servants.

"They might leave," Sanctu-Germainios allowed. "But they would be back, demanding more, and plundering when there was nothing more to give." He met Urridien's jumpy eyes with his steady ones. "They do not want slaves. They are traveling people, and slaves slow them down; they require food if they are to keep up with the Huns, and they take up space. Gold does not eat and a great deal of it can be contained in a small chest. The only thing to be said against it is that it is heavy."

"But surely we have something they want?" The question was more of a wail than an inquiry.

"We do have. On their raids, they take food, hides, cloth, cooking pots, iron, cases, and chests, and occasionally young women." He had seen that at Panticapaeum. "They may be more organized now, but their wants have changed little."

"Then we are doomed," Urridien said in despair, and made the sign of the fish in supplication to the Christian God.

"Not necessarily, at least not yet," said Sanctu-Germainios, and was about to explain when Beijos, the head groom, came rushing into the reception-room.

"Pardon, Dom, but a courier has just arrived from Maeia Retta. He is in the stable; his horse has an injured hoof." He managed to stop panting.

"Maeia Retta is how far east of here?" Sanctu-Germainios asked. "Six leagues?"

"More than five; it's very remote," said Beijos. "He has a message for you."

Sanctu-Germainios nodded to Urridien. "See that the men report to Mangueinic, and meet me in the forum at the close of the afternoon." He watched Urridien duck his head, then turned to Beijos. "Take me to this messenger from Maeia Retta." He fell in beside Beijos. "What has he told you?"

"Me? Nothing. Nothing."

As he walked out into the sunshine, Sanctu-Germainios could feel the gusty wind rising; that was the first real encouragement he had experienced that day—Huns, he knew, would not risk traveling through trees in strong winds, for it was dangerous for men and horses to risk being struck by thrashing branches. That might give Apulum Inferior another full day to prepare for their arrival. No matter what news the courier brought from Maeia Retta, the town might have a reprieve. Ignoring the discomfort of the sunlight, he lengthened his stride and made for the stable, Beijos jogging beside him.

Text of a letter from Atta Olivia Clemens at Emona in Pannonia Superior, to Feranescus Rakoczy Sanctu-Germainios at Apulum Inferior in the former Province of Dacia Superior, written with fixed ink on split leather, carried by hired courier, and delivered in thirty-six days.

To the foreign guardian of the region of Apulum Inferior, and my most treasured friend, ave, ave, from the Roman widow, Atta Olivia Clemens, presently at Emona in what has been Pannonia Superior, thirty days after the Autumnal Equinox in the 1191st Year of the City, or the 438th year of the Christians.

Do not tell me that all is well and that I should not be worried. The word here at Emona is that Attila is raging through the mountains to the northeast, his men slaughtering every human being and half the livestock they come upon. Two Gepidae merchants carrying furs and iron arrived yesterday with such tales of rapine and destruction that I have become anxious on your behalf, since, according to the merchants, Porolissum was entirely sacked, and the Huns have spread out through the mountains and onto the Dacian plains. Even allowing for conflation and the natural inclination to make accounts more exciting than the events they describe were, it is clear that there is real danger in the mountains, and that it is unlikely to end soon. I fear that there is worse to come for all of us.

There is a rumor that the Byzantine Emperor Theodosios will dispatch troops to relieve the Christian towns and villages in the Carpathians, but I must tell you that I believe the Byzantines are not likely to defend lands that are part of the Western Roman Empire. If you are anticipating relief from Constantinople, you are more apt to be disappointed than to be heartened.

Which brings me to the purpose of this letter: I had intended to send you word when I arrive in Aquileia in ten to twelve days, but now, with this alarming information, I believe it is fitting to communicate with you, while I have a chance of getting a message through to you. If what we hear is true, let me make the request that you leave your post and come to Aquileia with all due haste. Knowing you, I extend this invitation to your household as well, and as many others as you wish, and we will find a way to make them welcome and safe.

Remember that there is no Tribigild to stop this new wave of Huns as he did almost forty years ago, and no Goths willing to form an army to hold the land against them. The Sciri and Carpi—what few are left of them—are not likely to unite with Attila as their fathers and grandfathers did with the first lot, which may be an advantage for you, but with more Goths holding the old Roman forts, the degree of protection they provide is not as ordered as it was before, unless the Byzantines finally decide to mount a resistance. Withdrawal from danger of the sort you are confronting is a sign of wisdom, not cowardice, and you are a wise man.

I vowed that I would not rail at you, and I have done my best not to, but I know I cannot continue without upbraiding you, so I will end this, hand it to the messenger, and leave wine and oil for Magna Mater in the hope that it will reach you before the Huns do. Know that it brings my pious love and my enduring bond, secured by blood, for days and years and centuries,

Olivia

5

Mangueinic arrived at the central villa of Apulum Inferior before prandium, a harried look on his face, his determined limping almost as rapid as a jog. Soot clung to his hair and swiped his nose, making the scrape along his jaw less noticeable than it would have been otherwise; all were indications that the morning clean-up after the nighttime skirmish with a small company of Huns was well-underway. He looked around the reception-room that had been transformed into an infirmary, where a dozen women tended forty-three men—nearly a third of the men of the town—on cots and pallets, and Sanctu-Germainios provided medicaments, set broken bones, and stitched wounds closed. "The woodmen have come back from the forest with twenty more logs," he announced, his voice strained; he had been shouting orders since sunrise. "There is a band of refugees coming this way, they tell us. They have wagons and carts, well-laden, and probably wounded."

"How many?" Sanctu-Germainios asked with great calm; unlike most of the people in the room, he was impervious to the damp chill that promised rain by evening, and had not added a trabea over his black woollen pallium and femoralia to keep warm. "And do we know where they come from?"

"We have only guesses," said Mangueinic. "The woodmen estimate anything from sixty to a hundred. They are coming from the northwest. Possibly from Tsapousso."

"The northwest?" Sanctu-Germainios repeated, slightly emphasizing *west*. "Not Apulum?" Apulum was northeast of Apulum Inferior.

"Tsapousso," Mangueinic said again, and fell silent as the men on the beds around him who were alert enough gave him their full attention.

"Then the main body of the Huns have passed beyond us, and may circle back once they've secured their targets to the west."

"Ulpia Traiana, do you think?" Mangueinic asked. "We've had no news from there."

"It is probable. It is certainly the greatest prize, with the fortifications and the old Dacian sacred precincts." Sanctu-Germainios motioned to one of the women. "Will you fetch another roll of bandages for me, from the cabinet in the corridor? The captain of the Watch needs his leg rebound." His level voice and even look concealed the alarm he felt as he studied the stains on the bandages along the outside of his calf: puffy parallel traces made by smears of oozing pale-yellow pus.

"You needn't bother," Mangueinic grumbled. "Just let me have my mid-day meal and two cups of wine before I leave—that's all I need. We have to get the section of wall repaired today. I'll rest tonight, while it's raining."

"I would rather rebind your wound now than have to care for you in a high fever, which may be the alternative if you refuse this treatment. The rain will not give you the deep aches that are already beginning if the wound is cleaned." Sanctu-Germainios indicated a bench next to an array of oil-lamps next to the hearth, for unlike traditional Roman villas, this one was heated with fireplaces, and the light from the lamps and the burning logs provided the illumination he needed for his task. "If you will? You can dine afterwards, when you are improved."

Mangueinic huffed, but went to the bench with as much of a swagger as he could manage, although his eyes were worried. "If these refugees come here, what should we do?" he asked, as much to distract himself as to seek information. "If the Huns come back—and sooner or later, they will come back—these foreigners may take their part against us."

"I doubt that will happen. Take them in," said Sanctu-

Germainios at once. "They will have valuable intelligence for us, and coming here now, we can use them and the time to advantage. The Huns will not attack in a storm, at least not so small a village as this one: it is not worth the risk." He paused in his untying the outer bands that held the dressing in place; Mangueinic winced, as much concession as he would give to pain. "The refugees can help us arrange our defenses." The unwrapping began. "I will try not to hurt you, but some of the bandage may stick to the laceration."

Mangueinic tried to conceal a squinch as he shifted his attitude. "If there are strong men among the refugees, then they can help re-build the southern wall and the storehouse, and assist the woodmen in bringing in more logs to heighten the outer wall."

While Mangueinic spoke, Sanctu-Germainios tossed the long bandage aside and saying to the woman who picked it up, "Boil it with astringent herbs and dry it in the caldarium."

"Why do you want her to do that?" Mangueinic demanded.

"Because the pus from your injury contains elements of disease. The Egyptians teach that there are animalcules engendered in wounds that may spread to others if not contained. Boiling in strin-gent herbs eliminates the contagion." He had learned about the boiling more than five centuries ago from a physician with the Le-gions and had used the technique ever since: anything that touched blood or pus boiled with astringent herbs. He had learned about the animalcules while serving at the Temple of Imhotep, many cen-turies ago. He also washed his hands with medicated water between patients, as a precaution against mixing animalcules.

The woman ducked her head and was about to throw the ban-dages into a cauldron when Mangueinic stopped her. "I want to have Patras Iob bless it first."

"Dom?" the woman inquired.

"Have him bless the bandages after they have been boiled, but tell him not to touch them." he said, and added for Mangueinic's benefit, "It would not be wise to pass infection to the priest."

"No," Mangueinic exclaimed, his nose wrinkling as the odor of his wound reached him. "There is pus."

"Not a great amount," Sanctu-Germainios said, "but I think it would be best to treat it with a sovereign remedy, one that will reduce the heat in the wound and will halt its progress. I will make more of it, so that you will not deprive any others who need it," he added, stifling Mangueinic's protest.

"What sovereign remedy is that?" Mangueinic was suspicious now.

"You have nothing to fear from it. You will take only benefit from it, my Word upon it." He raised his voice. "Urridien!"

The house-keeper came hurrying along the corridor to the kitchen, his banded hair in disarray, the front of his sleeved tunica stained with orange grease. He ducked his head. "Dom, I am preparing the cauldrons to take food to the Watchmen; they are due their meal at mid-d . . . day . . ." His words trailed off as he saw the condition of Mangueinic's leg. "God on the Cross."

"And so you shall feed the Watchmen, after one small errand," Sanctu-Germainios said at his most reassuring, making no reference to the horrified exclamation the house-keeper had uttered. "For now, you will go into my office, where you will find a red-lacquer chest of Roman design next to my writing table. Open it and you will see on the second shelf from the top a group of glass vials about as long and as thick as three fingers held together; they stand in a wooden frame. There is a viscous liquid in them that is pale and opalescent, and the vials are stoppered with long-tongued glass lids. If you would fetch me one of the vials, I would appreciate it. Then you will be free to return to your usual duties." Again he found himself missing Rugierus and worrying that he had had no word from him—or if a message had been dispatched, it had not yet arrived.

Urridien looked back toward the corridor to the kitchen, then at Mangueinic, then at Sanctu-Germainios, attempting to resolve the dither in his thoughts. "If I can't find the vials, what then?"

"They were there in the chest earlier this morning, so I am sure you will have no trouble," Sanctu-Germainios told him.

"If I should bring the wrong—"

Sanctu-Germainios cut him off. "Nothing else in the chests is imilar to those vials. If you will take the time to do as I ask, you will oon be back in the kitchen."

"But—" Urridien bit his lower lip and his shoulders sagged. "On he second shelf from the top, in glass vials, you say?"

"Yes. It is in plain sight." Sanctu-Germainios turned to the voman again. "If you will bring me the bottle of rose-hip infusion nd a clean cloth? And the small pitcher of syrup of poppies? Thank 'ou, Hildren. I'll want my basin of herbed water when I have fin- shed redressing his leg."

Hildren, who had been Mangueinic's woman for several years nd found his wound distressing, nodded as if awakened from roubling sleep, and rubbed her dark-ringed eyes. "At once, Dom 'anctu-Germainios. I'll bring the basin when you've done with Mangueinic, unless . . ." She made a vague gesture toward the occu-)ied cots. "Syrup of poppies," she reminded herself, and went across he room to the table where their treatment supplies and medica- nents were laid to get what Sanctu-Germainios requested.

"Urridien?" Sanctu-Germainios prompted.

The house-keeper gave a startled yelp and all but sprinted away, eturning as the woman went off to fetch a cup of wine. He held out he vial. "Is this what you asked for, Dom?"

"Exactly," said Sanctu-Germainios, taking it and slipping it into he pouch on his belt as he went on cleaning out Mangueinic's in- ury with the infusion of rose-hips. "Thank you, Urridien."

One of the other men with extensive burns on his forearms noaned loudly in his enforced sleep; a quiver of dysphoria passed hrough the room, and the other patients studiously avoided looking it the burned man.

"May I . . . may I go back to preparing the Watchmen's)randium?" His voice shook as he asked, and he did his best not to ook at Mangueinic or what was being done to his leg. "I'm needed n the kitchen."

"Yes. And tell the Watchmen that their captain will not join hem until this evening. He needs to rest with his leg up. Thank you gain." He put the soiled square of cloth aside, brought out the vial,

and opened it, then spread a thin film of the contents on the in
flamed skin.

"It's slimy," Mangueinic complained.

Urridien blanched and fled.

Sanctu-Germainios watched Mangueinic's face. "I will bandage
your leg again after you have had some of the wine with syrup o
poppies. It will be less painful that way, and will allow you to rest."

Mangueinic ducked his head, his neck stiff. "Anything else?"

"When you get up this afternoon, I will give you some of the
sovereign remedy to drink. Then you will want to have something
hot to eat. Tomorrow I will want to change your bandages again."

"I have duties to attend to," Mangueinic protested truculently
"I can't be taking—"

"The rain will alleviate your most pressing ones for a day or two
if you use that time to recuperate, when we must be prepared to
fight, you will be capable of commanding the Watch."

Hildren came back with a large tankard of wine. "Dom," she
said, handing it to him. "Save my man, Dom."

"Thank you, Hildren," he said, and took the pitcher of syrup
of poppies from its place at the end of the bench. He removed
the lid and poured a small amount into the wine, then used a
long, thin, scoured stick to stir the mixture. "Here." He gave it to
Mangueinic. "Do not drink it too quickly. Sip a little, then wait a
dozen heartbeats, then drink a little more."

Mangueinic took the tankard and, disregarding Sanctu-
Germainios' instructions, drank a long, deep draft that consumed almost half the mixture, then put the tankard down. "It tastes musty."

"That is not unexpected. If you take in so much at one time
it will affect you sooner and more emphatically," said Sanctu-
Germainios. "Syrup of poppies is anodyne and soporific."

"Is there any harm in that?" Mangueinic asked, doing his best to
bluster.

"No, it will not harm you, but it will hit you harder."

Mangueinic scowled at the tankard accusingly. "In that case, do
you expect me to drink all of it?"

"Yes, I do," said Sanctu-Germainios.

There was something in Sanctu-Germainios' quiet response that quelled the objections Mangueinic had intended to raise; he finished the wine and set down the tankard. "What now?"

"Now you will lie down with a bolster under your leg to keep it from swelling. You'll drift off to sleep shortly, and should awaken toward the end of the day. This will do you more good than anything else. When you waken, I will have a potion of the sovereign remedy and willow-bark tincture for you to drink, and you may move around again, unless you run a fever." He rose from the bench.

Hildren spoke up, her manner deferential as custom required. "Dom; how will you know if he has a fever if he pays no attention?"

"I will know because you will seek him out from time to time to test him. If his palms are hot and dry and his breath is meaty, then bring him back here and see that he lies down again. Then inform me so that I may attend to him." Sanctu-Germainios pointed to one of the beds and turned to Mangueinic. "That will suit your purposes for now."

Mangueinic was already starting to feel the drink, and he nodded in assent as he struggled to stand up. "I'll get there on my own," he declared as Sanctu-Germainios reached out to steady him.

"As you wish," said Sanctu-Germainios, and spoke to Hildren again. "Please bring a bolster for the captain of the Watch. Then inform his deputy—"

"Oh, no," Mangueinic exclaimed as he made his way precariously through the rows of cots. "If something needs my attention, wake me." He sagged against the foot of the nearest cot, and muttered an apology to the carpenter who lay there with a splinted broken arm. Once he regained his balance, he continued on to the bed. He worked his way onto it, trying not to bang his leg against anything firm, finally managing to lie supine upon it.

Hildren came up to Sanctu-Germainios with the bolster and a blanket. "In case he should be cold."

"A very fine idea," he said. "Where did you put the basin? I will wash while you put the bolster under his leg from knee to ankle, and then cover him."

She pointed to a shelf across the room, and told him, "The under-cook says stew will be ready shortly. If any of these men are asleep when the scullions bring it, should I wake them?"

"No. Sleep is more healing than food for most injured people. Be sure you and the other women eat, and have wine and water with your prandium, so that you will gain restoration as you sleep." He gave her a one-sided smile. "You are all doing well, but do not be profligate with your strength: if you tend patients while exhausted, you are likelier to make errors in their care."

"I pray not," Hildren said, dubiety coloring her words. "I have the responsibility for the care all the women provide."

Sanctu-Germainios sought to reassure her. "There is no lack of virtue in being rested; if monks choose to keep vigil and fast, that is their way, but it is not for everyone. For those caring for the sick and wounded, concentration is needed, and for that, you cannot be fatigued."

"I'll tell the other women," she said, and went off to deal with Mangueinic.

When Sanctu-Germainios had washed his hands, he went out into the forum of the village, looking for the town's three messengers; he found two of them—Samnor of Porolissum and Vilca Troed—in the tack-room at the back of the stable, busy repairing girths and bridles, and waxing saddles. "Good messengers," he said courteously, "may I ask a service of you?"

"Dom," said Samnor as he looked up; he put the girth he was mending aside. "Both of us, or just one?"

"Both of you if you are willing, or one who is willing to travel farther and longer."

The two messengers exchanged a private look and Samnor said, "Tell us what you want," as he stood.

"Since my courier is presently at Sanctu-Eustachios the Hermit, I must ask you to undertake to carry messages for me. I will pay you for your service, of course, and you may use my horses." Since

ıe was known to have the best horses in the stable, this was a wel-
ome offer.

Vilca Troed had taken a little longer to get to his feet; his ex-
ɔression bordered on sullen. "It is going to rain again and the roads
ıre already fairly muddy. Where do you want us to go?"

"I want one of you to find the refugees coming this way and
ʒuide them here so that they will not become lost once it starts to
ˀain; that could bring danger to them and to us. The company of
Huns who attacked us last night cannot have gone far, and they will
ɔe looking for isolated people with limited defenses." He touched
ıis hands together. "I want one of you to bear a message to the Tri-
ɔune Rotlandus Bernardius at Ulpia Traiana. Later one of your
ɔomrades will have to carry a message to Apulum. Do you know
ʌhere either one of them may be?"

"Polynices is at the chapel; he should be through with his
ɔrayers by mealtime." Samnor paused. "Why Apulum?"

"To be sure it is still there," said Sanctu-Germainios.

Again the messengers exchanged glances, and again Samnor
ʒpoke for them both. "How far away are the refugees, and where do
:hey come from? Who are they—Goths, Daci, Gepidae, Romans,
Byzantines, Carpi, or some unknown barbarians?"

"I do not know, to all questions," said Sanctu-Germainios. "The
ʌoodsmen saw them from higher up the mountain, so I would sup-
ɔose they may be two or three leagues away, depending on how rap-
ɩdly they travel. I have no notion where they came from except that
ɩt is in some way north of here."

"What does the captain of the Watch say to this?" Vilca Troed
ısked.

"He is currently recuperating from the cleaning of the wound
ɔn his leg," said Sanctu-Germainios. "I am asking you to do this as
ˀegional guardian."

"How much will you pay us?" Vilca Troed watched Sanctu-
Germainios carefully, a sly glint in his eyes.

"A golden Byzantine Emperor to the one who guides the
ˀefugees, and three to the one who rides to Ulpia Traiana."

"Those coins are good metal," said Samnor.

Sanctu-Germainios regarded the two. "I would expect you to depart as soon as possible. If you have had prandium, then before the first quarter of the afternoon."

"A pack with food, water, a blanket, and a tent for the one going to Ulpia Traiana," said Samnor.

"Have the cook give you bread and cheese and smoked meat," said Sanctu-Germainios. "The man going to meet the refugees, get a sack of bread from the baker."

"I'll go to Ulpia Traiana," said Vilca Troed, making up his mind. "I know the way better than Samnor."

"Then choose your horses, take what supplies you need from the store-room, and start on your way." He left them alone, and had the satisfaction of seeing them ride out shortly before he went back into the reception-room to reset a dislocated shoulder, after which he sought out Polynices Ridion and dispatched him to Apulum. He returned to the reception-room to spend the afternoon with his patients, and when supper was served, he went to his private quarters and began to compound more of his sovereign remedy, beginning with gathering moldy bread in a ceramic pail and heating his athanor. As night fell, he continued to work on the remedy along with an array of tinctures and ointments in anticipation of more fighting and more wounded once the rain stopped. A short time later, while he combined camphor and woolfat in a deep stoneware jar, he heard Patras Anso singing the blessing for the dying; he wondered who among his patients was receiving those prayers.

In the middle of Patras Anso's orisons, a chorus of shouts went up outside the central villa, growing louder. The ritual broke off, and shortly thereafter one of the under-cooks was pounding on Sanctu-Germainios' door, shouting that Samnor had returned with a band of strangers. "They're almost to the gate! What are we to do? If Samnor is leading them, will the captain of the Watch admit them?" His confusion lent a higher pitch to his voice, and his questions were breathless.

"I will be with you in a moment," Sanctu-Germainios called out,

going to damp the athanor and set his new vials of sovereign remedy aside and placing his pan of ointment in his tallest oaken cabinet. He retrieved his key from its hook and left his quarters, locking
the door behind him. "Now tell me what has happened."

"There are strangers about to enter the main courtyard," the
under-cook, Thirhald, announced as if anticipating pandemonium.

"Who are they: do you know?" Sanctu-Germainios' stride lengthened. "Are they in the courtyard yet?"

"I don't know. They are at the outer wall," Thirhald cried out, a
worried excitement coursing through him.

"And Mangueinic—is he still sleeping? I do not wish to usurp
his authority."

"He was asleep when I came through the reception-room. He
may be wakened by the furor by now." The under-cook flapped his
arms in the direction of the growing shouting. "What's to be done?"
He stared at Sanctu-Germainios so intently, he almost tripped as
they turned toward the outer door that led onto the courtyard.

"We will determine that after the newcomers are identified."

"But once they're inside, how will we expel them?" Thirhald
shook his head repeatedly, like a horse bitted up too tightly.

"There may be no need to do that," said Sanctu-Germainios,
and opened the side-door onto the courtyard.

The people of Apulum Inferior had come out of their dwellings,
most carrying torches, a few with covered oil-lamps, for the clouds
had soaked up the remaining daylight. They were anxious and curious
at once, huddling together as the gates were pulled open.

"Who gave the order to admit them?" Thirhald muttered. "The
Watchmen should not do it without orders."

"Samnor did, I suspect," Sanctu-Germainios responded before
he walked toward the center of the courtyard, feeling the first sting-
ing drops of rain strike his face and hands.

Samnor was at the head of a bedraggled band: there were nine
carts in all, and five wagons; nineteen women and eleven children
rode in the wagons, with fifteen men riding horses and mules, two of
them sagging in their saddles. Twenty-eight horses pulled the carts

and wagons, and another eleven were tied to them with lead ropes. A flock of long-haired sheep tagged after them, kept in a group by a solitary woman riding a mule. They all drew up in the center of the courtyard, and Samnor dismounted and offered an off-handed salute to Sanctu-Germainios.

"Here are your refugees, Dom. All that remains of Tsapousso, they tell me." He sighed. "What are you going to do with them?"

"Put them in the old storehouse for tonight," said Sanctu-Germainios. "Tomorrow we will arrange things more equitably. For now, they should be given something to eat—Thirhald, if you would see to that?—and given a chance to bathe. Urridien, order the bath heated. I will want to talk to their leaders later."

"They told me their leaders died at the hands of the Huns. They are traveling without a leader, following the road hoping to find someone untouched by the Huns." Samnor's mirthless chuckle ended in a snarl. "The man with the patch over his eye is as much of a leader as they have, and the woman on the mule. They're Daci and Carpi, for the most part."

"Ah." Sanctu-Germainios moved closer to the wagons. "Welcome," he said in Dacian. "Dismount and let us extend you hospitality as custom requires." He went on in the Latin vulgate of the region, "Everyone here will be glad to help you. Watchmen, see to the gates! Urridien, escort our guests to the dining room. Herdsmen, see to the horses and the goats!" Activity erupted around him, and he stepped back toward the central villa, satisfied that the new arrivals would be taken care of. He was about to go back into the villa when the woman on the mule rode up to him.

"Good Praetor," she began in careful Latin.

"You do me too much honor. I am the regional guardian." He took the reins of the mule and offered her his arm to assist her to dismount.

She all but slid off the mule, and leaned against the saddle before she turned to face him. "Regional guardian, then. Where would you wish to assign me?" She looked up at him, the light of the doorway torches revealing her unusual features: her face was angular, and just now shaded by enervation, with broad, high cheekbones and a wide, ointed jaw. Her mouth was well-shaped, accented by a small, red irthmark in the shape of a leaf at its corner. Her hair, braided and oiled on her head, was a color that was not quite black. What was most striking was her eyes: pale gray and shiny, like quicksilver. She appeared to be about twenty-five or so.

"With your people, of course," Sanctu-Germainios said after a brief, intense pause.

"That would be impossible. My people are dead." She said it unflinchingly but with an air of profound grief. "I am a . . . a servant to the village of Tsapousso. They gave me a hut, a mule, three flocks of sheep, and two of goats to herd. I wouldn't mind sleeping in the stable, or the barn," she offered, taking the mule's reins from him. "If you will point the way?"

Sanctu-Germainios thought a moment, then said, "For tonight, I'll place you with the women of the household. There is a dormitory where you will find a bed. In the morning we will decide what is to be done." He opened the door behind him and began to think of how he would explain this to Hildren. "When you have been assigned a bed, you may go to the kitchen for something to eat."

"I thank you for that," she said, lowering her head and following him into the central villa.

At the end of the corridor, he stopped and asked her, "What shall I call you? The women will want to know your name."

She nodded in agreement. "I am Nicoris."

Text of a letter from Priam Corydon of the Sanctu-Eustachios the Hermit monastery to Feranescus Rakoczy Sanctu-Germainios, regional guardian of Apulum Inferior in the Kingdom of the Gepidae, written on cotton with paint, carried by Sanctu-Germainios' personal courier, Estaphanos Stobi, and delivered in eleven days, having been delayed for six.

To the honorable regional guardian Feranescus Rakoczy Sanctu-Germainios, ave and benedictions from the monastery of Sanctu-

Eustachios the Hermit on this second day of November in the 438th
year of the Christ:

*I have your request for the protection of the monastery for the
people of your region, who are much plagued by the Huns. Since
Christ enjoined His followers to succor the weary and the helpless,
what can I do but agree to receive you? If I refused I would not be
true to my faith, and unworthy of my calling, though I fear there
will be great crowding with so many inside our walls.*

*You may wish to consider the weather that has become cold so
suddenly. Two days ago we had our first snow—very light, but there
will be more and heavier, which may make your travel difficult. At
present, it should take you eight days to reach here, but after more
snow comes, that time may easily double. I advise you to consider
weather in your evacuation plans, and to send a messenger when
you leave Apulum Inferior, so that we will know to anticipate your
arrival. We may soon receive the people of Ulpia Traiana as well, so
our resources will be much strained. Anything you can do to diminish your demands on our limited stores would earn our gratitude
and the favor of God: your offer of food and the providing of your
own basic household equipment is greatly appreciated; also your offer of weapons, for we keep none here. If you have men who can
hunt, or animals that give milk, we ask you to bring them with you.*

*May God guard and keep you and your people, and so I will
pray every morning and every night.*

> Priam Corydon
> Sanctu-Eustachios the Hermit
> In the former Province of Dacia Superior

6

Three open braziers stood in the reception-room of the central villa of Apulum Inferior, the short logs burning in them adding their warmth to that of the embers in the fireplace, all throwing off enough heat to make the room only chilly instead of freezing in this dark hour between midnight and dawn. Sixteen of the cots remained set up and occupied, a patient lying on each wrapped in heavy blankets. All the other cots had been taken apart and now were stacked in anticipation of their coming departure the following day. A solitary scullion dozed at the entrance to the kitchen corridor, as far from the dying fire as possible, guarding the room and its occupants, but otherwise, nothing intruded—all was still except for an occasional groan from one of the patients.

Then Hildren came in from the dining room dormitory, groggy from too little sleep and shivering from cold, a heavy trabea flung round her shoulders over the woollen palla she had donned. She held an oil-lamp with two wicks burning as she made her way among the cots, evaluating the condition of her patients and trying to decide how best to transport the injured men.

A grumble from one of the cots attracted her attention, and she turned toward the voice; she gasped as she caught sight of Mangueinic, for he had thrown off his blankets and his face was flushed; above the bandage on his leg, distinct, dark-red lines ran up to his knee. She could tell he was delirious—his eyes were only half-open and only the whites were visible, and fragments of words slipped through his lips, angry and incoherent at once. Uttering a little shriek, she hurried from the reception-room and ran to

Sanctu-Germainios' quarters, pounding as loudly as she could o:
the door.

Sanctu-Germainios opened the door quite promptly, dressed i
a black-wool pallium and black femoralia, an abolla shrugged on a
an afterthought. He held an oil-lamp in his hand and a folded boo
in the other. "Hildren—what has happened."

Hildren began to tremble, tears spilling down her face. "O
Dom Sanctu-Germainios . . . You must do something. You must. I
you don't, he will not live more than a day or two, his fever bein
what it is . . . He can't travel . . . that would almost certainly kill him
But we shouldn't leave him behind, not with Huns in the regions . .
and who would be willing to stay with him? If the Huns should fin
him . . ."

Seeing how distrait she was, Sanctu-Germainios brought he
into his withdrawing room and urged her to sit down in his mo:
comfortable chair. He then went to a small cabinet and removed
bottle of strong, boiled-plum wine. He poured a small cupful fc
Hildren and took it to her. "Here. Drink this. It will calm you
nerves. Then you can tell me what has upset you."

She set her oil-lamp down on the floor beside her and took th
cup with trembling fingers. When she had drunk a small amoun
she coughed, then said, "He's much worse."

"Which man?" he asked, anticipating the answer with unhapp
certainty.

She summoned up her courage to answer. "It's Mangueinic." Th
breath caught in her throat. "He has fever enough for him to thro
off his covers, and there are Devil's Fingers running up his leg."

"How far have they gone?" Sanctu-Germainios asked, takin
care to conceal his alarm from Hildren; for in the six days sinc
Mangueinic was injured, his three lacerations had developed
deep infection that not even his sovereign remedy had been abl
to obliterate, although the progress of the infection had bee
much slowed. He had seen this kind of injury many times, treate
worse resultant fevers to full recovery. But in rare instances, th
wounds had remained open and feverish in spite of his best effort

ne recognized the signs and knew that they boded ill for the builder who was captain of the Watch.

"The longest looked to be above the knee a little way, the other two are shorter, but their color is dark, and . . . the skin itself is darkening . . ." She took more of the wine. "This is very potent," she said, sputtering a little.

"That it is. You may have more if you like."

She shook her head. "Much as it would steady me, it would dull me as well, and I need my wits about me, thank you. There is so much to do through this coming day, and more again tomorrow. As it is, this will be enough to make me bacchic," she told him, closing her eyes for a half-dozen heartbeats. "Can you come? It would be very bad if he dies, wouldn't it?"

"I can come, and yes, it would be most unfortunate to lose him. Eight dead already, and five men still hampered by their hurts—adding Mangueinic to their number would discourage the Watchmen; they depend upon him," he said, putting his book away and setting his abolla aside as he picked up a voluminous closed saie that hung on a peg near the door. He pulled it over his head and nodded to Hildren. "Let me get my treatment case and I will join you in the reception-room directly." He held the door open so that she could leave.

She drank the last of the boiled-plum wine and picked up her oil-lamp, then rose carefully and minced out of the room. "Will he die?"

"We will all die," said Sanctu-Germainios kindly. "I hope that day may be far off for Mangueinic."

"I hope so, too," she said, stumbling a bit as she turned into the corridor; she waited while Sanctu-Germainios locked the door, then asked, "Should I fetch a priest?"

"I will tell you after I have seen Mangueinic."

"Don't you need a lamp?" She held out her own.

"I can manage, but thank you." Like all of his blood, he had no difficulty seeing in the dark: he went along to his office, opened the red-lacquer chest and took out a wood-and-leather case that contained

his medical equipment and a number of medicaments. This in hand
he went to the reception-room, and to Mangueinic's cot, where Hil
dren was standing guard. "If you will bring a stand of lamps?" he re
quested not only to give her something to do, but to appear as needfu
of light as other men.

"I will. There is one stand with six oil-lamps. Will that be suffi
cient?"

"I should hope so," he said, and bent over Mangueinic, examin
ing his leg for inflammation and swelling: his calf was bulging
around the bandage that covered the unhealing wound, and the
Devil's Fingers, tracks of infection, ran up toward his knee, as Hil
dren had said; below the bandage, the skin was tight and dark a
roof-tiles in Roma. The odor of the wound was metallically acerbi
mixed with a cloying sweetness, the stink of suppuration. Straight
ening up, Sanctu-Germainios pressed his lips together, trying to de
cide what he ought to do.

Moving slowly so as not to extinguish any of the wick-flames
Hildren came back to Mangueinic's cot with the lamp-stand, he
face carefully blank. "Dom?"

"He is, as you say, very ill." Sanctu-Germainios hesitated, the
went on. "It may be that the only way to save his life is to remove th
infected part of his leg. Otherwise the infection will reach th
bones, and then he—"

Hildren stared at him, aghast. "You mean *cut it off*?" Her voic
rose as the enormity of the idea bore in on her.

"It may be that or death," said Sanctu-Germainios as levelly a
he could.

"But cut off his leg—" She put the stand of oil-lamps down an
put her hands to her face.

"It is the only way to save him, and it is no certain method. If h
becomes too consumed with fever, he will die no matter what is done
Such fires can consume more than flesh if they remain unchecked
To end it, the fuel must be taken away." The bluntness of his word
was mitigated by the kindness of his tone. "I hope that there is som
chance of a recovery for him, but there may not be."

"Patras Anso should be consulted," said Hildren. "In case such a drastic . . . if taking his leg might endanger his soul."

"Why should it?" Sanctu-Germainios asked.

"An imperfect body . . . who can say what that would mean to God." She made the sign of the fish to keep her from evil thoughts, speaking quietly as if to herself, "Some teach that only the Christ had a perfect body, that all others are marked by original sin, but others teach that those who aspire to be one with God, must achieve perfection in mind and body." Her face crumpled with grief. "He must be worthy to appear before God."

"If his leg is not removed, he will surely die of the fever. It will be a very hard death, much harder than the amputation would be." For a moment he said nothing, then observed, "God receives the men wounded in battle for His sake, and crowns the martyrs and saints. Why should He reject Mangueinic for a severed leg?" He studied her tormented face. "Talk to Patras Anso if you think it will be helpful, but realize that once the Devil's Fingers stretch beyond the knee to his groin he will be beyond anything I can do for him."

Hildren blanched. "Is it really so desperate?"

"Yes."

Their eyes met; she made an effort to regain her composure. "How soon must it be done?" Her voice was quiet now, and tentative.

"As soon as possible," said Sanctu-Germainios.

"God save me," she whispered. "And may He spare Mangueinic."

Sanctu-Germainios gave a hard sigh. "Then his leg must be sacrificed for benefit of the rest of his body. I will need help, if I am to do this. If my manservant were here, he would assist me, but with him far away, I will require—"

"I'll ask among the Watchmen, and the newcomers." She rubbed her face suddenly, as if to warm her skin, or to prevent more tears from coming. "If Patras Anso will permit it to be done."

Mangueinic thrashed feebly, then moaned before falling into a soft whimpering without waking.

"Oh. Oh." Hildren clasped her hands together, her self-possession deserting her. "He mustn't die. He mustn't."

Sanctu-Germainios reached out, laying his hand on her shoulder "It is difficult to remain calm, but if you do not, he will be at more risk than he is already. He needs to be treated, and soon. We can move him into the withdrawing room in the east corner of the villa. All that we are taking from there has been loaded into the wagons."

As if this reminder of Apulum Inferior's imminent evacuation spurred her to action, Hildren steadied herself. "I will find Patras Anso. He will be singing Mass soon; dawn is not far off. Then I will visit the Watchmen as they break their fasts, and I'll send Khorea to deal with the patients so you will be able to devote yourself to Mangueinic." She ducked her head.

"Have the bath-house heated and the fire"—he nodded toward the hearth—"built up in here."

"As you wish, Dom," she said before she turned abruptly and hastened from the room.

Sanctu-Germainios brought a small serving-table from its place against the wall and opened his treatment case atop it, looking over the items secured within it. He would have to order a cauldron of water boiled with astringent herbs; Khorea would deal with it for him. He would need to bring down his wire-saw and flensing knife to be boiled as well. Then he would have to have a metal platter heated to cauterize the cuts and burn away the fever of the infection. And all the while, the people of the town would be finishing their packing and making ready to leave. Travel would be hard on Mangueinic, but he would have a better chance of recuperation at Sanctu-Eustachios the Hermit monastery than here, where the Huns would undoubtedly return in the near future. He was so preoccupied with these problems that he was unaware of someone next to him until she spoke again, a bit more loudly; he turned to her in surprise. "Nicoris. I trust you are well?"

"Cold but well," she said. "I have just seen Hildren, who told me of what has happened. I thought I might be of some use to you. She said you would need someone to aid you."

"Did she tell you what I will have to do?" Sanctu-Germainios asked, impressed by her courage, but wondering if she understood what she was volunteering to do.

"You will have to cut off his leg," said Nicoris, resolution and revulsion vying for dominance in her demeanor.

"Such a procedure is bloody and difficult. Do you think you can endure it?" He watched her as he spoke, trying to decide if she would be able to stomach what he would have to do.

"I can." She paused. "I have had sheep savaged by bears, and had to minister to those who could be saved. The butcher took the others. And I helped to treat a mare with a damaged stifle."

"It is not quite the same," Sanctu-Germainios said with sympathy.

"I have seen men lose limbs before—with swords."

"You were not over-set by it?" he asked.

"Not while it was happening. Later, when it was all finished, I shook for half the afternoon." She was neither apologetic nor defiant, and though there was no eagerness in her, there was also no reluctance. "Someone must help you. This man is a stranger to me, so his suffering will not distress me as much as it would those who know him."

He looked down at Mangueinic's leg. "Some may disapprove."

"So they might," she said with the appearance of resignation, then brightened, a mordant cast to her tone. "But at least I will have spared them from having to help you themselves. That may count for something."

Sanctu-Germainios thought a bit longer. "You will need a working-woman's palla made of heavy cotton or linen to protect you from the blood. And you'll need a ricinium to cover your hair. Bathe before and after the task is undertaken." He noticed that Nicoris swallowed hard but did not flinch. "If you decide you cannot do this, tell me so that I may find another assistant. I will think no less of you if you choose not to help me."

"I can do this," she insisted. "But I have no such clothing. I do have a short Gepidean cloak much like the one you're wearing, and it should be adequate. It's boiled wool."

"Will you need it later? You should consider that, since you will want to discard it after the leg is removed; blood in that amount does not wash out easily." He slipped his hand into Mangueinic's arm-pit and shook his head in alarm. "We must attend to this soon. His fever is increasing." Saying that, he reached for his medicaments and selected a glass jar. "This is a fortified tincture of willow-bark-and-pansy. If he can be made to drink some, his fever should stop rising at least for a while, and his pain may be reduced. But he will bleed more freely because of it."

"That should help diminish the fever in his blood," she said. "Give me the jar and I'll try to make him take—how much would you recommend?"

"Half the contents of the jar," he said after considering for a moment.

"Half the jar." She took it from him and opened the lid. "Is the taste unpleasant?"

Sanctu-Germainios thought back to the many comments he had heard over the centuries, since he had never tasted it. "It is somewhat bitter and caustic, but not intolerably so."

"I'll bear that in mind," she said as she dipped her finger in the sauce-like solution, then spread it on Mangueinic's lips; he licked it away, and she did it again. "This should enable me to give him a fair amount."

"Very good," said Sanctu-Germainios. "I am going to the withdrawing room on the east corner to prepare it for the task. Hildren knows what will be needed; I will tell her to make the bath ready for you." He could feel a deep fatigue grip him, the accumulation of centuries and the weight of mortality. "We should begin as soon as we may. It is beginning to lighten and it serves nothing to delay."

"All right," said Nicoris, tipping the jar to Mangueinic's lips. "Half of this, you say?"

"Yes," said Sanctu-Germainios as he went off toward the withdrawing room. He found it empty of everything but a low table and a large, oblong hearth-shield of brass. The table would not be useful to him, but the hearth-shield could be heated for cauterizing the wound

ie would order a fire built up, and would bring in the trestle-table
rom his book-room. The thought gave him a pang, for he would
iave to leave almost all of his books behind, and he had no hope that
he Huns would not destroy them. He removed the shutters from the
vindows, taking note of the lowering, light-gray clouds that were
eginning to pale in anticipation of dawn.

"Dom?" The voice was Hildren's; she was standing in the door-
vay, her sagum drawn tightly around her, her face grave. "You are
oing to do it?"

Sanctu-Germainios turned toward her. "I think I must," he an-
wered softly. "The amputation may kill him, but the infection most
ertainly will."

"Are you sure?" She came into the room, stopping at the table.

"As sure as my experience makes me," he replied, approaching
ier. "Did you speak to Patras Anso?"

"He said he could not decide what ought to be done." She
ocked her head to the side. "He told me to pray, and I have tried,
ut nothing comes to me to ask God, except to spare Mangueinic's
ife."

"Then the only thing that might accomplish that is to remove
iis leg," said Sanctu-Germainios as gently as he could.

"There could be a miracle," she said in a small voice.

"There could," he told her, with no conviction whatsoever. "But
hat is a gamble that could cost him his life."

"So is your plan," she accused him.

"Yes. But at least if he survives the amputation, he may be able to
ndure the journey to Sanctu-Eustachios the Hermit. If his leg is not
emoved, he will have to remain here, for travel would not only be ag-
inizing, he would not live through it, and that is as sure as sunrise."

"I want him to live," she whispered.

"So do I."

Hildren gave a shudder as if releasing all the pent-up fear.
Then tell me what you need and I will see to it."

He told her the things he required, and added, "Nicoris has said
he will assist me. If you can find two strong men to help hold him

down, then I will start as soon as this room is ready and I have had a quick bath." He looked around the room, thinking that it would soon be splashed with blood. It would be a dreadful sight—not as bad as what the Huns might do, but hideous in its way; it would remind him of how long it had been since he had taken sustenance, and although this was not the kind of blood he would take, he felt famished for an instant. With an impatient motion, he returned to the reception-room, going to Mangueinic's bed and Nicoris. "How much has he taken?"

"Not quite half," she answered, holding up the jar. "I've tried to get him to drink more, but he gags."

"Then we must let him be for now." He tested his arm-pit again. "The fever is still quite high."

"Is that a problem?" She held out the jar to him, the lid back in place.

"Fever is always a problem." He set the jar with his other medicaments and studied the supine figure. "A table will be set up for him in the withdrawing room. I'll move him as soon as it is prepared."

Nicoris stared down at Mangueinic. "I'm ready," she said to Sanctu-Germainios.

"You will be when you have bathed." He put his supplies and medicaments back in his case, adding, "If you will bring the syrup of poppies before you go to the bath-house? We will have need of it."

She shrugged and did as he asked. As they entered the withdrawing room, she said, "You will need to build up the fire, won't you?"

"Yes." He stared at the window. "There will be more snow soon."

"Will that delay our leaving tomorrow?" She put the syrup of poppies on the mantel and stared around her.

"We would have to complete an outer wall in a few days if we did, and with the ground frozen, that wouldn't be possible. Wise as the Goths are to build outer walls, they are not easily maintained in winter." He turned to her. "Go gather up the clothes you will wear, then hie yourself to the bath-house and wash thoroughly."

Nicoris nodded. "If you're sure it's necessary."

"It is," he answered, and turned to see Khorea in the doorway. "Ah. Let me tell you how the room is to be set up, and then I will go to my quarters and then the bath-house." He motioned to Nicoris. "We will get this done as quickly as we can."

She gave a single nod and left the reception-room.

He regarded Khorea. "If any of these men should need attending, call upon Patras Iob. He has some experience with the wounded. I will give you my full attention as soon as I have the opportunity, but what Mangueinic requires will take at least a quarter of the morning." He then described what he needed her to arrange for him.

Khorea made the sign of the cross to call the protection of the Christ upon them all. "I will do my utmost. And I will pray that the Huns do not return today, or tomorrow."

"Very good," said Sanctu-Germainios, doubtful that her supplications would make any difference. He went to his quarters, chose his clothes, his special surgical tools, then went out into the frigid morning, all the while hoping that the amputation was not coming too late to spare Mangueinic from death.

Text of two identical letters from Feranescus Rakoczy Sanctu-Germainios to Rugierus, written in Imperial Latin on squares of sanded split leather in fixed ink, then entrusted to Patras Nestor for delivery to the crossing-fortresses at Drobetae and Oescus on the Danuvius. Only the first reached its destination, sixty-seven days after being dispatched.

Rogerian,

When you receive this, we will have moved on to Sanctu-Eustachios the Hermit, where we will spend the winter, and hope that the Huns will not follow us there. We have forty-six carts and wagons, and over four hundred people in our company. A few of the

Gepidae in Apulum Inferior have decided to take their chances on reaching Aquincum, and have already left.

Since I have received no messages from you, I must hope that this reaches you as you return from Constantinople. So much has been disrupted by the presence of the Huns that I am going to assume that the failure of messages is the result of their actions and not an indication of harm to you. Additionally, I am assuming that Dona Rhea has been established appropriately in the city of her birth—for which I am deeply obliged to you.

If matters go ill at Sanctu-Eustachios, then I will attempt to reach Olivia in Aquileia, and should that fail, I will strike out for Lago Comus. At every opportunity I will dispatch messengers to ports where my trading company has offices, on my own ships if possible, and ask you to do the same so that we may once more reunite.

Sanct' Germainus
(his sigil, the eclipse)

7

Glistering sunlight shone off the patches of new snow along the narrow road that led up over the ridge to the little valley where Sanctu-Eustachios the Hermit was situated, all but obscured by shaggy pines and ponderous oaks; the wagons and carts and flocks were strung out for almost a league along the way, forced into single-file by the narrow path. Humans and animals kept up a steady walk even as the road grew steeper; the herders strove to keep their animals from bolting into the trees, and mothers kept vigilant watch on their children, knowing how capable they were of mischief and how dangerous it could be for them all. This was their fourth day of travel and the weather was deteriorating, high, thin clouds increasing the glare of the sky, riding on a sharp, searching wind.

Mounted on a large mule, Patras Anso led the people from Apulum Inferior and the refugees from Tsapousso on the torturous road, followed by Enlitus Brevios, the new captain of the Watchmen and master mason, on a mountain pony. Watchmen with spears in their hands walked between the two leaders, alert to any disturbance on the road or near it. Behind them came an assortment of wagons, the third of which held Mangueinic with Hildren and Nicoris to tend him. Immediately behind that wagon rode Sanctu-Germainios on a handsome gray horse—one of six he had brought with him. To protect himself from the biting wind he wore a fine black abolla of boiled wool over his heavy silk pallium and black-dyed doeskin femoralia; his thick-soled boots were of dark-red leather from Troesmis. He carried his case of medical supplies on a strap across his chest. After him came more wagons, and the people from Tsapousso with their vehicles and animals, then the flocks and herds of the region of Apulum Inferior with their keepers flanking them, and finally the carts pulled by donkeys and driven by under-cooks and grooms, holding the foodstuffs, supplies, and household goods from the abandoned town.

Sanctu-Germainios moved his horse up close to the rear of the wagon and called out, "How is he doing?"

Nicoris stuck her head out of the leather panels that covered the back and said, "The syrup of poppies is keeping him asleep for now and the bandage you gave him is allowing the cauterized scar and the skin flap you have sewn over it to breathe, as you said it would. There is no sign of returning infection, though he complains of itching. He drinks when we give him your medicaments in water, and his fever is moderate, not high. Hildren tells me he has made water twice since we broke camp."

"Has he been awake for any period of time?"

"He has been groggy, not truly awake, about a third of the time; at those times he forgets that we're traveling. He keeps talking about reinforcing the outer wall. He wants it done before the Huns can return." A slight frown crossed her face. "If the road gets much rougher, it will take a toll on him."

"On us all," said Sanctu-Germainios. "Thirhald's woman could go into labor early if she has to endure much more of this."

"Agtha rides in the wagon behind us, doesn't she? All the injured are in wagons or on mules, isn't that right?" Nicoris asked, holding on to the frame as the trail dipped down toward a fast-running stream.

Sanctu-Germainios adjusted his seat in his Persian-style saddle with a broad, raised pommel to help him maintain his balance; he held his horse with his lower legs and leaned back as the gelding picked his way down the slope. "She does; Khorea and Dysis are with her. I may ask Isalind to ride with them when next we stop; she has had four children of her own, and has birthed six others—more than Khorea and Dysis combined." She was, he believed, the nearest thing Apulum Inferior had to a midwife.

"It will calm her, at least, having such good help with her. It will calm Thirhald as well," said Nicoris, and ducked back into the wagon.

From the front of the line, Patras Anso called out, "We will ford a stream ahead. The water will be cold, but not too deep. It should not rise above your knees. We will group on the far side so the animals can drink, and we may have a short rest before we have to climb to the ridge."

Four of the Watchmen turned and made their way back along the line, relaying the Patras' words to all the travelers; a buzz of conversation followed their progress along the line.

As predicted, the water was cold, flowing fast in a rocky bed; it rose a bit higher than the Watchmen's knees, but no higher than half-way up their thighs. The horses and mules had a dodgy crossing, finding poor footing in the stream; one of the wagons almost lost a wheel as it lurched across. Sanctu-Germainios, feeling queasy as he always did crossing running water, held the team of mules from the back of his horse while half a dozen men worked to keep the wheel in place so that the wagon would not founder. He avoided looking at the water, and instead concentrated on the mules in order to contain his sense of vertigo. If only he were not hungry, he thought, this passage would be less disquieting; the blood of horses that had sustained him on the trail thus far did little to offset his enervation.

By the time the herds and flocks were on the far bank, it was past mid-day and Patras Anso ordered that they prepare a meal before they resumed their journey. "No fires!" he shouted. "No fires! Cheese and bread and apples, but nothing hot! We want no smoke to mark our place."

There was a discontented rumble of protest, but everyone understood why Patras Anso had ordered it, and they went about putting together meals that needed no fire and that could be eaten quickly.

"Are you never hungry, Dom?" Nicoris asked as Sanctu-Germainios dropped out of the saddle; they were at the edge of the gathering, away from the bustle.

"Of course I am," he said, aware that he was now; it was more than a week since he had taken any sustenance from a human source.

"But I never see you eat." She contemplated him, her quick-silver eyes alive with curiosity. "You don't join the rest of the household for prandium, nor did you when there was a convivium in the town."

"No; those of my blood dine in private."

"That's haughty of them," said Nicoris as if remarking on the distance they had covered that morning. "How did they come to decide such a thing—are they afraid of poison?"

"Not that I recall," he said, realizing that she had been observing him more closely than he had supposed.

"Then do their gods demand it?"

"Possibly: they see it as respectful, in any case," he said, recalling the living god of his people who had brought him to his life before he fell in battle. He drew his horse's reins over his head and started to lead him to the edge of the stream.

Nicoris tagged after him, her saie dragging on the ground behind her. "Who are your people, that they have such manners?"

He paused, then spoke to her. "Long ago they lived in the

mountains east of here, but they were driven away from their native earth by powerful enemies who came out of the east and forced us to the south and the west, away from our native earth. There are not many of us left."

She had the grace to look chagrined. "I'm sorry. I shouldn't have asked."

"You had no way of knowing," he answered calmly, and resumed walking, his horse's nose nudging his upper arm.

"I know how I feel when I think of my family." Her voice was small and she looked over her shoulder as if she were afraid of being overheard. "The people of Tsapousso have been kind to me, but it doesn't change the loss of my family."

"No; it would not," he said, sympathy for her burgeoning within him. He shifted the reins so that his horse could drink from the cold, rushing stream. "Why not go get some food. Just because I do not eat hardly keeps you from doing so. You will need nourishment if you are to keep to your tasks. The climb ahead of us is rigorous."

Nicoris stared hard at him. "All right," she said, and went off to join the growing crowd around the two carts of foodstuffs that had only just arrived.

Once his horse had drunk his fill, Sanctu-Germainios led him to another one of the carts and removed a small bag of grain and a pail. Emptying the grain into the pail, he offered it to the gelding, holding it while the horse fed. When the animal was done, Sanctu-Germainios put the pail back in the cart, told his groom to see to his other horses while he went on a short errand, then vaulted into the saddle and rode a little way up the track to the first level spot on the road in order to have a clearer view of the mountainside: bare rock faces stood out above the tree-line, somberly gray under the massing clouds. In spite of the wind, he made a careful inspection of the road ahead and the road behind. When he was satisfied they were not being followed, he returned to the temporary camp and sought out Patras Anso.

"What did you see, Dom?" the priest asked in roughly accented Byzantine Greek. He was half a head taller than Sanctu-Germainios, making him easily the tallest man in all the people following him; his face was lean and deeply lined, his nose was pointed, and his large ears protruded as if providing handles for his head.

"Nothing troublesome, Patras; a small party bound to the south on the Roman road, either merchants or farmers abandoning their land," said Sanctu-Germainios in the courtly version of the same tongue.

"God is good to us." He blessed himself with the sign of the cross, and then made the sign of the fish. "When we reach the ridge tonight, if the weather holds, we will arrive at the monastery tomorrow afternoon. A good passage, considering what we have had to deal with."

"Not to discourage you, Patras, but I doubt the weather will hold, not with the way the wind is blowing; there will be rain before nightfall, and the snow may fall here as well as on the crest of the rise," said Sanctu-Germainios, not wanting to alarm the priest, but seeking to provide him warning. "As you can see, the clouds are gathering in the northwest, and they will reach us before mid-afternoon."

"Possibly," Patras Anso allowed. "But they may not. God has watched over us for most of the way. He may well continue to do so."

"What if the storm closes more quickly than we expect, and strands us on the upward track? There will be no place for us to make a camp, and we will have to manage for the night on the steep side of the mountain, all strung out along the way." He gave Patras Anso a little time to consider this. "If it is, as you say, God's Will that we reach the monastery, then He may seek to render us safe in our climb. In which case, He may well intend to keep us here," said Sanctu-Germainios. "This hollow can provide protection greater than the ridge will, or the road up the mountain."

Patras Anso folded his arms. "Why should that be the case? We must show our faith by pressing on. God will know that we trust in Him. He will bring us to the haven of His monastery once we have passed the test He has set for us."

"We would be almost two leagues closer to Sanctu-Eustachios the Hermit if we keep climbing: that is true enough, and we may arrive there before sunset if all goes well. It is a pity the ridge is so exposed. If we must make camp there, we will all be open to the weather and without the stream for water. And we will be more readily seen by any foe." Sanctu-Germainios waited as if something had just occurred to him. "If we stay the night here, we will be far more protected from the weather by the trees, we will have water, and we will be rested in the morning; so will our animals."

"But it would take at least another day to reach Sanctu-Eustachios the Hermit," said Patras Anso.

"Or more," Sanctu-Germainios said. "But it is likely that we will all arrive, which might not be the case if we try to ascend now. With so many injured and so many children, pressing on could mean a great risk to all of them."

Patras Anso glowered at the stream. "And if we are being followed, what then? You say there might be foes behind us. What if they are hidden in the forest as they hunt us? They would be upon us before we were ready to fight."

"Bad weather will halt anyone behind us as surely as it stops us," said Sanctu-Germainios.

"We will have to make fires if we stay here, and the Huns could use the smoke to find us." Patras Anso shook his head, weighing alternatives.

"Yes, and in addition, we will have to put up our shelters and set up pens for the animals. But we will have to do that no matter where we pass the night, and it will be more difficult to do that in a storm, and more demanding, since frightened animals tend to bolt. We have no hope of other shelter—there are no estates between us and the monastery."

They had reached an impasse and both knew it. They fell silent, and into that silence came Enlitus Brevios, his fair skin wind-reddened and his blue eyes watering. He addressed Patras Anso.

"Hovas' son is missing." He tried not to seem confused or ineffective, so he spoke bluntly and loudly.

"Are you sure?" Patras Anso asked. "Is it certain he isn't—" He waved his hand to indicate the confusion of the camp.

"We have searched and called everywhere among the wagons and carts, and there is no sign of him." Brevios held up his hand as if to swear an oath. "Bacoem is organizing a group of Watchmen to search for him. There's just the one son, you know, so Hovas is beside himself. His other three children are girls."

"You mean the nine-year-old? The one called Ionnis?" Patras Anso asked, looking alarmed. This was the second child to go missing since they left Apulum Inferior, and the first lost one had been found dead from cold.

Brevios nodded. "He was last seen when food was being passed out. He got his share and ran to the edge of the trees so that the bigger boys would not take it from him. He is an adventurous rascal."

"Do you think he wandered off on his own, or there has been something done to him?" The priest made the sign of the cross.

"I haven't any idea," said Brevios.

"What does Hovas say?" Sanctu-Germainios asked.

"He says that his son must be found. He and his family will not move on until they know the child is safe, and a dozen men swear to remain with him, and will order their families to remain as well."

"What of Hovas?" Patras Anso pursed his lips in thought.

"He is miserable, weeping and decrying his fate. His woman is as if she is asleep." Brevios put his hand on the short-sword that hung from his belt. "I have said we will find him."

Patras Anso made up his mind. "Sad as this is, it is a sign. We will camp here for the night, and we will send search parties to look for the boy as long as there is light. Have Hovas go with the Watchmen, and call for the boy often. How old are his sisters?"

"Thirteen, eleven, and six," said Brevios.

"That's right, that's right," said Patras Anso. "The boy is a clever child, as I recall, and given to mischief-making. If this is a trick, Hovas should beat him for his shenanigans as soon as he is found. Young as he is, he cannot be allowed such license." He gave Sanctu-Germainios a curt nod, and then he started back toward the greatest concentration of people where they clustered on the edge of the stream, Brevios two steps behind him.

For the rest of the afternoon the evacuees and refugees divided themselves between making camp and searching for Hovas' son. The clouds continued to thicken and the wind grew keener, so that in the fourth quarter of the afternoon, everyone in camp was seeking out the newly laid fires for warmth. The first odors of cooking rose on the whining wind.

Sanctu-Germainios had tethered his horses to a long remuda-line and was finishing putting down hay for them when Nicoris found him. He felt a pang of dismay as he caught sight of her, presuming her errand was not a pleasant one. "What has happened?"

"It's not Mangueinic; he's doing well enough," she said as she came up to him. "It's Kynthie, Thirhald's woman. She has gone into labor; it began a quarter of the afternoon ago, hard and sudden. Her pangs are still some distance apart, but that will change. Isalind is worried that Kynthie may not manage the delivery well: her heart-beat is very fast."

"That is not a good sign," Sanctu-Germainios said, wondering what he could do to ease her birthing.

"Will you come with me now?" Nicoris swept her arm to take in the bustle around her. "If you have other duties . . ."

"Yes, I will come with you," he said, putting down the last arm-load of hay. "Has Thirhald been told?"

"He's helping to prepare supper for the camp and I don't want to disturb him. He would be distraught."

"It would be wise to inform him; at least he should know her labor has begun," Sanctu-Germainios suggested. "I will go see to her now."

Nicoris remained where she was as she studied his face. "You're worried, Dom. You think she is going to die."

"Perhaps not worried so much as concerned," he said, aware how intently she scrutinized him. "This is not the place for a delivery, particularly if it has problems attending it."

"Then you expect problems," she said.

"Her labor is nearly a month early. That does not bode well under any circumstances. Hard travel has not helped her." Nor has the danger from the Huns, he added to himself. He patted his gelding on the rump, then started off to where the wagons were assembled. "Where is she?" he called out to Nicoris.

"Four from the far end," she replied, pointing. "What do I tell Thirhald?"

"Tell him that his wife may be going to give birth tonight—nothing more."

"He may want to know more," Nicoris warned him.

"So he may, which is why it will be better for him to learn from you than to hear of it later, by accident. When his work is done, tell him I will inform him of Kynthie's progress." He lengthened his stride, moving through the groups of people who were making ready for nightfall; in the distance he could hear the sound of calls for Ionnis, accompanied by the moan of the wind in the trees.

Through sunset and the arrival of the storm, Sanctu-Germainios stayed in the wagon with Kynthie, Agtha, Isalind, and Khorea. The women tended Kynthie, making her as comfortable as they could, while Sanctu-Germainios used all his skill to bring about a quick delivery. In the wavering light of oil-lamps, he tried to massage Kynthie's swollen abdomen in an effort to align the baby for birth; he could feel the infant and was troubled that its movements were so feeble.

"How much longer?" Isalind asked while a troop of Watchmen left the camp to continue the search for Ionnis.

It was the very question he had been debating with himself. "I wish I could say. It is not encouraging to see her so lethargic. You said she has no other children?"

"She's miscarried once," Isalind told him.

"That's inauspicious." He had attended difficult births before, some during his long tenure at the Temple of Imhotep, and he knew that the more exhausted Kynthie became, the more problems that could arise.

Isalind lowered her voice to hardly more than a whisper. "Is she going to die?"

"She may," said Sanctu-Germainios. "If we had a better place, with a tilted table and tincture of hawthorn to calm her pulse; willow-bark and pansy are anodyne, but will not ease her heart. It would be much better for her and the baby if her—"

Kynthie gave a moan, thrashing her legs and attempting to break free of Sanctu-Germainios' gentle, powerful grip; Isalind and Khorea endeavored to hold her steady while Agtha wiped her face with a cool, damp cloth. Kynthie howled, her voice more like the cry of wolves than anything human.

Khorea started to weep, her hands over her mouth to keep from sobbing.

"Shall I fetch Patras Anso?" Agtha muttered to Sanctu-Germainios.

"Not yet," he replied, and resumed massaging Kynthie's abdomen. "If a quarter of the night passes and she continues this way, it would probably be wise." He had noticed the small cross on a leather thong around her neck, and hoped the attention of the priest might help her rally.

"Where is Thirhald? She might respond well to his presence," Isalind suggested. "If he can bear to see her like this."

"He has gone to help the Watchmen search for Hovas' boy; they have taken the dogs to help them, and Thirhald has a good hunter," said Khorea. "When I spoke to him, he would not want to see her in her present travail, for it could bring him to despair."

This kind of response did not surprise Sanctu-Germainios; he had seen many men shy away from the process of birth, relegating its mysteries to women rather than have to be party to it. "When he returns, he should come here, for Kynthie's sake, no matter how late it may be."

"I will find him and bring him here," said Agtha, her mouth a grim line.

"Do you think he can wait so long?" Khorea gave Kynthie a worried glance. "She could fail, and if she does—"

"If she does, it will be rapid, I concur." He touched his fingers to the vein in her neck, shaking his head as he felt its rapidity. "If the babe will shift its position, there may still be a safe delivery." Sanctu-Germainios stared into the middle distance. With careful circumspection, he regarded Kynthie closely. "If the infant does not move, I could open her belly and take out the child; Kynthie might die, but if she continues as she is doing now, we will not be able to save her or the child. If I—"

"Patras Anso would never allow it," said Agtha sharply. "Opening the body is a sin. Those who do it are heretics and diabolists."

Sanctu-Germainios was well-aware of the strictures against surgery; he had encountered such censure during his most recent stay in Constantinople. As a result of that experience, he considered his arguments carefully. "It is a risk, but her present state is precarious and unless I take the baby soon, she will not have strength enough to recover. If she cannot deliver shortly, not only she but her baby will die."

Isalind gave Sanctu-Germainios a measuring look. "I have seen two women die from such difficulties as this. If you know any means to spare her, then do it and let the priest declaim. What may I do to help?"

"Go to the wagon where Mangueinic rides and ask Nicoris to bring my case and some of the sovereign remedy and the ointment in the red jar. Quickly." He did not watch Isalind leave, turning at once to Agtha. "I will need boiling water. Take a metal cauldron, fill it with water, and place it over the nearest fire. I will give you herbs to add to the water, and my instruments."

"This is against God's Will," Agtha declared.

"It is a skill I learned in Egypt, where the Christ was taught." He had studied in many other parts of the world for more than nineteen centuries, but he knew that Christians held Egypt in a kind of awe, and used this knowledge to his advantage.

There was an impressed silence, then Khorea said, "You are a regional guardian for Roma and Byzantium: how is it you have studied in Egypt?'"

"I am an exile. Exiles travel."

There was a silence, then Kynthie moaned again, and spasmed as blood frothed between her legs.

Sanctu-Germainios responded promptly. "Give me a knife. She and her child will be dead almost at once if I do not remove the baby," he said, holding out his hand; Isalind put her knife into it. "Move the lamps as near as you can," he ordered, and cut.

When the Watchmen returned with the terrified Ionnis, sometime near midnight, Thirhald hurried to the wagon where Kynthie lay. He called her name as he approached, faltering now that his goal was in sight.

"Thirhald. You have a son," said Sanctu-Germainios, coming out of the wagon to speak with him. "But I grieve to tell you that your woman is dead." He could see disbelief in Thirhald's face, and softened his tone. "The boy is with a wetnurse, and will remain in her care as long as it is needed." He watched as incredulity became shock and sorrow, and Thirhald swayed on his feet as if the ground had shaken beneath him. "You have my sympathy."

"Does Patras Anso know?" Thirhald asked blankly.

"He has blessed her and will supervise her burial when we reach Sanctu-Eustachios the Hermit, so she may lie in sacred ground." He met Thirhald's vacant gaze with his own. "I wish we could have saved her."

Thirhald nodded once. "Yes," he mumbled, and turned away.

Text of a letter from Verus Flautens, landholder of Drobetae, to Gnaccus Tortulla, Praetor Custodis of Viminacium, written in code on vellum with fixed ink and carried by Tortulla's confidential courier; delivered in eight days.

Ave to the esteemed Praetor Custodis of Viminacium, Gnaccus Tortulla, on the twentieth day before the Winter Solstice. I am honored to be of service to you once more, and thank you for giving me the opportunity to perform the useful deed you have informed me you require.

I can understand your fear regarding the large numbers gathering at Sanctu-Eustachios the Hermit monastery. Too many of those iving in the Carpathians and on the plains the mountains surround have gone over to the Huns of late, and I agree that the monastery could prove an opportunity for subversion. Those who have lost their lands and goods to the Huns may seek to regain them through Hunnic favor. I also agree that leaders of any such movement constitute a threat to the remains of Roman-and-Byzantine rule in the region and cannot be allowed to continue their illegal course. I am eager to comply with any actions that will bring about an end to the Huns' invasion.

This is not a task I can undertake personally, of course, for I would be viewed with suspicion by many of those seeking refuge at Sanctu-Eustachios the Hermit, but I will dispatch my newly freed manservant, Hredus, to go to the monastery and report on all he sees. Hredus has an elementary knowledge of letters and he may be relied upon in this undertaking as I relied upon him assisting me in my dispatching of Sergios of Drobetae, who would surely have betrayed Roman interests to Byzantium in exchange for the advancement he sought. If there is any skulduggery afoot, Hredus will root it out and get word to me as quickly as distance and weather allows. I will charge him also with learning all that he can about the location and number of Hunnic forces in the region and the nature of their attacks: with all the barbarians flocking to the Huns, it will serve us well to know how and where the Huns have enlarged their armies, and any changes they have made in their methods of making war.

Know by this that my devotion to you and the Roman cause is beyond corruption and unending,

Verus Flautens

PART II

DOM FERANESCUS RAKOCZY SANCTU-GERMAINIOS

*T*ext of a letter from Atta Olivia Clemens in Aquileia to Ragoczy Sanct' Germain Franciscus at Apulum Inferior in the Kingdom of the Gepidae, once the Province of Dacia, written in Imperial Latin on two sheets of vellum in fixed ink and carried by Iraeneus Catalinus, but never delivered.

To my most cherished friend and blood relation, the greetings of Atta Olivia Clemens from her estate at Aquileia on this, the Winter Solstice of the year 438 according to the Christians, the 1191st Year of the City, and the 2557th year since your birth:

How long it has been since I have had word from you—and I am assuming you have written—or received any letters from anyone in old Dacia. Were it not for the accounts of increasing Hunnic raids, I would think only that any messages sent to me had been delayed, but given the increasing alarms from that region, I have become more vexed than I was earlier in the year, which is saying a great deal, and now that word has come that the Western Emperor has hoped to bring about an alliance with the Goths or Gauls against the Huns, I am growing truly distressed; there have been so many assaults on Roma that I doubt any of the Empire is safe. You needn't remind me that I would know if you had died the True Death, but a great deal of harm could come to you without that happening, and I have imagined the most dreadful things.

A month ago I received a visit from a merchant, Demetrios Maius, whom I had known in Porolissum, who has lost everything that he owned that remained there. He is now attempting to gather what little he has left in the towns and cities where he has done business before this ruin came upon him, telling me that he fears for all of the Empire in the West. Assuming he can amass enough to salvage a small trading company for himself, he then plans to leave for Constantinople and enter into a partnership with a cousin who owns ships. His family and household were spared destruction by leaving Porolissum last July, and are now at Ravenna with the family of his mother and her brothers, most of whom are rich; once he has established himself, he will summon his family to join him. His experience is unusual only because he was so beforehand in his planning, and he made the most of the opportunity to depart ahead of the forces of Attila, the new King of the Huns, who he claims is responsible for their new ferocity. He asked me how many others I knew of had got out before the town was razed, and I had to admit that I knew of fewer than five households. Thinking of you, I provided Maius with ten golden Emperors as an initial investment in his new trading company, and the name of your factor in Constantinople, in case his cousin there reneges on his agreement. It is the sort of gesture you would make, don't you think?

How many of the fortunes in what was Dacia can still be secure? How many estates are truly safe? Seharic the Goth is in no position to hire soldiers beyond the ones allied to him by marriage or blood, and he is far from unique among his people. The Gepidae have soldiers, but they fight on foot, not on horseback as the Huns do, which puts them at a disadvantage, even if they had men enough to hold off the Huns. Roma cannot send Legions to protect what is no longer theirs in any case, and the Emperor in Byzantium is not about to risk his troops in Dacia. Stilicho is dead and there is now no General in Byzantium who is willing to take on the Huns as he did. For all his skills, Aetius is in no position to contain the Huns either, and is not likely to act unless he is attacked directly.

Do not, I beg you, consider this a challenge to you to take up arms against the Huns because no living man will do it. It is exactly the kind of foolhardy thing you would do. You have risks enough without making a target of yourself with the Huns. As regional guardian, you may limit your hazards to preserving Apulum Inferior and its extended vicinity, as you are sworn to do, which is dangerous enough without you taking on more. Remarkable though you are, you cannot oppose the Huns alone. Compassion for the living is all very well in its way, but it should include your own survival—not that I suppose you will consider such advice if you see peril increasing.

With most of the Roman Court now removed to Ravenna, depending on the Padus and its swamps around the city to defend it from attack better than walls could, Roma itself is ripe for another plundering. For that reason, I have decided to stay here in Aquileia for the time being. I have sent instructions to Adrastus Feo, the major domo at Sine Pari, to reinforce the villa starting with the outermost walls, and to do the same for Villa Ragoczy. I've ordered that the inner stockade at both estates be strengthened, and weapons provided for defense, for whether or not the Huns come to Roma, Goths or Vandals or Gauls or other northern barbarians may decide to plunder it now that it is so very vulnerable.

Cognizant of the hazards of Aquileia's location, Niklos Aulirios has engaged masons to put a stone wall around the central buildings on this estate. I must thank you again for reanimating him for me. It is more than a century since you restored him to life, and every day he proves his worth a thousand times. He believes stone is the better choice now, since the Huns are known to set wooden walls afire. It is an expensive precaution, but one I endorse, and which I encourage you to consider, as well. Were stonework not so dear in Roma, I would have ordered the walls of our villas ringed with it, but the cost is prohibitive, even with the funds you have provided to me. I may regret my decision in time, and Sine Pari may suffer for it, but I believe that a double wall of standing, close-joined trunks will suffice unless Roma is left entirely without defenders of any sort. It will mean cutting down the wood at Villa Ragoczy, I regret to say, but it is the only way to ensure the work is done quickly and properly, and without paying outrageous prices.

If conditions continue to deteriorate in this region, and Roma remains exposed, I will go to Lago Comus to the villa there; it is properly fortified and there is a company of mercenaries based near-by. If you need a place to come to and you decide not to go back to Constantinople—which, I remind you, would be prudent—then perhaps you would like to join me there, at least for a short while, say as long as a year? Ordinarily I would agree with your policy of separate lives, but surely two vampires can spend time together without attracting unwanted attention with so much of the world caught up in bloody turmoil; what we do is hardly comparable. We would have the opportunity to enjoy the tranquillity of accepting companionship, which is as advantageous in its way as the passion of the living can be. At least give it some thought, won't you.

You may send me an answer with the man who brings it, Iraeneus Catalinus, one of five couriers recommended to me by the Praetor Custodis of Aquileia. He knows the main roads of old Dacia and most of the minor ones, and has three strong horses for his journey, two from my own stable. He has been to Apulum Inferior and promises to find it again. If the roads are blocked by snow when he reaches the frontier, he will wait in Viminacium until the thaw to deliver this. I ask you to reward him handsomely, since many couriers now refuse to venture north of the Danuvius.

Be safe, my oldest, my dearest friend, and, on behalf of all your forgotten gods, be sensible. Let this anniversary of your birth remind you of the value of your longevity. Remember that I want to know where I can find you once you have removed yourself from harm's way. I should be here for two years unless the Huns come this way, in which case, seek me at Lago Comus. If I leave Lago Comus before you arrive, I will send word of where I have gone to your factors in all the ports where Eclipse Trading operates, so that one way or another, we will reunite, if only for a little while.

Eternally your devoted
Olivia

1

Priam Corydon rose from the slated floor of his monastery's church, his shoulders and knees aching; he brushed off the front of his rough-woven pallium, and went to open the doors for the rest of his monks to begin their daily worship. He could barely hear the novice singing the Psalms' worn-down Latin in the chapel behind the altar, for the wind was ululating so loudly that the icons seemed to be transfixed by the uncanny noise. It was half-way between midnight and dawn, so cold that the Priam's breath fogged in front of his face as he trudged toward the door, stamping his feet to help warm them, his wool-lined peri feeling woefully inadequate to keep out the razor-like chill. He told himself that this was the heart of winter, the hardest time that always came shortly after the year turned toward light again, and that he should be grateful that the days were getting longer, but at the moment, he found it difficult to praise God for his discomfort.

Monachos Egidius Remigos, the broad-bodied warder, stood outside the doors, his arms folded, the monks gathered behind him. He made the sign of the fish. "Priam Corydon. God be praised."

Priam Corydon made the sign of the cross. "God be praised, Monachos Egidius. Open the doors to our good monks, that they may receive the blessings of God." He moved aside and let the monks file through.

The last in line was Monachos Niccolae of Sinu, the recorder for the monastery. "I will need a word with you later, Priam Corydon," he said just before he entered the church.

"This evening," said Priam Corydon.

"It is a matter of some urgency."

"After Mass, then." Wondering what had happened this time, Priam Corydon nodded his consent, resigning himself to a busy day; all days had been busy since the refugees arrived. He stood still, watching Monachos Egidius close the door, then listening for the first drone of the Mass chanted in Greek. When he knew the ritual was under way, he went off toward the cross-shaped building that held the monks' cells, the refectory, the kitchens, the library, the infirmary, and the two small offices of the monastery. He would be permitted to sleep until the sky lightened in the east, and this morning, he needed all the rest he could get. With all the refugees inside the monastery's walls, the demands of his position had trebled, with the promise of more duties to come. He recalled that he would have to meet with the Tribune of the garrison from Ulpia Traiana after they all broke their fasts, and then the delegation from Apulum Inferior; perhaps he should see them at the same time, so that there would be no opportunity for anyone to misconstrue his actions. "Christ be merciful," he said, more loudly than he had intended, as he entered the dormitory wing of the building—the right end of the main cross-arm of the crucifix.

"Priam Corydon," mumbled the dormitory warder.

"Monachos Bessamos," said Priam Corydon, passing down the narrow corridor to his own cell at the far end, just off the intersection of the hallways. As he entered his cell, he made the sign of the fish, and then used a small knife to trim the wick on the single oil-lamp burning beneath the Greek crucifix next to the door. In the uncertain light, he made his way to his narrow straw-filled mattress atop a simplified table-bed. He recited his prayers, then lay down pulling up his single blanket, and did his best, in spite of his worries and the cold, to fall asleep. After a longer time than he had hoped he was dozing, when a sharp rap on his door brought him awake once again. "What?" he called out.

"I apologize, Priam, but there is a problem in the main kitchen." The monk's voice was strained by his effort to speak softly.

"The main kitchen? Not the dormitories' kitchen?" What or

earth could be wrong in the kitchen that it should require his attention so early? A chill that came from something more than the cold of the room came over him. He moved his blanket aside and got to his feet. "I'm coming," he assured the monk outside his door. He made the sign of the fish at the crucifix, then let himself out the door, his patience fading as he pulled the door open.

Monachos Vlasos, the butcher for the monastery, stood at the door. Even in the indefinite light it was possible to see he had a bruise over his eye. "I'm sorry, Priam Corydon, but I thought this couldn't wait: there has been an attempt to raid the pantry, undoubtedly by a group of refugees, since no monk would do so uncharitable a thing. Not that I actually saw the men who tried to steal our meat, but I believe they must have been among the groups of outsiders who now make their camp within our walls. I know they must be the culprits, since I can't imagine any of our monks resorting to theft."

Priam Corydon gave a long, tired sigh. "I suppose this shouldn't surprise us that the refugees might do something so reckless; they have so little. Those coming with the troops from Ulpia Traiana were nearly out of food by the time they arrived here, and had been on short rations. Not all of them have been fed well in the last two days, either." They went back to the hub of the cross-shaped building and turned down the corridor that led to the refectory and kitchens at the west end of the structure. "Was anyone seriously hurt, aside from you?"

Monachos Vlasos made the sign of the cross. "One of the novices, who keeps watch on the kitchen fires for the second half of the night—"

"Would that be Penthos or Ritt?" Priam Corydon interrupted. "Or that youngster Corvius?"

"Ritt," said Monachos Vlasos. "He has a broken arm, I think." They went on a few strides in silence, then he added, "He may have seen two of the men."

"Why do you say that: may have?"

"He is dazed and overwhelmed with pain, and has told me very little," Monachos Vlasos explained; they had reached the refectory and were passing through it toward the kitchens that were at the foot of the cross at the broadened rooms representing the foot-rest on the Greek crucifix.

"The monks in the infirmary have their hands full," said Priam Corydon.

"They say there is a good physician with the people from Apulum Inferior—their regional guardian, in fact." Monachos Vlasos knew better than to suggest that the Priam speak to the stranger, but thought mentioning the man would help. "Dom Sanctu-Germainios. He has . . . had land at Apulum Inferior, and a small trading company. Enlitus Brevios has told me that Dom Sanctu-Germainios saved the life of the first leader of their Watchmen, though it cost the man his leg, and he tells me that he yesterday removed two toes from Hovas, whose feet were frozen during the hunt for his lost son. I understand that the Dom has a trading company in Constantinople, though he isn't Roman or Greek."

"Most interesting," said Priam Corydon, trying to make up his mind if he should send for this man; as regional guardian for the region of Apulum Inferior, he would have to be included in their meeting in the coming morning, so he might as well summon him now. "Will you find him and bring him here?"

"I suppose I can do that. He has several wagons among those brought here, and a number of servants. No slaves, they tell me. He keeps himself in his own wagon. One of the night Watchmen should be able to point it out to me." He made the sign of the cross and hurried toward the side-door to the refectory, where he paused. "Shall I tell him what's happened?"

"No, I don't think so. Just say that one of the novices has been injured and requires special treatment. There will be speculation, of course, but at least it need not be too outrageous." The Priam watched Monachos Vlasos let himself out into the night, then he ducked into the corridor leading to the main kitchen, where he found the novice huddled, whimpering, near the largest hearth, his arm held across his body, his face white except for the pits of his eyes. "Ritt," he said, leaning over to inspect the young man, " am sorry you are hurt. I regret that you have had to suffer for your devotion."

"God have mercy," Ritt said, as if he doubted it were possible. Hunkered down as he was, he looked small for his fifteen years.

"How do you feel?" It was a foolish question, Priam Corydon decided, so he amended it. "How bad are your injuries?"

"I'm cold," he mumbled. "My arm is burning. Corvius ran away."

"He will ask God for mercy for such an act," said Priam Corydon.

Ritt's teeth chattered. "It's so cold."

Priam Corydon touched Ritt's forehead and felt a film of chilly sweat on it. "Then we must warm you. It's bad enough that you are hurt."

"Monachos Anatolios would say that hurt is—"

At the mention of the apocalypticistic monk, Priam Corydon stiffened but he said nothing against Monachos Anatolios; he would pray for patience later. "I have sent Monachos Vlasos to bring you a worthy physician. He will attend to your hurts."

Ritt nodded slowly. "Thank you, Priam."

"Thank Monachos Vlasos and God; it is my responsibility to guard you from harm. You ought to expect it of me." He realized as he said it that he felt deeply guilty, and that Monachos Anatolios would make the most of his failing. "You will have good care, and with God's Grace, you will recover without lasting harm."

"May God be praised," whispered the novice.

Priam Corydon went to the wood-box and pulled out two substantial branches cut to fit in the maw of the fireplace. "I'm going to build up the fire, so you will not be so cold."

The youth mumbled a response, his teeth still chattering as he tried to pray.

"Did you see who attacked you?" Priam Corydon asked as he put the branches onto the glowing embers of the night-fire.

"No. They weren't monks," he answered with some vehemence.

"Not monks," said Priam Corydon as he stepped back to avoid

the shower of sparks that accompanied his prodding of the coals with the fire-fork.

"No. They didn't smell like monks, they didn't sound like monks . . ." His voice faded suddenly, becoming a mewl of pain.

Priam Corydon abandoned his efforts on the fire and knelt down next to Ritt. "It won't be much longer. You will be better by dawn."

"May God spare me," the novice cried softly.

"We will pray for you at the morning Office."

Ritt nodded listlessly.

The sound of a door closing thundered along the corridor, and almost at once there was the sharp report of rapid footsteps from two persons; Priam Corydon had rarely heard such a welcome sound. He got to his feet, anticipating the return of Monachos Vlasos with the physician.

"Priam Corydon," said Monachos Vlasos as he entered the main kitchen, "this is Dom Feranescus Rakoczy Sanctu-Germainios, the regional guardian of Apulum Inferior."

"God reward you for coming, Dom," said Priam Corydon, liking the man he saw: a bit taller than most, sturdily built with a deep chest and powerful, well-shaped legs, his dark hair trimmed in the old Roman style; his cheeks were shaved, and his narrow beard was carefully cut; his countenance was regular, although his nose was a little askew. His most striking feature were his eyes: the most compelling dark eyes that seemed almost black but glinted blue. He carried a leather case under his waxed-wool byrrus.

"Monachos Vlasos tells me that he and his assistants were attacked by men seeking to steal meat from the larder." His eyes went from Priam Corydon's to the novice. "It looks as if the boy has taken the worst of the fight."

"I couldn't see them," Ritt grumbled.

Sanctu-Germainios crouched next to the novice and eased him out of his huddle so that he could examine his arm. "They bent the arm back and snapped both bones below the elbow; I think they may have intended to break the bone above the elbow, not the two

ower ones," he said when he had finished his scrutiny. "And they
unseated the elbow in its joint. I'll have to align the bones and splint
hem before I reset the joint."

"How long will it take?" Priam Corydon asked.

"No longer than it must," Sanctu-Germainios said, and looked
about the kitchen. "How long until the cooks begin the breakfast?"

"The monastery's slaves will rise in a short while. They will be
here well before sunrise," said Priam Corydon.

"Then is there a room nearby where I may take this young
man?" Sanctu-Germainios asked. "Preferably one with a large table
and torches or oil-lamps for light?"

Priam Corydon answered quickly. "There is a drying room for
herbs and fruit. It has a table and two trees of oil-lamps."

"How far away?"

This time Monachos Vlasos answered. "It is on the west end of
his extension—about twenty paces."

"That should do. When the lamps are lit, I will set to work there."
Sanctu-Germainios looked down at Ritt. "I will carry you, but before I do, I will give you an anodyne drink so that you will not have
much pain."

"Do you want me to summon monks or slaves to carry him?"
Priam Corydon asked.

"I can carry him," said Sanctu-Germainios. He opened his case
and took out a small, covered cup, which he held to Ritt's lips. "Drink
his. Not too quickly."

The novice did his best to comply, only once giving a sputtering
cough. "God spare me," he whispered before he finished the con-
ents of the cup.

Monachos Vlasos left the kitchen, saying, "I'll light the lamps."

A short while later, Sanctu-Germainios lifted Ritt in his arms
with little show of effort, and bore him into the drying room; he was
truck at once by the odor of fennel and thyme, rosemary and figs,
but he paid no attention to them as he laid Ritt out on the table,
ook his case from Priam Corydon, and said, "I have slats for splint-
ng, but I may need cloth for a sling."

"I will have someone bring it to you. Will linen do?"

"Very well." He paused. "Also, I may be a bit late for the meeting this morning. I hope you will explain my absence to the others."

"Certainly. God be thanked for you." The Priam made the sign of the cross, then withdrew from the room, praying that he had made the right choice and that Dom Sanctu-Germainios would be able to care for Ritt properly. He worried about his decision through prayers and breakfast and the first of his meetings that morning, trying to keep his mind on what the Tribune of Ulpia Traiana had to say rather than fretting about Ritt.

"It is for me to uphold the honor of the Legions, for the sake of my great-great-grandfathers, who served so well. Honoribus Romanum, as they would have said." Bernardius folded his arms to express his determination and pride of heritage, and a lack of awareness of his ramshackle Latin. "I'll be glad to organize a temporary garrison here, of course." He was a tall, substantial man with hazel-green eyes and a true Roman nose that was marred by an angled scar; his light-brown hair was thinning, so like Gaius Julius Caesar, over four hundred years before, he combed it all forward and kept it trimmed short.

"I had hoped it would not come to that," said Priam Corydon.

"So might we all hope," said Rotlandus Bernardius. "But the Huns might not feel so magnanimous. We should prepare for the worst, you know."

"I know," said Priam Corydon heavily.

"There are men enough to do the needed labor, and enough of them to man the battlements when they are completed." Bernardius made an abrupt turn about the confined space that was Priam Corydon's office. "I will speak with the Watchmen from Apulum Inferior, and between them and my men, we should be able to set up a successful defense for all of Sanctu-Eustachios."

Mangueinic eased himself more comfortably into his chair, taking care to adjust the soft shearling lining the socket of his wooden leg to prevent any binding against his healing stump. "Enlitus Brevios will welcome the chance to assist in protecting this place; it is fitting that we do our part to preserve Sanctu-Eustachios the Hermit. Our Watchmen are eager to demonstrate their gratitude for the haven you provide." Although he knew his presence was due to his new appointment as advisor to the Watchmen of Apulum Inferior, he was determined to make himself useful.

"That would be welcome," Priam Corydon conceded. "If we must fight, it would be better left to secular men."

"So I think," said Bernardius, and was about to continue when there was a knock on the door.

"Who is it?" Priam Corydon asked, wondering what had happened now.

"Sanctu-Germainios. Your novice is resting in his cell; his broken arm is set and splinted and his elbow is realigned. I will look in on him at mid-day."

"God be praised," said Priam Corydon, making the sign of the cross.

"Is this the regional guardian of Apulum Inferior?" Bernardius asked quietly. "I have been told he is an accomplished man for a foreigner."

"Yes. Would you like to speak with him?" He started toward the door before Bernardius could answer.

"He's an excellent fellow: excellent," Mangueinic informed Bernardius.

"Your people say good things of him," said Bernardius, "for all that he isn't a true Roman, a Byzantine, or even a Goth."

Not wanting to show any sign of favor, Priam Corydon said nothing to the Tribune and the former leader of the Watchmen; he called out to the black-clad foreigner, who was already some distance away from the door, "Dom Sanctu-Germainios, if you would join us for a short while . . ."

Sanctu-Germainios stopped and looked back. "As you like," he said, coming back to Priam Corydon.

To account for his request, Priam Corydon remarked, "I thought it would take longer for you to finish your care of Ritt."

"So did I," Sanctu-Germainios said as he entered the office.

"His break was less complicated than I had expected, and his elbow had not swelled much, so my work was quickly done." He looked at the man across the room and made a shrewd guess. "You must be the Tribune of Ulpia Traiana."

Bernardius gave a startled stare. "I am."

"It is a privilege to meet you at last, Tribune," said Sanctu-Germainios with a little salute, his right hand touching his left shoulder before he extended it to Bernardius.

"The Tribune was just explaining his plans for garrisoning the monastery," said Priam Corydon. "The refugees from Ulpia Traiana, Apulum Inferior, and—what was that other town?"

"Tsapousso," Sanctu-Germainios supplied.

"Ah, yes: Tsapousso," said Priam Corydon. "It seems to me that if you can come to an accord, it would be useful to all of us."

"I cannot speak for any of the refugees," Sanctu-Germainios pointed out. "But I can help us all agree on your plan's particulars."

"We need a clear statement, all proper," Bernardius agreed. "Something everyone can understand."

"Then let us address our concerns; I will send for the recorder for Sanctu-Eustachios to take down our discussion," said Priam Corydon, and decided to send for Monachos Niccolae of Sinu to record their agreement. "We will distribute our items of agreement throughout all the monastery."

"An excellent notion," said Mangueinic, trying not to fret as his missing foot began to itch once more.

"Then let us discuss our intentions while one of the novices brings Monachos Niccolae to us," Priam Corydon proposed. "The agreement could be read at supper to everyone."

"In Roman and Byzantine dialects, as well as Gothic, Dacian, and the languages of the Gepidae and the Carpi," Mangueinic appended. "We may need more besides."

"Yes," said Priam Corydon heavily. "In all those tongues, if we are to understand one another. Those of your men who know two languages will prove most useful to all of us." He was fairly sure that

Monachos Niccolae would resent such a demanding task. "Can any of you help him with other languages? We wish to make this task as undaunting as possible."

"I can," said Sanctu-Germainios.

Text of the agreement for conduct and order at Sanctu-Eustachios the Hermit monastery, written officially in Byzantine Greek with copies in five other tongues.

To the monks, novices, slaves, soldiers, and refugees currently resident at Sanctu-Eustachios the Hermit monastery, take heed to observe these terms of order to be enforced from this, the twelfth day following the Winter Solstice, in the new Christian Year of 439:

This is a haven for all who have come here, and it must be part of our purpose to keep it as safe for all those living within its walls. Comradeship must be maintained among all of us sharing the dormitories, the warehouse, the provisions for livestock, and all other aspects of civilized Christian life. To that end, we endorse and will impose the following regulations, all implementation of prescribed punishments to be administered equally, showing no favor to one group or person over another:

There shall be no physical disputes among any of the residents. Any residents who resort to fighting may be confined to cells for five days for a first offense, and exiled from the monastery for a second offense. Any resident whose fighting has caused a death will be exiled at the first offense.

Any abuse of any of the women abiding within the monastery walls will result in castration of the offender and immediate exile.

Any theft of monies or possessions will be put before a magisterial committee consisting of: Priam Corydon of Sanctu-Eustachios the Hermit; Mangueinic, advisor to the Watchmen of Apulum Inferior; Denerac of Tsapousso; and Tribune Rotlandus Bernardius of Ulpia Traiana. Anyone found guilty of theft will be confined to a cell for ten days for a first offense, confined to a cell for a month for a second offense, and exiled for a third. Anyone maliciously and erroneously accusing another of theft will spend five days in a cell for a first offense, and exiled for a second.

Any deliberate insults visited upon one group of refugees to another, or to a monk or novice, or to soldiers, will result in those offering the insults to have beer and roasted game withheld from all of the members of that group for a period of ten days for a first offense and for fifteen days for a second, the withholding to be supervised by Monachos Bessamos or Monachos Vlasos according to the preference of the offended group. Any monk insulting any refugee or soldier will be confined to his cell for a period of fifteen days, and fed on bread and water.

Any resident deliberately inciting fear in other residents will be confined to a monk's cell for thirty days.

Any resident resorting to lewd or irreligious behavior will be confined to a cell for a period of ten days for a first offense, thirty for a second offense, and exile for a third.

Any resident found stealing foodstuffs or hoarding needed food will be consigned to a cell for ten days for a first offense and exiled for a second.

Any resident withholding feed for the livestock of others in favor of his own will be fined half of his food supply for his animals for a first offense, and will lose title to his livestock entirely for a second. Any hunter holding back his kill from the residents of Sanctu-Eustachios the Hermit will be confined to a cell for ten days for a first offense and confined for thirty days for a second one, and be deprived of his bows, arrows, and spears for a period of two months.

Those who offend against these regulations may expect the punishments described to be meted out promptly. Enforcement of the regulations will be the province of the Watchmen of Ulpia Traiana and Apulum Inferior. Those who believe they have been wrongfully accused may engage an advocate to press that claim, provided the advocate is approved by at least three of the undersigned.

Agreed to by:

Rotlandus Bernardius, Tribune of Ulpia Traiana
  Mangueinic, advisor to the Watchmen of Apulum Inferior
    (his mark)
      Denerac, master of Tsapousso (his mark)
        Priam Corydon of Sanctu-Eustachios the Hermit

Witnessed by:

Monachos Niccolae of Sinu, recorder for Sanctu-Eustachios
    the Hermit
  Dom Feranescus Rakoczy Sanctu-Germainios, regional
      guardian of Apulum Inferior (his sigil, the eclipse)
    Enlitus Brevios, deputy to Mangueinic (his mark)

2

"That feels . . . wonderful," Nicoris sighed as Sanctu-Germainios' small, strong hands worked their way down her aching back, kneading out the tension that had taken hold of her. "It wasn't an easy day," she said with a sigh of pleasure as she felt another knot give way, "not with the mason smashing his arm between stones, and the farrier getting himself kicked in the head by a lame mule." Just speaking of these two dreadful accidents brought back the horror she had done her utmost to submerge during the time she had worked to assist Sanctu-Germainios with the injured and the ill. She tried now to shift her attention beyond the thick wooden walls, out into the night, where there was the muffled silence of snowfall that wrapped the whole valley in a thick cloak of smooth white. Mixed with the myriad flakes on the deceptively gentle wind was the scent of wood-smoke and the odor of grilled meat, a reminder of the nine hundred seventy-eight people—townsmen, their wives and children, farmers and their families, goat-and-shepherds, soldiers, servants, slaves, and monks—within the walls of Sanctu-Eustachios the Hermit, all shut up in close quarters against the growing storm.

"It is unfortunate that the farrier survived," said Sanctu-Germainios, his face revealing little emotion as he considered the man from Tsapousso.

She raised herself on her elbows and turned toward him. "Unfortunate? Why?—he's alive, isn't he? If his wound doesn't putrify, won't he recover?" The square-sleeved linen tunica she wore over her woollen stola had spots of blood and brain on it left over from treating the farrier; she had made a point of ignoring them until now, and wished she had removed the engulfing tunica when she had taken off her femoralia and calcea so she need not have such a reminder: surely the stola would be garment enough for propriety, and she would not feel so queasy. She wondered if Sanctu-Germainios was as sympathetic as he seemed, for his equanimity made her think that it might be a sign of indifference to her, or to the farrier's suffering.

"Because after such a blow to the head, he will not be able to function as he did before he was injured. It will be some days before we know how extensive his impairments may be, but without doubt he will have them. He may lose some or all of his ability to speak, or his coordination may go, and leave him incapable of working. He may forget everyone he knows, or where he is. He will probably have to learn his profession all over again, if he has concentration and energy enough to permit him to trim and shoe hooves, which he may not."

"You sound so positive that he will remain . . . damaged." She bit her lower lip. "How can you be certain?"

"A blow to the head often brings serious problems with it. Anything that cracks the skull can ravage the person who endures it. Given the extent of his hurts, it is beyond doubt that he will have lasting effects from them. At the very least, he will be disfigured." He thought back to the Temple of Imhotep, recalling the times he had seen devastating fractures to the head; he shook off the memories. "He may yet curse us for saving his life, and with good cause."

"You were so . . . so composed when you picked out the bone splinters with those little grabbers and then put in that piece of ivory to cover the—" Nicoris closed her eyes, trying to shut out the recollection of the farrier with the left side of his head broken and bloody, with his soft, whitish brains showing through the cracks. "Don't you ever feel the repugnance such injuries cause?"

"Yes," he said steadily. "But I have had more years to learn to quiesce my revulsion than you have." The L-shaped alcove off the old chapel near the barns that had been turned over to them to serve as a treatment room was warmer than most of the old wooden building, which was drafty as a tree and as empty; only a square stone altar gave any sign that the chapel was a place of worship. Here in the alcove at least there was a fire in the hearth, a stout door between them and the nave, and shutters on the windows; the low couch on which she lay was padded with goat-hair and covered with a cotton blanket, making it comfortable and warm, which even he found soothing.

She laughed a bit uncertainly, then leaned into his hands again. "If it weren't so cold, this work we do would be easier."

"If it were not so cold, we would have less work to do. The man with the sprained ankle we dressed this morning got his injury from skidding on the ice, and the mason dropped the block he was putting in place because his fingers were stiff, to say nothing of the coughs and fevers that are so prevalent. But we might have the results of a Hunnic attack to contend with, so . . ." He lifted her arm and put her hand on his shoulder. "Do not try to hold it: rest. Let me keep it in place."

"Do you think that spring . . ." she began, but changed her mind—thinking seemed to be too much trouble after such a demanding day. As he had promised, her over-stimulated exhaustion began to give way to lassitude. She started to smile as he worked down from her shoulder to her fingers, turning the stress of fatigue into relaxation; at the same time an unfamiliar thrill awakened within her, one she dared not identify. "Where did you learn to do this?"

"In Egypt and Roma, for the most part," he told her, starting on her other arm. "You are tightening your shoulders again."

"Could you teach me?" she asked, paying no attention to his admonition. Her quick smile brought a glint to her quicksilver eyes; she added, "If you teach me, I can do the same for you."

"Learn to give massages? Do you want to?" He sensed her enthusiasm was more than the impulse of the moment. "You will need practice to build up your strength, but if it is what you want, I will."

She attempted to swing around so she could stand up, but he would not move to let her do so. "I *do* want to learn," she said eagerly. "I have no wish to be a goat-and-shepherd forever."

"Then you shall learn, after you are rested. In the morning, if you and I are not needed elsewhere, we can begin with Isalind; she has need of such relief." He worked her hands, loosening them with a gentle shake, finger by finger.

"Why?" The question was sharp with a feeling that confused her.

"Because it is the result of her having one leg that is a bit longer than the other, so that every step she takes reinforces the ache in her back," he said.

"I have an ache in my back," she said.

"I know, but yours will fade—hers will not; every step she takes will renew it." He ducked his head. "I have an unguent for you to use, later, on your lower back. It will reduce the discomfort you may feel from all the hard work you have done today. You have a tightness of the hip that could mean stiff joints tomorrow." Finally he released her arm.

She lay down again as he began on the backs of her thighs, his fingers seeking out the tenderest knots. The sharp ache his first touch evoked quickly gave way to languor. "You feel it all, don't you? The places I'm most tense."

"You will learn the trick yourself, in time. You will discover how the body reveals itself." He had bent over her legs as he moved down below her knees and focused on her calves. "You have a bruise on the back of this leg," he went on, tapping her left ankle just below the purple smudge. "Do you know how you got it?"

Thinking back over her day, she took a short while to decide that "It had to have been when they were moving the farrier back to the infirmary; the stretcher-bearers had swung a stool out of the way and it banged into me." She twisted on the table so that she could see it. "Not as bad as some I've had."

"That stool could be the cause," he agreed, and took care not to squeeze that part of her leg.

"Yesterday I tripped on the enclosed channel from the spring to the lake; the snow covered it completely. I might have got a bruise then, as well." In spite of her determination to keep from giving herself away, Nicoris heard evasion in her answer.

"It is possible," he said, feeling her response to him intensify along with her attempts to disguise the cause of her heightened state.

To distract herself, she asked, "What do you make of this Antoninu Neves? Is he really what he says he is?" The man had arrived at the monastery the day before with a small company of mercenaries under his command, claiming to have come from the Roman garrison at Porolissum; they said they had been in the employ of a Gepid landholder at his estate since the city was sacked, but that their arrangement had soured: sent off on their own without pay, they had been given provisional shelter at the monastery until the spring thaw in exchange for their labor and scouting.

"He seems a reliable sort of man, and his soldiers will be most useful here. Better that they should guard this valley than turn brigands."

"Do you think they would do that?—turn outlaw?"

"It has happened before," he said, recalling the trade routes he had followed, which were infested with gangs of former soldiers, as well as remote tribes that stole as a matter of survival, and the cities where garrisons enforced the laws in ways that made up for the pay they often did not receive. "And those who come from the Legions' traditions have the habit of fighting."

She could think of nothing to add; her thoughts remained fidgety. "How much longer will it snow?"

"Probably another day, and then it will be clear for a time—at least it has happened that way in the past," he said.

"Then some of the men will go out to hunt boar," Nicoris remarked.

"If the snow is not too deep," Sanctu-Germainios remarked, and added, "You will need thicker wraps on your feet under your calcea; you have a blister forming on your heel."

"I'll be careful," she said, her concentration disrupted by his touch; she could feel that his hands were cool, but where he put them, her skin seemed hot. A short while later he asked her to turn over.

"You mean you're going to do more?" she exclaimed.

"If you like. If you would rather I not, then I will stop. There is hot water in the tub behind the confession-cell. You can wash away the soil of the day before you sleep. I have put a night-wrap next to the towel for you."

Nonplussed, she could think of nothing to say. She wriggled onto her back, taking the time to look up at him as she wrestled with her clothes, unaccountably self-conscious. "What more will you do?"

"Your feet, your face, and perhaps your shoulders," he said; he was aware of her confusion and sought to put her at ease. "If you are too tired to continue, I will leave you to sleep."

"No," she protested, repeating more calmly, "no. This is helpful."

"As you wish," he said, realigning the cotton blanket for her. "This will not take long, I think. You will want to sleep shortly."

"Oh," she said, between disappointment and relief. As he touched her foot, she quivered.

"Are you ticklish?" he asked, knowing the answer.

"No. It must be that the cold is fading and the heat prickles," she said.

He said nothing in response to this as he started working on her foot, flexing it gently before stroking the sole with his thumbs, following the long tendons from toes to heel, aware that everything he did was no longer wholly relaxing for Nicoris; her pulse was getting faster, and her breathing was deepening. So long as she did not recognize her own fledgling arousal, he would continue; once she realized what was happening within her, he would cease his malacissation, it being no longer effective. He watched her stretch, her back arched, as he moved to her other foot. "I think, when I'm done with this"—he tweaked her big toe—"that you may want to go off to your bed." It was in another alcove on the far side of the nave, less than half the size of this one, with its own small bed and fireplace, shutters over the tall, slitted windows, and a heavy wooden door to ensure her privacy.

Her yawn had a sigh in it. "You're right. I should . . . wash and get to sleep." That would get her away from his compelling presence so that she could regain her self-possession and bring her mind into order again.

"Very wise. The nights may be long, but you will need every hour of this one, or you will be tired still in the morning." He rubbed at her Achilles' tendon, keeping his mind on the feel of what was under her skin.

"All right," she said, trying not to sound disappointed. "I'll go bathe as soon as you're done."

"Very good," he said, continuing his ministrations. "You should sleep very well."

"I hope so," she said with a spurt of nervous laughter.

He finished in silence, standing back with his hand extended to help her to sit up; she took it promptly, pulled herself erect, then released it more quickly than was necessary.

"Thank you, Dom. It was a very . . . helpful . . . I'll be refreshed, come morning." That was more for his benefit than to express her conviction. She got down from the table, stepping back from him as she did, her marvelous lassitude now almost gone. "The tub has hot water, you said?"

"Yes: it was filled from cauldrons set above the hearth-fire to boil. It was done while you were at supper. The water should be hot enough, but not scalding." He inclined his head, sensing his flaring attraction to her. It had been four nights since he visited one of the women from Ulpia Traiana in her sleep, and his esurience was awakened, keyed by Nicoris' dawning excitement. "There are a brush and a cloth for you to use."

She flushed at this, and was baffled by the unexpected embarrassment that came over her. "I'll let you know when I've finished, if you like," she said, then turned abruptly and headed for the confession-cell, apparently unaware of the cold stones beneath her feet, or the chill that took hold of her as she got farther from the hearth; her breath came quickly.

A branch of oil-lamps stood beside the tub—an old tun cut in half, with a faint odor of wine still clinging to its ancient slats, with a rim a hand's-breadth wide around the top—and there was a bench with the brush, cloth, towel, and night-wrap set out on it, as he had told her. Above the black, shiny water, specters of steam writhed over the surface, promising heat, which she suddenly desired as a starving person desires bread. She had a moment of self-reproach, then dismissed it. Shivering, she skinned out of her clothes as quickly as possible, grabbed the brush, climbed up onto the stool beside the barrel, and eased herself into the warm water, trying to minimize splashing as she sank into it up to her shoulders, her skin tingling. The sensations that ran through her made her gasp with a frightening kind of delectation. Closing her eyes and holding her breath, she slipped under the surface, remaining there until her chest began to ache; she stood up, the water streaming and steaming off her. She reached for the brush and started to scrub, starting with her feet and working her way up her body, her skin becoming more sensitive with each stroke. A twinge very like a cramp shot up her leg from her calf, and she gave a little cry, sloshing water as she struggled to keep her balance.

"Nicoris? Are you all right?" Sanctu-Germainios called to her.

"Yes," she answered brusquely. "I . . ." What should she tell him? that she was flustered by his nearness? that she had become aroused by what his hands had done? that she wanted to share his bed? that she—? "I'm fine!" She took hold of the rim of the tub and steadied herself, preparing to emerge from the warm bath into the cold air.

"Have a care getting out," he recommended while he pinched the flames on all but one of the oil-lamps. He looked around the alcove, his dark-seeing eyes making out the faint paintings on the walls, faded with age, detailing the life of Sanctu Eustachios the Hermit, or so the monks claimed: to Sanctu-Germainios, the murals showed the life of the Maiden of the Spring, a much older figure than Sanctu Eustachios. Saint or Maiden, the miracle-working spirit of the place was depicted as being tall, thin, and in flowing white robes. The Maiden of the Spring had been worshipped while Sanctu-Germainios still breathed, and her place in this isolated valley had been sacred before he was born. He sat down on the table and let his long memories wander back to that vanished time when his own people still lived in the eastern hook of these mountains, to his capture by the invaders from the east, and his execution at their hands, more than twenty-five centuries ago. "Why do they so often come from the east?" he murmured in a language that no one else on earth could speak now, except Rugierus, who had learned it from him.

"Dom Sanctu-Germainios," Nicoris' voice cut into his reverie.

He shook off the hold of the past. "Is something wrong?"

"N . . . no, not wrong," she responded. "It's my mind; it won't be still. My thoughts are . . . jumping like locusts. I can't stop them." Moving toward him through the darkened alcove, she concentrated on the single burning oil-lamp rather than on the shadow he had become. In her night-wrap she was pale as the mists hovering over the snow, her damp hair hanging unconfined; she looked very young as she came up to him. "Don't tell me to pray."

"Are you worried, or are you edgy from so much work?" He took the hand she held out to him, once again aware of the turmoil within her.

"Neither of those." She went silent, summoning up the courage to tell him the truth. "I haven't the right to ask this of you, and I know it, you being Dom and regional guardian, and Priam Corydon wouldn't approve, and this being a holy place, but my body needs . . . *I* need . . . succor. Don't make me go to one of the soldiers; they're too rough. All the tenderness has been driven out of them." Her eyes glittered in the lamplight as they fixed on him. "You are not a man to deny me, are you?"

He felt the strength of her impetration, and his own ardor rose to meet hers. "If it is in me to release you, I will do what you ask."

With a soft exclamation, she went into his arms, clinging to him as if she expected to be pulled apart from him. "You needn't worry—I'm not a virgin." She burrowed her head into his shoulder, shivering with something that was not quite passion. "You can be quick, if you want."

"No," he said gently, touching her hair, and then her cheek. "I cannot."

"Why not? Do I offend you?" she asked flatly even while she strained her body to his.

"Because you will not be quick, no matter how urgent your desire, and my relief is tied to yours," he said, tilting her face upwards to kiss her, lightly at first, then growing more rapturous as her fervor increased. As he started to move back from her, she laced her fingers behind his head and renewed the kiss with determination. For a long, suspended moment, they remained together, her body locked to his, as if striving to melt into him. She trembled and slowly released him, her face revealing the depth of her arousal. "Where shall we go?"

"To your bed, if you like," he said, certain that the thin mattress that lay atop a chest of his native earth, which had served him when he slept, would afford her little comfort.

"It isn't much," she said apologetically.

"No bed here is much," he said, and lifted her easily into his arms. "But you have two blankets and a sheet, which is more than many have." As he walked, she hung on to him lightly, her arms around his neck, and pressed little kisses along his jaw and on his angled ear, growing more adventuresome with every step he took. He made his way toward the far end of the alcove, into a small space behind the confession-cell where her bed waited, smelling faintly of rosemary from the needles in the stuffing of her mattress.

She did not wait for him to lower her, but scrambled out of his arms, threw back her blankets, and patted the sheet as she stretched out on it. "Here, Dom. There's room enough for both of us if we lie close together." She opened her night-wrap and patted the sheet again.

Her offer was so obvious that he sat on the edge of the bed and leaned over her. "There is no hurry."

"But we should be quick . . ." she began, then was silenced, trembling as he slipped his hand inside her night-wrap, moving over her body, barely touching her, but evoking responses from her flesh that astonished her.

"Why lessen your enjoyment in the name of haste?" he asked as he leaned down to kiss her slowly and thoroughly, his fingers teasing at her breast while his lips provided a kind of fascination no other lover had awakened in her. Gradually, luxuriously, he worked his way down to her shoulders, and then his mouth began on her breast where his hand had been, his tongue more artful than his fingers were.

Her hands caught his hair and pressed his face hard against her breast. "I want to *feel* you, Dom."

"You dislike pain; I will not give you any," he said steadily, eluding her grasp. "This is to bring you joy, not hurt." His hand explored down her torso, over her taut abdomen, then dawdled among the soft, moist folds between her legs.

She inhaled sharply between her teeth, and she seized the edge of her blankets in a solid grip; she laughed again, her head thrown back euphorically, and suddenly the spasm was upon her, coursing through her in ecstatic waves. Suddenly she released the blankets and grabbed him, pulling him down on top of her once more; she hardly noticed his mouth on her neck. Her being was subsumed in greater fulfillment than she had ever experienced. Her body, made malleable by passion, sank down, more relaxed than when Sanctu-Germainios had massaged her muscles. As she loosened him, she kissed him soundly once, then looked at him critically. "Why didn't you . . ." She gestured to show what she meant.

He got up from the bed, taking a moment to gather his thoughts.

"Those of my blood have limitations—at least the men do." He had long since become accustomed to his impotence and spoke of it without embarrassment.

She took hold of his arm. "You . . . have nothing for yourself."

He caressed her admiringly. "Now there, Nicoris, you are wrong; I have fulfillment through your fulfillment," he said, his voice kind, his dark eyes full of understanding. "I have you." Yet even as he said it, he wondered why she was lying to him.

Text of a letter from Rugierus in Constantinople to Sanctu-Germainios in Apulum Inferior, written in code in Imperial Latin with fixed ink on vellum, carried by hired courier as far as Oescus and turned over to the Praetor Custodis, never delivered.

To Dom Feranescus Rakoczy Sanctu-Germainios, regional guardian at Apulum Inferior, this from your devoted servant Rugierus of Gades, now in Constantinople, resolving certain problems confronting Eclipse Shipping and the question of your private properties. It is one month past the Winter Solstice in the Christian year 439, and I am in residence at your house in this city.

My master,

I am sorry to tell you that I have had to deal with a zealous priest who enforces the taxation levied on foreigners by the Emperor's orders. Patras Methodos, priest though he is, is cut from much the same cloth as Telemachus Batsho in Roma, two centuries ago. He has a remarkable talent for finding taxation schedules that require more money from you. In addition, the Patras has made it his business to demand every tax he can think of from the earnings of your ships. He has inspected cargo frequently and inventoried goods in your warehouses. He will not allow me to leave until he is satisfied that you have provided all the monies that can be demanded of you. Your new factor, a prudent Greek called Artemidorus Iocopolis, who is acceptable to the Metropolitan, has tried to ask the Metropolitan to review what Patras Methodos has de-

manded, and as a Constantinopolitan, he cannot be considered a foreigner. But the Metropolitan is too pleased to have the money that Patras Methodos has required you to pay. I have stated that I am obliged to leave here by the end of February in order to report to you in a timely way of your affairs in this city. Fortunately the Metropolitan puts much importance on the dedication of servants and slaves to their masters.

I have to tell you that it is unlikely that you can return to Constantinople for some years yet. There are too many still alive who are likely to remember you and the upheaval that revolved around the Captain of the Hecate *and his fellow-smugglers. In fact, it seems to me that some of the rapacity of Patras Methodos arises from the assumption that you in some way benefited from those smugglers' crimes. I have ordered certain necessary repairs on your house, and told Iocopolis to monitor the house and maintain it in your absence. That will calm the Patras and the Metropolitan.*

Rhea Penthekrassi is now established in a house near Hagia Sophia, in a street of handsome houses most of which are owned by merchants. This permits her to live as a woman of quality lives. She has a small household—a major domo, a cook, a builder, a personal maid, a household maid, a gardener, and a groom to care for her stable and horses. She has found it difficult to go about in society, lacking a male relative or in-law to accompany her. I have attempted to find her an acceptable escort; I still hope that I will be able to find her someone before I must leave the city.

There are more rumors about the Huns, saying they are ransacking all the towns in the Carpathians and will soon move into the Balkans and do the same there. Given the depths of the snows at present, I am puzzled as to how they are to accomplish the raids that make up so many rumors. How the Constantinopolitans come to know such things is never explained. There is much fear in this place that the Huns will enlarge their forces and campaign against this capital. The Emperor Theodosios has been reluctant to send his troops to stop Attila, fearing that his Hunnic mercenaries may well rebel, join with Attila and his men, and render the army ineffective, thus leaving all Byzantium open to attack. When Roma is mentioned, very few of the people here want to take the risk of reinforcing the city.

I am eager to join you at Apulum Inferior again; I will bring you reports from your factor and the Patras, as well as some additional money to make your situation more secure. I am assuming that you will have need of it, with so much turmoil in the region. I anticipate arriving by the Equinox, barring any more military incursions. If there are too many conflicts under way, I will stay at Viminacium until I can join a northward-bound company of travelers. Until the day when we meet again,

I am, as I have been for almost four centuries,
Rogerian

3

Antoninu Neves strode purposefully toward the half-rebuilt battlements, explaining to those who followed him, "This snow will protect us for two months more, or so I guess. The Huns will not attack through these deep drifts, in the unlikely event they could get through the passes; it would be a waste of horses and men; if they got here, they could only wallow in the snow—they couldn't fight. There are farmsteads and villages farther down the mountains where they will strike first, so we will have a little warning of their presence. We will need to keep watch day and night. I have posted four of my men on the peaks around this valley, so that they can report any activity. I would like to send out a hunting party, but only if the weather holds clear, and they can reach one of the meadows down the eastern slope." He waved his arm, indicating the brilliant blue of the sky and the stark whiteness of the mountains. "The trees will have to shed the snow on their branches before anything can be seen in the forest. Logging and hunting in the forest is impracticable with so much snow." His vigor was contagious, and the four men with him took it in eagerly.

Priam Corydon, usually more careful in his manner, looked behind him to the others who accompanied him and Neves. "When the outer wall is finished, we will rebuild the gates, so that they will be as strong as our other fortifications. That will improve our protection and give us power over anyone who enters." Much as he disliked the notion of a fortified monastery, he saw the sense of it. Sanctu-Eustachios had been enclosed since before it became a monastery, when it was a stop-over compound for travelers, and before, when it had been a place of pagan worship. The foundations on which the current walls stood were ancient. "The warder-monks can keep the gates. You need not deploy your soldiers to the task."

"You will want to put a watch-tower at the gates when they're rebuilt." Rotlandus Bernardius nodded authoritatively. "A pity that work on the outer wall must be delayed. But no one can be expected to work in this snow." He glanced over his shoulder. "What do you think, Brevios?"

Enlitus Brevios coughed once. "My men will not be able to build in the snow, though they will as soon as the thaw comes. It would be as dangerous for them to attempt to work while freezing as it would be for anyone else." He stared down the mountain. "The Huns won't attack until the thaw."

At the rear of the line, Denerac of Tsapousso tromped doggedly in the uneven rift their passage made in the snow. Of all the men here, he was the least inclined to build defenses. He had already suggested that as soon as the thaw began, they should evacuate the monastery, leaving in small groups, heading south into Roman or Byzantine territory and the protection that could be found there. Better than most of them, he knew what Huns could do; he did not want his people to experience their ferocity again. He kept his mouth shut; he was being ignored and for now he was glad of it.

"Today and tomorrow," Brevios announced, "the Watchmen of

Apulum Inferior will work at repairing the south wall of the Pilgrim's Hall, and come evening tomorrow, we can all gather there to inform our people of how things stand."

"It will have to be a little earlier than evening," Priam Corydon said. "Let's settle on the last quarter of the afternoon. The monastery has an Office to perform at sundown. We keep to the Chanting Rite, and mark our sunsets with Psalms." He was a bit surprised that Neves had not been aware of the monastic routines.

"That suits me and my men," said Neves at once. "The church in Porolissum held to a different Rite, Priam. They sang Mass four times each full day: at dawn, at mid-day, at sunset, and at midnight. They opened their church for each Mass so that everyone in the town could attend at least once a day."

"More Roman than we are," said Priam Corydon. "We hold more to the old Twelve Gospels and the Apostolic Rites. Every hour of the day and night, one of the novices chants in the chapel behind the altar. At the canonical Hours, all the monks must chant."

"What happens if you haven't enough novices?" Neves asked, sounding slightly amused.

"Then monks must sing; we fill every moment with prayers and praise," said Priam Corydon, asperity sharpening his answer. "But for now, we have novices enough." He went a short way in silence, thinking that the men around him cared little for novices and Psalms.

As if to confirm his supposition, Brevios said, "Just as well the snow is so deep. Our activities will be shaped by it. We'll need to find work to occupy all the people, women and children as well as men, or they may fall to mischief. My Watchmen will be glad of a little less labor than digging in the snow, but I don't want them to be idle. That could be as troublesome as the Huns if it isn't avoided." He was holding his arms out to help him stay balanced; the drift they waded through was piled up higher than his waist.

Bernardius pointed to the inner walls ahead. "My men are on watch until mid-day, then those of Apulum Inferior replace them. That should serve to occupy their afternoon, at least." He swung around. "You are fortunate to have so many men with you."

Brevios hesitated. "It would be better if we hadn't lost nine of them coming here, and that none of them had taken an inflammation of the lungs."

"Better yet if we hadn't left," grumbled Denerac.

Neves heard this and came to a halt. "Don't say that," he recommended. "I know what the Huns do, I've fought them, so has Tribune Bernardius. You have spared your families horrible suffering by abandoning your village."

"The Huns came to Tsapousso," said Denerac, visibly bristling; his thick, white mustaches quivered and his shoulders rose.

"And sensibly, you departed," said Neves, unimpressed by his display.

"Yes. We left behind everything, including the dying."

Neves nodded. "Just as the rest of us would have done in your situation. Not an easy decision, of course, but something that you had to do. Any leader must be called upon to deal with unpleasant things from time to time. You chose the most sensible action, though it was difficult."

Before the two men became furious, Priam Corydon intervened. "No doubt each of you has had his own horrendous experience with these barbarians, and shares the desire never to have to engage with them again. Since we can't be the ones to decide that, it behooves us to prepare for the worst they can do. We do this by improving our defenses and our housing. Don't you agree?"

Neves and Denerac exchanged vitriolic looks, then Neves moved on. "You are fortunate that the spring is inside the inner walls; they will not be able to drive us out by thirst. We will have to lay in more meat—smoked or salted—so that we can't be starved out, either. We will have to try to hunt in the meadows. There must be boar and deer about. Are there fish in the lake?" He reached the stairs up to the new battlement, and leaned forward to steady himself for the climb.

"A few. We could chop a hole in the ice, I suppose; we have done so before," said Priam Corydon, setting his foot on the tread after Neves, heading upward.

The rampart-walkways were no more than eighteen hands above the ground, but high enough to raise them above the level of men on horseback, and the logs that made the walls were notched to allow for more effective use of weapons. Each upright log was bound to its neighbor by wide iron straps, making the wall especially sturdy. The heavy planks of the walkway were a hand thick and fifteen hands wide, supported by upended-log pillars and braces to the wall that added to its strength. A dozen men could stand upon this section and not fear a collapse.

Leaning forward to support himself on the steps above as Neves had done, Priam Corydon soon reached the platform, where he asked, "What of the monks living in caves around the valley?" pointing to the ridge beyond the lake, its crags towering over it. "Do you see that spur? Three of them have cells there. The rest are lower down, above the scree."

Neves and Bernardius looked shocked; Brevios and Denarac were not surprised at anything monks might do.

"How many are there?" Neves asked, recovering himself slightly.

"Nine, if they're all still alive," Priam Corydon answered. "They come here on major feast days."

Bernardius scowled out at the face of the mountain. "Nunc non fassi est," he muttered in mangled Latin.

"It isn't safe for them to try to reach this place, not with snow so deep," Brevios remarked, stepping out on the walkway and squinting out at the sawtooth tor in front of them.

"Try to tell them, if you like; you need only walk half a league through deep snow," said Priam Corydon. "They have been there for years, and only two have died in the last six years. Monachos Vlasos makes them meat, cheese, and bread on Sundays and the novices carry the food to them; in addition they're provided meals on feast days, when they come here. They are always welcome at our table, of course, but they usually avail themselves of the welcome on feast days alone."

"When is the next feast day?" Neves asked.

"In three days' time," said Priam Corydon. "It commemorates our founder, Sanctu Eustachios, who came here forty years ago." Warming to his topic, he continued, "He had been a disciple of Sanctu Ioannos Chrysostom, and when that holy man was sent into exile, he dispersed his followers so that none would have to suffer on his account. Sanctu Eustachios, faithful to his vows to uphold traditional Christian worship, came here from Byzantiu—"

"In winter?" Denarac marveled. "Why would he come in winter?"

"He followed God's promptings. The spring and its chapel and the walls and the warehouses and barns were here, and the dormitory; there was a small company of nine soldiers left manning it, and they were glad to have Sanctu Eustachios with them; they became his first monks. As he gained followers, the monastery itself was built. Not all pious men drawn here seek to live among others; they prefer their remote cells."

"Why would they do that?" Bernardius asked. "This valley is isolated already. Why not accept the safety and companionship of other monks?"

"Some of them are afraid of soldiers, and of strangers, some have secrets they want to preserve, one of them is troubled in his mind and unwilling to live among others, or so they have told the novices; only four of them attended the Nativity Feast. They will join us again before many more days go by, when you may ask them for yourself." After a moment, Priam Corydon continued, "And some of them disapprove of what we're doing here."

"Disapprove?" Bernardius blurted, much shocked. "Why on earth should they disapprove?"

"They believe that to do anything to interfere with the unfolding of events is to go against God's Will, and therefore anyone who doesn't surrender to the fate of the world falls from Grace. If they strive to save themselves in this world, they damn themselves in the next," said Priam Corydon. "They say that if God wants us to be saved, He will save us: we disrespect Him if we seek to defend ourselves. It is for us to acquiesce in the Will of God, not to defy Him."

"Then they're fools!" Bernardius flapped his arms to show his indignation. "The Huns don't care about God."

"Do you think the hermits could be a problem for us?" Neves asked the Priam. "Would they aid the Huns?"

"Actively aid them, no," said Priam Corydon. "But they would do nothing to stop them."

Brevios shuddered. "Would they be willing to warn us of anything they see that might endanger the monastery?"

Priam Corydon considered this. "I doubt it," he told them at last. "It is likely that they would pray for God to use them according to His Will if they saw trouble coming."

"All the better then, that I've posted men on the mountains," said Neves, being as practical as he could.

"Very likely," said Brevios. "If you need more men to stand guard, I will provide some of our Watchmen. Ours is the largest delegation here: it is fitting that we shoulder the greater part of the care of this place."

Last onto the platform was Denerac, who brushed off the front of his wolfskin byrrus, then glowered out at the rising crags and said, "We had a monk who came to Tsapousso and preached the same nonsense. A few of our people believed him and would not evacuate with us: they remained behind and that was the last we heard of them." He shook his head slowly. "What God would ask that of His worshippers? Martyrdom ought to have its limits."

"Monachos Anatolios would approve of what they did," said Priam Corydon dryly. "He says it is what he will do."

"Then I hope the Huns will be merciful and make short work of him," said Neves. "Since his God will not spare him."

Priam Corydon made the sign of the cross toward the mountains. "May he enter Heaven singing."

"Screaming, more likely," said Denerac, his glare daring Priam Corydon to contradict him. "If the Huns take him, he'll have a proper foretaste of Hell, and no mistaking."

"Preco ni Dei me induxerunt in multos erroris," Bernardius whispered in his chaotic Latin.

"Praying won't save you," Denerac grumbled. "Tell those monks that they may help us, or they may keep to their cells, but it must be one or the other."

Brevios cleared his throat. "There are two families with our group who have declared their intention to leave as soon as travel is possible. I cannot compel them to remain. If they feel they must depart, I will be unable to stop them."

"If they feel that way when the snows begin to melt, then let them go, so that they will not interfere with our efforts," said Neves. "The same with Bernardius' group. No one should have to stay here if the roads are passable if they would prefer not to." He sighed. "We may have still more wanting to depart, come spring."

"All of us may have to leave," said Bernardius dispiritedly. "There are certain enemies we may have to flee rather than fight."

"You're descended from Legionaries, and you say that?" Neves asked, rounding on him.

"My grandfather said only a fool fights a futile battle," Bernardius declared. "Prudenti caveat barbaram."

Once again Priam Corydon intervened. "Let's deal with the evils we have before us rather than argue about those that may not befall us. We are agreed that we will not seek out a battle, or pursue a bellicose course. We have more than enough to contend with as things stand now." He shaded his eyes as he looked toward the mountain again. "I want those hermits to be safe, for their safety benefits us all. I'll talk to them in three days, when they will be here."

"And you will pray that they will listen," said Bernardius. "You are a good man, from what I've seen. You will try to save them."

"And I pray they will allow me to do so, in the name of Sanctu Eustachios. The monks are my flock; it is my duty to care for them." Priam Corydon stepped under the roof at the angle in the wall, rubbing his hands together. "You told me we need more weapons," he said to Neves.

"We do," he said. "There should be time enough to make spears, bows, and arrows, possibly even a ballista."

"That wouldn't be much use against cavalry," said Bernardius.

"It might be," said Neves. "If we put it in the right place." He looked out toward the lake. "They'll have to muster somewhere, and the likeliest place is out there."

Priam Corydon shook his head. "In the spring a good portion of that land becomes a bog from the melting snows running into the lake. No. It would be too much trouble to climb the back side of that ridge: the drop is a steep one. There are too many hazards in that direction. They'll probably come in from the east, on the same road those from Apulum Inferior used, and that would give them the triangular foot of the pass to marshal their men."

"And the advantage of higher ground," said Neves.

"Could we force them onto the swale? Make them try to fight on boggy footing?" Bernardius asked. "It would slow any attack they made, and it might ruin their horses."

Denerac raised his voice. "Better to take down the buildings outside the walls. The Huns usually set out-buildings on fire."

"Do they?" Priam Corydon inquired. "Then the skinning shed and the quarantine-house will be taken down as soon as possible. The lumber can be used elsewhere in our defenses, and it will spare us the danger of out-buildings that can be set afire." The men all nodded their agreement, a little good-will spreading among them. In this more cordial atmosphere, Priam Corydon turned to Brevios. "Can you tell me how Patras Anso is doing?"

"He's improving," said Brevios.

"It is no small thing to have putrid lungs; he is fortunate to survive." He intended this remark sympathetically, but saw Brevios bristle. "If you will convey my wishes for his recovery to him and assure him of my prayers?"

Brevios stared at him. "I will do that," he said flatly.

Priam Corydon could not imagine what he had said that offended Brevios, for he had not wanted to slight the priest. "Thank you," he said properly.

"What plans have you made for evacuation? Has a route been

chosen?" Denerac asked purposefully, forestalling any protests by adding, "It is a possibility we must consider."

"I haven't thought much about it," said Priam Corydon, "since there is no chance of evacuating now. When the snows are gone, it will be otherwise." He flipped his hand toward the edge of the valley. "If we must leave this place, it will be later in the spring. Between then and now, if we shore up the walls and the outer fortifications, we will at least have security enough to keep us safe from all but the most concerted assaults the Huns can make. With so many stalwart men to fight, surely we can sustain ourselves until one of the garrisons relieves us."

Neves chuckled mirthlessly. "More hope of Legions, Priam?"

"Like you, I am the descendant of the Legionaries posted here in the time of Imperial glory," he said.

Denerac moaned. "Another fool."

"Hardly a fool. My grandfather served as a quartermaster in one army; I do the same in another, and for a grander master." Priam Corydon inclined his head toward Neves, then Bernardius. "We have been taught to uphold Roman rule, and each of us, in his way, does what he can to vindicate our purpose, though I cleave to the Second Roma, not the First."

"If you believe you will vindicate your faith, Priam," said Neves with a shrug.

Whatever Denerac would have said was cut short by a voice from beneath them. "Priam Corydon."

The Priam went to the edge and looked down. "Dom Sanctu-Germainios. What may I do for you?"

"It is not for me, it is for the people in the monastery," said Sanctu-Germainios, looking up from where he stood. "I fear there are four guards in the refectory who are competing in terrifying one another and all those listening with ever-more-horrific tales of the Huns. Half their stories are about rape and the other half are about torture. There are fifty refugees listening, and most of them are now ready to succumb to terror."

Priam Corydon clicked his tongue. "What are they claiming? That the Huns are devils and ride on demons?"

"Nothing so ecclesiastical. The same thing that was said of all barbarians: that they sew Christians into the opened bellies of gutted swine and roast them on spits; that they open the bellies of Christians, tie their guts to trees, and force the Christians to walk around the tree until their own intestines bind them in place; that they cut a ribbon of flesh away from a captive's back, attach it to a spool, and continue to roll the ribbon onto the spool until the captive is entirely flayed." He had an uneasy moment as he recalled his own death by simple disemboweling. "The women are pale and whimpering, and the men have that transfixed stare that may end in sudden anger."

Priam Corydon made the sign of the cross. "What fools. May God restore them to their senses." He shoved past Bernardius as he made for the nearest descent ladder. "I will have to speak to them at once. Comrades, if you will come with me and help me to quell this nonsense. We have regulations for this."

Denerac sighed. "Why not let them continue?"

"Because it will lead to chaos," said Priam Corydon, continuing downward.

Neves followed after him. "Why didn't you try to stop them, Dom?" he asked as he set his foot on the first rung.

"They would not listen to Mangueinic, who did his best to change the nature of their tales; they would not listen to Monachos Vlasos, who chastised them for frightening their women and children; and they would not listen to me," he said levelly. He reached out and steadied the ladder. "They were too caught up in their tales of torture and havoc, relishing their growing panic for its excitement." He had encountered this pattern of cultivated dread before and knew it led to nothing useful. "If you will speak to them, I think they may recover themselves."

Priam Corydon stepped onto the ground. "I suppose we should count ourselves fortunate that this didn't happen earlier." He squared his shoulders. "What of Patras Anso? Did he hear any of this?"

Sanctu-Germainios hesitated for an instant, then said, "He joined in the story-telling, and encouraged the four men in their contest." He kept slightly behind Priam Corydon, aware that Neves was following him.

"Humph," Priam Corydon uttered. "You'd think that a man of his position wouldn't want to encourage that sort of—"

A loud shout from the direction of the refectory halted the men in their tracks. As they stared, half a dozen men boiled out of the refectory door, trying to move and fight at the same time. Shouts and curses sounded from the developing melee. From other buildings people emerged, alarmed and curious about the sudden eruption from the refectory.

Priam Corydon gathered himself up. *"Enough of this!"* he bellowed, pressing forward through the snow. "All you men. Stop this. STOP."

The combatants wavered, then attempted to resume their battle.

"STOP." The sound of the Priam's voice was as absolute as a clap of thunder; this time the men lowered their fists and dropped their cudgels and knives.

"What possessed you?" Priam Corydon demanded as he came up to the flattened stretch of icy slush outside the refectory door. "Bacoem, you have only one arm—why abuse it? What idiotic notion came over you?" He trod up directly to the tallest of the scrappers and faced him unflinchingly. "If you were a monk, you'd be confined to your cell for a month, and given only water and bread to eat."

"It's the Huns—" the man began.

"You decided to do their work for them, did you?" Priam Corydon glared at him.

"No. Nothing like that. There was—" the man blustered, then went silent as Rotlandus Bernardius came up beside the Priam.

"Yes, Woliac of Gardmandus," he said with excessive cordiality. "Tell Priam Corydon what it was like. Then perhaps I will understand why one of my men should so disgrace himself. Calcitratus sum. I am ashamed."

Mangueinic, leaning heavily on his crutches, appeared in the doorway, a small crowd behind him. "You six have broken the stated rules for this monastery. You know what those rules are. I warned you when you began your fighting that you would have to answer for it."

Bernardius looked steadily at the man he had addressed as Woliac of Gardmandus. "The penalty for fighting is five days in a cell for a first offense. You and your three companions will be put in cells for five days. If there is a repetition of fighting, you will be exiled." He shook his head. "Four against two. You do not even fight honorably."

Woliac blustered in protest, "We had to fight. You don't know what they said about us, and—"

"Nor do I care. You were told not to fight. You were ordered not to spread fear. You disobeyed," said Bernardius.

"But we *had* to. Don't you understand?" Woliac importuned.

Mangueinic pegged over to Bernardius. "My two men are just as much to blame, and they, too, will have five days in the cells to think about the error of their ways." He turned to Priam Corydon. "I am sorry they forgot themselves."

Brevios, not to be out-done, declared, "And if any egged them on, they will stand extra Watches while Bacoem and Smardens keep their five-day isolation."

Mangueinic stood back a pair of steps, looking over the gathering around the six men. "Thirhald, Dom Sanctu-Germainios, will you escort Bacoem and Smardens to their cells?"

Thirhald hesitated, then stepped forward; Sanctu-Germainios came forward from the rear of the gathering. "Which cells are we to use?" he asked Priam Corydon.

"The ones on the third floor of the monastery. The cells for penance." The Priam turned his attention to the other men. "Tribune Bernardius, will you take these men in hand?"

Neves joined Bernardius, saying as he did, "Lead the way, Tribune."

The gathered people melted away as the group of ten moved

off toward the cruciform monastery and the steep, narrow stairs
that led to the penitents' cells.

Text of a letter from Gnaccus Tortulla, Praetor Custodis of Viminacium, in the Province of Moesia, to Verus Flautens, land-owner
near Drobetae, written on vellum and carried by official messenger
nine days after it was written.

*To the distinguished Roman and currently acting Praetor-Governor
of the Drobetae region of the former Province of Dacia Inferior, my
heartiest congratulations and my hope that you will enjoy the privileges of your office.*

*As I intimated to you last year, your appointment to this posi-
tion for Romans living within the frontiers of the former province is
an honor that is long overdue. I know that you will acquit yourself
brilliantly, with devotion to Roma and attention to the welfare of the
Romans living around you.*

*Notice of this promotion is being tendered to the Gepidae and
Goths now living in the region, with the assurance that you will receive their cooperation in all matters that bear both upon their concerns and upon Roman ones.*

*With this in mind, I urge you to dispatch your man to the
monastery we have discussed. I know the roads are not yet passable,
but I think you should consider authorizing his travel as soon as
may be, for once the roads are passable, your servant may have to
share them with the Huns, and we need to have information as soon
as may be in that regard. Remember, the service you do Roma will
bring Roman gratitude and honor for your family.*

*The refugees we saw in such number last autumn have dwindled
to a trickle, but I fear that with the warmer weather, we will once
again be overwhelmed with Romans, Goths, and Gepidae fleeing the
old province. Any warning of numbers that you can supply will be
most welcome.*

I hope to have the honor of attending your investiture once spring is truly under way. If circumstances intervene, I ask you to receive this as surety of my alliance to you and your gens.

On the fifty-fifth day since the Winter Solstice,

> *Gnaccus Tortulla*
> *Praetor Custodis*
> *Viminacium, Province of Moesia*

4

Aquileia spread out along the gentle rise above the upper end of the Adriatic Sea, a magnificent city, as elegant as Roma at her grandest, the handsomest port in all of the old Empire. It was the home to successful merchants and the newer nobility, and it showed their prosperity to advantage. Nothing about it suggested the trials that the Roman Empire in the West was undergoing, or that the true authority in the region was the Ostrogothic, not Roman; Aquileia remained lovely and serene. Even in March, the city turned the blustery weather into a setting for adventure and intrepid undertakings.

From the vantage-point of the open-ended atrium of her main house at her estate, Atta Olivia Clemens watched the sea through the peristyle; some two leagues away it was a dark slate-blue flecked with foam under thickening clouds and a freshening wind. It was a little past mid-day, and the light was already fading behind the clouds. Contemplating the gathering storm, she gave herself over to apprehension. The day's chill made no impact upon her, though the tenor of her reverie left her shivering, and the threat of rain before mid-afternoon only served to sharpen her worry for her most enduring friend—Sanct' Germain Franciscus, Sanctu-Germainios, whatever he called himself—an emotion she made no effort to conceal as she addressed her bondsman, Niklos Aulirios.

"They say the Huns are moving farther into the Carpathians, where neither Roma nor Constantinople is likely to reinforce the barbarians against them; it is not a good turn of events for Sanct' Germain, or any other client of Roma still living in the old provinces," she remarked as she studied the distant expanse of water. "The merchants report that the Hunnic plan supposes that there will be no new troops sent to aid the remaining Romans, although how they can be certain of it, I can't imagine." The Latin she and Niklos spoke was more than a century out of date.

"They pass through garrison towns coming south. They probably hear things," said Niklos. "Do you want to go in? The wind's getting stronger."

"Not yet." She continued to stare. "It doesn't seem very Roman, leaving the enclaves in the old provinces to fend for themselves."

"It could be worse than that: if the Huns can persuade more of the Goths and Gepids to join with them, they'll have fewer enemies to fight, and a better chance to find towns to serve as camps for them, to make their campaign against those towns that won't surrender more easily prosecuted," said Niklos, handing her a fan-folded scroll. "The inventories from winter. And the annual purchasing accounts."

"Very good; I'll review them properly in a short while, once I go inside," she said, taking them from him and studying the first open part of the fan. "You don't think any of the remaining Romans would surrender, do you?"

"Why not?" Niklos answered. "The Huns don't tax, and they reward good service, or so I've been told. Many have gone over to them."

"Um," said Olivia as a sign that she was reserving judgment. "What else do you have for me?"

"I have the sales figures from the harvest, and an accounting of the cost of the household for the previous year. There are recommendations for this year's planting to come. And the report on mares in foal and cows with calf." He smiled as he pulled out a small bound ledger.

"Is this Aristarchion's work?" The fussy Greek kept most of the estate's records, and had done so for more than twenty years.

"It is, as always." Niklos chuckled. "You know Aristarchion: he says every year he'll take an apprentice, and every year he puts it off again."

"I think he will need one this year. His handwriting looks like spider-webs, and his eyesight is beginning to fail," she said, scanning the faint, angular scrawl. A sharp gust of wind almost pulled the fan-folded scrolls from her hands. Taking a firmer hold, she said, "I think it might be better to go in. The weather is turning."

"I agree," said Niklos, nodding toward the door leading to her book-room. "Do you want the fire in the holocaust built up?"

"It would probably be wise. If the floors get cold, the whole house is miserable." She held the scrolls close to her chest while her lilac-colored woollen palla and trabea fluttered in the rising wind. "And order a small vat of wine heated and spiced for the household."

"As you like," said Niklos, holding the door open for her. "Do you think this will bring snow in the mountains?"

"It seems likely. Travel will soon be hard." She slipped indoors and touched her fawn-brown hair, knowing it was tousled beyond any excuse of fashion. "It might be best to have the grooms bring the horses in, and the mules." Then, as she regarded the clouds through narrowed eyes, "Better get the cattle into the barn and the sheep into their sheds. This is going to be a bad night."

"I'll see the men are set to it," Niklos assured her. "What can I get for you?"

She saw the sly shine in his eyes and she wagged her finger at him. "Don't you go playing with me, Niklos. You know that I am hungry, but I won't prey upon anyone of my household. Later this evening, if you will seek out Italicus Erbertus when he returns from the markets, and ask him to join me in my withdrawing room, I believe I may relieve my hunger without any intrusions among my servants and slaves, and to his satisfaction as well as mine."

"Bondama Clemens," Niklos responded with a respectful lowering of his head, modified by a quick wink, "would I even so much as imply such a thing about you? We have been together long enough that I know you will not approach anyone who would dislike your way of taking nourishment."

"And yet you have doubts about Italicus Erbertus," she said.

"I suspect you do, too," he said with a more serious mien. "I doubt he'll be here tonight, given the weather that's developing. There are inns in Aquileia that will keep him fed, and warm, and dry. He's not a man to put himself out when he has no inspiration to do so."

"I am not sufficient inspiration?" she asked.

"I doubt he would risk traveling in pouring rain to spend the night with you, not when he need not do so."

"Another aspect of the man you have your doubts about?" Olivia prodded.

"Enough to caution you. Do you question my motives?"

"Only when you want to beleaguer me," she replied baldly. "Or when you disapprove of my choices for a partner." She studied Niklos' face. "Why do you object to Italicus Erbertus?"

Niklos stood still for a long moment, his remarkably handsome features still. "I don't know precisely what it is that bothers me, but I can't quiet the vexation he rouses in me. He's a bit too smug—but he's a successful merchant, after all, and such men are often smug. He's boastful about women—but so is almost every other man in Aquileia, so that isn't the cause, little as I like his manner. In that regard, he behaves as if he is lord of your estate—but so have others before him. It may be that he is unworthy of you, or that I don't believe he will keep your secret." He shrugged, his expression puzzled. "It may be all of those things, or none. But there is something badly amiss in him. Be careful of him, Olivia."

Neither of them thought it odd that her bondsman would call her by her personal name; he would not have done it had they been overheard. "I will, but I think you're being over-cautious."

"As you are with Sanct' Germain," he suggested.

She tried to smile and almost managed it. "I take your point. I wonder," she added in a more speculative tone, "if I would care half so much about the Huns if Sanct' Germain weren't in their path."

"Wait until he is safe and find out." He escorted her to the couch near the main table in the room. "If you want to lie down for a bit, I'll see to the securing of the house, and then I'll report to you." He took a blanket from the foot of the couch and opened it.

"I will be glad to recline for a while; there is so much to do later," she said, exaggerating a yawn as she came up to the three couches in front of the empty hearth and chose the one with the most cushions. She sat down and prepared to lean back. "I suppose I'll be up most of the night."

Niklos grinned. "That will depend upon the storm, I think. Let me put the estate in order for you while you recruit yourself. May you have a pleasant rest, Bondama."

"Niklos, stop it," she admonished him playfully. "You are too willing to make light of our position."

"Not I," he objected. "I know that we must not remain here for more than a decade, or anywhere else, for that matter. You are older than I am, but our ages are sufficiently beyond the average that we would not want to be subject to scrutiny. And longevity is the least of it." He took the blanket and held it up for her as she settled onto the couch. "I'll deal with the stable and then the household."

"You are good to me, Niklos." She lay back as if prepared to nap, but there was only acuity in her gaze. "When you return, we must consider Sanct' Germain's problems more closely."

He touched his forehead respectfully and left her alone on the couch, her household records held closely to her chest. Moving out through the atrium, he shouted to summon grooms and cowmen to him, snapping out orders as he went toward the stable.

"The storm will be upon us shortly," said Tarquinus, the head-groom. "It will be best to get the animals in."

"So Bondama Clemens thinks," said Niklos, helping to pull open the side-doors of the stable. "And have the youngsters round up the ducks and chickens; get them into their coops."

"That I will. We should be closed up before the rain begins."

"And have warm mash for the horses tonight," Niklos added, hurrying on to the barn on the far side of the stable, where the cowmen were already herding their charges into the building. "Make sure you have hay enough for them. Check the loft. Get rid of the rats if you find any."

"There are always rats," said Bynum, the cowman from Gaul who was in charge of the barn. "But we'll kill as many as we can. We have ten cats to help us, and that scrappy dog Darios brought from the market."

"Very good. Make sure the windows have their shutters in place, and barred closed." Niklos went on to the sheep-sheds and the pigpens, making a cursory sweep of them, then he circled around back toward the main house. He stopped on the way to urge four young slaves to close the shutters on the windows of the house. "Then get indoors yourselves."

"Yes, Major Domo," said two of them at the same time.

Niklos knew it was useless to remind them that he was not the major domo for the estate—that titled belonged to Sylvandrus Polli and had for eight years—but the personal bondsman to Atta Olivia Clemens, the owner of the estate and all it contained. There was no reason to stop and explain again; he kept on, passing the footman as he entered the house on his right foot. "Make sure the door-lamp has enough oil to last the night, Sergius."

"And there will be someone manning the door until the weather clears," Sergius pledged, trying not to cough.

"Get yourself to Briareus and have him give you some tincture of hawthorn-and-honey. You don't want that cough to get worse."

"Yes, Bondsman," said Sergius, still doing his utmost not to cough.

Niklos went to the kitchens and summoned the main cook. "It is going to be a hard night, Patricius. Make sure there is a cauldron of hearty soup simmering all through the night. We may have travelers arrive."

"Not willing to go all the way into Aquileia," remarked the cook

"Not in the middle of a bad storm, no," Niklos agreed. "Have you seen Sylvandrus Polli about?"

"He went to the cellars at mid-day. He may still be there Aristarchion is with him."

"I'll find them once we're settled here." He looked around the kitchen. "Could you and Nicodemus manage another baking thi afternoon? Not a full one, a half, so that there will be small bread only."

"Probably," said Patricius. "Since there is no convivium thi evening." He did not add any such obvious word as *fortunately* o *luckily,* but his satisfaction at this arrangement was obvious in ever aspect of his demeanor.

"Had the Bondama arranged for one, she would most likely cancel it, given the weather. No one would want to come out of the city during a tempest." Niklos pointed to the box in which Patricius kept his recipes. "Mixed meats and root vegetables, I'd think, and wine to give it body."

"With onions and garlic as well as turnips and carrots. A good basic soup," said Patricius, both satisfaction and regret in his de meanor. "Not like the old days, when they stuffed ducks with larks tongues and sweetbreads."

"That dish hasn't been made in two centuries," said Niklos, and pointed to the handled bowls stacked on the shelf across the room "Plan to serve the soup before everyone retires."

"A late supper?" Patricius asked, startled at the suggestion.

"Yes. To help them all sleep a little more soundly on a hard night," Niklos ordered, and then said, "The main cellar, or the wine cellar?"

"The main cellar. Onions, apples, turnips, sacks of grain, boxe of honeycombs, and smoked meats. All the signs are for a late spring, and we'll need to know our reserves. We don't want to have to slaughter all the shoats and lambs." He nodded toward the mai hearth, where three large geese turned on spits manned by a bored scullion, dripping sizzling grease onto the bricks. "This will be ready for prandium, in less than an hour now."

"I hope you will have a pleasant meal," said Niklos, as good manners required. He nodded and started off toward the door that led to the main cellar. "Is there an oil-lamp I can use?"

"Just inside the door at the top of the stairs, on a hook; see you put it back," said Patricius, and began to make his way through the baskets of vegetables, selecting those that would go into the soup.

The stairs zigzagged down into the cellar—three large, stone rooms filled with barrels and sacks and baskets of all manner of foodstuffs. The place was cool even at the height of summer; just now it was chilly. Sylvandrus Polli and Aristarchion were in the second room, the only one with a window, and they stood next to a sealed vat of olive oil. One that had been broached was slightly behind them.

"Major Domo," Niklos called out, "the Bondama is closing the house for the storm, and is calling all the livestock in."

"There," said Polli. "I told you she wouldn't take any chances."

Aristarchion pulled at the edge of his short beard, now more than half white, and said, "It is a good precaution."

"There will be soup and bread for a late supper. If the storm turns more dangerous, a good part of the household will be up during the night." Niklos regarded the two men. "If you will be good enough to help arrange this?"

"It is our duty," said Polli somberly. "We have done about half the inventory down here, but under the circumstances, the rest can wait. We can postpone the rest until the storm passes." He took a piece of chalk and made a note on the vat in front of him. "We can resume with this in a day or so."

"It is going to be a long night," Aristarchion said, folding up the scroll in his hands. "How soon must we be ready to engage the storm?"

"As soon as it starts," said Niklos, going toward the stairs, holding his oil-lamp up to help light the way for the other two. "So my shadow won't block your lamplight."

When they reached the kitchen, three more scullions and a pair of under-cooks were huddled with Patricius, discussing supper and the second night meal. "This is all to the good," said Patricius as he caught sight of the major domo. "We should have a pleasant night, storm or no storm."

"So long as there are no disruptions," said Patricius.

As if to punctuate the cook's remark, there was a clanging from the main gate, and the sound of activity as a number of household slaves rushed to discover who had arrived.

"Is it raining yet?" Aristarchion asked. "The wind is rising."

"No rain, but it won't be long," said Patricius.

"Then it will be all to the good that we admit travelers now. Once the rain begins, there will be mud everywhere," said Orandus, the older under-cook.

"See that the vestibule is ready for visitors," said Polli. "And have guest rooms made up."

Niklos considered this, and added, "As soon as we know who has arrived and how many are in the party, inform me so that I may tell Bondama Clemens how many travelers will be stopping here for the night."

The wind was drubbing the house with heavy gusts, and more of the household staff came into the kitchen on the way to the dining room set aside for their use. The thick glass in the windows rattled and the shutters quivered against their iron braces.

"Pity the mariners at sea tonight," said Polli, whose nephews worked on merchant ships.

"True enough," said Niklos. "But let us prepare to welcome the travelers." He started toward the front of the house. "I leave you to tend to the evening meals."

"The baking is under way," said Patricius, paying very little attention to Niklos. "The ovens are heating and the doughs are being kneaded. They'll be in the oven by nightfall."

"When do you want to present the travelers to Bondama Clemens?" Polli called after Niklos.

"As soon as they are dried and warm," said Niklos, striding toward the main door of the house, listening to the roaring wind. He saw Sergius busily lighting more oil-lamps, and he paused long nough to say, "If you will learn the names of the travelers, where hey came from, and where they are bound?"

"Of course. We will have no strangers in the Bondama's house." He had donned an abolla over his sleeved tunica, but he still looked old.

Niklos went out through the main door, making sure to cross he threshold on his right foot. The wind struck him like a weighted lub, and he steadied himself against it. He saw the flickering oil-amp in its glass cage beside the door and wondered if anyone vould be able to see it when the rain began. He went out toward the nain gate, standing open to admit the small party of merchants; all he while he listened to the boom of the wind. When he was near nough to be heard, he called out, "Travelers! On behalf of Bondama Clemens, whose estate this is, you are welcome to shelter from the torm as her guests."

There were three men riding mules, huddled into their byrri, heir hoods pulled forward to protect their faces; they led seven nules, all well-laden. Their escort was five armed men mounted on orses. They, too, had heavy abollae to keep out the cutting wind. 'our grooms had run up to help the men dismount and to lead their nimals to the stable. The three slaves manning the gate were strug-ling to close it once again.

One of the merchants got down from his mule and turned to Niklos. He steadied himself by holding on to the broad pommel of is saddle. "Thank the Bondama for her hospitality," he said, his atin heavily accented with Greek. "I am Orestes of Naissus. We re bound for Ravenna and Roma. These are my companions, Ful-ius Gaudiensis, and Marcellos Basilios." He indicated the other wo merchants. "I fear Fulvius has taken ill, and is in need of suc-or."

For an instant, Niklos wished that Sanct' Germain were with hem and not in the remote mountains of the old Province of Dacia. Certainly," he said. "Kardens, see that the ailing man is taken to his oom at once, and make sure that Mater Rhodanthe is sent to care r him."

The slave who had finally secured the gate nodded. "Yes, Bondsman," he said flatly, and went to the last mounted of the merchants, where he helped the ailing man out of the saddle, then offered him his shoulder to lean on.

The escort had already dismounted and were leading their horses and the pack-mules toward the stable, following the groom with the enclosed oil-lamp. The day was dark now, with no trace of color in the clouds, but it was mid-afternoon. The remaining grooms took the riding mules in hand and went off after the others.

Orestes of Naissus regarded Niklos narrowly. "It is rare to find so . . . so fine a reception on the roads these days." He walked unsteadily, as if his back were sore.

"Bondama Clemens keeps to the Roman traditions," said Niklos, indicating that the two merchants should accompany him. "We will have rooms for you, and a simple meal in a short while, but no convivium."

"On such short notice, no one would expect otherwise. And I fear Marcellos Basilios and I are tired and would be poor company." He turned to Basilios and said, "I trust you are willing to have simple fare tonight."

"After what we have endured on the road, simple fare is splendid; some meat, some wine, and a bread and I will think myself blessed," Basilios answered.

Niklos was almost at the main door when he thought of something more to ask. "Have you any news of the Huns?"

Orestes moaned, "They kept winter at the foot of the mountains. Odessus and Tomi are thoroughly in their hands, where the cities are not in ruins. The Huns have spent their time improving their weapons and learning more about Roman defenses. They were boasting that by next winter they will control the Carpathians down to the Danuvius." He crossed the threshold on the right foot and made sure Basilios did the same. Sergius made a sign of approval and held out his hand for their byrri, saying, "There are laenae laid out for you in your rooms."

"Do you think they will succeed?" Niklos pursued, for once paying no heed to the courtesy the men had been given. "The Huns? coming so far south?"

Orestes nodded. "I would wager on it," he said grimly. "They are not inclined to idle bragging."

Sylvandrus Polli came up to the newcomers. "Be welcome in the house of Bondama Clemens," he said. "Your companion is being treated by Mater Rhodanthe, who will tell you of his condition later. If you will come with me, I will show you to your rooms. Your personal cases are being brought in from the stable. Will you need a servant to help you, or would you prefer to manage on your own?"

The merchants exchanged glances, then Basilios said, "If you could spare one to wait upon two of us?"

"Of course," said Polli. "This way," and he started off under the overhang of the atrium, leaving Niklos to go to Olivia.

She was seated at her writing table, a tree of oil-lamps providing illumination for the reports Niklos had given her earlier. "What have you learned?" she asked when he had explained the basics.

"They're worried about the Huns, that was conspicuous, and not just in words, but the whole of their expression: more worried than they are about Roman tax collectors." He paused, then added, "Orestes said that they have their sights on the Carpathians." As he said that, the first rush of rain washed down over the hillside, sounding like a continuous load of pebbles had been dropped across the land.

Olivia looked up at the ceiling and a shiver of discomfort went through her, but she spoke calmly enough. "I have been thinking that I should send you to Sanct' Germain with my next letter to him, as soon as the storm is over. You can see for yourself how he is faring, and you may add your voice to mine if you think he would be wiser to leave the mountains than to stay."

"And what of you? Do you intend to come with me?"

"No, much as I would like to do it. If you think Aquileia isn't safe, the roads north are much less so, and not only because of the Huns." She smiled without amusement. "Don't fret, Niklos. The household here will guard me well enough, though I will miss you while you are away." She smiled, and there was something profound in her eyes, an acknowledgment that she could finally be of use to Sanct' Germain, who had done so much for her. "If you have to be gone until winter, so be it, so long as you find him and determine he is safe."

"Rogerian is with him. Why should he need me?" Niklos asked.

"Rogerian has only recently left Constantinople, and he won't have reached the Carpathians yet; for all we know, the Huns have caught him," said Olivia with the kind of tranquil determination that Niklos knew it would be useless to dispute.

"All right. But speak to the merchants this evening, before you decide to send me off."

She considered. "Very well. But if I tell you that it must be done, I expect you to comply without complaint."

Niklos sighed. "As you wish, Olivia," he said, and began to plan what he would have to take with him on the coming journey.

Text of an arrest warrant for the detention of Rugierus of Gades, issued by the Imperial Secretary, Herakles Akacios, in Constantinople, copied with fixed ink on vellum and dispatched by Imperial couriers to nine cities in Thracia and Moesia.

To the Imperial Governors, the Praetori Custodii, Governors, regional guadians, the garrison Tribunes, and the Proconsuls of the Emperor, this notification of detention from the Imperial Secretary, Herakles Akacios, at the pleasure of the Emperor Theodosios.

Be it known that the servant of Dom Feranescus Rakoczy Sanctu-Germainios, one Rugierus of Gades, currently believed to be traveling alone toward the Danuvius River, is to be apprehended and returned to Constantinople to explain to the Imperial Questor certain matters put before the Imperial Questor by the factor Artemidorus Iocopolis, at the exemplary instigation of Patras Methodos, who has declared he is convinced that this Rugierus of Gades is part of an organization of smugglers who may or may not be allied with Rugierus of Gades' employer, the Dom Feranescus Rakoczy Sanctu-Germainios.

In order to determine the truth of this allegation, Rugierus of Gades must be held and returned to Constantinople. Failure to comply with this order will serve as an indication that the official refusing to carry out this order is no longer loyal to the Emperor Theodosios and the Roman Empire in the East.

Those who are willing to pursue this matter will be brought to the favorable attention of the Emperor, and will, in due time, be rewarded for that loyalty. Those who shirk this duty will be known as officials of tergiversation and no longer worthy of the trust bestowed upon them by the Emperor.

At ten days before the Vernal Equinox,

> Herakles Akacios
> Imperial Secretary to the Emperor Theodosios
> at Constantinople

5

For two weeks the mountains had been showing signs of spring: pines and oaks shed their mantles of snow; the little creeks lost their ice and ran chuckling down into the lake at the end of Sanctu-Eustachios the Hermit; a few early flowers struggled into the sunlight, leaving the snow in patches around them. The sounds of birds returned to the air, and the underbrush rustled with the passage of foxes, badgers, marten, deer, and wild boar; the first few bear emerged from hibernation and grumpily sought out streams for fishing.

Then, five days after the Equinox, winter returned in gelid fury. Snow rode horizontally on ferocious winds and the trees once again were swaddled in white. Occasional loud cracks came from the forest as branches broke under the weight of snow and wind. The many people at the monastery crouched indoors, crowded together, their tempers sharp and their states of mind alive with increasing fear. No one looked forward to the Paschal Mass that would be celebrated the following morning at dawn.

In the old wooden chapel, Sanctu-Germainios continued to tend those persons the monks in the infirmary would not touch; it fell to him to set broken limbs and remove frostbitten fingers and toes, to purge putrid lungs and poisoned guts, to sew up cuts and gouges, and to set misaligned joints. On the second day of the blizzard, Isalind was brought to him with a badly sprained ankle and a severe scrape along her shin.

"How did this happen?" Sanctu-Germainios asked her as he knelt beside her to touch her swollen leg. He motioned to Nicoris, who had been sorting lengths of linen, to come closer. "And bring the steady chair. She needs to sit down so she can raise her leg to keep the ankle from swelling any more than it has."

"I was carrying slops to the midden, and I slipped." Isalind scowled and ground her teeth, both in aggravation and against the pain. "My ankle twisted as I fell."

"I see that," he said, and glanced at the two monks who had brought her. "The skin is not broken, she has none of the signs of inward illness."

"We have no means to care for her in the infirmary," said one of the monks, his voice devoid of all emotion.

"Then it is fortunate that I do," said Sanctu-Germainios. "You may put her in that chair." He went in, pointing to a straight-backed, square-seated one that Nicoris had moved beside the raised bed he used for treating those seriously injured.

The monks did as he instructed, neither of them liking the work they were having to do. Both of them made an effort to touch Isalind as little as possible. As they put her down, they both made the sign of the fish. "That none of her ills pass to us," said the shorter of the two, then lowered his head and made for the door, his taller companion following him. Neither made the sign of the cross as they departed.

"It is because I'm a woman. The infirmary monks don't like

treating women. They say it compromises their chastity." Her aggravation was obvious from her face and the harshness of her voice.

"They're becoming more stringent about their vows," said Nicoris, raising her voice so that she could be heard. "They aren't comfortable having so many residents who don't want to practice their rites and rituals. They told Bernardius not to talk Latin."

"It is also part of their discomfort with having bodies. They believe holiness is attained through neglect of their bodies in all manner of ways," said Sanctu-Germainios. "It is a foolish thing to do; if you ignore the flesh, it will lead to all manner of unnecessary ills, and in the end it will shorten life." He had seen it before, in many places, and he knew beyond doubt that clean bodies resisted disease and infection better than bodies that were not.

"They are fools not to have a better bath-house and proper latrines," said Isalind, not only to agree with him, but to try to keep her mind off the gnawing ache from her ankle. "I wouldn't have to carry slops if they had latrines. No one would. And we would stink less than we do, and have fewer lice and lice fever. Our clothes could be kept cleaner, as well, if there were a laundry here."

"The monks won't agree to a bath-house or a laundry. They say it glorifies the body to have enclosed latrines and baths, and that clean clothes promote vanity, all of which they believe imperil the soul, and all of them fear for their souls with the Huns about," said Sanctu-Germainios, recalling his fruitless discussion with Priam Corydon, and the awkwardness that had resulted from it. "The monks prefer their dirt and their vermin. It comes from their peculiar understanding of chastity and their disdain for their well-being."

"An enclosed latrine wouldn't lead to debauchery," said Isalind, then hissed breath through her clamped teeth as Sanctu-Germainios slightly repositioned her leg.

"But they fear it would," said Sanctu-Germainios. "And their fear makes it a certainty."

Isalind took a deep breath and let it out slowly, striving against her pain. "It would make their winters easier. With their flocks and

herds, they have dung enough to tath their fields. Slops aren't required. A channel could carry the waste out of the valley and down
the mountain. If any of them have the courage to build such a
channel—with the Huns about, as you say." She scowled as she lifted
her leg until it was straight. "I have truly hurt myself," she said.

"That you have," said Sanctu-Germainios, rising and reaching
for a stool to put under her elevated foot.

"What will you have to do?" Isalind asked. She was pale; her
ruddy hair made her look pasty.

"I will tell you when I have discerned the extent of your injuries. Your ankle is clearly sprained, but you may have broken a
bone in your foot as well; I will not know if you have until the ankle
is less distended. And I'll want to clean that abrasion."

"The slops spilled. You can probably tell. I reek of them."
Isalind looked abashed at this confession.

"You'll have to give up your clothes, and not for the odor, for the
animalcules that may cling to them," said Sanctu-Germainios. "You
will need to keep the laceration clean for it to heal. Nicoris will
bring you an abolla to warm you for now. Being cold when there has
been an injury can be very dangerous."

She looked skeptically at Sanctu-Germainios. "My man won't
like me undressed before you."

"Tell him that your clothes were unhealthy; I will go into my
sleeping alcove when you change; I will not see you naked," said
Sanctu-Germainios, watching while Nicoris went to the one of his
traveling cases he had indicated and removed an abolla and a
long-sleeved tunica made of sand-colored wool; both belonged to
Rugierus, but Sanctu-Germainios knew he would not begrudge
them to Isalind, for he had more clothing to choose from.

"This should be enough for her to be properly dressed and
warm." Nicoris set the garments on the raised treatment bed.

"If you will heat some water so we can put her in it to wash,"
Sanctu-Germainios suggested. "Then we can add more hot water so
her foot can be soaked in restorative salts."

"The salts you use on the horses and mules?" Nicoris asked.

"The same. Tendons are tendons, no matter what animal or human contains them." Sanctu-Germainios laid his hand on Isalind's arm. "You will recover so long as that scrape has no infection. But to avoid that, you must be clean."

She sighed. "Patras Anso won't like it."

"Nor will Priam Corydon," said Sanctu-Germainios, who had had his share of disputes with both the Patras and the Priam, "but treating injuries is not a religious exercise, no matter what they may believe." As he said this, he thought back to his centuries at the Temple of Imhotep, the Egyptian god of healing and architecture, whose priests provided medical treatment for all Egyptians, no matter which of the gods they favored or what illness or injury brought them to the temple.

Nicoris rolled out a large wooden tub and set it near the stone hearth. "I'm going out to load the cauldron with snow," she announced, anticipating his need. "You can build up the logs for me, Dom, so the water can boil. I'll be back shortly." She hefted the large iron pot from its hook over the dying fire. As she opened the door, snowy wind shrieked into the old chapel, chilling it and making the lengths of linen flutter from their neat stacks into confusion.

Isalind glanced around her, taking stock of the chapel for the first time. "You are treating no one else but me?"

"I have at present nine other patients in the old dormitory. I carry them there once their hurts are dressed, where their companions and families may care for them." He smiled at her without any sign of concern. "You will be at your man's side by full dark."

She wrinkled her nose. "I suppose my clothes will be useless after this? Blood and shit won't wash out, will they?"

"Most likely not," he said. "If you need clothes, you may keep what I give you."

"My man wouldn't let me accept such a gift, neither would Patras Anso, but I thank you for your offer," said Isalind.

Sanctu-Germainios went to his red-lacquer chest and brought out a small jar. He then took a small pottery cup from the top shelf of the chest and poured a little of the contents into the cup. "I will mix this with a little wine and honey. I want you to drink it. It will lessen your pain and help the swelling in your ankle diminish."

She watched him as he prepared the mixture. "Is there anything in it besides what you say?"

"The medicament has ground willow-bark and pansy, which reduce pain and swelling, crushed juniper berries, celery seed, and ground pepper for swelling and stiffness, in a paste of sourberries which helps to preserve it and provides a lessening of fever if any should arise. It is useful in treating scrapes and strains, and tightening of the joints. I have been told that it has an unpleasant taste. The honey will help that, and the wine will aid the medicament to work for it eases the body and strengthens the blood." He used an alabaster spoon to stir the mixture, then gave the cup to Isalind.

She drank cautiously, pursed her lips after the first swallow "You're right. Its taste is unpleasant."

"Well, drink as much of it as you can endure," he recommended, then turned to see Nicoris struggling with the cauldron brimming with snow, the wind pursuing her, howling. Going to help her, he closed the door and set the brace, then said, "You have done a fine job, Nicoris." He took the cauldron from her and carried it easily to the hearth.

"There's more snow coming down," she said, watching him speculatively. "This is a very bad storm. The passes will be closed again for at least a week." She pulled off her byrrus and hung it on a peg near the door to dry. "I'll get more once the tub is full, so we may adjust the temperature of the water."

Sanctu-Germainios went to the stacked logs at the end of the fireplace stones and selected three lengths of good girth. He brought these back to the weakening fire and carefully set them to burn, leaning them on the embers to promote a good draw of air. Then he placed the cauldron on its hook once more and swung it into the fireplace over the logs. "I should have done this before you returned."

"You have been treating Isalind," said Nicoris, still scrutinizing him; she knew how heavy the snow-filled cauldron was, and she was amazed that he could lift it so effortlessly. "I was approached by a monk while I loaded the cauldron. He says that the hermits have come down from their caves. They're in the monastery in the upper cells, and they have announced they intend to remain until the storm passes."

"That shows some small measure of sense," said Sanctu-Germainios.

"They're claiming that God has sent the storm to show us His might." Isalind stopped herself from saying something more reckless.

"How did you find out about it?" Nicoris asked.

"Everyone was talking about it in the dormitory," said Isalind. "The Watchmen were complaining that Monachos Anatolios has been exhorting them while they've been on duty, telling them that they are betraying God."

"They want the world to end, so God will reign on earth," said Nicoris, her face set.

"You do not want that to happen?" Sanctu-Germainios asked, a touch of irony in his tone.

"Do you? They say only the most dedicated Christians will be chosen to share the Kingdom of God, all the rest will burn forever in Hell," said Isalind. "Monachos Anatolios has stated that only virgins can hope to be among the few who will attend upon God's Glory when the apocalypse comes. Those who try to forestall the Second Coming by opposing the Will of God will be among the first cast into the Pit." She managed to drink the last sip from the cup, then set it on the floor beside her chair.

"He expects God to prefer men like himself, I imagine. Men of his kind usually do," said Sanctu-Germainios.

"Don't let any of the religious hear you say that," Nicoris warned him. "Antoninu Neves has had two of his men sent away from this place because they would not honor the religion of the monks."

Sanctu-Germainios looked surprised. "When did that happen?" And why, he added inwardly, did no one tell him about it?

"Yesterday morning, while his men were bringing in more wood for all the fires," said Isalind. "They were accused of chastising the monks for praying instead of working at a time when labor was more necessary."

"How unwise of them," said Isalind.

"I must suppose it did no good," said Sanctu-Germainios.

"Since the soldiers were cast out, it's a double loss. There are two fewer men to cut and saw wood, and no monks are willing to take their place," said Nicoris. "Neves has said that such losses are damaging to all of us."

"And Monachos Anatolios says it is God's punishment for our lack of submission to His Will," said Isalind.

Sanctu-Germainios bit back the remark he wanted to make, and said instead, "As soon as the water is warm, I will wash your leg and then you can prepare for your bath. When I am done, I will leave so you may get into the tub."

"I'll remain with you when you come to bathe, in case you need any help," Nicoris said to Isalind. "You might have difficulty getting out of the tub."

"So I might," said Isalind, staring at her puffy ankle.

"Thank you for that," said Sanctu-Germainios, once again struck by her beneficent pragmatism and her unusual directness. If only, he thought, she would tell him the truth about herself, for after their second love-making, he knew beyond all doubt that she had not been veracious with him.

Isalind tried to flex her foot and let out a small mew of dismayed pain. "How long will it take before my ankle is well?"

"That will depend on how you treat it," said Sanctu-Germainios. "If you will follow my instructions, you may hope to be significantly improved in a month. You will feel better before then, but your ankle will not yet be strong." He saw her wince at his remark. "There are things you can do that do not require carrying heavy items. Devote yourself to making clothes and mending those that need it. That is as useful as carrying slops."

"My man won't like it," she said with foreboding.

"If you would like, I will explain your situation to him. But whatever he may think, you will only delay your recovery if you try to resume your duties too quickly."

Isalind looked troubled. "I have my tasks to do."

"Not while your ankle is injured." He regarded her steadily. "Neglect it now and it will never be fully strong again."

She shuddered. "The monks have told me I should pray."

Sanctu-Germainios gave a single shake of his head. "Pray if you like, but do not stress your ankle."

Although Nicoris had said nothing, she was clearly listening to everything. She used a poking-stick on the logs to get them to burn more fiercely. "Pay attention to the Dom," she advised. "He has great skill."

"All of us from Apulum Inferior know that," Isalind said brusquely, going on with a bit more cordiality, "All of us have seen what he can do."

"Then do as he tells you," Nicoris said, bringing a stool to the side of the wooden tub.

Isalind sighed. "It isn't that simple."

Nicoris clicked her tongue impatiently. "Then don't fault him when your ankle twists on you again."

"I will speak to your man, and to Priam Corydon," Sanctu-Germainios offered again. "The monks may have no regard for their bodies, but few of us can be so inattentive."

"Let me think about this," said Isalind. "It is a difficult matter. Patras Anso will put his faith above your medicaments, and my man will follow his lead."

Sanctu-Germainios did not bother to ask why; he knew that among the Gepidae, women were not coddled—as their men put it—the way Romans coddled their women. It would require persuasion of a most practical kind to arrange for Isalind to get the care she needed. "I will do what I can to explain the risks."

"He's good at that," said Nicoris. "He's explained a lot to me. I understood him, too."

Isalind shook her head. "You may try, Dom."

"I will," he said, and turned to Nicoris. "We'll need a drying sheet for her. You may take one from my copper-banded chest."

Nicoris nodded. "Yes, Dom," she said, and went to get it.

"She's devoted to you, isn't she?" Isalind asked.

"It seems so," said Sanctu-Germainios, adding, "Her knowledge of herbs is extensive, and she aids me in my work. I am very grateful to her."

"Grateful?" Isalind looked startled at the word. "Why should you be grateful?"

"Why should I not? She is capable and well-informed," he countered, and would have said more had Nicoris not returned with a drying sheet over her arm.

"There you are," she said, addressing Isalind as she put the sheet on the raised bed, then went back to poke the fire again.

"The water will boil in good time," said Sanctu-Germainios, regarding Nicoris with perplexity: what was she hiding, he asked himself, and why? What would be so dreadful that she would not tell him?

Outside, through the bluster of the storm came the eerie wail of wolves. The three in the old chapel exchanged uneasy glances.

"They're after the livestock," said Nicoris. "And they're near."

"But not inside the old walls," said Sanctu-Germainios.

"No. Not yet." Nicoris hunkered down beside the fire as if she were without protection from the blizzard or the wolves.

"What more will you do when I have bathed?" Isalind asked, needing to distract herself from the growing chorus of howls.

"Treat your scrape, soak your ankle, and bind it. Then I'll get you to the dormitory and talk to your man." He studied Nicoris. "I give the storm two more days; what do you think?"

"At this time of year, two is probably right; there isn't the northern bite to keep it blowing. A month ago it would have been four days at the least." She stood up and dusted off the front of her heavy, long-sleeved palla. "And it will melt quickly, flooding the streams and some of the villages down the mountain along with filling the large rivers. There'll be logs and branches floating in the current, and they may damage the four bridges crossing the Danuvius downstream."

"The bridges are in poor repair in any case," said Sanctu-Germainios. "Neither Roma nor Constantinople has seen fit to restore them." He walked down the length of the main part of the chapel, listening to the counterpoint of wolves and storm. No wonder so many thought these mountains were haunted, he thought. Even in his breathing days most of the inhabitants of the Carpathians had believed that powerful spirits awoke in the remote peaks and valleys during the winter. He remained near the main door for a little while, until Nicoris called to him.

"The water is about to boil."

"I'll come and pour the water into the tub," he responded, and started back toward the main fireplace.

"Dom, do I have to keep from using my ankle—really?" Isalind asked as she watched him heft the cauldron of simmering water and tip it so that it flowed into the wooden tub.

Nicoris took the cauldron. "I'll get snow, to balance the heat," she said, and went to the side-door to let herself out.

"There are too many of us in this place," said Isalind as the door thudded shut.

"I agree," he said to her. "But there is no place to go in such a storm."

"The exiled men are out in it, along with the Huns," Isalind observed. "If he fights again, my man will be one of them." There was worry in her voice, and although she kept her face averted, he could recognize her distress.

"Then it would be best for him to hold his temper." His tone was kindly and he made a point of moving around her chair so he could study her. "Spring will be here in a week or so, and then those who wish to travel may do so."

"And face the Huns alone?" She stared at him, her eyes glistening with tears. "I think, sometimes, that the Huns are just a story made up to frighten us. Other times I almost wish they would come, and end this hideous waiting."

"You have heard what those who have faced them have said of them." He went down on one knee. "It is all a gamble, Isalind. The Huns may pay no heed to this place, or they may attack. If people decide to leave, they may or may not be attacked by the Huns. No one can say what will happen, not with certainty. All we can do is prepare for the worst possibilities, and hope we have been too pessimistic." In his long life he had been in battle many, many times, and each time the battle had not gone as anyone had planned. He thought back to his time in Gaul with Caesar's Legions, and reminded himself that even that superb strategist Gaius Julius Caesar had often misanticipated the strength and disposition of his opponents. "But for our own survival, we must assume they will come and be prepared to fight them."

"Fight them and perhaps lose our lives, I suppose? My man says that the monks are trying to keep us here to fight for them."

"And that may well be part of their motives for allowing us to take refuge here," he said. "I would rather have stout walls and a supply of food and water than wagons in the open if the Huns arrive in force."

"Do you want to die?" She seemed repulsed by the very words.

He gave a sad chuckle and got to his feet. "Oh, Isalind: there are so many worse things than death."

She regarded him in shock as the side-door banged open and Nicoris lugged in a second load of snow in the cauldron.

"There are some of Neves' men on patrol. They claim that the carcass of a deer is missing and they're planning to find it and bring the thief before Priam Corydon." Nicoris lugged the cauldron next to the tub. "I'm going to put two pails of this into the water, and you can test it then, to find out if it is not too hot for you."

"Thank you," said Isalind.

"Whatever you don't want to lower the temperature now, I'll put to heat so you won't have to sit in cold water, or soak your ankle in it." Nicoris waved to Sanctu-Germainios. "You may leave, Dom. I will manage things here."

Sanctu-Germainios offered her a Roman salute. "Call me when ou want me to return."

"That we will," said Nicoris, picking up the pail to scoop out now. "I'll support you to the tub to test the water in a short while," he went on, talking to Isalind.

Sanctu-Germainios moved away, toward his sleeping alcove, gain missing Rugierus. He sat on the end of his hard, narrow bed set top a chest of his native earth, recalling the many times he had seen nmity erupt among men and women forced to live in contained pace under threat. He let his memories range from his living days to he long years of bloody vengeance that followed his execution, to the nany decades in the Babylonian prison, to his centuries in Egypt where he regained his humanity again, to the peripatetic existence which he still pursued; all the while his recollections were accompa- ied by the yammer of the storm and the ululation of the wolves.

ext of a letter from Gnaccus Tortulla, Praetor Custodis at Vimi- acium in the Province of Moesia, to Octavianus Honorius Regulus, ecorder to the Imperial Court of the Roman Empire in the West at Ravenna, written in code with fixed ink on polished linen, carried by mperial courier and delivered twelve days after it was written.

o the most august Octavianus Honorius Regulus, Ave! The Praetor Custodis at Viminacium in the Province of Moesia, Gnaccus Tor- illa, greets you with respect and esteem on this fourth day of April, the official year of 439.

It is my duty to inform you that in spite of continuing rumors nd new bands of refugees, there has been no direct attack on this de of the Danuvius farther west than Odessus. I am certain there ay come a time when this is not the case, but at present I see no roof to justify the constant alarm that I hear everywhere. You may iform the Imperial Treasurer that this region will continue to pro- ide revenue from taxes and other payments, such as from customs and assessments for defense. I have imposed a tax upon those refugees arriving here to cover the increased cost of provisions and more hired soldiers to man the defenses here.

From what I have been able to ascertain of his work, the newly appointed Praetor-General of Drobetae in old Dacia, Verus Flautens, has taken his task to heart. He has heard reports from merchants regarding the movements of the Huns, and transmitted them to me. He has sent his own men to the north to determine the amount of damage the Huns have done, and the present areas of their activities. He has compiled a list of towns that have been emptied and the current locations of many groups of refugees. He has also consulted the refugees coming to Drobetae to ferry over the Danuvius, and has made a record of their accounts, a copy of which he has provided for me, and which I will have a true copy enclosed with this. While I commend his thoroughness, it is my belief that he has placed too much trust in the descriptions of these unfortunates, for he has not yet learned that those who flee count three men as twenty, and twenty as an army.

My next communication will require an escort, for it will accompany the accounts of the last six months as well as the readiness reports of my Tribunes.

> *Gnaccus Tortulla*
> *Praetor Custodis at Viminacium in Moesia*

6

There was a steady drone of bees from the hives at the far end of the outer wall, not unlike the continual chanting from the church. It was late in the afternoon and the cowherds were starting to drive their charges back from grazing between the inner and outer wall to the barn; behind them, the goatherds and shepherds guided their charges to their pens. All around there were signs of spring bur geoning: the flowers on the fruit trees were filled with blossoms, and the raised beds of herbs and vegetables were attended by monks and refugees as well as insects. The air was filled with wonderful scents and the barnyard was redolent of livestock and manure. Lambs and shoats kept near their mothers as they moved; cows plodded steadily while their calves romped; foals rushed among the mares, improving their running. Occasionally the young goats rushed together, butting their heads in anticipation of horns.

"The monastery has a good number of young animals," Rotlandus Bernardius said to Mangueinic as they made their way toward the outer walls where two work-crews were putting up the stockade they wanted to complete before the snows melted in the pass. "I trust we will have had good progress today."

"It's to their advantage to have livestock," said Mangueinic, leaning heavily on his crutch. "Some of it belongs to us, of course." He steadied himself with difficulty, adding, "I would think there would have to be good progress. We had another load of logs brought in this morning."

"I saw the sledge being dragged by the mules. A good thing we have them to work."

"And a good thing we will have them when we leave, given the ground we'll have to cover," said Mangueinic, leaning on his crutch in anticipation of the long trek to come. "We'll need them to negotiate the mountains, as we discovered coming here."

"When do you think we should leave?" Bernardius inquired.

"Shortly before midsummer. The days will be at their longest, and there will be many more companies of travelers on the roads, which may provide us greater protection than keeping to ourselves." Mangueinic cleared his throat. "There will be goodly crops and enlarged herds, and if we make an equitable arrangement with the monks, we should all benefit."

"The monks may not see it that way," warned Bernardius. "Some of them have said that any baby animals should be regarded as a donation to the monastery, including the six mules the mares have dropped."

"Those of us who are going to remain here into summer wouldn't mind the monks keeping the babies, so long as we may take the animals we brought with us when we leave. It would be a fair exchange. They have given us a haven—that should be worth a spring's run of new livestock." Mangueinic slewed around, aware that half a dozen men were following them; the westering sun dazzled him so that he was unable to recognize any of the men. "I think there are men who want to talk with you, Tribune."

Bernardius stopped and swung around, shading his eyes as he regarded the men behind him. "Is there something you want of me, fellows?" He turned to Mangueinic. "I believe they're your Watchmen. They probably want to talk to you."

Mangueinic blinked and stepped aside so that the sun was behind him; he was startled to realize Bernardius was right. "What do you want of me, Watchmen? Is there some trouble?" he asked.

The men halted; they all had been serving as Watchmen since they arrived at Sanctu-Eustachios the Hermit and they clearly intended to speak to Mangueinic. "We want you and the others in charge to know that as soon as we can get through the pass, we and our families are going to leave. We've had enough. We'll go south to Viminacium and from there make our way to Pola, where we can take to the sea if the Huns should reach so far into Roman territory, though it doesn't seem likely that they will." The speaker, the former house-keeper Urridien, folded his arms. "Say what you will, we are committed to leaving. Our messenger from Apulum Inferior, Vilca Troed, says he knows the way. He will guide us."

"He knows the way from Odessus to Ravenna," agreed Mangueinic. "He is a fine guide." He looked squarely from one to the next as he went on, "So you, Urridien, and Corcotos, and Bacoem, and Thirhald, and Hovas, and you, Enlitus Brevios, wish to leave with your families—"

"Those of us who still have families who can travel," muttered Thirhald. "My infant son is too young to make such a journey, though my older daughter will be able to. As to Betto, Agtha will care for him. She has already agreed to it."

Rotlandus Bernardius stared hard at the six men. "You are willing to abandon your comrades from Apulum Inferior? Vertigino me facit. I should be ashamed to treat my people of Ulpia Traiana so shabbily."

"Do you think it's what we want to do?" Enlitus Brevios exclaimed. "We'll all be exiled on some excuse or other if we remain here much longer. The monks disapprove of us, and are looking for reasons to make us leave. We'd rather go of our own choice, with what remains of our property and our animals."

"What of the Huns?" Mangueinic asked.

"What of them?" Hovas shot back. "There has been no trace of them. For all we know, they have left these mountains and are searching the plains for better pickings. It would be a sensible thing to do. Coming this far into the mountains for mounted warriors is a tremendous risk. The sentries on the peaks have seen nothing of them. Why should we believe that they will bother to attack?"

"You heard the accounts that the men from Tsapousso gave, didn't you? They didn't believe that the Huns would bother with them. Tsapousso was smaller than this monastery, and as isolated, yet the Huns came. Why would they spare Sanctu-Eustachios the Hermit?" Mangueinic asked.

"All the more reason to leave as soon as possible—the monks as well as the rest of us," said Bacoem. "If we go, we will have a chance to be safe. If you're right, we will never be so here."

"If I'm right, you won't be safe in Pola," said Mangueinic.

"How do you know that? Have you been in contact with the Huns?" Urridien demanded, flicking his hands fastidiously.

"No more than you have," Mangueinic countered, his face darkening as his temper rose.

"Watchmen, please," said Bernardius. "We need not turn to anger."

Mangueinic glowered at the far wall, taking care not to engage anyone's eyes; he struggled to keep his voice even and his tone amiable. "If we had reliable, recent information, we might be able to find a solution that would put as few of us as possible at risk.

Since we have no such information, I think it might be wisest to wait before taking any action."

Hovas took a step forward. "We are leaving and there is nothing you can do to keep us here."

"Possibly not," Bernardius interjected, attempting to reduce the tension that was building between Mangueinic and the men from Apulum Inferior. "But since there is no reason to think that anyone can get through the pass from either direction, there is still time to discuss the matter and work out a plan that will expose you to the least risk. *Fas est cogit.*"

"There you are wrong," said Thirhald with a harsh smugness. "We do have current information. A man has arrived from Drobetae a short while ago. He made it through the pass, he and his two mules. He is with Antoninu Neves and Priam Corydon at present."

Bernardius and Mangueinic exchanged startled glances. "From Drobetae? What would he want here? Why not make for Apulum or Ulpia Traiana? They're more accessible." Mangueinic could not conceal his doubts about this new arrival. "What does he want with us?"

"He says he was sent here, and he carries a letter from the Praetor-General of Drobetae to Priam Corydon," Brevios declared. "In addition he has his own observations to report."

"I was unaware that Drobetae had a Praetor-General," said Bernardius, his observation laden with skepticism. "*Non credo.*"

"He is newly appointed, the messenger says. A Roman land-owner called Verus Flautens, long known to protect Roman interests in the former province of Dacia, which accounts for his advancement," said Urridien, a trace of satisfaction in his voice. "Dom Sanctu-Germainios affirms he knows the name."

"I, too, have exchanged messages with him," said Bernardius. "Although it startles me that the Romans would decide to make such an appointment at a time like this."

"It is one way to ensure that the old border is maintained on both sides of the Danuvius," said Mangueinic. "He will undoubtedly work in concert with Gnaccus Tortulla in Viminacium, who is well-established."

Thirhald laughed unpleasantly. "The man from Drobetae has said that he is charged with advising the Praetor-General, who has been assigned the task of keeping the road open and protected for those seeking to leave the former Province of Dacia, or to cross through it. It is our intention to take advantage of this extended protection before the Huns come along the Danuvius."

"Why do you say the Huns will follow the Danuvius?" Bernardius asked. "Or has the messenger brought news about that, as well?"

"It is believed that they will attempt to cross the river into Moesia once the river passes the danger of flooding,"

"How do you plan to travel?" Mangueinic asked. "Which way will you go?"

"We'll follow the old milestones on the Roman roads, and gauge ourselves every thousand paces in order to determine our speed of travel." Thirhald nodded twice. "Just the way the merchants do."

"Huns can follow milestones, too, and they travel faster than a band of refugees," Bernardius said in as steady a voice as he could produce. "As Goths follow white pebbles and notched tree-trunks."

"There are still some fortresses where we can find shelter if we need to seek protection." Hovas gave Bernardius a hard look. "We will have Vilca Troed to guide us."

Corcotos, who had been content to glare at Mangueinic and Bernardius, now spoke up. "You have no right to order us to remain here. It was never our intention to remain here. We only want to preserve what little we have left, and we cannot do that in this place, with the monks requiring we live according to their dictates."

"You may not be able to preserve your goods and chattel anywhere else," said Bernardius. "Some of the garrisons are as greedy as pirates on the sea, and some would not be above selling you into slavery if you will not pay them what they demand."

"You say that to frighten us," Hovas accused. "But Troed says that he knows all the garrison commanders from Porolissum—they are gone from that town now, but Troed knows them—to Durostorum, in Moesia Inferior. He will handle all our arrangements."

"Dorus Teodoricos can probably be trusted," said Bernardius, doing his best to be accommodating. "But there are others I wouldn't put too much faith in. Cave amicum."

"Because you're so frightened you can't see the advantage of leaving," Hovas said scornfully. "You'll stay here until the monks have everything."

"I think," said Mangueinic, "that you might want to hear what the newcomer from Drobetae has to say before you make any binding plans. He will undoubtedly have more information than any of us."

Enlitus Brevios achieved a pugnacious stance. "If we speak with him, then you must hear what we hear, or you may be deceived by the monks, who are not above telling you things that will cause you to take their side. I don't trust monks to be forthcoming about such matters."

"Then let us seek this stranger out now," said Bernardius. "I will ask Priam Corydon to allow us to join in the interview of the man." He began to walk up the slope toward the cross-shaped monastery, not bothering to turn to see if he were being followed.

They found Priam Corydon, Antoninu Neves, and the messenger in the office of the monastery, all three men looking troubled at the sight of the eight encroachers who hardly bothered to knock on the door. Neves put his hand on the hilt of his sword, but moved it away again when Priam Corydon gave him a severe look and said, "This is no occasion for fighting."

"They have come without being summoned," said Neves.

"They would have been informed of the messenger's presence before sunset in any case. I gather everyone within the walls is aware that our first visitor of the spring has arrived," said Priam Corydon, trying to make the best of the awkward situation. He motioned to the plain wooden bench against the far wall. "You may be seated. All of you."

Enlitus Brevios hesitated as if uncertain if such an offer were an insult. He considered the matter, then did as he was told; the others joined him. "Who is this man? They say he comes from Drobetae."

"That I do," the stranger said, absently chafing his forearm. "I am Hredus, a freedman in the household of the Praetor-General, Verus Flautens. He has dispatched me to discover where the people of Dacia are living now, and how well-prepared they are to defend themselves." He ducked his head in an habitual show of respect.

"He has been giving us news from the former Province of Dacia," said the Priam.

"And imparting all he has seen for himself as he made his way here," added Neves.

Mangueinic leaned his crutch against the wall at the end of the bench; he stretched to relieve the tightening in his back. "What have you seen, Freedman Hredus?"

"There are many encampments of refugees, most of them at lower elevations than this one, most of them fairly small—perhaps fifty persons and as many animals," said Hredus promptly. "I have noticed that the greatest number of refugees are from the high plateau, northwest of this valley, where the land is flat enough for a good cavalry attack. About half the refugees have been driven out by Huns; the others have left anticipating attacks." He paused. "They say the Huns leave few survivors where they have passed. And if they attack a second time, they come in greater numbers. They are like a plague on the land."

"So have we all heard," said Enlitus Brevios, an edge of defiance in his remark. "The Gepidae and Carpi have said it, and so have the Goths and Daci."

"According to rumor, this new Hunnic King, Attila, is organizing his forces along Roman lines, and is changing his manner of attack to confront fortresses and ground troops." Hredus nodded to Neves. "You have heard of this, haven't you?"

"That I have, but haven't been able to gather more information since the first storm of winter," said Neves. "No one could reach this valley, and no one could leave."

"Except the fifteen we exiled," said Brevios under his breath.

"We all have heard the same thing," added Mangueinic.

"Many garrison commanders are convinced that Attila is going to focus his efforts on Aquincum, from where he can strike out at all the Carpathians, and position himself to assault cities farther west, or so they have informed the Praetor-General," said Hredus. Three garrison commanders had offered him such speculation, which seemed enough to bring it to the attention of these men. He scratched at a patch of darkened skin on his forearm. "I'm told you have a healer here. Do you think he could do something to alleviate this infernal itch?"

"If there is anything to be done, Dom Sanctu-Germainios will do it," said Mangueinic.

"The regional guardian of Apulum Inferior?" Hredus asked, startled.

"The same," said Mangueinic. "The monks at the infirmary have nothing to match his knowledge of medicaments, and they have their hands full with those suffering from dry eyes and wet noses. You may need more than prayers and powdered angelica-root. Without the Dom's skill, I'd have lost my life and not just my leg."

Hredus concealed his interest. "If it's convenient, I'd like to consult him after evening supper."

"It will be arranged," said Priam Corydon, anxious to learn more from Hredus. "How long did it take you to reach us? How were the roads and the bridges? How many towns have been attacked?"

"I would have been here some days since, but the late storm prevented me from traveling at all for three days, and then the snow was so deep that I couldn't determine if I would get through the pass at all." Hredus scratched his wrist again. "There were wolves about, and bear, so I didn't want to risk making camp outside sturdy walls, and that, too, slowed me down."

"Better a few days late than dead," Bernardius said.

"As to the condition of the road, the nearer you are to Roman territory—East or West—the better the roads are, but they are not as fine as records say they were a century ago. Most of the roads are in need of repair, and in some areas, total replacement is required. Three of the small bridges between Drobetae and Gepidorum are no longer safe to cross so I ferried across some ten thousand paces below Ulpia Traiana, which has been raided, but I can't say who the raiders were. That was why I didn't remain near the town. The river was high but the main thaw had barely started. By now, it will be a torrent." Hredus could see the trenchant involvement of the men in the room, and he decided to make the most of it. "One merchant I encountered not far from Ulpia Traiana told me that the Huns are moving out into the plains to the northwest of here. He had it from a family of farmers from Auru Calida; the Huns burned them out."

"Others have suggested that," said Priam Corydon.

"Then it may be worthy of your attention. This part of the mountains is only two or three days' ride to the beginning of the plains; if the land were flatter you could cut that time in half," Hredus said. "Once they're set up in a camp, your valley will be one of the first they're likely to seek out."

"You must have a great deal to impart to the Praetor-General," said Bernardius. "Can you tell us why he sent you here?"

Hredus chuckled. "He wants someone he can trust to get close enough to the Huns to observe them, but not so close as to risk being caught." He said it very much the way Flautens had told him to answer such an inquiry. His eyes gave nothing away; his many years of slavery had taught him to conceal every aspect of his thoughts and emotions.

"Then he must trust you," said Priam Corydon. "We'll bear that in mind."

Enlitus Brevios spoke up. "We'll want to consult this man more closely, for some of us are planning to leave as soon as we can take our wagons through the pass, and we'll want to be prepared for what we should expect. We will be bound for Viminacium." His hard smile challenged Priam Corydon to forbid them to go.

"If you are determined, then I will not attempt to stop you. But I urge you to be sure that you will be as safe as possible during your travels. You will be responsible for the well-being of those going with you, and the preservation of their souls." Priam Corydon rose.

"Who among you is planning to leave?" Urridien answered first, then Bacoem, Hovas, Thirhald, and Corcotos. "And what of you, Mangueinic? and Tribune Bernardius?"

"We've only now heard of this plan," said Bernardius. "I still believe for those who wish to move on that midsummer is the time for us to go." He shrugged. "Neither I nor Bernardius have the authority to command these men to stay or to go. If it suits their purposes, then, no matter how reckless it may be, we won't have the right to keep them here."

Mangueinic pursed his lips. "I don't think it is prudent to set out so early in the season of travel, but there is little I can do about it, except to tell them my reservations, which I have done."

Priam Corydon made the sign of the fish and then the sign of the cross. "May your leaving not harm you, or us, and may God protect you on your journey." He went toward the door. "I ask you to take time for private contemplation, that you not discuss what you have heard here with one another until tomorrow, so that none of you reaches a conclusion that hasn't been examined in your own souls. You are worried and you are unhappy with living here. If you will implore God to grant you His Wisdom in your dreams, I will be content with your outcome whatever it may be, for it will have come from God." He made the sign of the fish again and left them.

Mangueinic leaned forward and shoved himself to his foot as he reached for his crutch. "Come," he said to Hredus. "I'll take you to Dom Sanctu-Germainios."

Hredus looked at the other men, tempted to disregard the Priam's orders. Then he hitched his shoulder. "The sooner he treats me, the sooner I will recover," he said, approaching Mangueinic. "I'll follow you."

Hovas took a step to block Hredus' leaving. "Tonight I'll think of questions to ask you in the morning. I will want answers, messenger."

"Hovas, don't badger the man. He's had a long, hard journey and is entitled to rest," said Brevios, who then addressed Hredus.

"You may rely on Dom Sanctu-Germainios to employ all he knows to rid you of the trouble you have with your skin."

"I pray it will be so," said Hredus as he moved around Hovas and fell in behind Mangueinic, making the sign of the fish as he went.

Mangueinic pointed out the old wooden chapel as he and Hredus approached it. "Long ago this was a pagan spring, and that chapel was put up for those who came to consult the keepers of the waters, and to find shelter in their travels through the Carpathians. Then a pilgrim stopped here, more than two centuries ago, and saw the Virgin Maria above the spring, and it became a holy place for Christians. Sanctu Eustachios had the monastery built when he retired from the world. Once the monastery was complete, the chapel fell into disuse."

Hredus had heard the story before, but he responded with interest. "That transformation has happened in other places."

Mangueinic nodded, and rapped on the side-door. "Dom Sanctu-Germainios. I have a new patient for you."

Nicoris opened the door and nodded a welcome. "You and the new patient are welcome. Dom Sanctu-Germainios is with Giraldus, Antoninu Neves' lieutenant; he hammered his hand while working on the outer wall." She stood aside to admit them.

"Is he badly hurt?" Mangueinic asked, coming through the door and leaving room for Hredus to enter with him.

"He has broken two bones in his hand, the Dom says, and he has made a splint to help the bones to heal straight."

"Poor man," said Hredus, because he knew a response was expected of him and would gain him the good opinion of Mangueinic, which would be useful.

"It is unfortunate," Nicoris said, encouraging the two to move toward the alcove where Sanctu-Germainios had his raised table.

Mangueinic stumped toward him. "I've brought you the messenger from Drobetae, Dom Sanctu-Germainios." He nodded to Giraldus. "I'm sorry to hear about your hand."

"It was a foolish thing to do," said Giraldus. "I don't know how it happened."

"You will need to wear that sling during the day, and to wrap your hand in cloth during the night," said Sanctu-Germainios to Giraldus as he got off the raised bed. "If you have swelling or pain, use ten drops of this tincture"—he held out a large vial—"and drink it in a cup of water or wine. Do not use it more than twice a night."

"Very well," said Giraldus, accepting the vial with his uninjured hand. "Lucky thing it was my left hand I struck. At least I can still use my sword."

"As you say: fortunate," was Sanctu-Germainios' dry answer.

Nicoris escorted Giraldus to the main door; she wished him well and went back to the alcove where Sanctu-Germainios conducted his examinations, waiting near the hearth and listening. When Hredus had finished his account of his trek from Drobetae, he held out his arm.

Sanctu-Germainios took it and held it up to the waning light; as he inspected the purplish area of skin, he asked, "Did you have a rash before the color changed?"

"Some chafing," Hredus allowed. "How did you know?"

He took on his most academic tone. "The rash was the cause of your infestation. As you scratched, you moved animalcules from the rash to lodge beneath your skin. I will need to open the skin and insert a curative ointment. It is not a pleasant procedure, but if it is not done, the animalcules will spread through your body and will rupture your organs." He saw the shock in Hredus' eyes. "I do not mean to frighten you, or to cause you distress, but you ought to be aware of the danger of delay, or superficial treatment."

Hredus' face went blank. "Then it must be done," he said without inflection.

"I have an unguent that will deaden the pain of the cutting, and syrup of poppies to relieve any pain you feel afterward. I will need some time to boil my instruments, as the physicians of Roma used to do." He regarded Hredus. "Would you rather have supper and rest until the first quarter of the night?"

"You said it was urgent that it be treated," said Hredus.

"It is, but if you are tired and hungry—"

"Let us be done with it," said Hredus.

Nicoris came up to Sanctu-Germainios and said quietly, "You have very little of the sovereign remedy left. Four vials are all that remain."

"I know," said Sanctu-Germainios. "And I have neither the moldy bread nor the athanor to make more." He sighed. "Still, there is enough to treat this man, and have a little left. If I must, I can pack wounds with moldy bread, if I can persuade the baker to provide me with some. For now, I will deal with this messenger."

"Then shall I put the flensing knives to boil, and the closing pins? Which astringent herbs shall I use?" Nicoris went to the red-lacquer chest.

"Nettles and tarragon," Sanctu-Germainios answered, then escorted Hredus to the raised bed. "If you like, I will prepare a composer for you."

"No need," said Hredus, and got onto the bed, watching Sanctu-Germainios, revealing nothing.

Text of a report from the factor Artemidorus Iocopolis to Patras Methodos, both in Constantinople; written in Byzantine Greek in fixed ink on vellum, and delivered by footman.

To the estimable priest, Patras Methodos, this accounting of the assets of the Eclipse Trading Company, as requested to facilitate the liberation of Rugierus of Gades, who is presently being held under house arrest, and to regularize the evaluation of the business.

The Eclipse Trading Company is presently owned by Dom Feranescus Rakoczy Sanctu-Germainios, regional guardian at Apulum Inferior in the former Province of Dacia, who has nine hundred aurea in deposit with the Secretary of the Metropolitan for its continuing operation.

The Company owns nineteen merchant ships, all plying ports from Trapezus, through the Black Sea, the Adriatic, the Mediterranean, into the Atlantic Ocean and as far as Gallia Belgicae;

additionally, the Company sponsors three caravan troupes that trade as far as Herat in Persia and Medina in Arabia. All tariffs on goods brought to market in Constantinople are current, in accordance with Dom Sanctu-Germainios' specific instructions, and all taxes on the property of the Company are current. Bona fides copies of bills of lading for the last year are included with this information, for your diligent review. Eclipse Trading Company maintains offices in twenty-seven ports; a list of these is provided in this report.

One hundred aurea accompany this as a donation to the law-courts and the Church, in the interests of justice.

By my own hand, sixteen days after the Vernal Equinox in the Christian year 439,

> *Artemidorus Iocopolis*
> *factor, Eclipse Trading Company*
> *Constantinople*

7

Three days after Enlitus Brevios and his little company of fifty-eight refugees departed for Drobetae, two of the sentries came down from the high peaks running, their eyes wide and breathing hard; they hurried to the travelers' dormitory and began to pound the platter of hammered brass that hung outside the main door and served as the alarm for all the monastery. In response to the clamor, monks, men, and women came at a rush, a few of the older women shooing children into the old chapel as they sped. The sentries continued to slam the leather-headed mallet into the hanging platter until more than half the residents of the monastery had reached them.

From his vantage-place on the roof of the old chapel, next to the drum-dome, Sanctu-Germainios shifted his attention from the distant clouds to the residents of the monastery, who surged into the central open square, some carrying weapons, and all of them restive. With a sense of distress, he climbed down from the roof, and stepped inside the building. "It's starting," he said to Nicoris.

"Are you going out to join them?" She seemed unflustered as she reached for his surgical tools. "I'll put these to boil."

"No, I won't join them. I'm too much of a foreigner for many of them, and just now, they are wary of foreigners." He said it readily enough, but there was an echo of loneliness in his admission.

"Then I'll stay in, too. I am also a foreigner." Her quicksilver eyes glittered. She came up to him.

Contemplating her from his vantage-point above her, he said, "Foreigner to foreigner, I can be counted upon to keep a confidence." He touched her birthmark with the tip of his finger.

She looked away from him. "That's good to know," she said distantly.

Outside, there was an increase in the noise as the crowd grew larger.

Luitpald, the younger sentry, began shouting as people gathered closely around them. "Horsemen! *Horsemen!* At least fifty of them! Coming this way!"

There were shrieks of dismay and demands for more information. The people moved closer to the sentries and one another. "Huns?" The question ricocheted through the crowd.

"It's God's judgment!" exclaimed Monachos Kyrillos, making the sign of the fish as he hurried toward the church.

"Huns or not, when will they get here?" Bernardius' voice cut through the general babble.

"Mid-afternoon!" the second sentry bellowed, his voice cracking. "If they keep up their pace."

"Call the herders in from the pastures and put the herds and flocks in the barn!" Bernardius ordered. "Then post all the Watchmen on the battlements! Women into the dormitory." Forgetting the ban on his Latin phrases, he yelled, "Cavi tempum!"

"We have time enough to man our posts, and guard the livestock!" Neves roared. "My company! Gather your weapons!"

"Not yet, not yet," exclaimed Priam Corydon as he pushed his way through the crowd to the sentries. He held up his hands for silence, and gradually the crowd went quiet. "Now, Luitpald, Oios, tell us what you saw. Keep your description simple, and do not report what you did not actually observe."

"Horsemen," said Luitpald. "Coming up the trail at the trot."

"Do you know which direction they came from before they took the road up the mountain?" Priam Corydon asked, unflustered and purposeful. "Just horsemen? Might they not be reserve troops sent to aid us? Why did you give the alarm?" He regarded the two sentries calmly.

Oios frowned. "They're too far away to be certain where they came from, but I think we should prepare to defend the monastery."

"They carried no Legion standards; a few of them had pikes topped with horsetails," Luitpald reported, the panic in his eyes unmistakable.

"Huns," said Neves loudly. "They have horsetail standards."

Another tide of whispers swept through the assembled residents, and Mangueinic, once again in charge of the Watchmen, bawled out, "Gather your arms! Bring in the livestock and brace the gates!"

There was an eruption of activity that only stopped when Priam Corydon slammed the mallet into the brass platter and cried out, *"Wait! All of you!"* This time the gathering did not go entirely quiescent, as many of the men began to fret. Occasional shouts burst through the growing mutters while Priam Corydon strove to gather his thoughts. "We have discussed how we are to mount our offense, and we've agreed to abide by our plans."

"Fifty Huns are coming this way!" shouted one of the men from Tsapousso. "Some of us can still escape!"

Now Priam Corydon drew himself up and spoke with finality. "We are not to abandon the plan we've agreed to when we need it most. Ritt, go to the infirmary and warn the monks there to be ready for injuries. Then warn Dom Sanctu-Germainios to prepare for many serious wounds. Ask what he may need from us to assist him in his work." He signaled the novice to hurry off. "Tribune Bernardius, dispatch your messengers to the herders and organize your men on the inner wall. Neves, assign posts to your men on the battlements and ladders, and deploy your lieutenants. Monachos Vlasos, take nine slaves and go to the kitchen to make ready to feed our defenders. See that there are slaves to carry water to the soldiers. Monachos Niccolae of Sinu, go to the office of the monastery and record the numbers of residents, monks, and slaves presently within these walls and put the accounting in the stone chest. Novice Penthos, go out to the hermits and warn them of what is coming. Monachos Egidius Remigos, summon your novices and delegate them to their posts and duties at the gates. Refugee women, order your dormitory, put your goods into chests and cases, and ready cloth for bandages. Do not be rendered hopeless; God will guard us all."

Someone at the back of the crowd bawled out, "Monachos Anatolios says God will desert us if we fight!"

Denerac of Tsapousso flung up his hands in outrage. "What of a courier? Won't you send one to Drobetae? You said you would. Are we to vanish from the face of the earth and our fate never known to anyone but the Huns?"

"An excellent reminder," said Priam Corydon. "Tribune Bernardius, choose your most skilled rider and mount him on the best horses; choose a loyal man who will cleave to his task. I will prepare a description of our circumstances for him to carry southward, and you may add what you will."

"If you send him out now, he'll meet the Huns on the road," Neves warned. "They'll make short work of him."

"Not if he goes over the western ridge, using the hunters' trail," said Priam Corydon. "The track is narrow and runs through the forest, but it will bring the messenger to the river at Bagna, and he can follow it south to the Danuvius." He held up his hand. "Let us be about our duties."

The crowd broke apart rapidly, but more purposefully than it would have done a moment before. Priam Corydon motioned to Bernardius, and joined him on the path to the monastery building.

"My best rider is Tiberius Valerios. I've asked him to ready himself to go." He pointed out a tall young man making for the stable. "He'll select his horses, then come to you for the message."

"Fine. God be praised." Priam Corydon noticed that Ritt was beckoning to him "Tell your rider that I will have my report ready by noon." He made the sign of the cross and went off to the novice.

For most of the time until mid-afternoon the monastery was filled with activity, the bustle fueled by anxiety and ill-concealed fear. Yet the mercenaries took their places on the battlements, the soldiers gathered their weapons, the refugees aided in cooking and herding. Before mid-day Mass was over, Tiberius Valerios had selected three horses, secured a bag of provisions, a wallet of coins, the report from Priam Corydon, and departed down the steep trail leading westward. By mid-afternoon, one of the nearer sentries had seen the horsemen three thousand paces away and coming along steadily; he reported counting sixty-seven men with a dozen more horses for remounts. Activity within the monastery became more sedulous than earlier in the day. The soldiers finished distributing weapons and settled down to wait for the arrival of the Huns while novices fussed among them, bringing small loaves filled with venison stew and skins of harsh red wine. Armorers took up posts between the two walls, where they could retrieve the enemy's weapons and turn them to the defenders' use. Monachos Archimedios, the master of the infirmary, went to the old chapel to inform Dom Sanctu-Germainios which of the wounded would be sent to the infirmary and which would be given to him; he suggested that Sanctu-Germainios have some of the young men among the refugees help him deal with his patients by carrying the wounded from the walls to the old chapel. Patras Anso went among the people from Apulum Inferior, delivering benedictions. The herders put stout beams across the stalls and pens to keep the animals in if they should panic, and three monks built up a large bonfire in the open space between the monastery building and the travelers' dormitory to provide light and torches when the sunlight faded.

"The pass!" Monachos Egidius Remigos yelled as the first of the riders topped the trail at the narrow gap and began the single-file descent into the valley.

"Stand to your posts! Stand with your comrades and kin!" Bernardius yowled before he set his helmet on his head.

"Three of them! They're starting down the road!"

At this cry, the mercenaries on the outer battlements rose to their stations, spears, bows, and pikes at the ready. The sound of chanting in the church rose in volume, and the rumble of furtive conversations got louder. The monks at the main gate put the heaviest brace across the upright logs and knelt to pray with their brothers in the church.

"Weapons up!" shouted Neves, climbing to the highest point on the gatehouse. "Kill the horses first!"

More than a dozen Huns were through the pass now, and the first few clustered at the base of the trail at the head of the valley. The men carried bows, quivered arrows, slings with stones, and swords; a few had maces as well, and others had weighted bags tied to their distinctive saddles. Eight riders carried the horsetail standards and each of them led one or two remount horses. They were more menacing as their pace increased, still circling, from a trot to a canter.

"Wait till they're close enough to hit!" Neves ordered. "Don't waste spears or arrows on them!"

Rotlandus Bernardius walked along the inner walls. "Have courage! Remember your heritage! Gloria ad Romanorum."

In the travelers' dormitory, Isalind and Dysis gathered the refugee children in the vestibule and set them to filling pouches with stones for the ballistas to fire, and gave the older boys the task of running out baskets of these pouches to Neves' mercenaries; Khorea, working in the main room, helped the women prepare beds and tables for their men.

As the number of Huns through the pass increased, they started up an eerie cry, between a whinny and a howl, and they kept their horses moving in a close circle, in and out of the shadow of the western peaks, which made it impossible to count their numbers.

Then, at a signal none of the defenders could see, the Huns started toward the outer wall of the monastery, the riders carrying the weighted leather bags riding in the van. As they approached the walls, these men suddenly spurred forward, shrieking, and flung the bags so that they landed inside the outer walls. None of the defenders bothered with them since none of the defenders were struck by them; their show of indifference helped to build their courage. Then the Huns began to circle the walls, riding in what seemed to be a disorganized mob, never gathered too closely together, never too ordered in their ranks.

"Use the nearer ballista!" Neves shouted.

"Can't," one of his men answered. "We can't get a fix on them to aim! They mill and—"

"Lead the volley." Neves tromped over to the catapult and took a few of the bags of stones and put them in the sling. "Tighten the skeins. Now!"

Two of his soldiers jumped to the task, both counting in unison as they worked the windlasses that drew back the arms. They set the trigger and swung the stock to aim, as Neves had ordered them, slightly ahead of where the Huns were swarming. They set the support-leg, ready. On Neves' signal, they fired, and had the satisfaction of seeing one man tumble from his horse.

"He'll mount again," one of the Watchmen shouted.

"Again! Farther ballista, make ready!" Neves handed another bag of stones to his men. "Keep at it."

"Until we run out of things to fire at them," shouted one of the soldiers manning the ballista, and laughed.

A boy carrying a basket of bagged stones almost tripped over one of the large leather sacks the Huns had thrown, and dislodged its contents. He stared, and then let out a terrified shout.

"Leave the bag alone," Neves barked at him, then saw the look on the boy's face; he rushed to the nearest ladder, scrambled down it, hastening to the boy. "What is it?"

"Fonalind," the boy whispered, pointing. "Thirhald's daughter."

Neves looked, and saw the girl's bloody head. "Perigrinos, Blazius!" he shouted. "Take three men and gather up the leather bags! Now!" As he spoke, he shoved the ghastly trophy back into its bag.

The men responded promptly, commandeering a large basket from a stack of them under the battlements. "What shall we do with them?" asked the nearest of the five men.

Neves considered an instant. "Take them to the Priam. He'll decide how to deal with them." Above them the second ballista fired. "Load up and fire again!"

Perigrinos had picked up a second sack, and realized at once what it contained. "What are we to tell him?"

"Take this lad with you, and leave it to him," said Neves, and made for the ladder once more.

Perigrinos took the lad by the shoulder and laid the baskets of bagged rocks on the ground. "We'll get the sacks away from here, to Priam Corydon," he said, uncertain if the boy heard him over the din of battle. Howls came from several points along the outer battlements as Hunnic arrows found their marks. The flights of Hunnic arrows continued and thickened.

"Archers!" Neves hollered. "Notch your first arrows, and fire at will!"

His bowmen loosed their arrows and notched more, firing steadily at the Huns, many trying for their horses. The ballistas continued to lob the fist-sized sacks of stones, and the noise of battle grew too loud for orders to be heard. Neves continued to walk along the outer battlements, showing no fear, his determination communicating itself to his soldiers. All the while, he watched the Huns, making note of which men they rallied around, and which men followed their orders. He stopped by his lieutenant assigned to this stretch of wall and pointed out one of the Huns on a spotted horse. "That man. Can you kill him?" he shouted in his ear.

His lieutenant, a hatchet-faced veteran from Illyricum called Drinus, nodded. "If I can see him, I can kill him." He hefted his Armenian bow.

Neves stepped away from him. "Good hunting," he called back, and continued on his rounds, finding his next lieutenant with an arrow in his side and blood staining his scale armor, spreading along the overlapping brass medallions rapidly. Neves signaled for one of the men from Apulum Inferior assigned to carry the wounded to safety. "This one is for the Dom. The arrow struck in the base of his shoulder. Tell the Dom he's lost a lot of blood. Oios! Take Accius' place!"

The look-out came from his post on the tower, ducking the Hunnic arrows sailing lethally near. "Nine men?"

"If you can, keep them alive," said Neves, and helped lower the wounded man to the refugees beneath, pausing long enough to see them carry him through the gate in the inner wall. He continued his rounds. When he had completed the circuit, he had a moment to take stock. Eleven men injured, two seriously; the Huns had lost one man and two horses. It was about what he had expected for a first sally. They could hold the outer walls until sundown, and then would use the gathering darkness to fall back. His evaluation ended abruptly as a flaming arrow shot overhead, thunking solidly into the inner stockade wall. *"Water!"* he screamed, and saw one of Bernardius' men come rushing, a pail slopping water as he ran.

Outside the walls, a thicket went up in flames, then another at the edge of the lake caught fire. One of Neves' men fell to the ground, a smoldering arrow in his neck. A dozen more sailed brightly into the space between the inner and outer walls, striking a novice and an armorer, and setting the trampled grass alight. Some of those assisting the mercenaries scattered, terrified by the fire as much as by the arrows.

A wail of dismay erupted among the Huns as a chain fired from one of the ballistas uncoiled among them; another volley of Hunnic arrows, some of them burning, soared over the outer wall, many landing again between the two defensive walls, where the refugees worked to help the fighters. More outcry signaled where the arrows had found their marks, and this time the response of those charged with tending the wounded was slower than before.

"Get to it!" Neves thundered at the refugees, crouched under the battlements. "The wounded need you!"

The refugees set out at a reluctant scuttle for the nearest ladder and the men above them.

Neves resumed his circuit of the outer wall, keeping his head down, and trusting his helmet and lorica to protect him from the continual flight of Hunnic arrows, now augmented with occasional spears. He wished now that they had a third ballista and many more chains to shoot at the mounted barbarians. They would need more bags of rocks and more arrows. He made himself keep moving, shouting to his lieutenants and dodging arrows. As he paused at one of the three towers, he saw Bernardius coming toward him.

"How much longer are you going to remain forward?" Bernardius yelled at him as he came up.

"We agreed my men would fall back at sunset," Neves reminded him. "We still have a little daylight left to us."

"But your refugee aides are retreating, and that leaves you without men to help your wounded." Bernardius swung his shield to deflect a burning arrow. "We're lost if they burn down the walls."

"Have the men who can be trusted to bring up cauldrons of water. We can throw the water on them as they light their arrows."

"Where did they get the fire? They had no torches when they rode in."

Neves cocked his head. "I think some of what we took for maces were readied torches that needed only a spark to light."

"A good notion. Nota bona," said Bernardius. "The bushes they set afire are dying down; that's something."

"Are your men ready to fight?"

"They claim to be. But standing and waiting is making them uneasy." Bernardius laced his fingers together and attempted a stretch. "I would like you to signal me before you fall back."

"So you can prepare your men?"

"Yes."

"And cauldrons of water?" Neves pursued.

"I'll see you have them." Bernardius jumped as a blazing arrow hissed by his head. "At once." He took a step back to return to his post, then halted as a sudden, triumphant howl burst from the two soldiers manning the nearer ballista, which was echoed by a scream from the Huns.

"Got him! Got him at last, by God!" The soldiers slammed their right fists into their left shoulders in approval, and cheering derision at the Huns, now clustering around their apparent leader, who remained in the saddle only because the high pommel and cantel held him erect; his body slumped, and the side of his head-guard was deeply indented into his temple. Blood ran down his neck as his men maneuvered his horse away from the outer stockade to the place they had put their dead, men and horses together. They took him out of the saddle, leaving him with two guards to watch over him while the rest resumed their attack with renewed ferocity.

One of the soldiers who had shot the heavy bolt at the leader was struck with three arrows, two of which were burning. More arrows threatened to set fire to the stockade, but cauldrons of water were rushed up, and the arrows embedded in the upended logs were extinguished.

By the time it was dark, Neves' men had retreated to the inner walls, bringing their ballistas with them and sending those with minor wounds off to be treated. A small holding force of ten remained on the outer walls, torches blazing, preparing burning arrows of their own. In the uncertain light, the Huns continued to circle the monastery, seeming to flicker in the last glow of sunset, continuing to pepper the defenders with arrows, not so often setting them alight as much to have the advantage of stealth in their flight as to continue their attempt to burn the place down.

Once he had fallen back, Neves went to the old chapel, requesting a salve and a bandage for a cut on his face and a welt on his arm. "Not the kind of injuries monks like to treat: too reminiscent of fighting." He touched the weal. "It's my own fault. Turned too quickly with my shield," he said, abashed. "As foolish as a recruit."

"Better than an arrow in the chest," said Sanctu-Germainios, inspecting the second injury. "I will give you an ointment for the bruise; you will be stiff tomorrow without it."

One of thirteen of Neves' men, lying on a pallet with a bandage around his head, called out, "How many did we kill?"

"The last count was eleven," said Neves. "Including their leader."

The men on the pallets did their best to whoop. "And our men?" one inquired.

"Eighteen wounded, I haven't got the count of the dead yet." Neves turned to Sanctu-Germainios. "Do you know the number?"

"Three who were brought to me wounded have died," he answered. "I do not know of any others."

Nicoris, who was giving water to the men, stopped her task. "Four," she corrected.

"Four?" Neves repeated, staring at her.

"Dead," she said by way of clarification, in case there was any doubt.

"The one with the arrow in the groin?" Sanctu-Germainios saw her nod. "I feared so. The main vessel was severed and stopping the bleeding was—"

"I've seen such wounds before," Neves said. "They are never good." He regarded Sanctu-Germainios. "The rest?"

"Speak to me in the morning; I will know more then." He pointed to five of the men. "They will be carried to the travelers' dormitory later this evening, assuming the fighting dies down. The rest I will keep here, in case there is trouble."

"Do you expect trouble?" Neves asked.

"To a degree, I do," said Sanctu-Germainios. "Otherwise I would send them to the dormitory." He pointed to one soldier, sitting up, but groggy and dazed. "He sustained a very bad blow to the head. I fear if he falls asleep, he may remain asleep for many days. Nicoris is watching him closely, and when he seems to fail, she gives him hart's-horn and water to smell to revive him."

Neves took a deep breath and let it out slowly. "I will return at midnight. And shortly after dawn. Bernardius may have casualties tonight. The Huns are determined on revenge for their leader's death, now, or later with more men."

"Do you anticipate heavy fighting?" Nicoris asked.

"They're Huns—who can tell what they'll do?" Neves said, taking the pat of camphor-laden ointment Sanctu-Germainios offered him. He managed a salute to his men before he trudged off to the door.

Text of an account of the Hunnic attack on Sanctu-Eustachios the Hermit, written with fixed ink on vellum in Byzantine Greek by Monachos Niccolae of Sinu for the archives of the monastery and entrusted to their stone vault for records.

In the Name of Father, Son, and Holy Spirit, Amen.

Yesterday, one month following the Vernal Equinox, this monastery of Sanctu-Eustachios the Hermit was viciously attacked by eighty-one Huns, well-armed and intent upon havoc, and answering to none but the Devil. The fighting having concluded, the account of the results are offered for the archives, with the ardent hope that God and Sanctu Eustachios will guide me in preparing a truthful report of the battle.

In addition to two hundred eighty-four monks and novices, this monastery has, as of this day, within its walls four hundred nine men, women, and children from Apulum Inferior, sixty-one from Tsapousso, one hundred sixty-seven from Ulpia Traiana, and the mercenary company of Antoninu Neves of one hundred fifty-three. As a result of the attack we are left with thirty-nine dead to whom to give Christian burial, and an additional forty-four who were among a company who had left the monastery but three days before, and whose heads were thrown over the walls in bags at the start of battle. What became of the others in the company, we have no knowledge, nor any knowledge of the few others who have left us since the thaw began, including a small number of monks who have set out for other Christian communities in the former Province of Dacia to obtain more information regarding our enemies, and to apply for help. Outside the walls there are a number of hermits, but we at present have

*no notion of their fate, for although they were offered the protection
of the monastery, they chose to remain in their caves, trusting to God
to spare them if He deemed they worthy, or to allow the Huns to
overwhelm them if not.*

*Actual fighting commenced at mid-afternoon as the Huns came
through the southeastern pass, and mustered for their charge,
shouting imprecations against God and Sanctu Eustachios. They
began to circle the outer walls which had been built specifically to
hold them out; they brought a vast number of arrows with them,
keeping up a steady flight of them for the last quarter of the day.
Their attack was answered by the men of Antoninu Neves' company,
who were manning the outer wall, and supported by the troops of
Tribune Bernardius of Ulpia Traiana, along with a good number of
refugees and novices, who did not actively fight, but busied themselves gathering enemy weapons, providing water to fight fires, and
to assist in carrying away the wounded and dead.*

*Having set fire to brush between the outer wall and the lake, the
Huns fired many burning arrows into the monastery, some killing
defenders, or grievously wounding them. They also threw spiked
stones from slings, threw spears, and once in a while struck at the
gates with swords and axes. They offered chants to their demonic
gods and performed vile rituals intended to destroy this monastery
and all the Christian souls within it.*

*Fighting continued through the later afternoon and into the
night, the Huns always circling the walls while attempting to light
them on fire, as restless as flames themselves, the defenders seeking
to reduce their numbers, and the number of their horses to such an
extent that they would be forced to withdraw. The fires outside the
wall spread to the sheepfold, and the Huns carried off a dozen lambs
and four ewes before Neves' men could recapture the enclosure and
extinguish the fire there. Through the Grace of God, Neves' men
were able to kill the leader of the Huns in a single blow, and many of
his favored men besides, which the remaining Huns burned in a fu-
neral pyre, with sacrifice of many horses to their damnable gods. We
counted some twenty-eight or -nine dead, and give thanks for their*

losses, which were roughly half their number. At the conclusion of their pagan rites, thunder and lightning rent the air long into the night, and the fires of Hunnic worship were extinguished by God's command.

While most of us believe the Huns will not think it worth their while to return, the refugees and soldiers inside the gates lack our faith and warn of another attack. They have said the walls need more reinforcement, two more ballistas have to be built, and the infirmary at the monastery, along with the hospital in the old chapel, require more beds and assistants, for we have some fifty-three wounded who will need time and tending to recover; if there are more, our resources will be extended beyond our limits, unless Sanctu Eustachios intervenes with God for our preservation, and so we trust.

A list of the dead and wounded are appended to this report; we pray for their souls and for all Christian souls.

I commend this account to Priam Corydon and the Christian Church, the Patriarch in Constantinople, and the Saints as a testament to my faith and the faith of those whose actions it describes.

Monachos Niccolae of Sinu
Sanctu-Eustachios the Hermit
observing the Rite of Sanctu-Ioannis Chrysostom

8

"No more patients left," Nicoris sighed, going to the center of the old chapel and turning around slowly under the drum-dome, her arms extended, reclaiming the floor where all the pallets had been spread out. She offered a tired smile. "And we only lost ten of them." It was six days since the Huns had attacked, and the sound of sawing and hammering was filling the little valley as the residents struggled to prepare for another, larger onslaught.

"So far," Sanctu-Germainios appended. "Two of them are still marginal. Oios' fever is too high, and I fear Drinus may not recover from his burns." He moved the last pallet into the rear of the old chapel and stacked it with the rest of them.

"Then why did you move them to the dormitory? Why not keep them here, where you could watch them?" Her hands were on her hips and her posture revealed her exasperation.

"Because their people want to care for them; they want to see for themselves that their comrades and kin are given adequate attention, which they fear they will not have among other wounded," he said quietly. "And I am a foreigner, for all that I have some abilities to treat sickness and injury."

"They distrust you, you mean? Though you're their regional guardian? You've saved many lives, haven't you?" Nicoris started toward him, her movements deliberate, provocative.

"All regional guardians are foreigners, to keep them in service to Roma, and unallied with anyone in their region; the people of the region are not expected to trust them," he said in the same steady voice. "Saving lives was the bargain I have struck with the people of Apulum Inferior, to keep their good opinion of me, foreigner that I am."

"They must not understand how fortunate they are," she said after considering what he said.

"Which they are entitled to do," he said, going on in a deeper tone, "It is no longer in our hands; for a while our work is done."

"That will mean we'll be alone tonight."

"So it would seem," he agreed, his demeanor less melancholy.

"Then I'll wait until nightfall, but no longer." She tossed her head, and met his gaze squarely.

His smile was fleeting, fading as quickly as it had appeared. "Will you open the door, Nicoris, so the chapel can be refreshed?"

"Main or side?" She was slightly more than an arm's-length in front of him now, tempting him with her nearness.

"Both would be best, to circulate the air." He nodded to the stack of rags he had used to clean the floor. "I'll take those out to the bonfire. I think we can sacrifice the basket."

Nicoris made a face. "Good. They all stink."

"That they do; warmer weather makes them worse," said Sanctu-Germainios, stepping back from her before going to pick up the large basket filled with filthy rags. He hefted the basket to his shoulder and went out through the side-door toward the bonfire laid in the central court of the monastery.

Luitpald and Hredus had been given the task of laying the bonfire for this night and were going about their work steadily; they were adding charred sections of logs to the fire, the last of the damage done to the walls by burning Hunnic arrows. Looking up as Sanctu-Germainios approached, Hredus swore comprehensively. "We need nothing of your tainted rags."

"Fire will purge the sickness from them, and from this place," Sanctu-Germainios answered unperturbedly.

"He knows what's needed to be rid of infection, messenger," said Luitpald staunchly, touching a half-healed patch of skin on his upper arm. "Here's proof." He took the basket and laid it on the bonfire. "Our friend from Drobetae hasn't had more need of your abilities since what he required when he arrived, which is fortunate for him."

Hredus shrugged in a display of indifference. "Whatever you did stopped the problem." He heaved a resigned sigh. "If burning the basket is what's required—" He glanced at the small, semi-circular scar on his wrist where Sanctu-Germainios had rid him of the animalcules causing his skin to darken and itch.

The afternoon was breezy, wiping away the morning's warmth; the bonfire would be welcome once the sun was down. Snow still capped some of the distant peaks, but around this valley, the thaw was almost complete.

"Some of the refugees are talking about leaving before the Huns return. They intend to be away in four days," said Luitpald, a speculative note in his remark.

"In spite of what happened to Enlitus Brevios and his companions—either a reckless or brave decision, depending on what the Huns do," Sanctu-Germainios countered.

"In spite of that," said Luitpald, a pugnacious thrust to his chin. "They plan to slip past the Huns at night."

"Tell me, Dom, do you think the Huns will strike again?" Hredus asked.

"I think it very likely," said Sanctu-Germainios.

"After they lost their leader?" Hredus persisted.

"Because they lost their leader." Sanctu-Germainios put a slight emphasis on *because*, then stood still, considered what more to say.

"And there will be more of them?"

"That is what I would expect," Sanctu-Germainios answered carefully.

"But none of the sentries have seen them, not even scouts," Luitpald protested.

Sanctu-Germainios regarded the young man. "They don't need scouts. They know where this valley is, and how we are situated. Their attack was intended to find out how prepared we are, not to break through."

"Why do you say that?" Luitpald wondered aloud.

"We outnumbered them ten to one. Not even the Huns take on prolonged battles against such odds," said Sanctu-Germainios. "They came to test us. Now that they have their measure, they will suit their force to that."

"But they rely on scouts to report on how things stand here, whatever their test may have revealed," said Hredus. "Anything else would be foolhardy. The Huns are audacious, not rash. They always scout where they plan to attack."

"There are no scouts," Sanctu-Germainios repeated patiently, giving voice to what he had realized had to be the case a few days ago. "The Huns have no scouts on the mountains around us because they have a spy inside these walls. They were too well-informed about the conditions here to have it otherwise."

"You mean there are Huns here?"

"Of course not," said Sanctu-Germainios quickly, continuing more steadily, "There is at least one person working for them, perhaps more."

"But we fought them off," Luitpald protested.

"They chose to retreat, having essayed our fortifications, and forced us to expend arrows and spears and bags of rocks and chains; we will have to work diligently to replace what we lost," said Sanctu-Germainios.

"There is work being done, Dom," Luitpald said. "We'll be ready if they return."

"They also learned something from their spy, I believe."

"Oh, yes. The spy." Hredus laughed cynically. "And what do Neves and Bernardius and Priam Corydon think of your theory, Sanctu-Germainios?"

"They have not told me," Sanctu-Germainios replied obliquely, having said nothing on the matter to any of those men.

"Perhaps the spy is outside, with the hermits?" Luitpald suggested, nodding toward the crest. "Monachos Anatolios has sought to encourage the Huns, hasn't he?"

One of the women approached, carrying a bundle of small branches and sticks. "For kindling," she said as she gave the bundle to Hredus.

"Good of you," said Hredus, shoving the bundle deep into the heart of the logs and debris. "God will reward you," he told her as he was required to do, then paid no more attention to her as Mangueinic came up to the bonfire with a sack of pine-cones slung around his shoulder.

"Why wouldn't it be Monachos Anatolios?" Luitpald whispered to Hredus. "He says that we lack faith because we fight them."

"Spying is for worldly men, not monks," scoffed Hredus.

"If that's so, it's got to be a soldier or a refugee," said Luitpald, and shook his head, uncomfortable with the implication of what he was saying.

"These will help get the fire going," Mangueinic said, tugging the strap over his head.

Luitpald swung round to face Mangueinic. "Do you think there's a spy for the Huns within these walls?"

Since Enlitus Brevios' departure, Mangueinic had resumed the position of leader of the Watchman, so he gave himself a little time to weigh the question before he answered. "It's certainly possible," he said at last. "Why do you ask?"

Hredus pointed at Sanctu-Germainios. "He thinks there is."

Sanctu-Germainios studied the three men. "I would like to discover I am wrong. It would be comforting to think that the Huns had underestimated our fortifications and our numbers, and that they have no current intelligence on this place," he said, and turned away. Little as he wanted to admit it, he was tired and hungry, which were starting to impair his judgment. He could hear the three men arguing behind him, and he hoped he had not added to the tension within the monastery's walls. As he entered the old chapel, he smelled the odor of roasted duck and saw Nicoris starting up the fire, a wooden platter resting on her arm.

"Perigrinos' woman brought this to us, in thanks for saving her man's life." She displayed the duck proudly.

"Generous of her, but unnecessary, at least not for me," he said, and saw Nicoris squirm in disapproval. Realizing he had offended her, he went to her, laying his small hand on her shoulder. "I am sorry. I am preoccupied. You deserve far more than duck for all you have done. Food is a conscientious gesture, and I know you are tired of venison stew. Enjoy your meal."

Nicoris offered him a mollifying smile. "You haven't even had the venison stew; you ask for none of this." She pointed to the duck. "There is nothing for you on that platter, is there? You think I don't notice, but I do. You retire to your sleeping alcove and you claim you dine in private, but I have never seen you so much as take a bite of bread or a sip of wine, and there are no crumbs or dishes left over," she said succinctly, blowing on the spark she had struck when he returned from the bonfire.

"I do not drink wine," he said quietly.

"I know that: that's what I'm saying," she responded with asperity. "I want you to know I've been aware of how tirelessly you've been working. What is your secret?" Her pale eyes seemed to turn darker as she realized she had gone too far; she changed her tone.

"You're exhausted. Why not rest for a while now you have the chance? I'll wake you if anyone needs you."

"That is a kind proposition; thank you, I will." He stretched, feeling his shoulders tighten, then release as he twisted to loosen his muscles, his black silken pallium shining with every movement. "I will be rested at the end of the first quarter of the night." Walking to his sleeping alcove, he decided he would remove his thick-soled peri and leather femoralia but leave on the pallium. Once he had taken off his boots and leggings, he put them in his nearest clothes-chest, and climbed onto his narrow, hard bed, slipped under the coverlet, and lay back, enjoying the aroma of roast duck as he sank into the stupor that passed for sleep among those of his kind.

He awoke precipitously some time later, his breath returning in a gasp; he smelled the bonfire's smoke and realized the old chapel was lit not with sunset but fire and oil-lamps.

"Oh, good," said Nicoris, "you're awake." She wriggled into position next to him, clinging to him to keep from falling off the bed that was hardly wider than a coffin; she wore a pale linen palla cut short, and her hair was loose.

"So are you, it would seem." He looked into her face, the darkness having little impact on his vision. "How was the duck?"

"Delicious," Nicoris said, adjusting her body along his. "I've longed to lie with you since the Huns came, for sympathy as much as satisfaction. And you," she added more briskly, "you must want to lie with me for what you require; I saw that you took nothing from those brought to you for help. You could have, and none the wiser. But you didn't."

"Not now, no, I would not. I might have done, long ago: but no more." Memories tweaked at him, of being turned loose on a battle-field to finish off the Egyptian wounded for the High Priests of his captors; they had thought of him as a demon, keeping him caged except when there were dying to be disposed of; there had been the oubliette where he had been kept in darkness, given a terrified sacrifice at the full moon. Chagrin pressed through him afresh as visions of his long years of slavery in Nineveh and Babylon rose in his mind.

From outside came a chorus of shouts and the sound of a scuffle, followed by Mangueinic's stentorian order for the fighting to stop.

"What's wrong?" Nicoris asked, feeling something of his dismay and paying no attention to what was going on around the bonfire.

"I was recalling distant days," he said, "in distant lands."

"How distant?" she persisted. "You tell me you're an exile, have been a student in Egypt, and have lived in Roma, which a man might do in a lifetime, of course, but then you say that you have a business in Constantinople and that you have been to the Empire of Silk, and you claim that you're older than you appear to be." She faltered, then asked the question that had been haunting her for many days. "How much older?"

Wry amusement and despair warred within him; his answer came from this turmoil: "Aeons."

Nicoris wedged her arm along his shoulder. "More than a century?"

He chuckled. "Much more."

"More than a millennium?" There was so much disbelief in her voice that he cracked a single laugh.

"More than *two* millennia," he said.

She stared, trying to read his expression in the darkness. "Really?"

"Yes."

The silence stretched out between them, thin and strong as a spider-web. Finally Nicoris gathered up her courage once more. "How many years have you been alive, Dom?"

He answered her truthfully. "Thirty-three."

She gave him a half-playful, half-angry slap, perplexity puckering her brows and turning down the corners of her mouth. "You just said you've been alive for more than two millennia."

"No, Nicoris, I did not," he corrected her gently, confining her hand in his own and fixing his compelling gaze on her silvery eyes. "I said I am more than two thousand years old."

"But—"

"The enemies of my people and my family killed me when I was thirty-three," he said remotely, "but they did not know how to do it, and I rose after they—"

"Rose," she repeated with incredulity. "Like the Christians' God—"

"Not quite," he said dryly. "Not. Quite."

"Then *what*?" Aggravation gave her demand an edge. "What are you keeping to yourself? What could be more incredible than what I've heard already? You tell me amazing things and I believe them, or I want to. But if I sum them up, you would have to be more than a century old certainly, and I have doubts. You are no stripling, but you are full of vigor and your strength is greater than most of the people here realize, and there are no signs of great age upon you. Your skin is both smooth and leathery, but your travels could account for that, not your years. Yet you say it is more than two millennia since you were born." She interrupted herself, asking impishly, "I have got that right, haven't I? You *were* born."

"I was—at the dark of the year, in these mountains, some distance to the east, more than twenty-five centuries ago." He paused. "So now you have my secret."

If she understood what he was implying, she gave no sign of it. "How did it happen, that you . . . lived so long?"

Concealing a sigh of disappointment at her continued reserve, he said, "When I was thirteen, I was initiated into the priesthood of our people, all of whom were undead." He fingered a stray tendril of her hair, musing on the recollections that flooded his mind. "My father called himself a King, but he was more a warlord, and as such he maintained a chain of fortresses to protect his lands; until the mercenaries of the Hittites came he controlled a large part of the eastern hook of the Carpathians."

"Carpi, or Daci?" she asked.

"Neither. Nor Goth, nor Gepid. They were the Erastna; you have heard nothing of them, for the name of my people is all but forgotten in these mountains. They left long ago, routed by enemies from the east. Some went south into Anatolia and some went west into Italia; none remained here." This admission troubled him more than it had in five centuries, and he decided that this was because he was so close to his native earth he could feel its pull.

Perplexed, she pulled on his ear. "You're alive, Dom. You can't deny that."

"I am undead: not quite the same thing."

"Because you *rose*?" She stared at him, incredulous. "Only you, of all your people?"

"Yes," he said quietly.

The enormity of his acknowledgment bore in on her: quite suddenly she moved atop him and gave him an impulsive, wet, enthusiastic kiss and wrapped her arms around his neck, her legs straddling his hips. "I don't know how you stand it," she said when she came up for air.

"Stand what?" he asked, bemused.

"The loneliness." She regarded him narrowly. "I have lost my family, and . . ." She stopped herself, then resumed speaking. "Sometimes it is unbearable to remember them. I have no knowledge of what became of my sisters and brother; our father may have sold them, if they lived. Not knowing is almost worse than being an orphan. But you—you have lost so much more: everything is gone."

"The earth remains," he said pensively, aware that some of what she was telling him was untrue.

"So much the worse, I'd think; all the world is a graveyard," she said, propping her head on her hands, her elbows flanking his ears.

"Not for those of my blood. We are bound to the earth, and it sustains us, as you will learn if you decide to become one of our number. The earth is as nourishing as blood is," he said, feeling the strength of it from the chest underneath them through the thin mattress. "We are creatures of the earth and we draw our endurance from it. Separate us from our native earth, and our . . . durability goes with it."

"If that is what sustains you—the earth—then I want to know about the blood: how can both of them nurture you?" she said, her breath coming more quickly. "What do you gain from the blood?"

"Life," he said.

"Truly? You don't need much of it." Her skeptical observation was punctuated by a kiss to his nose.

"No, not if it is . . ." he said, faltering as he tried to explain, "Apodictically given."

"What do you mean by that?"

He took a long, ruminative breath. "Blood is more than blood for me, and those of my kind: it is the totality of the person whose it is, the most undeniable substance of personal uniqueness. If in taking blood there is genuine intimacy, when something of each passes to the other, my needs in terms of quantity are quite small; it is the whole person that sustains me, not the palmful of blood. If there is pleasure but no touching beyond dreams and flesh, then I require a little more—not much more, perhaps half again as much as what knowing closeness compels—to be nourished. If there is nothing but anguish and dread, then I need more, but then it is a hunger for poison, and if I succumb to it, blood taken in agony passes that pain to me and blights my soul."

Nicoris stared at him, fascinated. "Do I nourish you?"

"You do," he told her, smiling up at her. "The whole of you." He hoped again that she would reveal what she was striving to hide.

"Do you want sustenance now, Dom?" She was teasing him with her nearness, deliberately leaning down to kiss his throat; she offered nothing more of herself.

"Yes," he said. "But there are a few things I have to tell you before we continue."

"What things?" she asked, annoyed at any delay.

"I warned you that there was a risk in lying with me more than five times, and this is the fifth time for us." He could see curiosity and irritation in her face; he touched the sharp crease between her brows. "Let me explain, Nicoris, for both our sakes."

She relented. "All right—but don't take too long."

"As you wish." He paused to order his thoughts. "This is the last time we may touch without that part of me that has passed to you reaching a point that when you die, you, too, will rise and be undead, as I am."

"What do you mean?" she asked, laughing breathlessly.

His dark eyes were enigmatic, his voice musical. "I mean that you will become one of my blood. You will live as I live, be what I am."

"Undead."

"Undead." When she remained silent, he went on, "Those of my blood also sustain themselves through the most profound touching, through the communion of making love."

"We've done that already," she said, dismissing his concerns.

"But it will not continue after you die," he said somberly.

Her eyes glinted with dawning outrage. "Why not? Do you not love those who are like you?"

He could feel the tension in her body; he took a little time to answer. "With those of my blood there is always a bond, and it endures until the True Death."

"And what is that: the True Death?" she demanded.

"It is the end of our life. Even we die, in the fullness of time."

"But you've died already," she protested.

"Yes, but not fatally." He began to stroke her back, easing the tautness from her muscles. "One day, the True Death will come, as it comes to everyone, and all things." He waited again for her to speak.

"Then you *can* die?"

"Most certainly; all vampires can."

The word made her flinch. "Don't say that."

"Say what—vampire?" He gave a single, sad chuckle. "What word would you prefer I use?"

Her aggravation was confined to a sniff. "If you must call yourself that, I suppose you must," she allowed, then kissed him again, this time with turbulent passion; as their kiss grew more intense, she reached around behind her to grab his hand and pull it to her breast, panting a little as the kiss ended. "None of that matters right now—what matters is that you love me."

"I do love you," he said, feeling her rapid pulse and mounting desire flood through her.

"Then show me," she said, and pressed her mouth to his again.

This kiss was more ardent as it lengthened, deepened, became more complex; Nicoris pressed herself into his hand, moaning as she awakened to the first quivers of rapture. "You know what gives me pleasure, Dom."

He moved, still holding her, so that they were lying side by side, with only space for his hand between them. "Slowly, Nicoris. There is no cause to rush."

"But it has been many days, and I—"

His hand between them worked down to raise her palla, lifting it gradually from her knees to her hips, finding the soft inner folds at the meeting of her powerful thighs. There he lingered, exploring the recesses, persuading her body to release its secrets to him.

After a time, she became more languorous, except for an occasional frisson of excitement. "Are you going to . . ."

"All in good time." He eased her palla farther up her body so that most of it was crumpled under her arms, revealing her breasts; he slid down her body to tongue her nipples while his hand quested for the core of her.

Her fulfillment, when it came, came quickly, coiling tightly like the skein on a ballista, then releasing in pulsing flourishes that were accompanied by little cries, like the calls of birds, her hand caught in the loose waves of his hair as the last of her spasms encompassed her. Finally she sighed and lay back, quivering in the glorious aftermath of their rapture; she clung to him, caressing his face, kissing his fingers, whispering endearments to him in the language of the Huns.

Text of a dispatch to Metropolitan Evangelos in Constantinople from Praetor Custodis Mauritzius Corvo at Narona, Province of Illyricum, written in Imperial Latin in fixed ink on sanded linen, carried by the Imperial bireme *Princeps Gloriae,* and delivered fifteen days after it was written.

To the most reverend Metropolitan Evangelos of the Emperor Theodosios at the City of Constantine, Praetor Mauritzius Corvo, resident at Narona in the Province of Illyricum, on this, the twenty-ninth day of April in the 439th Year of Salvation: Ave.

I have recently received a request from one Patras Methodos of your city that is of so startling a nature that I am compelled to bring it to your attention, for it appears to me that in his zeal, Patras Methodos has overstepped his mandate to the detriment of his office, to wit: he has commanded all records of the Eclipse Trading Company operating in this port as well as many others, with accounting of all monies transferred to and from that company's treasury for the last ten years; he indicates that he has made similar demands of factors for the company in all cities allied to the Roman Empires, East and West, along with official tax records, to be sure that there has been no attempt to defraud the government, nor to conceal smuggling or other wrong-doing.

I am familiar with this company, and its factor here, Pollux Savinus, who has been factor for twelve years and is a man of impeccable probity—I could wish that many another merchants' factors were as upright as this man. To bring his character into question is offensive to anyone who knows him, and an insult to the company for which he works.

The company itself is an exemplary one. I have only once met its owner, Dom Feranescus Rakoczy Sanctu-Germainios, who called upon me when he was returning to his post as regional guardian at Apulum Inferior in the former Province of Dacia, where presently he has been engaged, so I am informed, in battling the barbarian Huns, which is a service to Roma, East and West. To call his character into question is unthinkable.

All of this is by way of saying that it appears to me that Patras Methodos has exceeded his authority and has earned at least a reprimand, and the assignment to other cases than this one, for clearly he has exercised poor judgment and abused his position. There is no wrong-doing at Eclipse Trading Company, so the detention of any of its personnel—and Patras Methodos informs me that there has been such a detention—dishonors the laudable conduct of this company, its owner, its staff, and its employees.

Most gratefully, and commending my information to your good consideration

> *Mauritzius Corvo*
> *Praetor Custodis at Narona*
> *Province of Illyricum*

PART III

NICORIS

*T*ext of a report from Hredus at Sanctu-Eustachios the Hermit monastery to Verus Flautens, Praetor-General of Drobetae, written in a simple Greek code on a thin plank of wood using a charring sty-lus, entrusted to the deputy Watchman leaving with a company of refugees to carry with other letters and reports, delivered forty-nine days after it was written.

To my revered Praetor-General, Verus Flautens, two weeks before the Summer Solstice, Ave.

This region is still on alert, for it is feared that the Huns will at-tack again, and in larger numbers than when they came before. Al-ready the people here have doubled the number of attackers they fought by repeating the tale among themselves; they have rebuilt the portions of the walls that were damaged during that first attack, and have also built two more observation towers in order to keep watch not only on the road through the pass but on the lake end of the valley. The men are largely busy with the defenses, the women help with the farming and cooking for all the residents. Those chil-dren who are old enough have been set to making shafts for arrows and fletching them. The monks are not pleased that they must deal with women, but their help has made a great difference in the state of the fields and flocks.

Over the last month, more than two hundred thirty of the refugees have left the monastery, diminishing the number of men available to fight and to help the fighters. More have plans to leave, including the ones who will bear this to you. The mercenaries are still willing to defend this place, some say because Dom Sanctu-Germainios has pledged to pay them if they survive. None of the soldiers have fled, though many of them are not happy to stay here. Antoninu Neves, their leader, has told Priam Corydon that his men will not desert the monks. Tribune Bernardius of Ulpia Traiana has said his soldiers will stay until an evacuation is ordered, but the others, the refugees, from Ulpia Traiana must do as they think best. He cannot force them to stay, or to go. The leaders of men, not the soldiers, from Ulpia Traiana have gone already, all but two, and one is planning to leave shortly.

Those refugees who remain here do so more because they fear to encounter the Huns in the open more than they wish to stay. All the refugees are awaiting the return of the Huns, and all are afraid. The monks say they would welcome the departure of the refugees and soldiers, but I think most of them are secretly glad to have help. Monks do not often make good fighters, and the Huns would defeat them with little effort if the refugees and soldiers and mercenaries left them without the protection they have given the monastery so far.

Presently there are eight hundred twenty-one men, women, children, and monks within these walls. The party leaving that will carry this to you will reduce that to seven hundred seventy-four. There are roughly thirty residents of the monastery who are ill or impaired and therefore unable to fight.

Only one merchant has stopped here since I have arrived, a man known to Priam Corydon from previous visits; he remained only two days before continuing his journey to Aquincum. He came from Thessalonika, crossed the Danuvius at Oescus, and came to the monastery by secondary roads, for he says the Roman ones are haunted by outlaws of all sorts; he said that this spring he has met with fewer merchants on this trip than in previous years. He had an escort of three men-at-arms, and nine well-laden mules, bearing not only the man and his escort, but all his wares. They travel at a rate of fifteen to twenty thousand paces a day on good roads, and between ten and twelve thousand paces a day on poor roads. They have three times had to fight off attacks of various robbers, but they have not yet seen any Huns. If this journey goes badly, he told the Priam that he would not come north of the Danuvius again.

If it is your intention to dispatch troops to add to the defenders' numbers, then I recommend that you do so as soon as may be. The summer will quickly be upon us, and the monastery could shortly be attacked. The Huns will not wait for much longer, I fear, if they intend to raid this place again, though they may hold off until the fields are nearer harvest, so they will have rewards for their efforts. They can use the grain in the fields before the lake, and the fruit in the orchards as well as items of value they can take from the refugees. I, for one, do not want to have to fight them if they come in their numbers as they are said to do.

The monastery is also being visited by the hermit Monachos Anatolios, who has declared that the defenses must be taken down, or God will not protect the monks and the other residents. He says that to build stockades shows a lack of faith, and that only those who will have utter faith in God will be worthy of His Mercy. By building defenses, Monachos Anatolios says, the monks expose themselves to the fires of Hell for apostasy, as well as to the fury of the Huns. He has four followers among the other hermits, and some of the monks here are inclined to agree with him. Because of that, stress between the monks and the refugees is getting worse, and it is likely that it will continue and worsen. Since I came here, four men have been exiled from the monastery for repeated fighting with those monks who think that the monastery should not be defended, to show their faith. No doubt more men will be turned off until the Huns come. The monks who fight are sent to penitential cells in the main building of the monastery.

There are rumors that the Huns have a spy in the monastery, but such rumors are always rife in circumstances like these, and I do not give the idea much credit. In so confined a place as this, it would be difficult for a spy to work without exposing himself. Not that the Huns would hesitate to employ spies, but I doubt that there is such a man in this place: the advantages appear to be few and the hazards many. Roman taxes may be high and arbitrary in former provinces, but they are not as destructive as the Huns can be.

From my view, from all I have seen and heard, this region would need a full Legion at least to defend it, the country being so mountainous that foot soldiers may have a good chance against cavalry, not that the Gepidae would welcome a Legion on this side of the Danuvius. The Gepidae and Goths have negotiated with the Hunnic King Attila, and pay him tribute to avoid fighting his men. Some of the Goths have gone over to the Huns, accepting their promise of safety in place of protecting their territory and kin. If anyone is to stop Attila's advance it will have to be the Roman Empire, East or West. The people in this region are growing weary of fighting, and many have already gone over to the Huns. If no action is taken now, in these mountains, then there will be no stopping Attila from attacking within the Empire, perhaps as far as Roma itself, or Constantinople. I do not say this to alarm you, but in warning.

I have fulfilled the first condition of my mission, so in accordance with your pledge, prepare a writ of manumission for my sister and procure a loom for her. I will leave here within the month, and will expect word of your compliance from my sister before I depart; should I have nothing from her, I will seek you out to discover the reason.

In all devotion to you and the Roman cause,

>   Hredus
>   Freedman of Drobetae

1

"With the death of the farrier's baby, we are down to seven hundred fifty-four souls within our walls," Monachos Niccolae of Sinu said as he presented his weekly census to Priam Corydon; he was weary, his hair and beard were grayer, and his face was more worn than it had been a month ago. "We have lost six weavers and a fuller, and are now reduced to two smiths. The refugees from Apulum Inferior have lost the greatest number, and they are still leaving in higher count than the others." Early Mass had been over for a quarter of the morning, half the monks were at private devotions in their cells, and it was almost time for the mid-day meal.

The monastery's office was dim although it was late morning; the shutters were closed against the weather. A warm summer rain was falling, the fine drops more of a mist than a proper downpour; this meant that the usual sentries were not posted on the peaks around the valley, which made many of the residents uneasy, for in conditions like this, the Huns could be upon them without any warning, so they went about their tasks quietly, talking in hushed voices when they had to speak, but generally saying very little.

Priam Corydon sighed as he looked at the sheet of vellum. "The last lot went down the hunters' road, didn't they?"

"Yes. They believe it is safer," said Monachos Niccolae. "There is another party from Tsapousso preparing to leave, a group of eighteen. That will leave fewer than two dozen from that village in the monastery." He moved nervously, his face tight with worry.

"When do they plan to depart?" Priam Corydon asked, trying to conceal his worry.

"They plan to leave in four or five days, or so they have told Mangueinic. They believe it is no longer safe here. Mangueinic told me that he wants to dissuade them; he is concerned that they will be waylaid by outlaws if they escape the Huns, being so few in number." He made the sign of the cross. "The Huns are still in the region; we know that. So anyone leaving here puts himself in danger if he goes, no matter which road he chooses."

Priam Corydon stared at the report, seeing nothing of it. "If he must, I suppose it wouldn't be wrong to attempt it."

"It is his duty," said Monachos Niccolae.

"How do you see that?" Priam Corydon asked.

"He is now once again leader of the Watchmen, and the man most responsible for the refugees from Apulum Inferior—" Monachos Niccolae began.

"What of Dom Sanctu-Germainios?" Priam Corydon interrupted.

"He is important to those dealing with Roma, but he is a foreigner, and that absolves him of responsibility." Monachos Niccolae looked down. "Or so I believe is the case."

Priam Corydon lapsed into contemplation, his gaze drifting. "Do you think the refugees who want to leave can be persuaded to remain?"

"It is in God's hands, not in the words of men," said Monachos Niccolae, and made the sign of the fish.

For some little time, neither man spoke, then he went on, "Monachos Anatolios told Ritt that he will come to the monastery before mid-day."

Priam Corydon put down the vellum and rubbed his face, resisting the urge to pull on his beard. "Did he say why he is coming?"

"He might have, but Ritt didn't mention what it was, if he did."

"He's going to preach," said Priam Corydon with complete certainty and growing dismay. "He has been waiting for an opportunity, and now he has one."

"He may only want to get dry," suggested Monachos Niccolae.

"Not he," said Priam Corydon. "Sitting in his cave, in the damp, is a wonderful opportunity to mortify the flesh. He would hardly deprive himself of it." He knew he should do penance for so uncharitable a remark, but he found it difficult to admire the irascible hermit, whose zeal was so intense that he prayed daily for the apocalypse to occur, ending the world, and for the damnation of all Christians who did not share his vision.

"Mangueinic will not be glad to see him," Monachos Niccolae remarked. "There is always trouble among the refugees when Monachos Anatolios preaches."

Priam Corydon said nothing in response; he rose from his writing table and took a turn about the small chamber. "Can you tell me if any of the refugees have gone out hunting today?"

"Not that I know of," said Monachos Niccolae. "They are working on the outer walls still, and some of them are inspecting the livestock; necessary tasks, all of them, and ones that have been neglected these last several days. The rain gives them a good reason to keep the animals in pens and paddocks."

"So it does." He could not shake the sense that he was not seeing a danger that was directly in front of him. He told himself it was the result of many weeks filled with anticipation of Hunnic attack.

There was a tap on the door; the two men turned toward it.

"Mangueinic here, with Dom Sanctu-Germainios," the gruff voice announced. "Will you admit us?"

"Enter, enter," Priam Corydon called out, and motioned to Monachos Niccolae to open the door; he resumed his place in his chair at his writing table, trying to compose himself, and reluctant to show any sign of misgivings. "God save you," he said as the two men came into the room.

Making the sign of the fish, Mangueinic stumped across the room to the writing table. "God save you, too, Priam." He steadied himself on his crutch and said, "We've stopped another fight, this one over a woman. The Dom has treated the loser, who has been stabbed."

Sanctu-Germainios nodded. "He has two wounds, painful but not serious unless there is pus, and then he could be in danger." He paused. "I am told there is malachite in these mountains: is that true?" He knew there were deposits all through the mountains from his breathing days, when it had been prized for providing copper for trade and warfare.

"There is," said Priam Corydon. "Why do you ask?"

"I would like your permission to mine for it. If I can dig some out, I can make a poultice that will lessen the chance of infection in his wounds, and those of others." The remedy was not as effective as his sovereign one, but without an athanor to create the sovereign remedy from moldy bread, powdered malachite in woolfat would be a good secondary treatment, as he had learned in Egypt many centuries before.

"Who has been fighting?" Priam Corydon asked. "Who is wounded?"

"Who is the woman?" Monachos Niccolae asked.

"Severac, Tribune Bernardius' armorer, and Adrastos, the goatherd," said Mangueinic. "It's the second time for Severac."

"Who is the woman?" Monachos Niccolae repeated.

"Dysis. Her man died—" Mangueinic began.

"During the battle with the Huns," said Priam Corydon, and made the sign of the cross.

"The same," said Mangueinic.

"Which of the men is wounded?" Priam Corydon asked.

"Severac," said Sanctu-Germainios. "In the hand and along the hip. Adrastos is badly bruised, but his injuries will heal quickly. The cut on Severac's hand may be a problem; I have not had a chance to dress it thoroughly yet; I have set Nicoris to soaking the injury in an anodyne solution, so what I say now is conjecture. He seems to have grabbed the knife-blade; his palm is deeply cut. The cut on his hip is painful but less troubling than the one in the palm of his hand."

Priam Corydon shook his head. "An unfortunate thing." He caught his lower lip between his teeth, mulling the situation.

"I think it best that he remain in the old chapel until his wounds are truly healing," said Sanctu-Germainios.

Monachos Niccolae scowled. "If this is his second time fighting, he—"

"Pardon me, Monachos," said Sanctu-Germainios diffidently, "but it is his right hand that is cut, and if he is turned out of the monastery, he will starve. He will not be able to hunt, or fish, or live on anything more than roots and berries."

Priam Corydon looked up, his face set with an obstinate sorrow. "That is true, and in this case, it's unfortunate. But our rules are clear."

"That's what I told him," said Mangueinic.

"But he's right—with an injured hand, the man will surely die, for he won't be able to make a fire, even if he had something to eat," said Priam Corydon thoughtfully. "That will expose him to wild beasts. He would be fortunate to be taken captive by outlaws or one of the gangs of raiders."

"Exactly. He could not go over to the Huns; unless his hand is sound, they will not accept him," said Sanctu-Germainios.

Monachos Niccolae glowered in his direction. "And how is it you know such things?"

"I know them from listening to what has been said about the Huns for the last four years," said Sanctu-Germainios. "As you do."

Priam Corydon held up his hand. "As we all do," he said, making an effort to enlarge on his observation. "Every traveler has tales about Huns and we listen to each word as if they were angels and their revelations gospel. There is no reason to be suspicious of anyone purporting to have knowledge about the Huns, particularly this man, since he has served as a regional guardian and therefore has heard more than most of us about the Huns."

Sanctu-Germainios lowered his head. "You are most kind, Priam."

"Kind? I am a sensible person, nothing more." He folded his arms. "If you can mine safely, then you may have your malachite." Then he looked at Monachos Niccolae. "You are circumspect, Monachos, and that is a laudable trait, but neither of these men is an enemy of this place, or anyone in it."

Monachos Niccolae made the sign of the fish. "As you say," he muttered, and backed toward the door. "Until our next prayers."

"God save you," said Priam Corydon automatically, then, as the door closed, gave Mangueinic a hard look. "So what do you recommend be done about Severac? Do we give him time to heal and then turn him out into the world, assuming his hand is strong enough?"

"I haven't decided upon anything yet; not until the Dom tells me how much of a chance Severac has of getting the use of his hand back."

"It may not be a popular decision," Priam Corydon warned. "No other man sent away from this monastery has been allowed to delay his departure."

"No other man had such injuries," said Sanctu-Germainios. "If he leaves now, I can tell you without doubt that the cuts will putrify and that he will not survive."

"Then sending him away would be sentencing him to death." Priam Corydon stared at the elaborate Greek crucifix above the door. "I understand that. You made it clear."

"The others at least had a chance. Severac has none." Mangueinic slammed his fist into his palm. "But we must uphold our rules, or there will be chaos here, and we needn't wait for the Huns to destroy us."

"Very true," said Priam Corydon. "Very well; I will pray on the matter and give you my decision tomorrow. Will you be able to assess his condition by then, Dom?"

"I should think so," said Sanctu-Germainios. "I ought to know how severely his hand has been damaged by then—what ligaments have been cut."

"I thank you for that," the Priam said. "If he is truly crippled, then we must regard his case differently than those of able-bodied men." He glanced toward the window. "I'll be glad when the weather clears. Having almost everyone indoors in such close quarters sours people, like animals kept stalled too long."

"Truly," Sanctu-Germainios said. "As does constant worry."

Priam Corydon made the sign of the fish. "As we have reason to see every day." He sighed, "It shows a lack of faith."

Mangueinic cleared his throat. "No cause for us to become morbid about it," he growled. "It isn't fitting that we should succumb to despair."

"You're right," said Priam Corydon, pushing himself to his feet again. "In fact, it is a sin. Your rebuke is righteous."

"I'm not rebuking you," said Mangueinic, shocked at the idea.

"Well, it would be fitting, in any case," said Priam Corydon, going toward the door. "Best not to be laggard all day; it presents a bad example." He stopped next to Mangueinic and laid his hand on his shoulder. "Difficult though it has been, you've shouldered your task well, Watchmen Leader; you deserve far more gratitude than you will probably see."

Feeling abashed, Mangueinic mumbled, "Most kind, Priam."

Priam Corydon turned to Sanctu-Germainios. "You, too, deserve the gratitude of many and will not see enough of it."

Sanctu-Germainios said nothing as he followed Priam Corydon and Mangueinic out of the office, though he found himself considering the many hazards he had experienced as the result of gratitude. As they reached the intersection of corridors, he said, "There are many problems still to be dealt with—assuming Severac is not in fit condition to be exiled."

"There are," said Priam Corydon. "I've been reviewing the various possibilities since I left my office, and I think this may satisfy all those concerned: if Severac were to profess himself a penitent and join this monastery as a monk, I think the people will agree not to enforce his exile. What do you—"

They turned toward the foot of the Orthodox-cross–shaped building, bound for the refectory, when they heard a harsh voice announce, "God is displeased with you all! He has seen your sins!"

"Monachos Anatolios," said Priam Corydon, and lengthened his stride, waving to the men with him to hurry.

"God has offered you Salvation, and you spurn His gift! You set yourselves up in pride and rebellion to Christian teaching, and then you add to your error by imploring His aid in your endeavors." The voice was rising in volume and pitch. "He will not be merciful forever. Every day that you cling to your defenses here, you reveal the failure of your faith."

Monachos Vlasos was standing in the door to the refectory, a wedge-shaped kitchen knife in his hands, his arms folded. "Priam," he said as Priam Corydon came up to him, "I could not stop him. He insisted on addressing the monks."

"And you chose not to fight with him," said Priam Corydon, resignation in every part of him.

Monachos Vlasos looked abashed. "Fighting isn't permitted. Otherwise, I would have—"

Priam Corydon held up his hand. "I can't dispute that."

Monachos Vlasos made the sign of the fish. "He is a most demanding man. His faith is powerful within him." He kept his voice low so as not to interfere with Monachos Anatolios' harangue.

"—in the Name of God. With your surrender to His Will, nothing will be denied you. You will walk on water, as Christ did, you will stand amid fire and remain unscathed, and you will vanquish armies with a shepherd's staff. Yet you prefer to cling to the ways of the world, forgoing the exaltation of His Glory in Paradise!" Monachos Anatolios held his thin arms up, the palms toward the ceiling, his lopsided face suffused with a rapture of rage. "But you fail Him! You impose your will on His Will, like ungrateful children. You do not believe His promise!" He stared at the men seated at the long tables, a hard light in his deep-sunk eyes. "Look at you! Huddling behind walls like rats, giving power to men of violence, not men of prayer. None of you has the courage of your religion to walk beyond the walls armed only with the Gospels. You will not face the Huns but on their terms, blood and fire. And you claim you are Christians!"

Priam Corydon stepped into the refectory. "Monachos Anatolios," he said firmly, "you are welcome at our table. We are pleased to have you pray with us. But this is not the place for you to preach."

"What better place?" Monachos Anatolios rounded on Priam Corydon. "Our Lord preached while his Apostles were at table. I seek only to emulate His perfect example."

"You seek to disrupt the spirit of community that is present here; you have lost your humility in your pursuit of holiness," said Priam Corydon, resisting the urge to take a step back from him. "In the name of Christ, you must not bring rancor here."

"I bring no rancor," declared Monachos Anatolios, his face becoming red with ire. "I bring only the duty of monks, to submit to God in all things. How can you call that rancor?"

"If you want to make yourself a martyr, so be it," said Priam Corydon, straightening his posture and meeting Monachos Anatolios' glare with one of his own. "The monks here are pledged to defend and protect the souls of their fellow-Christians, the refugees and soldiers who are within—"

"Christians!" Monachos Anatolios jeered. "Those soldiers you protect make sacrifices to pagan demons. I have seen them in their red caps, giving up offering to the Persian Mithras. Their heresy has brought you to this sorry pass, for God punishes apostasy."

"Whatever they do, so long as they honor our faith, God will not be so uncharitable to deny them Grace for fighting our enemies. Their diligence in our cause will bring them Salvation through God's Mercy." Priam Corydon made the sign of the cross, holding Monachos Anatolios' gaze unflinchingly. "Your devotion may compel you to expose yourself to needless danger as a sign of your faith, but I have sworn an oath that I will succor those in my charge, and keep them from the pains of the world, and that is what I will do while there is breath in my body."

"A false oath, made to men in finery and jewels, living amid the corruption of the Imperial Court, claiming to be true to Christ and His Redemption."

The monks seated at the table were becoming restive; although speaking was forbidden, a murmuring joined with the whisper of the rain as the men listened to this confrontation.

Priam Corydon noticed this, and he spoke more quietly but with no loss of authority. "You must come away from here so that the monks may take their meal in peace. If you insist on prosecuting your intent, you may address the residents—all of them—in the main courtyard before sunset. I will guarantee that rain or no rain, you will have listeners." He motioned to Monachos Vlasos. "Take Monachos Anatolios to the kitchen and feed him fish soup and bread, then take him to the church so he may join with our novice in perpetual prayer."

There was no protest that Monachos Anatolios could make to such offers that would not compromise him in the eyes of the monks, so he made the sign of the fish. "I pray that God will reveal Himself to you so that you will no longer remain in stubborn, willful error."

"As I pray the same for you," said Priam Corydon. "May we both become wise enough through Grace that we may be capable of such understanding." He stepped aside for Monachos Vlasos to provide escort to Monachos Anatolios, then he looked around the room and three times made the sign of the cross.

"If you do not surrender to His Will, God will send you despair and ruin before the end!" Monachos Anatolios promised as he went with Monachos Vlasos toward the short corridor leading into the kitchen.

Monachos Egidius Remigos, the gate-warder, rose from his seat on the bench. "I ask the forgiveness of all the monks here for letting Monachos Anatolios inside the gates."

"You needn't do that," said Priam Corydon. "Monachos Anatolios is entitled to enter the monastery; no one can forbid him access to this place so long as monks live here."

"He wants the Huns to kill us all," called out one of the monks.

"He wants us to be martyrs and have crowns in Paradise," cried another.

Priam Corydon held up his hand. "Whatever may be the case, eat in silence, and meditate on what is owed to the body in the Name of God, Who gave them to us."

An uneasy silence settled over the refectory, and three of the novices put their hands over their mouths to stop the impulse to speak more.

Mangueinic moved away from his place at the door, signaling

Sanctu-Germainios to come with him. When he spoke, it was in an under-voice that hardly carried to the man he addressed. "Dom, something must be done about that hermit-fellow. He's going to cause more trouble, I can feel it in my bones."

Sanctu-Germainios did not respond at once, and when he did, his dark eyes were troubled, and his words were sad. "I wish I could disagree with you."

Text of a letter from Artemidorus Iocopolis, factor in Constantinople for the Eclipse Trading Company, to Rugierus of Gades, presently detained in the Magistrates' Palace in Constantinople, written in Greek in blue paint on Persian vellum and delivered by Eclipse Trading Company courier.

To the manservant of the distinguished foreign trader Dom Feranes-cus Rakoczy Sanctu-Germainios, Rugierus of Gades, the greetings of factor for the Eclipse Trading Company, Artemidorus Iocopolis, on this third day after the Summer Solstice,

I have spent the last month in negotiations for your release, and I am pleased to report there has finally been some progress. Most accounts from the Eclipse Trading Company factors throughout the region in which the ships trade have arrived and been perused by the various officers appointed to the task, and they report that the information is exemplary, both in content and in compliance with the law by the factors.

You will not be released immediately, but I am assured that once they have the one hundred twenty golden Emperors in hand to cover the cost of your detention and investigation, you will be permitted to leave the city, and the Eclipse Trading Company will be free of all suspicion. I have pledged to produce the money within ten days, which is not as large an amount as I had suspected we would be asked to provide. I must assume that Dom Sanctu-Germainios has powerful friends in the ports where our ships call, for nothing his associates in this city have said has been able to bring about your release. If you will inform me who among your guards and attendants is to be given a token of your gratitude, I will see to the amounts at once so that no one will have reason to keep you from leaving.

I understand that the priest who spearheaded the inquiries into Eclipse Trading Company has been assigned to the Imperial Magisterial Court in Tarsus in the former Imperial Province of Cilicia, to monitor the terms of trade in that port, so you may be easy in your mind about coming to Constantinople again. Inform Dom Sanctu-Germainios of these developments, but use an Imperial courier to carry any message you dispatch before your release.

My congratulations on your deliverance,

> *Artemidorus Iocopolis*
> *factor, Eclipse Trading Company*
> *Constantinople, Roman Empire in the East*

2

As summer took hold of the Carpathian Mountains a few more travelers fetched up at Sanctu-Eustachios the Hermit, bearing tales of Huns and refugees in ever-more-colorful details. More refugees straggled into the monastery in groups of three to twenty, seeking the only true asylum to be found in the whole of this part of the mountain range; there had been raids on villages three and four leagues away, but no large company of Huns was seen on the road to the monastery, and no Hunnic scouts wandered this part of the mountains. Encouraged by this apparent indifference of the Huns, another ninety-six people left the protection of the monastery's double walls and set out southward for Roman-held territory, leaving the monastery unevenly staffed, and the defenders troubled by the loss of men to fight in case of another attack; most of the new arrivals had had their fill of fighting and were set to more commonplace labors.

Antoninu Neves and Tribune Rotlandus Bernardius strove to integrate their two groups of men, arriving at an arrangement that they hoped would be most likely to work in the event the Huns returned in force. The Watchmen of Apulum Inferior were added to the company of soldiers and mercenaries. Priam Corydon set up a council among his monks to help ease their dissatisfaction with the refugees, promising his followers to enforce stricter codes of behavior on those living within the walls. Four huntsmen from Tsapousso were injured while hunting for wild boar when the animal they sought turned on them; they brought home the boar and were treated by Dom Feranescus Rakoczy Sanctu-Germainios, who occupied a portion of each day digging in the slopes around Sanctu-Eustachios for malachite, which he powdered into medicine and used on those coming to him with injuries; it was not as effective as his sovereign remedy, but it was better than nothing.

Two days after the refugees' festivities for the Summer Solstice— which offended the monks, being given over to rowdiness and lasciviousness and other pagan excesses—a lone man riding an ash-colored horse and leading a well-laden bay horse and two mules arrived at the gates of the monastery. He was dark-haired and dark-eyed, dressed in a pallium and trabea of heavy linen, leather braccae decorated with lavish embroidery, and calcea laced from ankle to knee. Although he had no escort, his air was prosperous, and when he presented himself to the warder-monk and Watchman, he offered a handsome sum for admission. "I prefer to pay for a bed within than to camp outside."

"Sanctu-Eustachios the Hermit will—"

Mangueinic, summoned to the gate for his advice, interrupted, "Two horses, two mules, no guards. He seems harmless enough. Let him in. If nothing else, he should have news for us. And he says he's willing to pay." He signaled to the Watchman manning the gates to pull them open.

Once inside, and the gates secured behind him, the stranger dismounted and saluted first the monk, then the Watchman, saying, "Thank you for admitting me. I am come from Aquileia at the behest of the Roman noblewoman Atta Olivia Clemens, with supplies that may help you in this difficult time. I am her bondsman, Niklos Aulirios, and I bear a greeting from her." He spoke the regional dialect with a strong Greek accent, and noticed that he had attracted some attention from the guards in the gate-tower.

Monachos Egidius Remigos nodded brusquely. "Give me the greeting from your bond-holder. I will present it to the Priam. You are welcome to Sanctu-Eustachios the Hermit." He indicated the leader of the Watch, who stood next to him. "Mangueinic will see to your housing." And with that, he took the letter and the gold coin Niklos proffered with equal disdain for each, then trod off toward the monastery church, saying something under his breath as he went.

"Cordial fellow," said Niklos.

"He's tired of dealing with the laity." Leaning heavily on his crutch, Mangueinic offered Niklos the suggestion of a salute. "Your animals can be taken to the stable to be unloaded, watered, groomed, and fed. I will show you where you can sleep for the duration of your stay." He swung away from Niklos and took his first step away, heading toward the main barn and stable.

Niklos gave Mangueinic a glittering smile as he took the lead-reins of his four animals in hand, tugging them after him. "I am told that Dom Feranescus Rakoczy Sanctu-Germainios is here. He is a blood relative of Bondama Clemens; I have messages from her to deliver to him. Perhaps it would be possible for me to share his quarters?"

"Do you know Dom Sanctu-Germainios?" Mangueinic looked startled.

"We have met occasionally over the years," said Niklos, who had been restored to life by Sanct' Germainus more than a century before. "No doubt he would recognize me, if you wonder at our connection."

"Dom Sanctu-Germainios is out on the eastern ridge, digging for malachite," said Mangueinic, watching Niklos through narrowed eyes. "But his assistant is in the old chapel. You could tell her you are here, and then wait for the Dom to return and decide what he would like you to do." He considered for a long moment. "It would be easiest if you were to stay with him and the woman in the old chapel."

"If that is what will suit you, then I will comply, with thanks," said Niklos, his face showing the most cordial expression he could muster; he wondered who *the woman* was. "If you'll accompany me to the stable, or direct me where to find it, and whom I should speak with there, I'll see to the unloading of the mules and horse."

"There are slaves who will do that," said Mangueinic.

"No doubt there are," said Niklos, maintaining his geniality, but with a touch more decisiveness in his tone. "Nonetheless, I would prefer to do the task myself."

Mangueinic shrugged. "Whatever you say, Bondsman. If you seek more work for yourself, who am I to deny you?" He went on down toward the barn and stable, remaining silent until they reached the stable-yard. "There are line-stalls within, and paddocks behind. You'll want to bring them in at night; it may be summer, but wolves and bears and cats are hungry all the same."

"I'm aware of that," said Niklos, stepping into the shadow of the stable, clucking to his animals. "Come up," he said in Latin to the four of them; his ash-colored horse craned his neck, wary of this new place. Then he whinnied, and was answered by a chorus of others from inside and outside the stable. "Conduct, Vulcan, conduct," Niklos admonished him, kissing to him to urge him forward. "Remember: we are guests here."

Vulcan minced into the alley between the line-stalls, pulling the bay and the mules after him; three slaves rushed forward to help him.

"Just tie them and tell me where I may store my tack," said Niklos, once again in the local patois, forestalling their efforts.

"You may store it atop your chests, once you have unladed them. No one will touch it, or them; we have strict rules here regarding theft," said Mangueinic, then scratched his beard, giving Niklos another thorough scrutiny. "Yes. I'll leave you to your animals. When you're finished here, ask one of the slaves to show you to the old chapel, or have anyone point the way." He stumped toward the door, then faltered. "You really do know the Dom, don't you?"

"Yes; as I said, he and the Bondama are blood relations." Niklos was tying Vulcan to a long railing that ran half the length of the middle of the stable. "I haven't seen him in some years, but we aren't total strangers."

"Very good," said Mangueinic, and went back out into the sunlight.

Niklos separated the leads of his other equines and handed them to the slaves. "Just secure them. I'll manage the rest," he said.

"What food for them?" asked the nearest slave.

"If you have grain, a handful of grain and a flake of hay for each, in the manger where they'll be tied. And some raisins, if you have any. They like raisins. For now, a bucket of water for each." He patted Vulcan on the neck and went to unfasten his bedroll from the back of the saddle, dropping it onto the ground before loosening the girth and pulling it free from the buckles. The mules—both a version of dun: one butter-colored, one dust, both with charcoal manes and tails—dropped their heads as the slaves tied them to the railing, with enough length in the lead to enable them to reach the full buckets of water set hurriedly beneath the rail. The bay horse whickered as Niklos came to unload his pack-saddle. "Where do I stack the chests and cases?"

"There," said one of the slaves, pointing to a recess in the line of mangers. "Put your animals on either side of your things."

"I will; thank you," said Niklos, ignoring the surprise in the slaves' eyes. By the time he finished unpacking, untacking, grooming, feeding, and stalling the horses and mules, a number of residents of the monastery had come by the stable to ask him where he had come from, how his journey had been, and why he had made it; Niklos answered them the same way, with honesty: "I am here on an errand ordered by Bondama Atta Olivia Clemens, Roman noblewoman, presently living on her estate near Aquileia, who has entrusted me with a message and supplies for her blood relation Dom Sanctu-

Germainios." By the time he left his horses and mules in their stalls to eat, he was sure almost everyone in the monastery knew his mission, and had begun adding their imaginations to what they knew.

Leaving the stable, he asked one of Antoninu Neves' men where he might find the old chapel. The mercenary—a Goth with braids in his orange beard—pointed the way, and in exchange, wanted to know how conditions on the roads were. "Are there many travelers abroad?"

"Not as many as I have encountered in years past. The Roman roads are in poor repair, but I suppose you know that. Every traveler deplores their condition. The secondary roads are no better; some are much worse. There are four bridges I wouldn't care to cross between here and Drobetae, and a fifth that I'd use only in dire need."

"There is a man here from Drobetae," the soldier remarked. "He says much the same thing."

"I should hope so, unless he's been here for years, or isn't being completely candid about himself," said Niklos, aware that the inquiry had been a trap to see if he had actually come from the Roman south. "And I doubt there'll be much improvement over the next year, not with the Huns continuing their raids. No one would be foolish enough to take work-gangs out."

"Then you believe they still might come here?" The mercenary sounded as if this were in question. "The Huns?"

"Oh, yes," said Niklos. "They have built up a major camp to the northwest of here, at the edge of the plains, or so everyone I met coming from that direction has claimed. They are gathering forces there, enlarging their armies, and recruiting local soldiers to their ranks. They've already sacked most of the towns in this quarter of the mountains; they'll pick off these small valleys at their leisure." He started walking toward the old chapel; the mercenary fell in half a step behind him.

"So, do you think we'll have to fight?"

"I fear so, if you remain here," said Niklos.

"But when? Other places have fallen, but not . . ." He gestured to finish his thought.

Niklos shaded his eyes to look at the small fields and the orchard in the widest separation of the two defensive walls. "I'd expect the Huns to come in the autumn, after the harvest, to take your crops as well as your animals. They have many mouths to feed, and they aren't farmers." He said this as bluntly as he could, and saw the suggestion of a smile cross the man's face. "You want to fight them?"

"Certainly—so we can win," he said almost merrily, his hand on the hilt of his Byzantine sword.

"Are you sure you will? Be able to defend this place from them?" Niklos asked. "I've seen what the Huns do to small places like this." He made no attempt to suppress a shudder; he had passed through Hunnic devastation only four days ago and the vision of the havoc they had left was still sharp in his mind. "Other village fortresses had defenders, too, and they're nothing but rubble now, rubble and ash, with bones strewn through them." He had passed through five other such ruins on his travels north; he knew that the monastery would not be able to withstand any concerted attack by the Huns or any other company of barbarians or rogues.

"We've had some time to prepare ourselves for another onslaught. We've turned the time to good use." He made the sign used to signal readiness to fight. "The Huns will be surprised, I think."—nodding in the direction of the ancient wooden building with the barrel-dome atop it—"That's the old chapel."

"Thank you," said Niklos, and went on with a wave to the mercenary. He studied the thick, weathered planks that made up the walls; its shape was irregular, there were few windows piercing its flanks, and those in the barrel-dome were of old, thick, greenish glass, one or two with jagged cracks running through them. There was a small door in an oblong projection at one end of the building, which Niklos assumed must be a side-door on account of its size, for it was narrow and inconspicuous. He went toward it, whistling so that he would not alarm anyone inside. At the door, he paused, gathering his thoughts, deciding how to introduce himself, and was startled when it opened, and a pale-eyed young woman with a taut, broad-shouldered body and neatly clubbed dark hair, dressed in an embroidered muted-lavender linen palla over blue femoralia, stepped out, taking her stance directly in front of him.

"Yes?" she demanded, meeting his gaze squarely.

"I am—"

"A stranger, yes, so I've been told. You've come to see Dom Sanctu-Germainios. He isn't here."

"I understand that," said Niklos. "May I wait for him?"

"If you like," she said. "But not alone with me; they think enough ill of me already." She stepped back and closed the door with an emphatic bang.

Niklos stood looking at the door with a mildly distracted air, doing his best to pay no heed to the many eyes turned on him or the occasional whispers of those who were watching him. He took a little time to walk around the building. He noticed it was older than the rest of the monastery, and that suggested to him that this place was yet another ancient shrine adopted by the Christians as one of their own; this part of the world, as he had seen, was strewn with them. The large doors at the end of the chapel convinced him of it; worn carvings of vines and flowers and flowing water adorned the ancient oak. He was about to proceed around the rest of the structure when he heard his name called. Turning toward the sound, he saw Sanctu-Germainios, in a black cotton pallium, black femoralia, and peri, all dusty, coming toward him, a sack slung over his shoulder, a wide-bladed trowel in his hand. "Sanct' Germain!" he called out in Latin.

"Niklos! What an unexpected arrival!" Speaking the same language Sanctu-Germainios came up to him and clapped his shoulder. "I need not ask what brings you here."

"Olivia," said Niklos unnecessarily. "I have a few things with me she thought you would want to have. And three letters, one from Rogerian . . . Rugierus. It arrived shortly before I left Aquileia. She said you'd want to have it, along with all the rest she ordered me to bring."

"How . . . how very like her," said Sanctu-Germainios, slipping the sack off his shoulder and lowering it to the ground with a noisy thunk. "What things are these, that you have brought?"

"They're in the stable. Earth, medicaments, bandages, clothes. Money."

Sanctu-Germainios nodded. "All very practical and all much needed. I thank you profoundly for bringing them here." He smiled, but the smile faded rapidly.

"Part of your preparations for resistance?" Niklos guessed.

"A very crucial part, much of which are in short supply," Sanctu-Germainios said. "Without an athanor, I have had to rely on my stores of medicaments and gold; both are running low." He shrugged. "What do you think of our fortifications?"

"Outer wall reinforced, with raised battlements for the soldiers inside, the plantations and orchards between it and the inner wall built up and strengthened, giving the crops a measure of security in an attack," Niklos mused aloud. "You're making plans to hold the Huns off, I understand?"

"Yes." He paused. "At least while there are people here to protect."

"They slip away, don't they?" Niklos observed.

"By twos and threes, some of them, and in groups of fifty and more, carrying their goods on the backs of their horses and goats," Sanctu-Germainios confirmed. "They go into the forests, along the hunters' tracks to small villages, and abandoned towns, and from there, toward the old Roman fortress-towns." He turned away. "Some go to the Huns, of course."

"Of course," said Niklos.

"I think the greater number still try for Roman territory," said Sanctu-Germainios, "but that may change. Others arrive, but in smaller numbers, and many of them pass on to the west and the south."

"The company of refugees who told me where I might find you were heading for Viminacium. I encountered them in a fortified village near Drobetae called Sisincum." Niklos paused. "They said you had agreed with the Watchmen of Apulum Inferior that the town couldn't be defended and had decided to come here, at least for a time. They said they had decided to make for Verona. I don't know how many of them actually reached their destination."

Sanctu-Germainios gave a single laugh. "How could you know? How could any of us?"

"Apulum Inferior faced the same dangers as Porolissum," Niklos pointed out. "Olivia took your advice and left. And good thing, too, as it turned out."

The side-door of the old chapel swung open and Nicoris said, "I heard voices."

Sanctu-Germainios held out his hand to her and, speaking in the local dialect again, said, "Nicoris, come out. I want you to meet Niklos Aulirios, an old . . . associate of mine."

Nicoris did as she was bade, watching Niklos suspiciously. "As you wish, Dom Sanctu-Germainios," she said, a bit too formally.

"He is the bondsman to my blood relative Atta Olivia Clemens," Sanctu-Germainios explained. "He has brought us supplies from Aquileia, from Olivia."

"And news from Roma and Rogerian," Niklos added, and saw Sanctu-Germainios smile.

"And where are they, these supplies?" Nicoris asked, making no apology for her confrontational question.

"At the moment they are in the stable, stacked up between a pair each of horses and mules," Niklos said affably. "I'll bring them up to you whenever you're ready to receive them."

She studied him carefully, then held the door wide. "For now, you should come in. Shouldn't he, Dom?"

"Indeed he should," said Sanctu-Germainios. "I have a great deal to ask him, and better to do it inside, in reasonable comfort, than to stay out here in the sun." Little as he wanted to admit it, the sunlight was beginning to wear on him, whittling away at his strength and making him ache from its relentless might; the lining of his native earth in the soles of his peri was nearing the end of its efficacy and would need to be changed shortly.

"Thank you, Sanct' Germain," said Niklos in Latin.

"It is my pleasure. Mind the right foot," he said, stepping over the threshold in the approved way of Imperial Roma.

Nicoris laughed at this custom, but said nothing as she closed the door behind them and went into the center of the chapel where the room was most light. "I can get some beer for you, Dom Aulirios, if you would like."

"I'm not Dom, I'm a bondsman," said Niklos. "And thank you, but I need nothing just now."

"You might want something to sit on," Sanctu-Germainios suggested, still in Imperial Latin. "That short bench is the best we have to offer. There are pallets stacked up, if you would prefer I get one ready for you."

"Then I will accept the bench gladly for now," said Niklos, adding, "I may ask for a pallet for the night, or discover if the refugees will grant me a bed in the men's dormitory, though a fellow with a crutch—I didn't catch his name—told me I should stay here with you."

"That would be Mangueinic. He's leader of the Watchmen from Apulum Inferior, and part of his job is to assign new arrivals to their quarters." Very deliberately, he changed to the local dialect; he had seen that Nicoris was growing restive. "How long have you been on the road?"

"Thirty-four days. Not too bad, considering the conditions." Niklos patted his clothes. "Is there a bath-house here? And a laundry? I can feel the grime all the way to my skin." He saw Nicoris out of the corner of his eye; she kept to the shadows, watching him.

"There is a small bath-house," said Sanctu-Germainios. "The monks disapprove, but the refugees have demanded it. Mangueinic will arrange for you to use it. There is no laundry, but one of the refugee women will gladly wash your clothes in the lake for a couple of silver Angels."

"Speaking of coins," said Niklos, "I should probably fetch the sacks of them that Olivia sent to you." He got to his feet. "I'll return shortly with two of the chests I brought you. No doubt you will be pleased with their contents."

"Do you need any help?" Sanctu-Germainios asked.

"If you think it wise, come with me and carry one of the chests. We can bring them up here before nightfall." He thought again. "Is there someone whose help it would be prudent to ask? Someone who's curious enough to want to help?"

Sanctu-Germainios chuckled. "Perhaps one of the Watchmen might be willing to assist us, for a few coins."

"Naturally," said Niklos, trying not to sound cynical, and glanced again at Nicoris. "Where should we put them?"

Before Sanctu-Germainios could answer, she spoke up. "Next to the hearth, as the Gepidae do. Otherwise the monks might claim you are setting up a pagan altar."

Sanctu-Germainios nodded at once. "Nicoris is right. The monks are always looking out for signs of paganism. A stack of chests and cases in this chapel would raise their suspicions unless they are at the hearth, where household goods are kept."

Niklos shrugged. "If that's what will spare us suspicions, then that's what we'll do." He smiled at Nicoris, but received only a troubled look for a response. "It's what Olivia would do."

Although he was keenly aware of the growing tension between Nicoris and Niklos, Sanctu-Germainios gave no indication of it. "How *is* Olivia?"

Niklos turned to Sanctu-Germainios. "Olivia is well, but worried, and not solely for you. She is convinced that neither Ravenna nor Constantinople will risk the men and arms to drive the Huns from these mountains, and that will turn out to be great folly, for which everyone will pay dearly." He stretched, beginning to ease the strain of travel from his body. "She's already planning to go to Lecco next year."

"A beautiful place, Lecco," said Sanctu-Germainios.

"Surrounded by mountains," said Niklos. "She thinks they're safer than the plains."

"She may be right," Sanctu-Germainios said, a wry turn to his mouth. "The monks here believe it."

"They believe their Christian God protects them," Nicoris said.

"That's all they care about. Monachos Anatolios says that the stockades show a lack of faith."

Niklos looked to Nicoris, a quizzical tilt to his brows. "What's this?"

"Oh, there is an apocalypticistic hermit living in a cave above the lake," Sanctu-Germainios said, and explained Monachos Anatolios' disputes with the residents of the monastery, and his determination to be a martyr. "So far few of the monks within the walls have joined with him, but—"

"But they might," said Nicoris, frowning fiercely.

"Does this hermit have many followers among the refugees?" Niklos asked.

"Not that I know of," said Sanctu-Germainios. "But there may be." He started toward the side-door. "This is not bringing the chests."

Niklos went to him. " 'The sooner begun, the sooner completed,' " he said, quoting an old Roman aphorism. As he followed Sanctu-Germainios out of the old chapel, he could almost feel Nicoris' penetrating gaze on his skin, like tiny, hot flames.

Text of a letter from Rugierus to Atta Olivia Clemens, written in Imperial Latin in blue paint on scraped vellum, carried by the Eclipse Trading Company ship *Magna Mater* and delivered thirty-eight days after it was written, then forwarded to Sanctu-Germainios with Niklos Aulirios.

To the most noble Roman noblewoman, Bondama Atta Olivia Clemens, the greetings of the bondsman to Dom Feranescus Rakoczy Sanctu-Germainios, Rugierus, Ave.

Bondama Clemens,

As you must undoubtedly know, I have been detained by the Emperor's authorities in Constantinople, so that my efforts to rejoin my master in the former Province of Dacia are for nothing. I am suspected, it appears, of aiding the enemies of the Eastern and Western Roman Empires, according to Patras Methodos, a priest of unusual zeal, and an adherence to the minutiae of the law. I understand it is you who has authorized the payment of a bond for my release, from my master's extensive holdings, and for this I am most appreciative.

I believe there have been communications sent from you and from my master that have not reached me, and so if I discuss issues that have been addressed already or that may have been resolved, I ask your indulgence for my ignorance: Patras Methodos is a man who is inclined to eke out news to me, when he provides any at all. He has limited the visits of Artemidorus Iocopolis to one every two weeks, and would curtail them more if money were not involved in the Eclipse factor's visits; there is a donation required for every time Patras Methodos opens the door. I must also assume that all communications that I have been allowed to receive have been read and that all I have sent have also been perused.

Stories have reached this city that the Huns are breaking through everywhere in the Carpathian Mountains, and because of that, I am taking advantage of your kind offer to receive letters to my master; I must suppose that he is no longer in Apulum Inferior, and might have been driven to any one of a number of havens. If anyone knows where he can be found, it must be you, and so I trust you will send him word that you have heard from me, and that efforts are now under way to end my confinement. Once I have secured my release, if I have heard nothing from him, I will take ship for Aquileia, trusting that you will be able to tell me where my master has gone.

The amount to secure my release is a large one; I am shocked that Patras Methodos should demand so much money. Let me say that it is my ardent wish that the amount can somehow be reclaimed, at least in part, when it can be proven that the accusations laid against me were false. Until that time, I am most humbly grateful to you for your prompt action on my behalf.

Rugierus of Gades
bondsman to Dom Feranescus Rakoczy Sanctu-Germainios

on the Feast of Hagia Scholastica, the Christian year 439

3

Thunder had growled in the low-hanging clouds for most of the morning; the air was hot, close, and humid, making for bad tempers and lethargy among the residents of Sanctu-Eustachios the Hermit monastery. The refugees went slowly about their chores, although a few of them hardly bothered with their assigned tasks, but stayed under the trees, dawdling over the morning beer; when monks patrolling the grounds admonished them for sloth, many of them compounded their sins by cursing. Soldiers manning the battlements no longer looked for Huns approaching, but for fires ignited by lightning, or the tatters in the cloud that promised the relief of rain. The largest company of monks kept to their scheduled rituals, praying for rain along with other blessings.

Mangueinic had come to the old chapel when the morning was half-gone; he had turned surly, claiming his severed leg was aching where the foot had been; his patience was wearing away and he was damp with sweat. He stared at Sanctu-Germainios, daring him to provide relief. "I can't bear it," he said loudly. "I can't sleep. My whole leg is sore, even the part that's gone. My good leg is swollen, so are my hands, and my calceus doesn't fit."

"I have something that may be anodyne," said Sanctu-Germainios. He went to his red-lacquer chest and took out a jar of greenish pellets. "These are powdered willow-bark, juniper berries, and hawthorn berries mixed with a paste of parsley and ground celery seed. If you take three of them now, and three when you go to bed, you should be less uncomfortable, and your hands and feet less swollen. I can also give you a salve for your scars."

The leader of the Watchmen held out his hand and counted aloud as Sanctu-Germainios measured them onto his palm. "That bondsman—the one who came last week from Aquileia to seek you out?—he's making himself useful in the stable. He's a better farrier than Monachos Cleander. He's trimmed all the horses' hooves and all the mules'. He's got a way with the foals, as well. They're behaving much better since he took them in hand."

"It was his calling, training horses, before he became bondsman to my . . . kinswoman," said Sanctu-Germainios, recalling his first meeting with Niklos more than a century ago, when he was teaching Olivia to ride as well as drive; his death and restoration to life had provided Olivia with the devoted male companion she required, someone who was increasingly necessary for women in the Eastern and Western Roman Empire. In the decades since his return to life, Niklos had proved to be her loyal friend as well as her defender. "Since he came to her service, he has broadened his skills."

"Well, whatever accounts for it, he's a capable fellow, and we have need of him. I'm pleased he came. I didn't think I would be, at first, but I see he has his uses." He looked at the pellets in his hand. "Three now and three when I go to bed."

"Yes. If you want more, come to me tomorrow," said Sanctu-Germainios.

He picked three pellets and dropped them into his mouth, biting down on them and then swallowing hard; his face squnched at the taste. "Can I take them with my beer? They're pretty bitter."

"As you like," said Sanctu-Germainios. "Or eat them with an apple. That should sweeten them."

"An apple will do," said Mangueinic. "How long before this eases? It's wearing me out, the hurt and the heat together."

"Once the rain comes, you will be better," Sanctu-Germainios promised. "When the air is moist and hot, no one is entirely—"

"I mean, how long before I feel more . . . comfortable?"

"You should notice some improvement before the cooks serve prandium, sooner if the weather breaks," said Sanctu-Germainios, wondering again where Nicoris had gone. With the weather turning ugly, his concern for her was increasing; he knew how bad weather discomfited her.

"Good enough." Mangueinic made a positive sign with his hands, then sighed as if under the weight of a heavy burden. "If only it *would* rain, and rain hard and long. Then the chance of fires would go down, and the air won't be so oppressive. A good heavy thunderstorm would help us all."

"Then let us hope for the storm to come soon," said Sanctu-Germainios, handing Mangueinic his crutch, noticing the slight hesitation before he took it.

More thunder bludgeoned the clouds; outside someone screamed.

"I'd best go and find out what that's about," said Mangueinic, hitching himself toward the main door. "Thank you for these pellets. I hope they work."

"You will know by mid-day," said Sanctu-Germainios, watching Mangueinic depart. Once the door was closed, he went to his chest once again and inspected the jars, bottles, pots, and vials that remained, shaking his head. Olivia's provisions had been most helpful, but even they would not last through the end of summer. Another, louder cry demanded his attention.

"*Smoke!* There's a *fire!*"

A second voice cut in, barking out, "It's three ridges away, to the east, you fool! The wind is out of the west! It'll move away from us!"

"The lightning did it!" cried another, from some little distance away.

"Lightning? The Huns, more likely," shouted someone near the old chapel.

There was an eruption of questions, hollers, and shrieks, the cacophony almost loud enough to rival the next mutter of thunder.

Sanctu-Germainios went toward the door, his curiosity and his growing apprehension for Nicoris getting the better of him. As he stepped out of the old chapel, he saw the level of confusion had increased sharply, with men and women milling about, wringing their hands, glowering at their comrades, or cursing the heavens. A dozen monks were making their way through the churning refugees, ineffectively admonishing those they could get to listen to pray, to entrust their souls to God, to calm their distress. He doubted these pious exhortations would do much good, but he listened to them long enough to realize that more order was needed, for the disruption was spreading, increasing with the band of smoke to the east. Wading into the pandemonium, he sought out Mangueinic, raising his voice to be heard. "You and Neves and Bernardius need to join with the monks to restore order. Look at how the residents are behaving, and it is not simply the thunder that causes them to fret. There will be fighting soon if the refugees are allowed to go on this way."

Mangueinic thought this over for several heartbeats, then said, "You're right, Dom. I'll find Bernardius. You get Neves and we'll meet at the monks' church, where Priam Corydon is. We'll accost him as soon as he's done with Mass."

"Very good," said Sanctu-Germainios, threading his way toward the dormitory assigned to the mercenaries that had the armory attached to it. He found Neves in the armory busy with three of his men in sharpening swords and spear-points on the three turning stone wheels set up for that purpose. Critical gazes turned toward him, watching him for any sign of treachery.

"Dom," Neves greeted him with a show of bonhomie, "the rabbits are scampering, aren't they? Imagine being spooked by a little thunder. Or by a foreigner." This last was pointedly directed at his men.

"If you mean that the refugees are agitated, you have the right of it, and their fright is increasing," said Sanctu-Germainios. "That is why I would like you to accompany me to the monks' church, so that we may forestall the kind of disruption we've dealt with before, but on a grander scale." He saw the three lieutenants exchange a sardonic glance. "Order must be restored or there will be trouble for all of us." He could see that his warning caught Neves' attention. "The people are afraid, and frightened people are—"

"Skittish and volatile, as we see," Neves finished for him. "You're right." He stopped working the foot-pedal and set aside his

Byzantine sword, then wiped his hand across his brow, leaving a grimy smear behind. He rose from the stool on which he had been sitting and said to his lieutenants, "I'll be back in a little while, with some kind of plan, I trust. In the meantime, Linus, find Luitpald and go out to the men and tell them to keep to their posts unless some danger threatens us from outside the walls, in which case, sound the alarm." He wiped his fingers with a worn cloth, then said to Sanctu-Germainios, "Let's be off."

They kept to the edges of the increasing chaos, passing the dormitories and the small warehouse before they reached the church, where they found Mangueinic and Rotlandus Bernardius waiting for them.

"The Priam is still saying Mass," Mangueinic announced. "He'll finish up shortly." As if to confirm this, the droning chant of the liturgy grew louder at the *Blessings and Honor*, enumerating the various Saints, Martyrs, Patriarchs, Metropolitans, Priams, Patrases, Emperors, and Empresses whom the Church singled out for this ritual attention. "Nothing more now than the *Have Mercy on us* and *Go in the Peace of God*."

The others nodded; Neves said, "They're going to need the Peace of God if this keeps up." He angled his chin toward the churning tide of people.

"I'd like to see it rain, rain hard enough to put out any flames in the trees," said Bernardius. "Carpi diem," he said, then looked around to see if any of the monks had overheard him, for they disliked hearing even his mangled Latin spoken since their rites were Greek.

The next crack of thunder was louder, shuddering along the mountain as if to break the very stones asunder. For a long instant, there was complete silence from all the residents of the monastery while the peals rolled over them.

"That struck to the west of us, about half a league away, by the look of it," Sanctu-Germainios said as screams and shouts were renewed, and the monks in the church continued the *Have Mercy on us* with far more fervor than usual.

"Any sign of fire?" Neves asked of no one in particular. "Other than the one to the east of us?"

"Isn't that bad enough?" Mangueinic asked; he expected no answer and got none; he peered westward. "No sign of smoke."

"Not yet," said Neves.

The four men waited, but no cries from the gate-tower sounded the alarm. Their postures slowly relaxed.

"Fire to the west could be a problem," said Neves.

More thunder battered overhead, accompanied by shouts and shrieks.

"Or to the south; the wind sometimes swings around to the south in the evening," Mangueinic remarked. "A pity we hadn't time enough or men enough to build in stone, as the monks did when they made their monastery."

"We didn't know when the Huns would be upon us," Bernardius said. "Semper pre—" He broke off as lightning flickered through the clouds, pursued by thunder.

"Nor do we know now," Neves added when the noise abated.

Before the two could begin an argument, the door of the church opened and one hundred thirty-eight monks, led by Priam Corydon, filed out by twos, their heads bowed, their pace stately. They paused to turn and make the sign of the cross to the door of the church before it was closed by two novices. The monks were about to continue on to their cells when they caught sight of the four men waiting. Priam Corydon halted his monks and made the sign of the fish. "What has happened?"

"There is trouble among the refugees," said Neves.

"And it's getting worse," said Mangueinic.

"Fourteen of my monks were sent to calm them," said Priam Corydon. "The rest are at their duties in the monastery." He frowned, thinking of the forty-six monks who had left Sanctu-Eustachios the Hermit since the arrival of the refugees. "What do you require of us now?"

"Well, your monks didn't succeed in calming the residents," said Neves.

"They—the refugees, not the monks—should probably be confined to their dormitories until the rain has passed, and the air is cooler," Bernardius recommended. "You know, limit the chance for disturbances."

"Do you think that would help? They might still fight among themselves," said Mangueinic.

"Double the Watchmen on the towers," Bernardius suggested. "That way, if there is any trouble beyond our walls, we'll know it at once."

Priam Corydon held up his hand, his features set into lines of resignation. "Not here. Bernardius, Neves, Mangueinic, come along to my office. Sanctu-Germainios, it would probably be best if you remained in the old chapel. If there is trouble, you'll be needed there more than with us."

"As you wish," said Sanctu-Germainios, and stepped back from the church. "If you would like my observations as regional guardian—"

"I'll send a novice for you when we're ready," Priam Corydon declared, and motioned the men and monks to follow him, Neves, Bernardius, and Mangueinic bringing up the rear.

Sanctu-Germainios watched them go, attended by a low grumble of thunder, then took himself back to the old chapel. He understood Priam Corydon's preference for the company of Mangueinic, Neves, and Bernardius: those three commanded men with weapons, and he did not. Making his way down the gradual slope toward the old chapel, he could see that the refugees were still discomposed, balking at every sound from the clouds, lamenting at every bolt of lightning they could discern. As he went into the old chapel, he was startled and relieved to discover Nicoris standing at the small table near the rear wall, a sack lying open in front of her, out of which she was sorting herbs.

"Oh, Dom," she called as she caught sight of him. "Look what I found down the hunters' trail: monkshood." She held up the plant for his inspection. "You can make the syrup to treat Hluthaw's cough."

Her pleasure had a brittle edge to it, and she continually looked about as if she expected the old chapel to be struck by lightning.

Sanctu-Germainios nodded his approval. "Excellent. But take care to wash your hands after you touch it. The virtue of the plant is very strong, and can harm those who do not need it. You shouldn't handle it more than necessary."

"That's not all I found." She laughed, her tone a bit too shrill. "There's water-lettuce from the stream. And nettles, hawthorn, tansy, and purge-root. I saw bear tracks around a large thicket of berry-vines, so I didn't stay to pick any." She held out a slightly wilted plant with yellow flowers. "Primrose. You said you can make a healing salve from primrose."

"Most impressive; I will turn it to good use," he remarked, coming to her side to see what else she had brought. "Mountain thyme. Pennyroyal." He sniffed the delicate leaves. "Angelica-root. Feverfew. You've been very diligent."

She flushed. "Thank you for saying so."

"There's no reason for thanks," he said, and saw a flash in her quicksilver eyes and a firmer set to her jaw. "You have no reason to be offended, Nicoris."

"You remind me that I'm beneath you. I know that. I can't forget it, Dom." She put heavy emphasis on his title, and glanced up at the barrel-dome, then back at him.

He met her glare with kindness in his eyes. "I meant only that it is I who should be thanking you."

It took her a short while to speak up again. "You are a perplexing man, Dom. As much as you are a man at all."

"Accepted," he said, knowing she wanted to wound him as she had felt herself to be wounded.

This time the percussion from the clouds rattled all the buildings of the monastery, followed by wails of dread.

Nicoris reached for him and hung on while the thunder rolled away in echoes. "I hate that sound. I *hate* it," she whispered, her face pressed against his shoulder.

"It will pass. The rain will come and the thunder will stop," he reassured her, his arms lightly around her. "The heat makes it worse."

"God is displeased," Nicoris exclaimed.

"That seems unlikely, or we must suppose that God is displeased every summer," he told her gently. "The seasons have temperaments of their own, and I doubt that any god bothers with them very often."

"There is only one God," she said, pulling away from him, becoming more discomposed. "All others are false." She looked around as if she were afraid of being overheard.

"All worshippers say that, of all gods but their own."

Her eyes widened. "Think where you are, Dom," she admonished him. "To speak heresy, and with the thunder treading through the heavens . . ."

This time the lightning and the thunder came at once, leaving a sharp odor in the air, and more lamentations. Then the skies let loose their bounty, not as rain but as hail. It rattled on the roof and walls of the old chapel, it ricocheted off the ground and buzzed on the roofs of all the buildings of the monastery; screeching and howls were quickly drowned out by the steady seething of the hail.

Nicoris yelped and flung herself once again into the haven of Sanctu-Germainios' arms. "Lord of the Heavens, have mercy on me." In a kind of desperation, she kissed him, her mouth hard on his while the hail bounced and thrummed.

The kiss was a long one, imbued with as much terror as desire; Sanctu-Germainios could feel her need rising, and he felt memories stir, memories that were as unwelcome as they were intense, of long days and nights enclosed in darkness, a darkness that was only alleviated by the monthly offering of a victim to his hunger. Feeding on repulsion and terrified loathing, his loneliness had grown through the decades until all traces of sympathy had drained out of him and he dreaded the burden of companionship even more than he yearned for it. Her fear recalled those years to him, and the wretched desolation that had overcome him; the memory sickened him and he strove to break their embrace without giving her more distress. Finally he ended the poignant, appalling kiss, stroking her hair as he moved a step back from her. "Not this way, Nicoris. Please. Not this way."

She stared at him wildly, her face working. "I'm so scared," she hissed. "The storm is—"

"I know," he said.

Thunder banged like a closing door, and the hail got louder, and then rapidly slacked off to a murmur.

She shrieked and covered her ears. "Make it stop!"

"You know no one can do that," he said. "If it were possible, I would."

"It is God's footsteps. He reminds us that He knows everything." She made the sign of the fish. "He tells us of our sins."

"Lightning ignites the air, and the thunder is the sound of it." He had heard that theory seven centuries before, and over time he had come to believe it was the most accurate of all the hypotheses regarding lightning that he had encountered.

Nicoris shook her head. "God knows all; He warns us of His displeasure at our sins. The monks say so. The monks listen, and they hear the warning God sends, and they bow to His Will." She bit her lower lip. "Sometimes I think they know when I lie; God whispers to them, and they heed Him. *You* know when I do; I can feel it," she said, slowly pacing toward the main door, not looking back at him. "You say it doesn't matter, that you accept it as part of me, but it does; it matters."

"Then why do you lie?" he asked, wondering if she would finally tell him the truth, whatever that truth might be.

"Because they'd kill me if they knew." She turned and came back toward him, her gaze fixed on the floor. "You might not, but . . ."

"I will not kill you if you tell me the truth: my Word on it." He regarded her steadily, adding, "And I will keep your secret."

She shook her head. "No. No, you won't."

"I will."

"I can't." She looked at him for a searing instant, then turned away.

He went to her but did not touch her. "Shall I tell you what I think your secret is? Would that make it easier for you?"

Although she nodded, she said, "No. You can't know. You'd despise me if you knew. You'd betray me."

"I would not," he said, his voice low and solacing; as he spoke, he sensed his protests were fruitless.

A distant mumble of thunder marked the end of the hail and the start of the rain.

"Is it over?" she whispered.

"The rain should go on for some time," he said, and lightly brushed her upper arm with his fingers.

She flinched as if she had been scalded. "Don't! Don't treat me well when you know I'm not worthy of it. If I told you—" Then she studied his face, her curiosity mixed with contempt. "Why don't you force me to tell you? No one would blame you, not even I would."

"When has force ever gained truth?" he asked her, compassion in his dark eyes. "You would tell me what I want to hear, not the truth." He had a brief, troubling memory of Srau. An ineluctable sadness came over him, and he regarded Nicoris heedfully. "When you decide to tell me, I will be honored to listen." He could not tell her that he knew because he had tasted her blood, knowing how much such a revelation would distress her.

"Why? Because you take your pleasure with me?"

"No: because I love you, and the pleasure I receive is yours to give." His compelling gaze rested upon her.

"You love what I provide you," she countered, unnerved by his serene demeanor.

"Yes: because it is the essence of you."

She began to weep, making almost no sound, her hands shading her eyes as if to block the sight of her tears from him.

"Nicoris—"

"Promise me," she said as she cut him off. "Promise me you won't tell anyone about this."

"That you have a secret? I will not."

She whispered, "I wish I could believe you."

He held out his hands to her. "So do I." He waited, and when she remained still, he added, "You know my secret, and you have kept it."

Slowly she put her hands into his. "Dom, why do you endure my insults?"

"Because I hope to keep your good opinion," he said, and realized Nicoris would be puzzled by this explanation, and so added, "To retain your respect."

"You can command my respect," she said.

"If I must command it, it is not respect but concession." He slowly enfolded her in his arms, remaining silent while she cried.

When her tears had given way to sniffs and hiccups, she finally looked up at him. "I wish we could leave this place."

"So do I," he said. "But until we know that we may travel without risk of being attacked, it is safer to remain behind the double walls here."

She sighed. "Do you think you could go with the soldiers? If Neves and his company left, couldn't we go with them? Wouldn't we be safe?"

"Possibly," said Sanctu-Germainios, cradling her close to him. "But they will not be departing until the crops are in, at the earliest." And when, he added to himself, the risk of raids would be at its height.

Nicoris thought about this for a brief time. "All right," she said, "but must we stay here for another winter?"

"I . . . ," He faltered. "I hope it will not be necessary."

The wind was picking up and the rain swept the mountains in angled waves; inside the old chapel it sounded as if the storm were breathing.

"It *is* God, making His Presence known." She twisted in his arms, listening to the susurrus of the rain. "The monks are right about that."

"It is the nature of wind and rain," he said.

"How can you be sure?" She shivered from fright.

Instead of renewing the debate, he kissed her forehead. "It will pass, Nicoris, and if it rains long enough, the fire to the east will be put out. If the wind lessens, we will have a fine day tomorrow."

She relaxed a little, her body no longer bow-string taut. "It would be a fine thing to have the fire die."

"The wind has shifted to the north, which will also serve us well." He turned her face to his. "Let me give you a tincture to help you to rest. By the time you waken, the storm should have lessened and we will have time together."

"Will I have dreams?" Her apprehension was less apparent than it had been while the thunder was beating the mountains, but it had not faded entirely.

"You may," he said gently.

"Can you make sure I won't dream?" she pleaded.

He considered. "I can make it so you probably will not dream."

She thought about this, then she nodded. "All right. I will take your potion." She moved out of his arms. "And tonight I'll welcome you to my bed."

"If that is what you want," he said.

"It is. It will be," she said with conviction.

He started toward the red-lacquer chest. "Then it is what you shall have," he said.

As she watched him, she said suddenly, "You could give me poison, couldn't you?"

"I could, but I will not," he said, turning toward her.

"How can I be sure?" She trembled, but held his eyes with her own.

Certain now that she felt threatened by more than the thunder and lightning, he opened the chest and took out a chalcedony cup, his curiosity about her apprehension quelled for the moment. Selecting his ingredients, he said, lightly and painfully, "I suppose you will have to trust me."

Text of a letter from Verus Flautens, Praetor-General of Drobetae in the former Province of Dacia, to Gnaccus Tortulla, Praetor Custodis of Viminacium in the Province of Moesia, written in Greek code on sanded linen and carried by Flautens' personal courier and delivered twenty-two days after it was written.

To the most esteemed Praetor Custodis of Viminacium in the Province of Moesia, the Praetor-General of Drobetae in the former Province of Dacia, on this, the last day of July in the Christian year 439, Ave!

My colleague and friend, I fear I must once again beseech you to send us troops to guard and to provide escort for the many refugees who are flooding into Drobetae from the north. We have no place to shelter them, and still they continue to come. We have had to house them in all manner of places, from the halls of the basilica to the stables of the inns. There are many among these refugees in need of more care than we can provide, and I despair of their safety if at any time the town should be attacked.

Our supplies of food are also growing crucially low, and with the Huns raiding through the mountains, no one can tell what crops they may actually be able to reap, so it is essential that we have food brought to us, or that places south of the Danuvius agree to take in as many of these refugees as they can. Otherwise we may be facing starvation among many of those who have come to us for safety.

Some several days ago, a Hunnic scout was taken by one of my mounted patrols. He was brought to Drobetae to be questioned, but killed himself before anyone could question him. I find it worrying that he was only four leagues from the town when he was captured, and I have doubled my patrols to search out any others that may be lurking in the hills.

Patras Fortunatos has warned that the churches can no longer provide the charity they are commanded to do, and will have to close their doors to those seeking the succor of the churches. Other priests have said much the same, although a number of mendicant monks have offered to seek out the sick and do what they can for them.

That is another concern I have: that in such close conditions, fever could arise suddenly and spread before we would be able to isolate those who bear the disease, thus making it certain that more of the people in the town, as well as the refugees, would take illness. I have no means of treating such an outbreak, but with the summer in full heat and the people worn and tired, I cannot believe that such a terrible outcome may be completely avoided.

Whatever you have that you may spare to help us would be appreciated beyond anything you can imagine. I pray you will do all that you can to relieve some part of the misery that has come to Drobetae.

Verus Flautens
Praetor-General of Drobetae
the former Province of Dacia

4

By the time Drinus made it down from his outpost at the narrow pass leading to Sanctu-Eustachios the Hermit, the three arrows in his shoulder and back had him reeling in the saddle from pain and loss of blood. He all but fell off his horse as he came through the gate, leaving a trail of blood to mark his progress; three monks and half a dozen mercenaries rushed forward to help him. Dazed as he was, he was able to say, "Huns. With scouts. I got two. Of them. But two more. Got away."

Oios, now recovered from his wounds of the previous attack, took the time to help Drinus to the ground and position him to lie on his side. "Someone! Fetch Sanctu-Germainios! Tell him to bring his medicaments! Perigrinos! Get Mangueinic! Monachos Benignos, summon Priam Corydon!" He bent over his comrade and said as calmly as he could, "Don't worry. The Dom will take care of you." The early afternoon was hot, the sky was clear, and most of the refugees were busy in the orchard, bringing in the first of the ripe fruit; women with baskets collected the peaches and plums and pears so that they could take them, remove their seeds, and set them out, halved, to dry. This violent intrusion brought many of them running from their tasks, while Rotlandus Bernardius' men rushed to their positions to man the inner walls, weapons in hand.

The flurry of activity rapidly became a maelstrom, monks rushing to discover what had happened, refugees attempting to find out when the Huns would arrive, soldiers hurrying to their stations on the walkways on the stockades, youngsters running for the fenced fields to drive the livestock into the barn, stable, and pens. Someone had begun to sound the alarm, the brazen echoes sounding over the valley in counterpoint to the murmured distraint of those gathered around the fallen look-out.

"Are we ready? to fight them?" one of the novices asked as he knelt beside Drinus. "How many are coming?"

Before Drinus could answer, Oios pulled the novice back. "Leave him alone! Get the Dom!"

The youth stumbled to his feet, then started running toward the old chapel, calling for Dom Sanctu-Germainios, his voice made strident by his fear.

"We have to tell the Priam," the nearest monk said in a manner that rebuked all those gathered around Drinus for not thinking of this first.

"I'll go," said Monachos Erigolos, who had once been a fowler and was now almost blind. He used his stick to find his way, moving as fast as he dared.

"Tell him it's urgent!" Oios shouted after him.

There were fragments of questions buzzing around Drinus, although no one was willing to raise his voice to ask Drinus anything more; the man had turned a pasty color, and his scars stood out, starkly white in his chalky face. Blood was slowly spreading around him, not so fast, Oios hoped, that it meant Drinus would surely die, but steadily. "Drinus!" He knelt down once more. "Drinus, listen! Help is coming!"

Drinus' eyelids fluttered and he gave Oios a muzzy stare. "What. Do you. Want?"

Oios bent down so that Drinus would hear him. "I want you to live, Drinus. Hang on!" He emphasized his words by taking the nearer of Drinus' hands. "Don't slip away on me. Stay here."

"What did he see?" one of the refugees shouted.

"Huns," Oios answered curtly, then once again gave his full attention to Drinus. "Hold on. Drinus. Drinus. Listen to me! Help is coming!" He felt the lethargy that was coming over Drinus in his fingers; he looked up, searching for a volunteer. "Someone fetch a blanket. He's getting cold." He waved his arm to emphasize the need for haste.

"I'll go," called out a woman's voice.

"Huns," Drinus muttered, struggling for breath. "Large. Numbers. Two. Three. Hundred."

"Where?" Oios demanded. "How far?"

"Half. A day. Or more. Not all. Pass." He looked into Oios' eyes. "More. Scouts. Need. To. To." Then there was a sound in his throat, he spasmed once, and his body went slack.

"Need to what?" Oios asked, aware that the question had come too late. He made the salute of Mithras and rocked back on his heels, letting Drinus' head drop from his hand. Those gathered around him made the sign of the cross, then the sign of the fish, and a few of them wept for the mercenary.

A short time later, Sanctu-Germainios pushed through the crowd, and stopped beside Oios. "I see I am too late."

"Unfortunately," said Oios, rising. "He must have lost more blood than I thought he had."

"He has lost a great deal of blood," said Sanctu-Germainios, who could sense his depletion, but added, "Look at the color of his face and you can tell."

"I should have brought him to you at once," said Oios, ashamed of himself.

"It would not have made any difference," Sanctu-Germainios said as he put his case of medicaments down and dropped onto one knee beside the body. "He did not have enough left in him to rally."

"Are you sure of that?" Oios asked.

"As sure as anyone could be." He moved Drinus' corpse enough to examine the arrows that stuck out from his shoulder and back. "They penetrated deeply, so they were probably loosed at close range. Perhaps they closed in on his position and all fired at once."

"Do you think he . . . he saw what he said he saw? that the Huns are coming at last?" Oios caught sight of Neves approaching from one side of the compound, and Priam Corydon coming from the opposite direction.

"I think he must have," said Sanctu-Germainios.

"Because he died?" Oios asked.

"Because the arrows in him are Hunnic. Because there is dust rising on the road to the east, a great deal of dust," said Sanctu-Germainios. "A large number of travelers are coming this way. We need only determine who they are." He had first observed the dust not long after sunrise, perhaps five or six leagues away, and had mentioned it to Priam Corydon when the Priam came from his private sunrise prayers.

"Do you know they're Huns?" Priam Corydon had inquired.

"No; I only know they are raising a long plume of dust," Sanctu-Germainios had told him.

"Then they could be more refugees," Priam Corydon had said.

"It is possible," Sanctu-Germainios had conceded, thinking it would be prudent to make ready for a real attack. "It is more likely that the Huns are moving this way." He could feel fear clutch those around him.

"I noticed the dust," Oios said, cutting into Sanctu-Germainios' reflection. "Tribune Bernardius said it was probably from refugees who had abandoned their town to the Huns. Huns, he thought, would be moving faster, and would raise less dust, their fighting forces traveling at speed. He is of the opinion that dust means wagons, not horsemen. He said that Priam Corydon would have to decide if they are going to be allowed in, the refugees. If they take the turn-off toward us, that is."

The two men said nothing for several heartbeats, then Sanctu-Germainios asked, "What does Antoninu Neves say?"

The mercenary leader coughed delicately. "I think we had best prepare for the worst. I'll post my men on the slope above the pass, not only to keep watch, but to roll the rocks down to block it if we must."

Priam Corydon stared at him, his expression aghast. "What do you mean, roll the rocks down?"

"I mean my men have set up barriers for falls of stones. All they need do is release the braces, and heavy rocks will descend on anyone foolish enough to try to come through the pass." Neves smiled, satisfied. "Bernardius' men helped us with building the barriers and gathering the rocks."

"But that would block us in," exclaimed one of the refugees.

"Only on the main road. There are still three other tracks that lead away from here, and, if it comes to that, we can evacuate using those paths," Neves declared.

"Hunters' tracks," scoffed another of the refugees.

"Which the Huns could use," Oios cautioned.

Before Neves could counter this remark, Priam Corydon said, "There isn't room enough in the mortuary just now to lay him out." He pointed to Drinus. "I will assign some monks to preparing a place for him, and readying his shroud." Stepping back, he addressed Neves, his whole demeanor condemning. "They say one of your men made the sign of Mithras over him."

Neves shrugged, unimpressed by the Priam's disapproval. "You know the aphorism: Mithras in war, Jesus in peace."

"Some of the monks will not want to let him lie in consecrated ground if he is a follower of Mithras." Priam Corydon was already striding back toward the monastery, Neves pursuing him.

"However you decide, neither my men nor I will protest it," Neves assured him. "If you want him buried beyond the outer walls, we'll attend to it."

More of the crowd around Drinus moved away, leaving Oios and Drinus at the center of a widening circle; Oios took a step toward Sanctu-Germainios. "What are we to do with him? We can't leave him here."

"Bernardius may have a place for him," Sanctu-Germainios suggested. "He may be willing to let you leave him where he puts his own dead to await burial."

"I should find out," Oios answered, but stayed where he was, reluctant to leave his fallen comrade. He squatted once more and began to break off the shafts of the arrows so that Drinus could lie nearly flat, then rose, wiping his hands on the hem of his heavy cotton pallium. "There. That's better."

The crowd was thinning now that Drinus was dead. As the refugees began to drift back to their interrupted labors, the woman who had gone to get a blanket came through the diminishing crush, a rough woolen blanket over her arm. "Here," she said, holding it out and casting a careful eye on Drinus as she made the sign of the fish. "It should be long enough to cover all of him."

"We don't need—" Oios began.

Sanctu-Germainios took it from her. "Thank you, Brynhald." He unfolded the blanket and placed it over the corpse. "I will see this is returned to you."

"No. No, don't bother," she said promptly. "Keep it for others who may also . . ." She made a gesture to finish her thoughts as she started away.

"Where shall we take him for now?" Oios asked, looking directly at Sanctu-Germainios.

"Priam Corydon will tell us where he is to lie when he and Neves have agreed," Sanctu-Germainios said. "If you would rather not appeal to Tribune Bernardius, you might wish to move him out of the sun, at least; we can carry him to the old chapel."

Oios nodded, and bent to lift Drinus' shoulders. "Take his feet, Dom. It isn't fitting for him to lie in the dust."

Sanctu-Germainios did as he was asked, lifting the fallen man carefully so that he would not appear to be as strong as he was. He felt the remaining people part behind him as he backed toward the old chapel, moving deliberately slowly for Oios' sake; it would have been no difficulty for Sanctu-Germainios to carry Drinus' body himself, but that would cause unwanted scrutiny for him, so he continued to back up cautiously. Once in the old chapel, the two men laid the body out on a pallet, and adjusted the blanket over him.

"I wish it weren't so hot. Where bodies are concerned, the heat benefits no one."

"Truly," said Sanctu-Germainios.

"It is unfortunate that Patras Anso is taken with fever just now: we may have need of him." Oios looked down at Drinus' shrouded corpse. "I best go inform Neves of what we have done." He stared at Sanctu-Germainios. "Thank you, Dom. This was a kindness."

"Hardly a kindness: a practical necessity," said Sanctu-Germainios with a spark in his dark eyes. "If the monastery must be defended, then it is just as well to keep as many bodies out of sight as possible."

Oios blinked. "I suppose that's true," he said, making for the main door. "Do you think the Huns know about the rock-falls?"

"They may; it depends on how much their spy knows, and what the spy has been able to tell them." He spoke without inflection as if to lessen the significance of what he said.

"Then I suppose we should assume they do," said Oios unhappily, shoving open one side of the main door.

"Let me know what the Priam decides," Sanctu-Germainios called after Oios as he stepped back into the sunlight.

It was sometime later that Nicoris returned from the women's dormitory, her manner flustered and her face pale. "They say the Huns are coming again," she stated by way of greeting him. "This waiting is almost as bad as another attack."

"They also say that there are rock-falls ready to be released upon them," said Sanctu-Germainios, interrupting the laying out of his medicaments and supplies. "As soon as the sentries see them coming near, they'll signal the soldiers and mercenaries to don their armor and man their posts." Privately he doubted this strategy would be useful, for once the rocks were set to falling, the pass would confine the residents of the monastery as surely as an iron prison door would do; the hunters' tracks were steep and difficult to traverse, and their destinations uncertain.

"Must it come to that?" She made the sign of the fish.

"I hope not, but it may. I think Neves will have posted his sentries back to the peaks by now, to prepare for battle, and to make a count of their numbers." He saw her agitation. "Are you frightened?"

"Of *course* I'm frightened: aren't you?" She flung the words at him as if they were weapons.

"I am worried," he said.

"Just worried," she said with an attempt at sarcasm.

"If the Huns are truly coming, I will have more than enough opportunity to be frightened later; I have no reason to anticipate their arrival with fear—not yet." He turned toward her, and saw her shaking. "What is it, Nicoris?" When she looked away, he said, "Another secret, or the same one?"

She swung back toward him. "I can't tell you."

He said nothing, remaining still.

"Especially not now," she added. Making an effort, she steeled herself. "Tell me what you want me to do to get ready for the attack; you will want to have all prepared in case the Huns do come."

Sanctu-Germainios wished she would accept comfort from him, that she would be willing to allow him to ease the dread that transfixed her, but he realized that it would be folly to add to her dejection with what she would perceive as trespass. "I want you to prepare a dozen pallets for the wounded," he said, resigned to her obduracy. "Then bring in five buckets of water, and set the cauldron to boil with bitter herbs so my surgical tools will be—"

"I know what to do; more Roman medical nonsense," she exclaimed brusquely. "Need I do anything more?"

"Not just at present," he said. "If you would feel safer, I have a leather tunica with brass scales on it that you can wear during any attack. It is in my second clothes' chest, at the bottom."

"Don't you want to wear it?"

"It does not fit me. Nor would it fit most grown men." It had belonged to the son of the leader of the caravan who had guided him and Rugierus back from Herat to Sinope, twenty years before; his father had presented it to Sanctu-Germainios for saving the youngster's life.

"Then why do you have it if you can't use it?"

"It was payment for services provided." And, he added to himself, he had not, until now, found anyone sufficiently slight to wear it.

"All right," she said. "When the order to arm comes, I'll put it on." Her face was unreadable and her demeanor gave nothing away. "I can help you bring the wounded to be treated if I have it on."

"Good," he said.

"What kind of armor are you going to wear?"

It took him a short while to frame his answer; he busied himself measuring out portions of syrup of poppies into small cups, rationing out the little he had left; much as he would have rather not, he decided to hold his Egyptian remedy in reserve. "I have a lorica, and a helmet. They're both old-fashioned, but they guard my spine." He had received them from Gaius Julius Caesar himself, during his time in Gaul.

"Good," she approved with more emotion than either of them expected.

He removed a very old jar from a recess within his red-lacquer chest. "If we run out of syrup of poppies, we will have to use this." He held up the jar; the lid was marked with hieroglyphics. "It is very powerful, more than syrup of poppies, and therefore harder to gauge its dosage. It brings on euphoria, but it can easily be deadly."

"What is it?" she asked, coming toward him to look at the alabaster jar he held.

"It is made from the blue lotus and another water-plant. If you rub this on a burn or torn skin, the pain will stop at once, but you must be careful with the amount, not only for the person with the injury, but for yourself, as well. I would prefer you not handle it except in a dire emergency, and then if you do use it, to wash your hands at once when you have medicated the injury. Do not keep the water you use for your hands."

Nicoris studied the jar, permitting herself to stand next to him. "How much before it is deadly?"

"An amount of the substance in this jar that is half the size of a walnut will kill a large man." He saw her blanch. "I will make a dilution of it, to lessen its dangers."

"I won't touch it unless you order me to," she said, her pale eyes shining.

"That may be best," he said, resisting the impulse to touch her. "I'll fetch the armor for you, shall I?"

"If you would." She faltered. "And set out your own."

"As you wish," he said, and went to his clothes' chest first, troubled by the way they were speaking to each other, as if they were little more than strangers. What was it about their intimacy that terrified her so that she was more willing to face Huns in battle than to seek out his embraces? The fervor she had shown in the past had not faded, but her dread of what—exposure? censure? condemnation?—had overcome her desire, and now left her filled with panic. "I hope," he said as he resumed his task, "that you may decide to trust me."

"I wish I could," she said, and deliberately turned away from him.

"And I," he said, but made no push to compel her to explain beyond what she had said already.

They worked until the last quarter of the afternoon in almost complete silence. Nicoris set up the pallets and prepared doses of standard medicaments, taking care not to draw Sanctu-Germainios in for discussion of any kind. When she was finished with the basic tasks, she said, "I am going to get my supper."

"Very good. The sun will drop behind the peaks in a little while, and we must be ready for the Huns to arrive with the darkness."

"Are you so sure of that? That they will come with the night?" she challenged, but did not bother to wait for an answer. She pulled a trabea around her, for although the night was warm, there was a cool breeze coming down from the high peaks, and it made the evening seem chillier than it was.

"For settings of this sort, yes, I am," he said, his tone and manner level. "Shadows and dusk will make it difficult to judge their numbers, and their positions."

"Surely the rocks will stop them," she said.

"Perhaps." He watched her leave, once again hoping she would not hold herself apart from him, and from all the rest of the people inside the walls of Sanctu-Eustachios the Hermit. With this distressing rumination for company, he set about preparing the dilution of the Egyptian remedy, taking care not to breathe while he stirred the ointment into a mixture of springwater and berry wine.

Nicoris returned as the monks began their Angelus service, saying as she came into the old chapel, "The sentries say that riders have taken the turn-off leading here."

"How long ago did they say that?" Sanctu-Germainios asked, wondering why the alarm had not been sounded.

"Not long. I was finishing my meal when one of them came into the refectory. As I came here, I saw Niklos go to tend to the horses; he looked troubled." She moved nervously but without the signs of consternation that had marked her behavior earlier. "The Watchmen and Bernardius' soldiers are being called to their stations, as Neves' mercenaries will shortly be. They expect the fighting to begin before nightfall. Where is that scale armor you said you had?"

"I will get it for you," he said, leaving his array of medicaments and instruments where he had set them out. He put some of his garments aside and removed the tunica, holding it out to Nicoris. "Here. Would you like me to help you don it? There are buckles at the shoulders."

She gave an abrupt shrug. "You'll want to buckle on your lorica." She glanced toward Drinus' covered body. "No one's come for him, I see."

"They're preoccupied with the living," said Sanctu-Germainios, watching Nicoris wrestle herself into the softly jingling tunica.

While she struggled with the buckles, he removed the segmented lorica from his first clothes' chest and reached for the short, padded tunica that was worn under the lorica to prevent its metal bands from chaffing. "In a little while, I will seek out Mangueinic and inform him of where he should have the wounded brought."

"Don't you think he knows?" Her incredulity was caustic. "He's no—"

She was interrupted by the brazen clamor from the alarm, followed by sudden shouts and the sound of many people running; the chanting from the monks' church stopped abruptly.

"I will not be long," Sanctu-Germainios said, striding toward the side-door. He emerged from the old chapel into a sea of activity: men hurried toward their places on and between the walls, the older children secured the livestock, women gathered the youngsters and herded them into the dormitories, monks worked the buckets over the three wells, filling buckets and small barrels with water, novices laid four large fires and bound pitch-soaked rags to staves for torches, and the few old refugees began soaking hides to put on the roofs in case of fire. Working his way through the commotion, until he reached the gate-tower, he found the leader of the Watchmen securing torches in their sconces, and checking the supplies of arrows and spears.

"What do you want?" he asked, beset with too many tasks and not enough time.

"We are ready for any injured. Use the novices to carry them to us." Sanctu-Germainios paused. "Are there sentries on the hunters' tracks as well as the road through the pass?"

"That's Bernardius' job," Mangueinic snapped. "Neves' men have the peaks and the main road, Bernardius the lesser routes. For the next ten days, those leaving here will have to consult Tribune Bernardius, not Neves." He motioned to one of his Watchmen, saying, "Take two torches and affix them to the outer wall at the battlements."

The Watchman nodded and grabbed two of the torches.

"Men coming through the pass!" the gate-sentry bawled out, his cry passed along the ramparts to alert all those making ready for battle.

A loud crash of falling stones announced the release of the rock-falls, with shouts and screams almost lost in the noise.

"That'll give them something to think about," said Mangueinic in great satisfaction. "Wruntha! What do you see?"

From his position on the roof of the gate-tower, Wruntha shouted, "There are horsemen coming! Some got through the pass. Not too many! Probably thirty or so, no more!!"

"Thirty!" Mangueinic crowed, all but dancing on his single leg. "They'll need time to clear away the rubble and renew their attack, if they come that way for their next assault. In the meantime, we'll post archers to the peaks above them. Reduce their numbers before they reach the pass." He laughed. "You see, Dom? Even so small a place as Sanctu-Eustachios the Hermit can keep the Huns at bay with a little planning."

"I hope you are right," said Sanctu-Germainios.

"We'll keep the torches lit through the night, and by dawn, we'll be able to keep the upper hand."

Then the alarm clanged again, and shouts from the other end of the compound erupted. *"Huns! On the hunters' tracks!"*

Everyone in the gate-tower went quiet as the full importance of the cries was borne in upon them.

"A *diversion!*" Mangueinic spat as if it were a curse. "The pass was a diversion! They're coming in from the hunters' trails!" He looked around and began shouting orders to shift his men to the other end of the inner wall, to carry torches, to join with Bernardius' soldiers in manning the far end of the wall to augment what Neves' mercenaries were just now massing to face.

Sanctu-Germainios descended the steep flight of stairs all but unnoticed, and ran with uncanny speed for the old chapel, thinking as he went that the Huns' spy was earning his reward this night.

Text of a report from the spy at Sanctu-Eustachios the Hermit, calling himself Romulius, to the commander of the Huns in the immediate region, written in Latin and Greek with fixed ink on vellum, carried by Hredus three days after the battle and delivered two days later.

To the courageous leader of the Huns in the western region of the former Roman Province of Dacia, Ave, on this, the second day of August in the Year of the City 1192.

As your soldiers have told you by now, I have fulfilled my end of our bargain in keeping the resistance from the defenders of this place to a minimum. As I pledged, I have stopped many of the refugees from leaving, and I have taken several opportunities to lessen the number of Watchmen standing duty. When you last assailed the monastery the soldiers on duty were short of weapons, which I arranged. That your men were eventually driven off was no fault of mine: your soldiers were able to seize ten goats and six foals, with a force of just over one hundred twenty men; by attacking from two directions your men were able to create confusion, and I was able to slow the response from the soldiers manning the walls without appearing to be doing anything detrimental to the residents here.

Your losses were minimal, under the circumstances—again, in good part through my apparent inept attempts at defensive deployment of those under my command—only thirty-one men and seventeen horses. We, on the other hand, lost ninety-four men, have another one hundred forty-four with injuries, and our supply of weapons is seriously depleted.

The man who carries this is applying to join your ranks, as I will do when my task here is completed. He is able to read and write in several tongues, and although his skills are not advanced, I am certain he may be most useful, discreet, and reliable. He will read this to you if you cannot. His name is Hredus, and he is a freedman from Drobetae where he served the current Praetor-General, Verus Flautens, before being sent here to observe and report on the state of this place. His knowledge will be most useful to you.

If you will wait a month and attack again in stronger force, I am certain you will conquer this monastery and be able to lay claim to its crops, livestock, supplies, and wealth. You may be sure I will do my part to bring that triumph about, as a further demonstration of my loyalty and gratitude to you and your King, Attila. You need not worry that I will renew my allegiance to the Roman Empire, either in the East or the West, for I did my utmost to serve it for most of my life, and was rewarded with steadily rising taxes, diminishing support, onerous responsibilities, and a general abandonment of my town and my people, hardly honorable recompense for my service. Your assurance of advancement and respect is worthy of my pledge of service as well as my help in any manner that will suit your cause.

Should circumstances here change in any way that bears on your ambitions, I will find another messenger to carry word to you; there are men among the refugees who would be eager to join with you, but are afraid to let such sentiments be known. I will not prove lacking in attention to your efforts so long as you will be guided by me and not press for an advantage until the monastery is more truly weakened. Already refugees are planning to leave in groups of ten to sixty; three or four such departures and you will not need to risk more than a hundred men, if that, to secure this place with a minimal chance of losses either of men or horses.

May your gods smile upon your endeavors and upon your people,

Romulius

5

"The men won't go into the woods to cut more trees," said Mangueinic, his frustration revealed in every line of his body. "They say it isn't safe. And they're right—it isn't." He looked around at the faces gathered in the small warehouse that stood between the monks' church and the largest of the travelers' dormitories. Half of the building was taken up with the stacked crates and chests of the refugees' belongings; the rest had been pressed into service as a council chamber. "Five have been wounded since the Huns' last attack, and one is dead from it. And someone loosed an arrow at them as they came in from felling today."

"But we must have logs to repair the outer stockade; two of the main supports are weakened from the fires the Huns started with their flaming arrows. We have to replace them, and the braces behind them," Neves protested, looking around at the others, leaning forward, elbows on knees, seeking their support. "Don't they understand how important it is that the walls be repaired and made stronger? We need logs to do that. It isn't safe to stand on the battlements without reinforcing the braces, not if we have to increase the number of men fighting from there."

Mangueinic looked ashamed. "The Watchmen say that since the outer wall is manned by your mercenaries, they should be the ones to cut the trees for its repair. I tried to convince them that the walls protect us all, but none of my Watchmen would listen." He turned to Priam Corydon. "I've tried to persuade them to reconsider, but they're too frightened. They know the Huns have scouts in the region, and that they have orders to fire on anyone from the monastery they see."

"They leave the hermits in the caves alone," said Denhirac, Denerac's son, who had taken over his father's position since his father and a company of men and women from Tsapousso had left Sanctu-Eustachios the Hermit for the plains to the west, and the old Roman city of Aquincum in the Province of Pannonia Inferior. He wore his responsibilities awkwardly and often said he would have preferred to go with his father and the twenty-one others; now only thirteen remained.

"The hermits have nothing the Huns want," said Bernardius. "They are safe where they are."

"Not that Monachos Anatolios would allow them to fight; it would be contrary to God's Will," said Neves, making no effort to hide his contempt.

"Would that still be true if the Huns take this monastery?" Mangueinic asked.

"Would it matter? We'd all be dead," said Neves.

"We're getting off the point," Priam Corydon said patiently. "Our present predicament is to deal with the need for trees to be felled and brought back here to make the needed repairs to the outer stockade, and we must bury the last of the dead. What the Huns may do is up to them, and nothing we do can change that."

"What about Patras Anso?" Mangueinic turned his eyes on Priam Corydon.

"Patras Anso may lie with the monks of this monastery," Priam Corydon said.

"That's all well and good," said Bernardius. "But we must do what we may, and trust to God to keep us from ruination."

Priam Corydon made the sign of the cross and motioned to Monachos Niccolae of Sinu. "We ought to prepare another dispatch for Verus Flautens, explaining the urgency of our plight. As Praetor-General, he is obligated to provide us what protection he can."

"Do you think he's in a position to send soldiers? Assuming he has any to spare?" Bernardius interjected.

"He hasn't sent any recently," said Neves.

"Is that man from Drobetae—Hredus, I believe he is called—still missing?" Bernardius asked.

"I believe so: why?" Mangueinic frowned.

"It is just that if Priam Corydon is preparing a report, Hredus would be the most useful courier." He clicked his tongue. "Well, if he is missing, we must find someone else."

"True," said Priam Corydon. "Monachos Niccolae, make a full catalog of our lacks; have it ready by sunrise tomorrow." He considered the others. "One of you might provide a courier for us."

"What about the bondsman who is caring for the horses? Niklos Aulirios. The one the Dom's relative sent to him. Do you think Sanctu-Germainios could spare him?" Neves asked. "We have men enough to care for the horses without him."

"We can ask," said Bernardius doubtfully.

Priam Corydon sighed. "There must be someone who will

take our report to Drobetae." He motioned to Monachos Niccolae. "Be sure you include the need for more messengers as well as
soldiers."

"Yes, Priam; I will," said Monachos Niccolae, his short-sighted
eyes straining to make out the faces of the others.

"That is all to the good, but it doesn't resolve the need for more
logs, and a more fortified wall," said Neves. "They're our most immediate problems."

"Tomorrow morning, some of our men must go into the forest,"
said Mangueinic emphatically. "They will have to be in the company
of guards, which I will order my Watchmen to be."

Bernardius hesitated, then said, "Of my soldiers I think I can
convince a dozen to log for the benefit of the monastery. Most of
the refugees from Ulpia Traiana know what happens when the defenses fail, for they saw it happen. They, like the rest of you, want
the inner wall reinforced, and that will not happen until the outer
wall is fortified. They will understand the advantage of helping the
wood-cutters."

"Do you think they will actually do it?" Neves asked, surprised
at this offer.

"I think they will, if I provide sufficient incentive," Bernardius
said, making the gesture for bargaining.

"And what incentive would that be?" Denhirac asked, his manner tentative although his words carried conviction. "I have six men
who could log, and they might agree to help Bernardius' soldiers if
there were reward enough for their labors."

"Something can surely be arranged," said Neves.

"If you pay them to go into the forest, then the harvesters
will ask for the same when they bring in the crops," warned
Mangueinic.

"There are many kinds of pay," said Denhirac. "Money isn't much
use here, but there are things that can be exchanged for labor."

"What did you have in mind?" asked Mangueinic.

"First chance at the beer and the cooked food, or a wheel of cheese," said Denhirac at once. "A chance to select some of the yearling sheep and goats."

"Or the right to hunt ducks on the lake," suggested Mangueinic.

"That would deplete our flocks," Priam Corydon warned. "You may plan to move on, but I and my monks expect to remain here; we cannot give away all our food."

"You will have many fewer mouths to feed once the refugees are gone. A great many of us plan to leave as soon as the whole harvest is in, and that should be two months at most," Denhirac pointed out. "You can spare a lamb or two, or a few ducks. You may be sure the Huns will take much more than any refugee would."

Bernardius held up his hands, struggling to smile genially. "No more, I ask you. We need no more devisiveness. All of us must be prepared to bend a little to guarantee our safety. We understand what you, Denhirac, have explained, and all of us second your sapience; we know that you, Priam Corydon, wish to protect your own people. Volemus. Both of you have valid points to make, and we should consider everything as we determine how to proceed. But we have to decide, and quickly. The longer we delay, the more exposed we are."

Mangueinic thumped his crutch on the floor. "The Tribune makes sense," he said firmly. "It's something for all of you to keep in mind. The Huns will know what we do shortly, if they don't know already."

"They're worse than vermin, or shadows," said Bernardius, adding defiantly in his own version of Latin, "cavi ombram."

There was a brief silence, then Priam Corydon said, "For now, we will turn our attentions to tomorrow and whatever arrangements must be made to repair the walls. We will determine the recompense for the work now and let the men know before they go to have their supper."

"Then we'd best agree quickly. Food is being prepared right now, and there are two deer turning on spits outside." Neves rose and clapped his hands together. "Yearling goats and sheep would be an acceptable trade for a week's work, I believe. Hunting privileges will also be a reasonable exchange for labor; we all benefit when a deer or a boar is killed. What do the rest of you say?"

"I will ask my soldiers if they're willing to agree to any or all of these terms, and report their answer to you after supper is ended," Bernardius said. "Mangueinic, see if your Watchmen will concur."

"That I will, and make them answer for it if they cavil," said Mangueinic, his glance shifting to Priam Corydon. "Will your monks be willing to spare some of the livestock and ducks so that they may be safe?"

Priam Corydon turned to Monachos Niccolae. "What do you think? Will they consent?"

"If they understand the danger, I think they might; they know that prayers alone will not deter the Huns, and that soldiers do not fight for the Glory of God alone, to all our ignominy," said Monachos Niccolae. He looked down at the vellum spread on the writing board in his lap. "Shall I record the terms here, for the archives?"

"It would be prudent to write this down. It will help us avoid later disputes or misunderstandings," said Priam Corydon, trying to ignore the condemning glare of Denhirac, who associated writing with magic.

"Then I will," said Monachos Niccolae, reaching for a jar of fixed ink and thumbing the lid open.

"Do you want the courier to leave tomorrow at dawn?" Mangueinic asked Priam Corydon.

"Ideally, yes. We can decide which road or path to tell the courier to use later this evening. The sooner we send our dispatch, the sooner we may have an answer," said Priam Corydon.

"Even if that answer is no, as it is likely to be," remarked Bernardius, then lifted his head as if to defend himself. "What makes any of you think that Verus Flautens will send us soldiers? What if he hasn't any more to provide? Drobetae itself may have been attacked by Huns, and all the soldiers are needed to protect the town from another assault."

"Like us; we beg for more soldiers because we are losing ours too rapidly," said Neves. "I'll ask my men, and Bernardius can ask his, who among them is willing to carry the report to Drobetae. One of them must be willing to risk being chased by Huns." He snapped his fingers. "Oios knows the roads in this region. He may be willing to go. He's a brave enough fellow." He turned toward the door. "When the payment agreement is ready, I'll put my name to it."

"Thank you," said Priam Corydon, making the sign of the cross in his direction, and then the sign of the fish.

"I'll sign it, as well," said Bernardius.

Mangueinic shifted uncomfortably on his crutch. "If there is reason for me to put my mark on it, I will."

"How will I know that you are going to abide by your agreement?" Denhirac asked testily.

"You know because I will swear by Christ the Savior to do so," said Priam Corydon, his countenance becoming severe. "I will bind the salvation of my soul to the terms of this agreement, if it will allay your reservations."

"Then I will speak to those few of my men who are still here; if any of them are willing to cut wood for a lamb, I'll let you know before we retire tonight. One way or another, the work will be done." He saluted the others with great formality and left the warehouse.

"That," said Mangueinic, "is an impatient man."

"Not without reason," Neves said. "We have work to do, comrades, and we had best be about it."

Priam Corydon made the sign of the cross. "Come, Monachos Niccolae." He rose from his bench, gesturing to his recorder. "You and I will have to explain our decisions to the rest of the monks and novices."

"Yes, Priam," said Monachos Niccolae as he gathered up his vellum, goose-quill pen, and jar of fixed ink and prepared to follow him.

Bernardius, Neves, and Mangueinic were left alone in the warehouse. The place was growing dark as the last of sunset faded from the sky, leaving the two clerestory windows aglowing deep-blue. The three took a little time to gather their thoughts, then Neves said, "At least work will continue on the walls."

"That's something," said Mangueinic.

"We can train some of the refugees to man the ballistas; that would be helpful just now," Neves went on.

"Not all the refugee men want to fight," said Bernardius, "but it's probably worth a try. I'll ask among my townsfolk."

"If we stay in here much longer, people will think we're plotting against the Priam and Denhirac," Bernardius remarked.

"True enough," Neves said, and started toward the door.

"Do we meet here later, or at the monastery?" Mangueinic asked, working his crutch to gain more speed.

"Probably at the monastery. I don't think the Priam will seek us out." Neves sounded annoyed, but he continued out into the deepening twilight, the increasing darkness banished by the large fire at the center of the compound where the carcasses of deer turned on spits and the smell of smoke, venison, wild garlic, and thyme filled the air.

"When do your men change their posts?" Bernardius asked. "Is it the same as most evenings, or have you assigned another hour?"

"It is the same as it has been," said Neves. "As I assume it is for your men."

"Most of them, yes, but not all." Bernardius cleared his throat and spat. "Our ranks have thinned, as have all ranks, and I am hard put to fill the posts on the battlements, so I have lengthened the watches stood to a half a day or half a night and staggered the times of service so they overlap, giving the appearance of more guards than we have. Or so I hope. Having more of the refugees to add to their numbers will embolden my soldiers."

"So that's what you've been doing—lengthening the watches your men stand," Neves exclaimed. "A good precaution. Astute of you."

"More necessity than cleverness, I fear," said Bernardius, opening the door for the three of them. "After supper, when we've spoken to our men, we should meet at the horse-trough, and decide how to deal with the messengers and the woodsmen. I hope we have some volunteers."

They stood together outside the door, looking serious. Neves finally broke their silence. "I trust we'll have good news by then."

"Truly," said Mangueinic, and would have said more but the loud, unmelodious clang of the alarm sounded.

"The outer walls are burning!" came the shout from the gate-tower.

"Huns!" Mangueinic started toward the center of the compound.

"No," Neves said, loudly enough to be heard. "No sentry or guard reported them approaching."

"There has been no lightning," Mangueinic said. "It has to be Huns."

"Then they killed the sentries and guards," growled Bernardius.

"All of them?" Neves asked, starting toward the lower gate that led to the fields and the outer wall where smoke was beginning to churn into the twilight sky. "And no one noticed?"

"It doesn't matter the cause: the fires must be put out," said Mangueinic, and started off as rapidly as he could go toward the inner gate, bellowing as he went, "Men of Apulum Inferior! To your posts! Bring water, and form a line to quench the flames!"

"But if there are Huns . . ." Bernardius began, then his words faded as the fire began to shine along the tops of the outer stockade. "We must be careful, in case this is another deceptive tactic."

"Then we must have the men take up their positions on the inner walls!" Neves shouted, running after Mangueinic. "We must put it out!"

Men came running from the center of the compound, their hands still shining with the grease of the basted deer they were dining upon. Some carried weapons, others held buckets of water, and still others had baskets of stones. Bernardius took up the task of directing them toward the outer walls or the battlements of the inner walls, all the while shouting encouragement and scrambled Latin phrases.

"What would you like me to do?" The voice came from a short distance behind Bernardius, and it shocked him to hear so reasonable a question. He swung around and looked into Niklos Aulirios' face.

"Are the horses safe?" Bernardius asked.

"For now. I put the grooms to wetting down the outside of the stable and the barn, though neither is very near the flames." Niklos paused. "I also ordered two of them into the roof, to stamp out sparks."

"A good idea," said Bernardius. "If you're willing, would you go around from the main gate to the fire and see if you can find anything that might reveal who did this?"

"You mean you want me to find out if the forest is full of Huns," said Niklos, faintly amused.

"Or brigands, or Gothic outlaws, or—well, who can say?" He coughed as the smoke thickened.

Niklos reverenced Bernardius as elegantly as a Byzantine courtier would have done. "I shall inform Dom Sanctu-Germainios of my mission, and will report to you as soon as I am finished with my inspection."

"If the fire enters the forest, things will go badly for us," Bernardius warned. "We must have trees to repair the walls—more so now than this morning."

"I'll observe as much as I can, and I'll tell you what I find, but you probably shouldn't hope for too much." He turned away and strode off to the old chapel, entering by the side-door and finding Sanctu-Germainios setting out medicaments. "I suppose you know?" he asked in Greek.

He sighed and spoke in the same tongue, "About the fire: how could I not? This will bring trouble."

"As if we didn't have any already," said Niklos. He studied Sanctu-Germainios narrowly. "Bernardius has asked me to go outside the outer walls to assess the damage."

"Because he can spare you, I suppose," said Sanctu-Germainios.

"I'm not one of his soldiers, or one of Neves' mercenaries, or one of the refugees, so I am more expendable than most." Niklos chuckled his exasperation. "I think I had better do it, don't you?"

"It would probably be advisable," said Sanctu-Germainios. "But be circumspect."

"I know: Olivia would kill me if I died again." Niklos ducked his head. "If I'm not back by midnight, look for what's left of me in the morning." He took a step back. "Where's your ice-eyed companion?"

"In the women's dormitory," said Sanctu-Germainios. "There has been an outbreak of fever there."

"The fire won't help that," said Niklos, and departed. He walked quickly to the horse-trough and drenched himself with water, then went to the main gate and slipped out through the warder's door to the outer wall of the monastery. Above him on the ramparts, a few of the guards still remained, but most had gone to fight the fire; Niklos kept in the shadow of the wall, not wanting to take an arrow in his flesh because a soldier thought he was an enemy.

The outer walls were more than half a league around, but Niklos covered the distance to the fire quickly. Nearing the shallow end of the lake, he saw the first of the flames gnawing away at the standing logs; the fire crackled and spat as it reached pockets of resin in the newly cut trunks. Niklos peered through the smoke, glad for once that ghouls did not have to breathe very often. The trees nearest the lake had been cut down during the most recent rebuilding of the fortifications, and most of the underbrush had been cleared away as well, so there were no signs of the fire spreading—at least not yet, he reminded himself. He approached as near to the burning stockade as he dared, noticing that the wind was blowing toward the buildings inside the walls rather than toward the forest. "That's something to be pleased about," he said aloud, and continued down toward the lake, wanting to wet himself down again before he continued his survey. Wading into the shallows, he crouched down and began lifting handfuls of water and pouring them over his head and shoulders. He rose slowly when he was soaked again, and looked around the edge of the lake, searching for any sign of men waiting for the breach in the wall to widen sufficiently for them to storm the defenses. He caught sight of what appeared to be a mound of rags at the edge of the lake, a dozen strides from where he stood. Frowning, he started toward the heap, and halted as he heard an agonized voice come from within the pile.

"God's Will. God's Will." The voice cracked, and the mass of rags lurched.

Niklos moved quickly, going to the fallen man, who lay supine, half in and half out of the water; Niklos was aware as he did that this could be a trap, that the man at the edge of the lake could be one of many others bent on catching him unaware. He felt for the dagger in his belt, prepared to use it. He reached the ragged figure and saw that his monkish garments were dreadfully burned, as were his hands and face. After he had taken a little time to look around, wishing as he did that he had a vampire's night-seeing eyes, he bent down next to the man. "You're badly hurt," he said, slowly and distinctly. "Do you understand me?"

"God's Will," the man whispered.

"Do you hear me?" Niklos persisted.

"I hear," the man answered. "The fire . . ."

"Yes, there is a fire."

"Is it still burning?"

"It is," Niklos answered, fearing the man's eyes had been damaged; his eyebrows were singed away and most of his face looked as if the skin had been melted.

"Is the wall destroyed?"

"It's . . . damaged," said Niklos.

"Oh," said the man, his tone remote.

Making up his mind, Niklos said to the man, "I'm going to pick you up and carry you into the monastery where your burns can be treated."

"No. *No!*" The man thrust out with his scorched hands; he writhed desperately as Niklos took hold of him.

"I promise you I will hurt you as little as possible," he said, and dragged the man upright as he wailed. In another abrupt motion, he slung the man up and over his shoulder, his arm holding him in place.

"No! God's Will! God's Will!"

Moving slowly so that he could maintain his hold on the squirming man, Niklos made his way back toward the main gate, trying not to listen to the howls the man made. Getting through the warder's door was difficult, but after two tries, he succeeded, emerging inside the walls to see that the flames were dying, and as much steam as smoke was rising from the outer wall. He started toward the old chapel, but slowed as Priam Corydon approached him with Mangueinic. "I saw no signs of Huns," he said as they came up to him.

"Then what's that?" Mangueinic asked, pointing to Niklos' miserable burden.

"I found him at the lake. He's badly burned."

"Let me look at him," said Priam Corydon.

"He's not a pleasant sight," Niklos warned as he lowered the man from his shoulder and helped him to stand upright.

Priam Corydon stared at the tarnished silver crucifix hanging from a braided leather thong around the man's neck; he made the sign of the fish. "Monachos Anatolios," he mumbled as if his lips had lost all feeling.

"Priam Corydon?" the man asked, cocking his head to hear.

"What have you done, Monachos Anatolios?" Priam Corydon asked, horrified. He studied the ruined face for some vestige of expression and found none.

"God's Will. Since you wouldn't do it, I have," he said, standing more erect as he spoke.

"You've killed us all," Mangueinic accused.

"God's Will," Monachos Anatolios said with apparent satisfaction, then fainted, falling to the ground before Niklos or Priam Corydon could reach him.

Text of a letter from Rugierus in Aquileia to Artemidorus Iocopolis in Constantinople, written in Greek on sanded linen with fixed ink and carried by the same ship that brought Rugierus to Aquileia, the

Celestial Crown, and delivered thirty-one days after the letter was written.

To the most worthy factor Artemidorus Iocopolis of Eclipse Trading Company at Constantinople, the greetings and thanks of the bondsman Rugierus of Gades on this, the 27th day of July, in the Christian year 439.

My esteemed Factor Iocopolis,

This is to inform you that I have arrived safely in Aquileia and am now staying at the estate of a blood relative of Sanctu-Germainios just outside the city. I am arranging for Captain Kakaios to carry not only this letter to you, but the sum of one hundred gold Angels as a sign of my gratitude, and to recompense you for all the expenses you incurred in your superlative efforts to gain my release. Without your continued endeavors, I might have languished in captivity for years. If I am ever in a position to extend myself on your behalf, you have only to inform me and I will do my utmost to return to you the exertions you performed for me.

In a month I plan to leave for the former Province of Dacia in the hope of rejoining my master, at which time I will inform him of all you did on my behalf. No doubt he, too, will want to offer some token of his appreciation. I have heard, as everyone has, of the ravages of the Huns, and so I believe I may not locate Dom Sanctu-Germainios readily. My one consolation is that Bondama Clemens has sent her most trusted servant to find Sanctu-Germainios and provide him with his assistance, whatever he may require. That is as much comfort as I can hope for at this time.

At Cnossus we learned of a fever spreading from Egypt, one that is marked by lethargy, great thirst, and general pain. Alexandria has already instituted measures against the fever by limiting public gatherings to religious services and confining all travelers to the foreign quarter of the city. I advise you to be on guard against this fever, and to warn the captains and crews of all Eclipse Trading Company ships about the disease, for it is said that half of those who contract it are invalided by it, or killed. If you suspect any ship *of carrying this fever, do not allow its crew ashore, and send a physician to treat those who suffer. I would also take care in sending ships to Egyptian ports, for fear of contracting the fever, and to report any information on the fever's spread. I know my master would issue such orders, so I give them in his name, certain that you will abide by them, for prudence if for no other reason.*

I am deeply obliged to you, good Factor,

> *Rugierus of Gades*
> *bondsman to Dom Sanctu-Germainios*

6

"The repairs to the outer walls are insufficient," said Bernardius, wiping his brow with the cuff of his pallium and looking out over the anxious faces in front of him. "And we haven't men enough to do what's needed to keep us safe *and* bring in the harvest; even if we abandoned all repairs, we'd have to employ the women and monks in the fields. Our numbers are too much reduced to do both. With the outer walls breached, and so few men to defend us, it would make taking this monastery easy for the Huns; they could slaughter us all." He studied the gathering of men crammed together in the available space in the warehouse, hoping they grasped the increased peril they all faced. "I see no other course: we have to evacuate."

This was met with shouts of agreement and dissension, the noise rising until Neves shoved himself to the front of the gathering and bellowed for quiet. When the level of sound had decreased, he said, "Then I agree: we must evacuate, and quickly."

"If the Huns see more of us leaving, won't they attack sooner, knowing they would have an undemanding raid, a quick battle that they could accomplish without much risk to them?" one of the remaining men from Tsapousso asked.

"They may decide on such an attack, in which case we will very likely be over-run. We have lost almost a hundred people from this place in the last few days, four of them my own men. That shows how dangerous it is to remain, so I am willing to provide what protection we can to those who leave," said Neves. "But if we arrange the evacuation to be unobvious, using hunters' trails, and taking only what is absolutely necessary, we might be able to buy a little time, enough time for most of us to get away. If we postpone the moment they—"

"We'd have to give the monastery the appearance of being still manned as fully as possible," said Imperus, one of Bernardius' soldiers. "The Hunnic scouts continue to patrol the ridges and crests around us, and they keep track of what happens in this place. If they notice the numbers here are lessening, they will attack sooner rather than later."

"They might wait until the monastery is empty, if they can get our harvest. Why put your troops in danger when it isn't necessary," said Luitpald. "Patras Anso, before he died, asserted the Huns wouldn't fight if they didn't have to."

"That might have been so before we killed some of them," Bernardius countered. "Now they have blood to avenge. They'll demand blood for blood."

Priam Corydon rose and made the sign of the cross. "I pray that your evacuation plan will succeed, but I will not allow the monks here to be used in any way that abuses their calling. All of us renounced the conflicts of this world when we came here. The monks can work the fields and tend livestock, but they will not use weapons against other men, not even Huns. For their sake, we will not remain after the rest of you have gone, for that would leave us open to attack and reprisal. I am charged with protecting the monks in this monastery, and I refuse to sacrifice them for you."

More cries and catcalls greeted this declaration. The heavy heat of this mid-August mid-day had penetrated the warehouse, draining sweat and strength from the men, sparking rancor, shortening tempers, and stirring resentment and frustration. A voice rose above the buzz of under-voices. "What'll you do with Monachos Anatolios then?" Mutters of support accompanied his next questions. "Do you plan to protect him? After what he did to this place?"

There was an abrupt silence; Neves looked over at Mangueinic and then at Priam Corydon. "Yes. What will you do?"

From his place next to the door, Sanctu-Germainios spoke up, and though his voice was not loud, it commanded the full attention of all the men in the warehouse. "Monachos Anatolios is dying. The burns on his hands and face are too deep to heal and he has lost all feeling where the fire entered his flesh too severely; six of his fingers and one of his thumbs are gone. The lesser burns bring him agony that can only be alleviated with soporific anodyne tinctures, which are strong enough to be dangerous if taken too often." He had been using a dilution of blue lotus on Monachos Anatolios, his supply of syrup of poppies being nearly gone. "He is almost blind. I may have to remove the remaining three fingers to keep them from taking rot and spreading it to the rest of his body. Nothing else can be done for him."

"You could end his suffering," suggested a Watchman.

The susurrus of conversation grew louder, becoming an indignant roar of accord.

Bernardius held up his hands and called for quiet; when the noise abated, he addressed Sanctu-Germainios. "How long does he have left?"

"Not long. He could die tonight, or tomorrow, or in the next three or four days at most; I do not think he will survive longer than that."

"He should be killed for what he did!" one of the men shouted.

"He's willing to kill us—he should die for that!" another cried.

Sanctu-Germainios kept his tone neutral, not wanting to add to the volatile atmosphere around the men. "That will happen soon enough; he is far enough gone that half the time he is delirious, but at other times, he says he has restored faith to this monastery, and returned the fate of its occupants to God, in accordance with his duty as a Christian. Jesus, he says, did not turn from his death on the cross, and none of his followers should disdain what God decrees for him."

"What man can know what God decrees?" a monk asked.

"He is confident his suffering will bring him greater glory in Heaven, so he is at peace with what he did. He is convinced that he acted for the benefit of all the Christians in the monastery." Sanctu-Germainios folded his arms.

"More delirium," said Mangueinic. He cleared his throat and spat. "I propose that we make plans to evacuate this place beginning in two days and completing our retreat by the end of ten days. We will leave in companies of no more than twenty, using three of the hunters' tracks, and depart shortly before dawn."

"Sixty people a day will not be enough to evacuate all the refugees. You will need larger parties if all the refugees are to get away in that time. And what of the monks?" The question came from Niklos Aulirios. "Priam Corydon says he will not remain here when the rest of us are gone."

Priam Corydon rubbed his beard. "I believe it would be best if my monks and I left when the monastery is nearly empty. We will put on the habits of pilgrims, which should buy us a modicum of safety."

"The Huns will be waiting," Neves warned him. "Pilgrims or not. And they may come before you leave."

"I've considered that, as well," said the Priam. "And I have a . . . a ruse in mind that may work. If God will forgive us this little deception, we might yet live to sing His Glory."

"And what deception is that?" Mangueinic asked suspiciously.

"I propose we fly the fever flag at the gate," Priam Corydon responded, so readily that it was apparent he had been thinking about this for some little while. "There *are* six monks and eleven refugees who have fever, so it is not completely false; it will be enough to keep the Huns from attacking, even if our numbers seem fewer. If the Huns' scouts have doubts about fever, they will probably hesitate coming too close, misliking the possible risk." He looked a bit uncomfortable at this, but he kept his poise. "It could make our position less precarious."

Neves laughed heartily. "Priam, you are a man after my own heart. The Byzantine army lost a great commander when you took the cloth."

Mangueinic slapped his thigh. "A clever dissimulation, and simple enough that it may well work. I am for giving it a try." He addressed Sanctu-Germainios, raising his voice to be heard through the renewed conversation. "Dom, what do you think? Will such a device work?"

"I think Priam Corydon is right: flying the yellow flag would put the Huns—and other travelers—on guard; a large fighting force is vulnerable to sickness of all sorts." He recalled the Babylonian and Egyptian soldiers laid waste by disease from contaminated water, and the Seventh Legion of Roma, losing one man in five to pustulant fever. "The Huns would be cautious if they were convinced that they would be in danger of spreading illness from coming here."

"Then is it settled?" Mangueinic asked, and grinned as the men sounded the affirmative. "We will spend tomorrow making up the lists of who will depart and when, and make the arrangements for where they will go. All of the dormitory guards will help to choose how much they will be allowed to carry with—"

"Are there guides enough remaining here to lead so many parties of refugees along the trails? You can't intend to let the refugees go off on their own, can you?" Niklos interrupted. "The hunters' tracks are unmarked beyond the paths through the trees, and not all of them lead to safety."

"He's right," Bernardius said, punctuating his agreement with a loud clap of his hands. "We don't have enough men who know the trails well. We will have to have those who do teach others how to find the way to Aquincum, Drobetae, Viminacium, Sirmium, Singidunum, and any other fortified town still in Roman hands. Otherwise the refugees may fall prey to more than Huns—there are robbers and slavers in the forests who can be dangerous, too."

"And many other refugees," added Niklos. "Desperate men who have lost all will not hesitate to take from other desperate men."

"Let each of you ask for volunteers to be guides, and have them meet tomorrow with the guides we already have," Bernardius exclaimed. "We must implement the first of our withdrawals the day after tomorrow."

"Everyone to go on foot but the injured and women with infants," Mangueinic added. "All children under six should have one older brother, or one parent to accompany them. We must be sure there is someone to carry the youngsters who aren't strong enough for long treks." He tried to ignore the aroma of ducks broiling for prandium; this meeting was more important than the mid-day meal.

"No group to have more than three such in it: injured, infant, or child," Bernardius said. "Otherwise it won't be possible to care for them."

"Do you truly think this will work?" Imperus asked Bernardius.

"I think we have a better chance to survive by evacuating than remaining here for the Huns to come. It is a risk to leave, but remaining is a certainty of our defeat. We've lost too many people to the Huns already." Bernardius cleared his throat. "This way, using the evacuation as best we can, some of us will probably survive. When the Huns return . . ." He left the rest to his soldiers' imagination.

"What if the Huns discover our evacuation plan? Everyone says there is a Hunnic spy in our midst, don't they?"

"There may be," said Neves, "but if we let that consideration stop us, then we will surely be killed."

"Find the spy!" Imperus shouted.

"That would waste valuable time, and undermine our efforts to spare as many of the refugees here as can be managed." With an emphatic salute Bernardius declared, "Carpi horam." He licked his lips. "At least we'll all dine well today."

"And there's new beer," called out one of the refugees.

"We must keep our evacuation uppermost in what we do," Mangueinic reminded them.

"Everyone!" Neves shouted. "Let's get our food. We can meet again this evening, and work out the details of our strategy."

Priam Corydon coughed discreetly. "I'll order Monachos Bessamos to inform the monks and determine when we are to depart."

"There is now one question we must decide before we organize our retreat," said Bernardius. He waited until he had the full attention of all the men, then said, "We must decide who is to be left behind."

There was a long, uneasy silence. Then Mangueinic asked, "What would that entail?"

"Trying to make it appear that the monastery is still occupied, that the refugees haven't left," said Bernardius, not willing to meet anyone's eyes.

"And if the Huns come?" The speaker was one of the men from Ulpia Traiana; he folded his arms as he waited for the answer.

"Whoever is left behind needn't wait to be killed. Once he sees the Huns are coming, he should not have to wait for an arrow in— If he can escape, he should." Color mounted in Bernardius' face.

"Do you think it likely that he—or they—could escape?" This from the novice Ritt. "It seems to me that anyone remaining here for very long will die."

Mangueinic glared at the young man. "It is a chance that such a man or men must be willing to recognize."

"But who will stay?" Imperus challenged.

In the quiet of the warehouse, Sanctu-Germainios said, "I will." "And I," said Niklos.

Bernardius stared at the two of them. "You? Both of you?"

Sanctu-Germainios came away from the door, walking slowly toward the Tribune. "I was appointed regional guardian by the Emperor; it is fitting that I protect those travelers bound for Roman territory who come into the region, as I did in Apulum Inferior." He straightened up, his voice purposeful. "It is my sworn duty to see to the safety and welfare of those who leave here."

Bernardius frowned. "You are a foreigner, Dom."

"To you, yes, but not to this place. My people came from these mountains to the east of this place; that was many years ago, but the ties remain," Sanctu-Germainios said, aware that it was nearly two thousand five hundred years since he had lived in these mountains, and that his people were vanished from the earth, except for him. "This place is near enough my native earth that I wish to protect it. I know a few tricks that would make taking even an empty place, as this will be, more costly than the Huns anticipate."

"He's told me that before, in Apulum Inferior, that his people came from the eastern hook of these mountains," Mangueinic said with an emphatic nod. "He would want to defend them on his people's behalf."

"Then he is a courageous man," Neves said sincerely, then rounded on Niklos. "What about you?"

Niklos smiled, ready with his answer. "My bond-holder sent me to Sanctu-Germainios to serve him in whatever way he required for as long as he was in danger. If I'm to remain true to my mission, I'll have to stay with him. It is what Bondama Clemens would expect me to do."

The men in the warehouse faltered. "That's most honorable," said Bernardius at last. "I accept your offer, on behalf of those you brought here."

This time there was a general vociferous approval from all the men, including the few monks who stood with Priam Corydon.

"Good!" Bernardius shouted. "Then we will gather again tonight, before retiring, and discuss how we plan to proceed!"

"God bless, keep, and save you," Priam Corydon declared, making the sign of the cross.

The door was thrust open and the men hurried out of the warehouse, many of them conversing urgently as they dispersed to their posts and tasks throughout the monastery. Directly overhead, the sun glared down on them, a disk of molten metal turning the mountains to an anvil for a vast celestial smithy.

Niklos caught up with Sanctu-Germainios not far from the old chapel. "Do you really have some tricks to use against the Huns, or was that only to assuage the guilt of the men who're willing to let you stay here for them at the risk of your life?" He spoke in Greek, and not so loudly that he could be easily overheard. "What would you like me to do to assist you?"

"I do have a trick or two that you and I can use, if you truly want to remain here with me," said Sanctu-Germainios. "I cannot swear that you will take no hurt for doing this: the Huns still might kill us, but that is not as easily done with you and me than it is for the rest of them."

"I can't dispute that," said Niklos, not quite laughing. "And speaking of such things, what about your companion? Will you send her away?"

"Nicoris? I hope she will consent to go with the last of the refugees from Tsapousso tomorrow. I would like to be with her when she comes to my life, but in this case, I think she will have a better chance at changing without having to fight off the Huns while doing it." His tone was light enough, but there was a somberness in his dark eyes that banished all traces of levity.

"Then what will you tell her?" Niklos asked. "If she knows you're staying, she may want to remain here as well."

"I will tell her the truth," Sanctu-Germainios answered, and opened the door to the old chapel, noticing as he did the lingering odor of fatally burned flesh. He called aloud, "It's Sanctu-Germainios and Niklos."

"Not Niklos," he corrected. "I'm off to the stable, to be sure the horses are ready to travel: hooves trimmed, teeth floated, and manes and tails braided to keep out burrs and brambles. I'll ready packs of grain for them, too, and repair any worn tack." Stepping back, he turned and strode off down the gradual slope, no trace of worry in his demeanor as he went.

Sanctu-Germainios pulled the door closed; the light from the windows in the barrel-dome was sufficient to reveal the shadowy interior of the building for eyes less able to pierce the dark than his. A quick glance around the room revealed Nicoris standing off to the side of the room next to the pallet where Monachos Anatolios lay, a ceramic cup in her hands.

She spoke without looking at him. "Dom, he has been complaining of thirst. I've tried to give him water, with three drops of the blue lotus dilution in each cup. It's helped him to sleep, and eased his pain."

"How much have you given him so far? How many cups has he drunk." Sanctu-Germainios asked as he came to her side.

"This is his fourth cup since morning Mass," she said.

He nodded. "I wouldn't give him any more until sundown—not that I think he'll wake up before then. He may need the water, but he is weak, and the blue lotus, even much diluted, can prove fatal in cases like his."

"As you wish," she said cautiously.

"Is something the matter?" He studied her face, his expression unreadable.

She did not answer at once, but continued to stare down into the cup. "They say we'll all be killed by the Huns if we don't leave."

"They've been saying that since we got here," he reminded her.

"Um. But they mean it now." She looked directly at him.

He took a moment to consider how to respond. "Given the number of people who have left here already, I would think it likely that this monastery will be abandoned by winter."

"Completely abandoned?" Her voice was small.

"Probably," he said, turning to her and taking the cup from her hands. "If you want to live, you should join one of the parties bound for Roman forts."

"*I* should? What about you? Are you sending me away?"

"No. But I hope you will go. I hope you will choose safety, and arrange to leave." He set the cup down next to the pitcher of water at the end of the pallet before he laid his hands on her shoulders. "The Huns will be back. There will be more of them than before, and there will be fewer defenders. For your—"

She pulled away from him, blurting out as she did, "But don't you see? I can't go! I'm a Hun! What do you think would happen if anyone found out? Do you think anyone here would let me travel in their company?" As soon as she realized what she had said, she recoiled, clapping her hand to her mouth, watching Sanctu-Germainios with fearful eyes. "I didn't . . . I don't . . ." No explanation came to her.

He regarded her tranquilly, his expression unchanged. "You have nothing to fear, Nicoris, not from me." He fell silent, waiting for what she would say next. "It is in your blood."

When she spoke again, she was incredulous, edgy, and disheartened. "You mean you know I'm—"

"—a Hun; yes, I know; I've known for some time. And I am aware that you want to keep that information secret." As her eyes widened, he went on, "I have tasted your blood, the very essence of you, and we have touched each other as deeply as anyone can touch." He saw her catch her lower lip in her teeth. "Ah, Nicoris. How could I not know you are a Hun, and recognize your desire to conceal that knowledge? It is as much a part of you as your quicksilver eyes."

Disgusted with herself for the distrust she felt, she asked him, "Have you told anyone? anyone at all?"

"Why would I do that?" His words were gentle and his dark eyes engaged all her attention; there was no hint of remonstration in any aspect of his behavior; kindness emanated from him like faint music. "You were unwilling to tell me; I know you fear what the people in this monastery might do to you, not without reason, so I have kept your confidence, as you have kept mine."

"Kept yours?" She was baffled.

"The refugees most certainly hate Huns, but they dread vampires." He took a single step toward her. "If you have not considered this, then I ask you to do so now. Each of us has a secret for the other to keep."

She turned away, her chagrin threatening to overwhelm her. "You're trying to bewilder me."

"I would not do that to you."

"Don't say that." She hunched her shoulders. "Not if you're going to send me away."

"I am not going to do that, but I do hope you will realize that you will have a better chance at living if you go than if you stay here." He sighed. "I would hate to see you throw your life away here."

"You're prepared to do that," she told him bluntly. "Why shouldn't I?"

"Because I intend not to die," he responded. "Niklos and I will remain here only until the Huns are on their way to this valley, and then we will leave."

"And they will pursue you," she said. "They will ride you down." Her eyes softened.

"I think not," said Sanctu-Germainios.

She swung around to face him. "You'll be chased by Huns. *Huns!* Don't you understand?"

"I have been chased by Egyptians and Babylonians and Hittites and Carthaginians and Greeks and Persians and Chinese and Arabs and Assyrians and many, many others, all sworn to deliver me the True Death, and I am still here," he said.

"But you can die: you told me so," she said.

"Everyone, everything dies eventually." His half-smile was quickly gone.

"You're most vexing, Dom," she said, coming toward him again.

"I do not mean to be," he assured her.

"That," she said, feeling disheartened, "is most vexing of all." Before she could stop herself, she went into his arms, resting her head on his shoulder, her face averted from his. "I don't want to lose you."

He stroked her hair. "You will not."

"How can you be so certain?" She wanted to believe him, but her experiences told her that it would be reckless to rely on him. "Once we are separated, we may never find each other again."

"The Blood Bond will remain as long as we . . . live our lives. While we can breathe, you will always be a part of me, and I of you."

She shivered in the hot afternoon, clinging to him, wanting to quiet the turbulence within her. "So you *do* desire me?"

"Of course," he said softly.

"Then why don't you take what you want?" She tightened her hold on him. "Why do you have to wait for me to want you?"

"It is my nature," he said. "I thought you understood that?"

She turned toward him without releasing him, and kissed him near his mouth. "Then I want you. You can waken my desires: you know that. Do it. If you aren't afraid to." This was a direct challenge, one that she expected him to answer. "If you really accept me, show me."

His gaze was enigmatic as he lifted her into his arms and carried her to his bed, setting her down gently on the linen sheet atop his firm mattress. He sat beside her. "I want you to understand that I would accept you no matter what does or does not pass between us; I would continue to love you as you are, without your acquiescence to desire, but since you will have it so—" He leaned toward her, drawing her into a long, persuasive kiss, one that illuminated degrees of excitement she had never recognized in herself. When he finally ended the kiss, Nicoris was breathing more quickly and her face was flushed. Very slowly, Sanctu-Germainios unfastened her broad leather belt and set it aside, then lifted the hem of her palla.

This time when Nicoris shivered, it was in anticipation of pleasure. "Dom . . ."

"Tell me what would please you," he whispered, working the hem upward.

"You know what pleases me," she breathed, taking his hand in hers and sliding it across her shoulders, then down to her breast; beneath the heavy linen her nipple swelled, and she shifted her posture so that he could remove her palla and unfasten the cotton femoralia, leaving her naked, languid in the sultry heat. "Let your hands tell me what I want."

"If that will bring you joy," he said, and lay down next to her as she stretched out. Compliant to her desire, his hands, light as murmurs, passed over her body, imparting sweet secrets to the nape of her neck, the curve of her shoulder, the rise of her breasts, then moved on, his caresses still featherlight, to awaken sensations in her belly, and the cleft between her legs. Softly, persuasively, he made poetry of her flesh, delineating nuances of excitement that she had not permitted herself to feel until now. What his hands could not accomplish, his lips did, exploring, savoring, delighting in her increasing arousal. His esurience made him keenly aware of how much more ardor had been ignited within her, and he did what he could to prolong her stimulation, to bring her to new heights, to give her all the rapture she was capable of achieving.

"I'll shatter," she said quietly.

"You will have fulfillment," he promised, moving down her body, sliding up from between her legs to engage her passion at her culmination, sharing the ecstatic pulsations that swept through and over her. His lips on her neck were as light as his fingers were, and as evocative.

As her transports faded she snuggled next to him, seeking for the first time to maintain the intimacy of their love-making. She was damp all over, and her eyes shone, their silvery color glowing like stars. As her exultation faded, the early afternoon warmth and the aftermath of her gratification made her drowsy; she felt herself drifting into sleep. "I'm not frightened anymore, Dom." She half-expected him to say, *I know;* when he did not, she kissed his cheek. "I guess you know already—from my blood."

He made a sound between a sigh and a chuckle. "Yes," he said, moving a little so that she could rest more comfortably.

"Will you wake me at the end of the second quarter of the afternoon?"

"If that is what you want," he said, securing her in the curve of his arm as she closed her eyes.

Text of a dispatch from Clutherus son of Einhalt, of the Third Gothic Company of Emperor Theodosios, stationed at Oescus in the Province of Moesia Inferior, to Verus Flautens, Praetor-General of Drobetae in the former Province of Dacia, written in Gothic Greek on thin wood with black paint and delivered by courier six days after being written.

To the Praetor-General of Drobetae in the old Province of Dacia, the greetings from the Captain of the Third Gothic Company of the Emperor in Constantinople, Clutherus son of Einhalt twenty days before the Autumnal Equinox:

    Worthy Praetor-General,

    I regret that the terms of our contract with Emperor Theodosios does not allow our Company to abandon our post to defend any other Roman fortress without specific orders from Constantinople. I will see that your urgent request is passed on to our General in Constantinople, along with our prayers that it will be possible to send troops to you, for we have been told that the Huns have been active all through the summer and may continue to be so for some time to come.

    You say the Emperor in the West has refused to help you with any of his Legions or hired companies, which is unfortunate; know that if it were my decision to make, I would gladly spare you fifty of my men to reinforce your soldiers.

        Captain Clutherus son of Einhalt (his mark)

by the hand of Patras Tullius, scribe

7

Neves took the life-sized, straw-stuffed figure dressed in old, torn garments and attempted to lean it against the wall of the battlements. "It's going to fall," he warned Sanctu-Germainios, who, after handing up the doll, had climbed up next to him, two straight tibiae in one hand, a spear in the other. A single lamp was burning, providing wavering illumination in the pre-dawn darkness.

    "Not once I pin its left hand to one of the upright logs, and the other around the shaft of a spear." Sanctu-Germainios set to work doing just that, setting each short, sharp tibia firmly in the heavy cotton, and had the satisfaction of seeing the awkward figure remain on its feet. "There."

Below them the last of this morning's departing refugees were going out through the improvised gate that had been hastily constructed where the outer wall had burned; there were twenty-four of them—men, women, and five children—with two horses carrying all the goods they were taking with them.

"How many of these things have you made?"

"Forty-two," said Sanctu-Germainios. "Nicoris and Niklos Aulirios have worked with me; I could not have finished so many on my own. We should be able to make another six of them before we run out of cloth."

"I'd lend you one of my men to help, but most of them are hopeless with needles," Neves said, watching the cumbersome gate close behind the refugees. "I hope they make it to safety." He yawned and rubbed his eyes. "They have a long way to go, and Aquincum may have already been razed by the Huns."

"It is a risk," Sanctu-Germainios agreed, his countenance enigmatic.

"So is remaining here." Neves sighed. "Are you sure you want your woman to go with me and my men? The Huns might move against us because we're a company of mercenaries."

"So they might, but they might move against anyone, and at least you and your men know how to fight, and there are more of you than there are men in most of the refugee companies. I also believe your company will be easier to find than some of the others when I leave here." Sanctu-Germainios patted the straw-filled figure, paying no heed to the flash of pathos in Neves' eyes. "I only wish that he and the rest of them could be made to throw spears."

Neves made himself laugh. "A wonderful notion. Perhaps you could have more made: enough to make it appear that there's still a force here to be reckoned with instead of a token presence. If there were a hundred of these, they might be enough to keep the Huns from an all-out attack for a while—long enough that you and

Aulirios could get away." He clapped his hands. "How many women remain? Do any of them have cloth to spare? Will they sew for you?"

"Thirty-nine grown women are here still, and five girls," said Sanctu-Germainios. "Sixteen go tomorrow, and the day after that, the first group of monks. Eighty-one of them."

"And the rest two days later, along with Tribune Bernardius and his lieutenants—the last to leave here, but you and your comrade— the day after I take my men toward Viminacium," said Neves, chafing his hands together. "I know the schedule. I'm counting the hours until we go. Three days more, that's all. If only the Huns will hold off until then. We've chosen an hour between midnight and dawn, to slip past the scouts."

"A reasonable precaution," said Sanctu-Germainios.

"My men are being more diligent than ever, watching for scouts, and they know that the scouts are least active from midnight until dawn. My men want to get away from here without incident."

"And Bernardius' men still on guard?" Sanctu-Germainios asked. "Do they report more scouts?"

"So far they haven't said they've seen anything troubling, whether they have or not." He waved his hand at the mountains. "But where would we look, to be certain?"

"I suppose we must continue to hope," said Sanctu-Germainios; he could feel the first stirring of dawn as the eastern horizon began to lighten.

"At least we've been able to get in a portion of the harvest, so those leaving will have some provisions beyond hard bread and old cheese. Out on remote roads, the chance of finding food is slim, and there won't be many opportunities for hunting." With another yawn, Neves slapped the back of the dummy next to him. "Hunting and dressing takes time, so vegetable stews will have to keep them going until they reach the next safe fortress." He paused again. "They say the Huns kill their meat, then put it under their saddles to cook as they ride."

Sanctu-Germainios gave a crack of laughter. "The heat of a

horse will not cook meat, but it can fill it with rot and make it deadly; that is assuming the horse would tolerate something like a joint of venison under its saddle." He knew Neves still had doubts. "These tales of the Huns are more the result of exaggerated reports and stories based on rumors than on any actuality—"

"They train their horses to tolerate the meat under the sad—"

"No one can train a horse to ignore a lump under its saddle. It would be the same as having a large stone under your armor." He regarded Neves steadily, sensing his uncertainty. "Think: what does a horse do when there is a burr or a pebble under his saddle—bucks and kicks. A joint of meat would cause—"

Neves nodded. "All right; Huns don't cook their meat that way. But they fight like the Devil's own minions, however they get their food."

"They probably carry smoked meats with them, or dried strips of meat," Sanctu-Germainios suggested; he recalled seeing nomads from the steppes riding with smoked meats hanging from their saddles, and Rugierus had eaten the dried, raw meat during their travels, as had Niklos. "And, of course, they raid for food and take few prisoners, since prisoners have to eat."

"So they do," Neves agreed, his face hardening.

"All the better, then, for those who are leaving here, to use as much of the harvest as possible," Sanctu-Germainios said.

"So the Huns won't have anything to plunder here," added Neves. "We'll have refugees in the fields later today, bringing in as much as is ready to be gathered. Bernardius' men are supposed to guard the harvesters, although most of the day-Watch are already gone; there aren't enough guards for all the fields. We'll have fewer than fifty men in the fields today, guards and harvesters, whose labors will be less than anticipated, their numbers being so few, and they will not remain outside the inner wall beyond mid-afternoon. There will be still fewer tomorrow, so the number of guards won't matter so much. All but two of Bernardius' hunters have left, and those two leave tomorrow, to guide two of the departing companies."

"There are eighteen of Bernardius' men left to serve as guards in the fields and on the walls, and thirteen of Mangueinic's Watchmen; with your men, and those from Apulum Inferior, one more full day of harvesting is still possible," Sanctu-Germainios reminded him. "They should be able to bring in half the current crops by tomorrow if the Huns keep their distance."

"I hope they'll be enough, those guards, on the walls and on the road," said Neves. "There are so many preparations we need to make. I've been thinking about what the refugees will need if they have trouble during their journeys . . ." His thoughts trailed off; he regarded the dummy attentively. "More than forty of these, you say? They won't fool the Huns for very long."

"No, but it will buy Niklos and me a little time—perhaps, as you say, enough that we can escape." He saw Neves' expression change to something grimmer than it had been.

"I pray you will get away." Neves did not say to whom he would address his prayers.

Sanctu-Germainios decided not to dwell on this. "Are you going to go mounted, or leave some of your horses for Bernardius' last four men, who will leave after you do?"

"I've decided that most of my men—those who are left here—will ride. We need to cover ground as quickly as possible, and that means riding. Some of them will have to ride double." He looked down, ashamed. "Seventeen of my company have already fled. I wouldn't have thought they were so craven."

"Why not mount all of your—" Sanctu-Germainios began, only to be interrupted.

"Because some of them are injured, and will have to ride in carts, with our supplies, or go with one of the refugee companies. And we're short of horses." He stopped abruptly. "Sorry, Dom. I'm worried, as everyone here is, that the Huns will attack again before we can empty the monastery. We'd surely lose this time, unless the monks suddenly decide to fight."

"That is—"

"—not going to happen. I know. We can hope that the fever flag will hold them at bay for a few more days, even if these straw-men do not." Neves peered out into the waning night as if attempting to find any Huns lurking among the trees. "Do you think either the flag or these dolls will—? The Huns are single-minded fighters. Is that flag alone enough to stop them?"

"Would it not keep you from trying to take this place, if you were a Hun?" Sanctu-Germainios asked. "Fever is as deadly as arrows, and lasts longer than battle."

Neves considered this, and nodded. "What about the spy? Won't he tell them that the flag is a deception?"

"If he has contacted the Huns, then yes. But he may have left already, or he may be here, waiting to leave to deliver his report himself," Sanctu-Germainios said distantly.

"Have you thought who the spy might be?"

"No. I have not." He hated to admit it. "What troubles me more is if any of the escaping refugees are caught, they might trade their lives for information."

Neves swore. "Wouldn't the Huns just kill them?"

Sanctu-Germainios shrugged. "It would depend on what they wanted most. If the refugees are clever, they would say they are escaping from the fever, not the Huns, but they would need to keep their wits about them, and that is not easily done in such circumstances."

This time Neves' laugh was angry. "Do you think any of them will? keep their wits if they're caught?"

"Some may," said Sanctu-Germainios. "If they are caught by Huns and questioned, which is, itself, unlikely."

"Do you mean caught or questioned?" Neves asked, and before Sanctu-Germainios could answer, he nodded emphatically. "You mean if the Huns find them, they'll be slaughtered and their goods and livestock taken. The Huns won't bother with questions."

"It is what they have done in the past," said Sanctu-Germainios, going on more pragmatically, "I should find a helmet for this straw soldier. The Huns may see that he has no features if his face is not partially covered." He looked at Neves, contemplating his scarred visage.

"I almost wish they would attack again. At least we could fight. This waiting and planning, it's worse than battle. Battle is chaos, but there's no doubt what's going on. What we're doing now . . . It erodes the will. Whether the Huns come or not, we must get away before we turn on one another and do the Huns' work for them."

"Then I wish you a safe withdrawal and the chance to engage the Huns elsewhere," Sanctu-Germainios said with genuine sincerity. "You have done well by us. Thank you."

"So have you, Dom," said Neves. "Done well by us. I'm obliged to you."

Sanctu-Germainios stepped back and reached for the top of the ladder; before he descended, he offered Neves a proper Roman salute. "May you find triumph, Neves."

Neves returned the salute as Sanctu-Germainios continued to climb down. As he reached the ground, he turned to the east, and heard the chanting of the monks grow louder as the first Mass of the day began.

By noon, twenty of the straw-filled dummies had been clothed, armed, helmeted, and pinned in place on the battlements. "This evening," Sanctu-Germainios told Niklos, "we must shift their positions so that their . . . inactivity will not give them away."

Niklos chuckled, looking up at the gate-tower. "What about reducing the number of them showing above the stockade for the night? The scouts might be suspicious of a full complement of soldiers on night duty, particularly with the fever flag up. No need to bring the dolls down to the ground. We can lie them down on the battlement walkways and set them up in the morning before dawn."

Sanctu-Germainios rubbed his chin, feeling the stubble of the last two weeks beneath his fingers; once again he missed Rugierus, who shaved his slow-growing beard once a week; he also missed Rugierus' practicality, planning, and good sense. Again he scraped his thumb along the stubble. He had managed for himself since Rugierus left, but he was not satisfied with the results. Realizing that Niklos was waiting for a comment, he said, "It would probably be wise. I'll speak to Mangueinic about it."

"He leaves tomorrow, doesn't he," said Niklos.

"Yes. He and thirty-one others from Apulum Inferior," said Sanctu-Germainios, a touch of sadness in his voice.

"Will you miss them?" Niklos was surprised. "They don't regard you as one of them."

"No one regards me as one of them," Sanctu-Germainios told him with the resignation of centuries in his tone. "But they have not cast me out."

"What of those who come to your life: what of them?" Niklos asked. "Olivia—"

"Coming to my life usually brings isolation, as my change brought me, long ago. I know Olivia has said much the same thing."

Niklos almost offered a witty rejoinder, but saw the expression in Sanctu-Germainios' dark eyes, and held his tongue. "Do you plan to put the rest of the straw-men into position this afternoon or to-morrow?"

"I think tomorrow. With laborers in the fields, adding to the fig-ures on the battlements might raise Hunnic suspicions. Besides, we will need to find clothes and helmets for the rest of the straw-men we have before putting them in place. They will have to look like men on watch, ready for anything, which means armor of some sort or another. And I will have to find out if Priam Corydon will give us some of the old monks' clothing. I doubt the Huns know the differ-ence between a pallium, a sagum, and an abolla." He himself had donned his most austere paragaudion and braccae, both in his ha-bitual black. "Tonight, while we stuff a few more of the straw-men, there is something we must discuss."

"Has it to do with how we manage here once the rest have gone?" Niklos gave Sanctu-Germainios a quick, fierce smile.

Sanctu-Germainios nodded. "I have a few things in mind," he said in Greek, then went back to the current dialect of the region. "For now, armor and clothing are needed. I will ask the monks first."

"Given that peasants and monks wear garments that are much the same, why not?" Niklos grinned. "The monks may object be-cause you want to use their old garments for defense."

"So they might," Sanctu-Germainios said quietly, lifting his head. "The wind is shifting."

"If it means cooler weather, it's welcome," Niklos said, squinting into the sky.

"It could mean rain." As Niklos looked at him, startled, Sanctu-Germainios added, "It is not unusual for there to be a day or two of rain toward the end of August. This rain is not like the thunderstorms of high summer, but more a first herald of autumn, spawned by cool winds. It could be an indication of an early season."

"Rain could damage the crops," Niklos remarked.

"It could also slow down the Huns," said Sanctu-Germainios, contemplating the gate-tower and the yellow flag flapping above it.

"So it could." For a short while neither of them said anything, then Niklos declared, "I'm going to help the grooms ready the chests for tomorrow. I'll help you with these large dolls after nightfall."

"I will be in the old chapel; Nicoris wants my help in choosing what to take with her and what to leave behind." Sanctu-Germainios looked up once more. "If the wind continues to rise in that quarter, there will be rain."

The day slipped quickly away, sunset partially obscured by gathering clouds to the northwest. The chanting of the monks went on throughout the afternoon while Priam Corydon went about organizing those of the monks who were to leave in two days; he dispatched novices to the remaining hermits in the caves above the lake, once again asking them if they wanted to depart with the rest of them; he supervised the packing of the various ritual objects that they would require for worship; he sent monks to help Monachos Vlasos secure as much food as possible for their journey; he visited the infirmary and made arrangements for the accommodation of those who were ill; he met with Mangueinic, Tribune Bernardius, and Neves; then he went to the stable to requisition horses and carts. By the time night came on, he sought out Sanctu-Germainios, entering the old chapel by the main door.

Sanctu-Germainios dropped the cloth he held and got to his feet. "Priam."

"Dom," said Priam Corydon, making the sign of the cross. "Are you alone?"

"I am. Niklos and Nicoris are off collecting more straw for our false soldiers. The slaves in the stable should be helping them. They will return shortly." He patted the cloth, then set the ivory needle in it and motioned to the bench near the fireplace as he laid the half-finished life-sized dummy down. "I have water and some wine, if you would like either, or both."

"If you have some of each to spare, I would thank you for them; it has been a demanding day," said Priam Corydon, taking his seat on the bench. "I want to extend you my thanks for your willingness to remain here when the rest of us are gone. If you should fall here, you will surely be a martyr in Heaven."

Sanctu-Germainios paused in his selecting two cups for the Priam. "I think I would prefer to continue as I am," he remarked with an ironic smile as he pulled out the jug of wine from the large standing case next to the red-lacquer chest.

"I can understand your feeling on that point," said Priam Corydon. "No doubt you'll still earn your place among the sheep, not the goats."

"The wine is red: will that suit you?" He held the jug poised to pour.

"Very well," said the Priam.

Sanctu-Germainios poured the wine, replaced the jug, and took out the ewer of water, and poured the larger cup almost full. "I fear I have nothing else to offer you; I have sent most of the food we have here to Mangueinic to distribute among the companies leaving in the morning."

"No matter; we take no food from sundown to sunrise; I thought you were aware of that; my monks and the refugees have locked horns about this several times," said Priam Corydon, looking a bit surprised as Sanctu-Germainios brought him the two cups.

"You have not required the refugees to maintain your Rule." He handed the cups to Priam Corydon.

"Won't you join me?"

"No, Priam, I will not: I do not drink wine."

"Not even your own? How remarkable," said Priam Corydon, taking a deep sip of the water, and then a taste of the wine, approving it with a single nod. "They've told me, some of those you have treated, that you are generous with drink of all sorts. Do you refrain from other kinds of imbibition?"

"Almost all, Priam; almost all."

"But you advise wine and other inebriants for your patients, don't you? Wolfsbane and syrup of poppies and something Egyptian, I've been told." He had more of the wine and followed it with water.

"When it will be helpful, not harmful, I believe the right intoxicant can aid recovery from injuries, and ease the pain of the injured." He drew up another stool and sat down across from Priam Corydon.

"Suffering is our lot in life, because of our sins," said Priam Corydon. "Penance is necessary for Christians to enter the Kingdom of Heaven."

"Do you think so? Does that not belittle the sacrifice of your Jesus, to seek out hurt and anguish? You teach that His death redeemed all men, or so I have understood."

Priam Corydon thought this over, and kept his conclusions to himself. "My monks tell me that you've requested our worn-out garments—the ones we save to give out to beggars and other unfortunates—to put on your straw soldiers; you left such a message for me."

"That I did," said Sanctu-Germainios. "These straw-men need clothing to make the counterfeit believable for the Huns. Clothing and armor," he added.

"I will authorize the use of our old clothing, since we will not take it with us, and no Christian here has need of it, but we have no armor to offer you." He sighed. "In spite of faith, the world imposes."

"We live in the world, Priam, and must answer to its demands," Sanctu-Germainios reminded him, and would have said more, but the side-door opened and Nicoris and Niklos came in, a large sling between them laden with straw. Sanctu-Germainios rose and went to assist them.

"Dom, we have another sling with as much straw as we have here," Nicoris cried out as she and Niklos set the sling down on the floor next to the whip-stitched dolls.

Sanctu-Germainios offered her a quick, delighted smile. "Wonderful! We can stuff the rest of the dolls tonight and have them in place before the next parties leave the monastery. Assuming we have hoods and helmets enough to disguise them."

Priam Corydon drank the rest of his wine and took a large gulp of water, then got up. "You have much to do. I'll leave you to your work. One of the novices will bring you the old clothing. If there are hoods to spare, I will donate them, as well." He made the sign of the cross, and then, more circumspectly, the sign of the fish.

"May you and your monks travel safely, Priam," said Sanctu-Germainios as Priam Corydon went out of the old chapel toward the monastery.

"So he'll give us the old clothes," said Niklos with a kind of wry enthusiasm that did not completely conceal his relief.

"So he tells me," said Sanctu-Germainios. "Since the deception was his idea to begin with, he is probably inclined to help us execute it."

"Will it be enough?" Nicoris asked, her face paling as she looked at the empty dummies spread out on the floor.

"The straw or the clothes?" Niklos flung up his hands. "One more sling to go, and then we can set to work filling the dolls."

"Or do you mean the dissimulation we are attempting?" Sanctu-Germainios asked her. "It will have to be enough; there is little else we can do."

She nodded mutely, and followed Niklos out of the old chapel, leaving Sanctu-Germainios to finish sewing the doll he had been assembling. He checked his supply of thread and realized that, too, was running low, although it would be enough for the remaining figures. He took out the long spool and fingered the fine Coan linen thread that he usually employed to close wounds, then returned to his sewing, working quickly so he would be done with this figure by the time Niklos and Nicoris returned.

By the third quarter of the night all the figures were in place; Sanctu-Germainios and Niklos cleaned the old chapel while Nicoris slept. While he swept up the last of the straw, Niklos said in Greek, "She doesn't want to go."

"Yes; I know."

"She'd probably be as safe with us as with Neves," Niklos continued.

"Do you think so." Sanctu-Germainios studied him.

"I do." Niklos brushed the straw into the fireplace. "We could take her with us when we leave."

"You assume our plan will be successful," said Sanctu-Germainios.

"Of course I do. Don't you?"

There was a long silence between them. "I think Nicoris will have a better chance of getting away if she travels with Neves' men."

"Perhaps she'd prefer to be with you," Niklos said, being as blunt as he dared.

"Did she say so?" Sanctu-Germainios asked.

"She . . . implied it."

"And you agree?"

Niklos set his long-handled brush aside. "Yes. I do."

Sanctu-Germainios stood very still; the sound of the monks' chanting reached them, disturbingly serene. "If that is what she truly wants, then she shall stay with us. But I suspect she will not."

Text of a letter from Atta Olivia Clemens in Aquileia to Sanct' Germain Franciscus at Sanctu-Eustachios the Hermit monastery in the former Province of Dacia, written with fixed ink in Imperial Latin on split leather, never delivered.

To my oldest, dearest friend currently calling himself Dom Feranescus Rakoczy Sanctu-Germainios, the greetings of Atta Olivia Clemens in Aquileia, although not for much longer:

Sanct' Germain,

I have just sustained a most annoying visit from our Praetor Custodis, informing me that as I live beyond the walls of Aquileia, I and my estate are not included in the city's protection, although I pay taxes that are supposed to ensure me security from all threats that are associated with the city. The Praetor Custodis also informed me that nine of my horses are being requisitioned now with another nine to follow in four days, for the city Guards to increase their patrols beyond the gates. It was all I could do to keep from railing at him. But I was mindful of the jeopardy of my position, and kept my words and manner civil—you would have laughed to see me so placating. I very nearly simpered. He puffed out his chest and gave orders like a sea captain in a wealthy port. Magna Mater, I am glad he has finally left, though I am rancorous about the horses! I am irritated by that officious, greedy fool, for it is a reminder of my situation here; this region has enough pettiness among its officials without the efforts of Sixtus Gratian Fulvius Draco.

As you should know by now, Rogerian is with me. I find it curiously amusing that I have your bondsman and you have mine. I trust that Niklos Aulirios is proving useful as well as providing you understanding company. I have to admit that I am uneasy on your behalf—not about the Huns—what with you being at a monastery at present, for Christians are becoming increasingly inflexible in regard to what and whom they deem deviant, such as vampires and ghouls.

In acknowledgment of hazards here, I am about to leave Aquileia for the villa at Lecco on Lago Comus; I expect to arrive there on the twenty-third or -fourth day of September. It will mean giving up more than half my harvest to local farmers, but it may be that they will need it more than I. Everyone here is afraid that the Huns will soon be upon us, thanks to the Praetor Custodis, and that has brought about serious disagreements among the more important personages in the city. Some want to reinforce the walls and prepare for battle, while others want to hire more mercenaries to keep the

Huns away from Aquileia entirely, and others think that we should treat with the Huns to arrange tribute so that we may lose only our money, not our lives and property. Since all those stances seem to me to be short-sighted, I believe it is time I found a more congenial place to stay until the danger is over. Whether or not any Huns will attack us, or when, disputes, such as the current ones, are not beneficial to those of our blood; when the living are afraid they turn first upon those unlike them, which bodes ill for me, and for Rogerian, or Rugierus, or whatever you wish to call him. Following your good advice of four centuries past, I am removing myself from the fray.

Which is what I hope you will do. That monastery may be protected in its valley, but once the Huns have a taste of gain to be had from a location, they will make every effort to obtain all that they can. For my sake if not your own, do not remain there any longer than you must. As soon as it is practicable, leave the place and get beyond the region controlled by the Huns. I have no doubt that you will conduct yourself honorably, for you have done so for all the years I have known you, and I have no expectation that you would change now, much as I might wish that you would. But please, ask no more of yourself than you would of any living man in that valley. As I read this over, I wonder why I bother to ask this of you; you will do what you decide is necessary, the peril of little consequence to you. Yet I know my warnings will go unheeded, though I give them because of my love for you, which has never wavered from the first time we lay together, when Nero wore the purple and my loathsome husband was still alive.

And now, before I become maudlin, I will commend myself to your good opinion in spite of my hectoring, and look forward to the day when we can exchange bondsmen and enjoy as much time together as will be prudent.

Your most allegiant
Olivia

on the tenth day before the end of August in the 1192nd Year of the City, or the 439th year of the Christians

8

A gelid mist hung over Sanctu-Eustachios the Hermit, not substantial enough to be called even a drizzle but more than fog; buildings were shrouded in clammy wraiths as if they were the artifacts of a ghostly dream. The little daylight that penetrated the obscuring haze was so diffuse, it was impossible to tell what time of day it was. The whole valley was silent, for the last of the monks had gone and there was no more chanting or ringing of the Mass bell to help mark the canonical Hours; no refugees called, no soldier shouted orders, no women supervised playing children. Emptiness haunted the place as much as the murkiness did.

"Do you think the straw-men are too damp to burn?" Niklos asked Sanctu-Germainios in the Greek of his youth as they made their way around the broad space between the two walls, carrying large jugs of oil; they would ladle the oil over each of the dummies. In the hush, his voice sounded unnaturally loud.

Sanctu-Germainios shifted his pluvial of waxed wool more tightly around his shoulders and scrutinized the moist air. "If the rain does not grow heavier, and the Huns arrive before mid-day we ought to—"

"And how do we know when it's mid-day?" Niklos spoke sharply. "I don't like this weather, and I don't like having to wait for the Huns to try to kill us."

"Before the last of the men left at the end of the night, the guards in the gate-tower saw a large company of mounted men moving up the Roman road. Making allowances for the weather—as you mentioned—they should be here about mid-day, since they will not risk coming too rapidly, with visibility so poor," said Sanctu-Germainios as calmly as he could. "You heard the guards." He climbed up the ladder onto the battlement walkway, carrying the jug of oil carefully so as not to spill any of its contents.

"How do we know that the men they saw were Huns? They could be Goths, or Gepidae, or Daci, or Carpi. Or any number of other refugees." Niklos followed him up.

"They could be," Sanctu-Germainios allowed. "But it is unlikely; most refugees are trying to cross into Roman territory, not go to ground here." He poured a ladle of oil over the nearest straw-man. "There is an advantage to the damp: it will tend to keep the fire from spreading."

"That is most worthwhile," said Niklos with heavy sarcasm, "considering."

"Dying in fire would be the True Death for us both," Sanctu-Germainios observed.

"I'm aware of it," said Niklos brusquely. "That's what I mean. What good is it to escape the Huns if we are killed by fire?" He straightened the next straw-man before emptying his ladle over the shoulders of the figure. "I reckon that's why Nicoris changed her mind about staying; you told her what we were planning to do."

"Not all of it, but enough," said Sanctu-Germainios. "She knows that you and I may not . . . be able to leave here."

"She might be attacked on the road, or have to fight the Huns in another place," said Niklos.

"That is why I asked her to go with Neves and his men. She would have a greater chance with a company of armed men than with just the two of us. She saw the advantages of that."

"Don't you want her here, with you?" Niklos dared to ask.

"If everything were settled and the monastery still a haven, then yes. But as matters stand, this is not her risk to take; she deserves protection, and here I cannot give it to her." He paused. "I hope I have done what will spare her from harm."

"And I suppose you paid Neves and his men to guard her?" Niklos guessed aloud.

"She is safer with Neves and his men than she would be here," Sanctu-Germainios reiterated, no emotion in his voice; he told himself again, as he had told her, that he did not want to be the cause of the death that would bring her to his life.

"I guess that means you did pay them, and knowing you, very well," said Niklos, saying nothing more as he continued on until he reached the next ladder. "Do we do the figures on the outer wall as well?"

"As many of them as we have time to; oil will keep them burning in spite of the damp," Sanctu-Germainios replied, wondering if Niklos would be willing not to remind him of Nicoris; his anxiety for her had been growing since she had left with Neves and his mercenaries. He concentrated on his immediate situation, trying not to fret for Nicoris. "Once the Huns break through the outer wall we—"

"—set these on the inner wall alight, and then the dormitories, and under cover of the flames, we make our way toward the lake, setting fire to the straw-men on the outer wall, trapping the Huns between the two blazes—that is, if the Huns cooperate. If they fight from outside the walls, we will have to think of another way." He coughed to express his discomfort at that notion. To keep from dwelling on their chance of failure, he said, "I trust our horses are well enough concealed to escape the notice of the Huns, otherwise we'll be in a worse situation than we are now. I don't wish to try to get out of the mountains on foot, not with the Huns about."

"One of the hermits has them in his cave. I gave him feed and water for the five animals: three horses and two mules; they are saddled, bridled, haltered, and laden: we can ride as soon as we reach the cave. For his service, I offered Monachos Guilielmos the last wheel of cheese from the larder—the one Monachos Vlasos left for us—and the gold crucifix from the wall of the refectory. Money would have insulted him." He followed Niklos down the ladder.

"Do you think the hermit is reliable? Does he have any idea of what could happen here if he fails us?" Niklos' nervousness was becoming more apparent; he fidgeted with the tails of his belt.

"He used to be a merchants' factor before his family died of pustulant fever: he may be a little mad, but he knows the importance of this duty."

Niklos nodded, going on an instant later, "Do you think we'll be able to get out of this place unnoticed?"

"I hope we can. The weather favors us." His hand slid around the hilt of the Byzantine long-sword hanging from his belt in a scabbard. "I have a dozen caltrops as well, and a dagger." He tapped the satchel slung across his shoulder.

"Then you anticipate a fight," said Niklos.

"Not necessarily, but I am prepared for one, just as you are," Sanctu-Germainios said as they crossed the narrowest part of the space between the two stockades.

"Do you think we're being watched now?" Niklos asked, hesitating a little as they reached the outer wall.

"In this?" Sanctu-Germainios waved his free hand through the air. "They are welcome to try: I can barely make out the stable from here."

Niklos made a sound between a laugh and a sigh. "Why have they waited so long? They must suspect the monastery is empty."

"Very likely they do. They want to strike when the monastery is most exposed and its defenses are at their weakest." He stopped at the foot of the ladder and looked closely at Niklos. "You know this. Why do you continue to—"

"Pester you? For reassurance. I don't know you well, but I realize that you're not like Olivia. You are a self-contained man, you don't reveal yourself as readily as she does. You keep your own counsel. If you are hopeful or discouraged, you make no show of either. You don't dissemble, but you aren't forthcoming, either. Olivia is much more open; she opines on everything. You puzzle me often, she never. I've tried to discern your purpose, and half the time I'm unable to figure it out. So I tell you what I understand and hope you'll confirm it for me." He turned away, shocked at his own outburst. "I intend no disrespect, Dom."

Sanctu-Germainios contemplated Niklos' restless movements, saying at last, "I did not think you did." He began to climb toward the battlement walkway. "We will be through here shortly. Then we can take our place on the battlements to watch for the arrival of the Huns."

"What if they don't come?" Niklos asked. "What do we do then?"

"If the Huns are not here by nightfall, we will set fire to the walls, collect our horses and mules, and take the southern hunters' track leading toward Drobetae."

"In the dark?" Niklos climbed up behind Sanctu-Germainios. "Why don't we just set fire to the place and leave now?"

"Because the Huns would know that the fire had been set, and they would search for us. Given their numbers, they would find us." He reached the walkway, turned, and offered his hand to Niklos, pulling him up the last few rungs with no apparent effort.

Niklos swallowed once, hard, then scowled. "I'll try not to keep badgering you, Dom."

"And I will try to explain myself," Sanctu-Germainios promised him as they began their work of applying oil to as many of the strawmen as possible. They had completed half of their task when the sound of hoof-beats reached them, at a distance, but moving at a trot.

"Huns," said Niklos.

"Down the ladder. Leave the jugs. We need our torches." Sanctu-Germainios had already dropped his and was making for the ladder, his satchel swinging along his side.

"At the gate-tower?"

"Yes. Hurry." He was on the ground, prepared to run. "Hurry," he repeated, starting away from the outer wall with amazing speed.

Niklos rushed after him, but could not keep pace with Sanctu-Germainios' uncanny speed. He continued to run with dogged purpose, reaching the gate-tower as Sanctu-Germainios emerged from the tower onto the battlement walkway, a burning torch in his hand. "Are you going to light them now?"

"No; as soon as they break through the outer wall; we need as many of them in the space between the walls as possible,"

Sanctu-Germainios answered. "For now, will you go to the monks' church and ring the bell twice?"

"Why?"

"So that it may seem that there are more men here than is actually the case; the longer they are confused, the better it is for us," came his answer. "Then go to the alarm and sound it loudly, so that it might seem that there are soldiers still here to defend this place."

"All right," said Niklos, and ran off to the monks' church. He found the bell-rope quickly, rang it twice, then rushed on to the courtyard between the dormitories where the alarm hung. He struck the hanging brass tube four times with the mallet beside it, and for a moment he could no longer hear the sounds of horsemen approaching. "They're coming up the river track," he said to himself, troubled by the ease with which the Huns were advancing. With the main approach still blocked by the rock-fall, the river track was the most well-marked and the easiest of all the hunters' trails. He heard the abrupt orders shouted to the horsemen; the sound goaded him into speeding back to the gate-tower and up the ladder. "Do you see them?" he asked as he came up to Sanctu-Germainios on the platform.

"Not clearly. They are too far away from us for me to determine what—" He stared intently. "They are gathering at the top of the lake, and that should bring them to the makeshift gate in the outer wall." His night-seeing eyes were less hampered by the dark, but the mist blurred all that moved in the distance.

"Do you think they know about the stockade getting burned by Monachos Anatolios?" Niklos looked directly at the torch flaming near them in its iron sconce.

"If the spy inside the monastery did not tell them, their scouts must have done so," Sanctu-Germainios said.

"Doesn't that worry you?" Niklos demanded, finding comfort in talking more than in any response he was given.

"Yes, it does, but for now, I must put my attention on the problems actually confronting us here, not on what I speculate could happen. We have anticipated as much as we could, and done what we can to prepare for any contingency." He thought back to the many battles he had fought, in his native land, in Anatolia, in Egypt, in Greece, in Gaul, and as quickly as he recalled them he wished them away, knowing he needed to center his vigilance on the Huns and the stratagem he hoped would succeed. He realized that Niklos wanted to hear more from him, so he said, "You know what our plans are; you can carry them out whether I am able to or not. Use your good sense and you will win free of this place."

Niklos glowered. "You're not planning something rash, are you?—something I don't know about. Something Olivia wouldn't approve."

"I am planning to do the things we have agreed upon, but that does not mean that the Huns will permit us to best them." He went silent, listening to the shouts and war-cries of the Huns as they started up from the lake toward the damaged outer wall of the monastery.

"I wish this fog would lift," said Niklos, needing to keep conversing.

"I hope it will not," said Sanctu-Germainios. "The less the Huns see clearly the better for us." He drew his sword. "Get ready."

Niklos took hold of the battle-axe that had been slung across his back; he unfastened the hook and swung the weapon around. "Ready," he said, and started along the battlements, working his way toward the mid-section of the inner wall.

"At least it is damp enough to render their bows inefficient," Sanctu-Germainios said as he checked the straw-men along the wall.

"The damp softens their bow-strings, doesn't it," said Niklos to show he grasped Sanctu-Germainios' meaning.

"Yes. Just as it softens the skeins on the ballistas." He went into the small tower that stood at the half-way point along the inner wall; he climbed up to the platform and peered into the thickening fog. "I can see about thirty mounted men headed this way, but I hear many more than that."

Niklos listened. "Many more than thirty," he agreed, becoming restive. "A lot of men for the two of us to take on."

Sanctu-Germainios swung his sword, testing its heft. "Wait until most of them are inside—"

"—the outer wall. I remember," he said testily, although he knew he had been about to set the oil-soaked straw-men alight.

Sanctu-Germainios listened, his full attention on the sound of the company of Huns. "There are more arriving, I would guess another forty," he said a little bit later as he came down from the platform. "They are about to circle the outer wall, to decide where to break through."

"Do you think they'll set the wall on fire?" Niklos asked.

"You mean before we do?" Sanctu-Germainios shook his head. "No. They are not carrying torches. Take heed of everything you hear."

"Do you want to remain here, or shall we—"

"We should stay in position until we know where the Huns will break through. Keep in the cover of the tower if you can. The longer we can remain undetected, the more chance we have to get away. We do not want to draw their attention yet." Sanctu-Germainios motioned for Niklos to be silent. "They have started to move."

The noise of their horses' hooves grew louder, pulsing like the sea. There were occasional shouts as the van of the company followed around the outer wall toward the gate-tower, their mounts at the canter.

Niklos was still, as much from fear as in response to Sanctu-Germainios' order. "There're more than a hundred of them."

"At least a hundred," said Sanctu-Germainios. "I think there may be as many as one hundred fifty."

That total increased Niklos' dread. "So many." He lapsed into a brief silence. "Do you think we'll actually get away?"

"I hope we will," said Sanctu-Germainios, lifting his sword again. "The more we can avoid confrontation the greater our chances are."

A wailing cry arose from the Huns as they encircled the outer wall, a sound similar to the howls of wolves, but deeper and more menacing. There was very little echo, which made the sound yet more disconcerting.

"What if they don't come in the new gate? If they come in the gate-tower, how will we get to the outer wall to set the second straw-men afire?"

"I hope they will take the new gate; it is less formidable than the main gate. The new gate is better-placed for a raid, as well, since it allows the Huns to reach the river track without being exposed to defensive assault. It is the easiest to bring down, as well." Sanctu-Germainios moved quickly, rising in the archers' niche to look out on the enemy horsemen.

A sudden, shattering moan punctuated by axe-blows rent the air; the Huns not at the new gate went rushing back to it to help to break it down. A few of them were screaming encouragement to their comrades.

The battering continued for a short while, then the wood groaned and cracked.

"Be ready. They will get through quickly, now the gate is gone." Sanctu-Germainios seized his torch.

Niklos was shaken; the determined vehemence of the horse-men scared him badly; to reassure himself, he muttered, "Light these straw-men, then down to the dormitories and set them on fire. Then, using the smoke for cover, go to the outer wall and light the straw-men there before we go out through the open gate."

"Exactly," said Sanctu-Germainios. "You will need your torch."

"I have it," he said, trying not to listen to the new gate being pulled apart, the cheers of the Huns marking its destruction more than the scrape and thud of its collapse. The clamor of the Huns grew louder as they poured through the hole left in the wall, fanning out as they got into the space between the two walls. Most of the men rode toward the small fields and the paddocks and pens, where their jubilant victory turned to wrath as they discovered that the livestock was gone and the fields were empty.

"Now," said Sanctu-Germainios, and flung his torch some distance along the wall into two straw-men fastened over a small catapult; the figures seemed to resist the flames; the torch began to smoke.

"What do we—?" Niklos whispered, watching as a number of Huns rode toward the inner wall, drawn by the noise and the momentary flare of light.

"Wait; wait," said Sanctu-Germainios. He started toward the ladder, observing the straw-men expectantly. "Keep your torch out of sight. Stay in the tower."

"But you—" Niklos began, only to be interrupted by a whump as the two straw-men startlingly flared alight.

The Huns pulled back from the inner wall and the spreading tongues of fire that fanned out from the two figures along the walkway to the next straw-man held in place; the first sparks struck. Abruptly one of the nearest Huns shouted something, and the words passed among the ranks in troubled, angry yells.

"Niklos! Come!" Sanctu-Germainios called to him from the foot of the ladder. "Bring your torch."

"Right!" Niklos replied, seizing his torch from its sconce, thrusting the handle of his axe through his belt, and descending as rapidly as he could. He was a little breathless as he touched the ground and accounted for it by the presence of increasing smoke instead of keyed-up nerves. "They know, don't they?"

"That the figures on the battlements are dolls? It seems so." Sanctu-Germainios opened the tower door a slit and watched the Huns milling, most of them keeping their distance from the increasing fury of the fire.

"They'll see us if we run for the dormitories. We're on foot." Niklos bit his lip to stop talking.

"Then we wait until the smoke is a bit thicker. They will stay away from it, and it will cover our—"

Much of the inner stockade was starting to burn, and the first two straw-men were little more than ash; one of the Huns threw a spear into one of the figures, and screamed out incomprehensible words as the straw-man tore open.

"They're furious," Niklos said.

"They dislike being fooled," said Sanctu-Germainios. "And they do not want to leave here empty-handed."

The Huns retreated to the open space between the dormitories, crowded close together, watching the inner wall nervously.

From his place at the tower door, Sanctu-Germainios saw the horsemen milling, their perplexity increasing with the fire. "We can move shortly."

"Good; I'm getting hot," Niklos complained, for the nearness of the flames rattled what little equanimity he had been able to maintain. "The stockade is starting to burn."

"Yes; the fire is getting nearer than the Huns," said Sanctu-Germainios. He raised his head, staring up into the thickening air. "There will be guards at the edge of the main company," he said, then slipped out of the door. "Be aware of them. They are the most dangerous for us."

"Why?" Niklos asked, more from jitteriness than any lack of understanding.

"They must know that there are still people here," said Sanctu-Germainios. "How else would that fire get started? In this weather it could hardly be an accident. So the guards will be looking for us." He edged away from the tower, through the roiling smoke, going toward the largest dormitory; he could hear Niklos' soft steps behind him. He was relieved that neither he nor Niklos had to breathe, for it meant they would not cough as the smoke became denser. He touched the side of the dormitory and felt for the large pile of rags he had laid at the door after the last party of refugees and monks had left. They had been soaked in pitch and would burn quickly and tenaciously as soon as Niklos put his torch to them.

"What do you think? Do I light them now?" Niklos almost ran into him.

"Yes. The stack is right—" He stopped, shoved Niklos away, and swung his sword, feeling its impact and hearing a yelp of pain and surprise, followed at once by the whump of a body falling.

Niklos had staggered a few paces away, his torch still clutched in his hand, its light revealing a Hunnic warrior splayed on the ground, a deep gash in his abdomen. Niklos gawked at the dying man. "Did he almost—"

"He did his best," said Sanctu-Germainios, wiping the blood from his Byzantine blade. "If he has found us, others might. Get the pitch burning, and we will go on to the outer wall."

The Hun on the ground moaned, but the sound was weak; blood fountained ever more slowly from the wound across the middle of his body.

Niklos shuddered. "The dormitory and the outer wall." He thrust his torch into the pile of rags, holding it there until it smoldered, sparked, and combusted. Niklos jumped back and almost slipped in the spreading pool of blood around the fallen Hun.

"Compose yourself," Sanctu-Germainios told him, not unkindly. "You can crumple when we are safely out of here."

It was a demanding effort, but Niklos managed to gather his scattering thoughts. "I'm ready."

"Good." He looked around the end of the dormitory. "Keep as near to the next building as you can. The smoke is not as thick on the other side."

"Shouldn't we wait until there's more smoke?" Niklos knew the answer, but had to ask the question.

"If there were fewer Huns or more of us, yes; we cannot afford to give them any opportunity to regroup and start an organized hunt for us." He hesitated, then added, "Your torch and your axe are both necessary to our escape."

Niklos ducked his head. "I'll be right behind you."

Sanctu-Germainios pointed in the direction they were to go. "Once the second dormitory is alight, then on to the outer wall."

"I know," said Niklos, trying to ignore the howls and shouts of the Huns, and the crackling roar of the fire.

As soon as he broke from cover of the dormitory, Sanctu-Germainios turned around as he ran, taking in all the increasing chaos between the walls of the monastery. He stayed as close to the surging smoke as he could, and slammed into the side of the next dormitory. He sought out the entrance to the building, and felt for the pile of rags as Niklos thumped into him. "These," he said, pointing to the pile of rags.

Niklos shoved the torch into the rags, and tried to keep from fretting while he waited for the rags to light. "The Huns are gathering in front of the stable."

"I saw," said Sanctu-Germainios, gesturing to Niklos to move on as the fire came alive.

"The wall; by the hunters' door."

Sanctu-Germainios slapped his arm. "Go!" He watched Niklos rush off into the smoky mist, then went after him, his sword up, to ensure Niklos as much protection as he could provide. They were almost at the outer wall when two mounted Huns bore down on them, thin, metal-tipped lances aimed at them. "Keep on!" he yelled to Niklos, then drew out three caltrops from his small satchel and flung them in the path of the charging horses, and an instant later saw the first horse rear, screaming, throwing his rider, and then rearing again as his on-side hoof touched the ground.

The second Hun drew rein, prepared to turn about and summon help. Sanctu-Germainios reached into his satchel, pulled out the dagger, and struck the second Hun between the shoulder-blades. The man jerked in the saddle, then sagged and slid off his horse, which went trotting, head up and ears back, toward the rest of the company. The first Hun lay unconscious, while his horse continued to shriek in pain.

Niklos appeared at Sanctu-Germainios' side, his torch gone, his battle-axe in his hands. "Let me take care of the horse," he said, distressed at its suffering.

"I will do it. You go open the hunters' door." Without waiting for a response, he swung his sword and went up to the wretched animal, cutting its throat in a tremendous upward swipe of his sword. He backed away as the horse fell, blood spraying in all directions. He looked toward the outer wall and saw one of the straw-men burning. There was no time to lose, for the hunters' door was directly beneath the part of the walkway already smoking. He bolted toward the hunters' door just as a few more Huns rode toward him. Those in the lead reached the caltrops, and crippled their mounts, one of the men screaming as he fell onto another caltrop. Sanctu-Germainios continued on, half-expecting to be fatally impaled on a lance before he could get out of the monastery.

"This way!" Niklos shouted, and Sanctu-Germainios ran toward the sound of his voice, lurching through the door as the battlement platform started to rain burning embers down on the Huns behind him.

Once outside the door, Sanctu-Germainios shoved Niklos ahead of him toward the narrow trail that led to the hermits' caves. Within the walls there was increasing panic as the Huns strove to get out of the new gate they had come in before the entire wall was blazing. "It will all be gone before nightfall," Sanctu-Germainios remarked, pausing to look back.

"Unless it starts to rain," Niklos reminded him.

"Our horses and mules are waiting," said Sanctu-Germainios.

As they climbed away from the fire, the smoke lessened, the heat vanished, and Sanctu-Germainios and Niklos were less than shadows in the mist.

Text of a report from Hredus in the Hunnic camp near Potaissa, to Verus Flautens, Praetor-General of Drobetae in the former Province of Dacia, written in the regional Gothic/Latin dialect with fixed ink on vellum, delivered ten months after being dispatched.

To the Praetor-General of Drobetae from the freedman Hredus,
    To Verus Flautens, Ave:
    This is to warn you to evacuate all Roman citizens in the former Province of Dacia to safer towns and forts south of the Danuvius River before the autumn rains make the roads impassable. The Hunnic King, Attila, has been taking advantage of the slow response from Roman officials and troops; he intends for his lieutenants to drive toward all the Roman towns north of the Danuvius before

winter. Since there are insufficient forces to stop them, the best course is to remove the Romans in this region from the path of danger. If only the Thirteenth Legion were still at Apulum to defend those faithful to the Roman Empire, East and West. Attila has paid the Praetor Custodis of Viminacium, Gnaccus Tortulla, handsomely to keep his troops south of the Danuvius, so any help you seek from him will surely be denied or postponed until all action is futile. In the meantime, Attila himself has taken his best companies and gone westward to strike at the Roman borders from here to Aquitania.

So it is that Huns are growing in strength daily, not only from an increase of their own numbers but from nobles and officers in the region giving their loyalty to Attila in exchange for rank and favor. Not three days ago, Tribune Rotlandus Bernardius of Ulpia Traiana arrived here with fourteen of his soldiers, and was welcomed as a hero not only by the Huns but by the Gepidae and Goths who have joined Attila's companies of foreign allies. Bernardius informed Attila's advisors that the Sanctu-Eustachios the Hermit monastery is all but deserted and ripe for the picking, and that if a company of soldiers were dispatched at once, the remaining goods and treasure could be taken without any true opposition; it would gain the valley and lake for the Huns, and the advantage of a place high enough to offer a superior view of the whole region. Since the monastery can be reached in two days' steady riding, a company was ordered out, charged with that task. They are expected back in five days with plunder from the monastery, especially foodstuffs and livestock.

Tribune Bernardius is not the only Roman officer assisting in the dismantling of the former province: I have seen three Praetors, seven column commanders, fifteen Tribunes other than Bernardius, twenty-two Centurions, and in excess of fifty soldiers. There are even nine scribe-monks and four former tax collectors among those who have made themselves allies of the Huns. They are shown respect and offered titles and privilege for their treachery.

This camp has upwards of four thousand men—a considerable number with Attila and many of his troops gone westward—and as many horses in it; all of them have the smell of victory and plunder in their nostrils; it is well-known that the intention of Attila is to have his men take and hold all the towns, villages, forts, and monasteries in this part of the Carpathian Mountains while his army makes its main push to the towns the Huns do not yet control. I have seen that Attila has been altering his methods of fighting to give him equal footing against Roman and Byzantine soldiers, increasing the danger they pose to us all. They have already surrounded more than half of the territory in these mountains that they wish to hold and there are only a few safe roads out of the Hunnic noose. For that reason, I will have to send this to Aquincum with instructions to have it carried to Drobetae by courier, and pray that none of the Hunnic armies have got to Aquincum or Drobetae ahead of the courier. I trust you will have it in time to make arrangements for your defense before winter sets in. I will leave camp after the first snow and I will hope to greet you at the start of the New Year, when I look forward to the reward you have promised me for my clandestine service to you and to all Roma. And I trust that when I see you, I will find my sister well.

This on the eighth day before the Autumnal Equinox,

> *Hredus*
> *freedman of Drobetae*

EPILOGUE

Text of a letter from Ragoczy Sanct' Germain Franciscus at Sa-lonae in the Province of Illyricum to Atta Olivia Clemens at Arae Flaviae in Noricum, written in Imperial Latin with fixed ink on vellum, carried by private courier, and delivered ten weeks after being dispatched.

To my much-loved Olivia, the greetings of Ragoczy Sanct' Germain Franciscus, or as I am still currently styled in this part of the Empire, Dom Feranescus Rakoczy Sanctu-Germainios:

The search is over at last. I have finally found her, and it is as you supposed—although I am unfathomably saddened to learn that Nicoris has come to dislike the necessities of her vampire life, and that the Blood Bond is insufficient to compensate for the burden her existence has become. Her death four years ago was not so terrible that it left her shocked and appalled with her changed state; she has said she would have preferred to have my company when she first woke to our life; she succumbed to the same fever that killed Antoninu Neves, a kind of complicated lethargy that was marked by pain in the guts and muscles of the legs. A number of mercenaries died of it at about the same time. Nicoris was hard put to explain her survival to Neves' comrades, and has sought the privacy of setting herself up once again herding goats, gathering herbs, and weaving. In the five nights I spent in her tent, I could not change her mind. She said of Neves that her time with him, more than five years, was better than she had thought they would be, but that generally she disliked the life of a mercenary's woman.

I offered to provide her with a villa and servants, but she said she would not accept either from me, for that would seem to her as if I were paying her for her companionship at Sanctu-Eustachios the Hermit, which would cheapen our passion in her memory. That is also the reason she says that she intends to end her undead life: she has no desire to remain in her current state, dependent on the passion and generosity of spirit from others. She has said she did not mind supplying my needs as she did, but that she does not want to be the one requiring the blood and the intimacy it corroborates.

She has not told me how she plans to achieve the True Death, but assures me that she will be gone before the year is quite out. Were I younger than I am, I would try to persuade her to give this new state some time, but as she says her intimate encounters have become worse, not better, in the last four years, and that the more she fuses her desire with others, the more she feels the loss of herself, a slipping of her own distinguishability that has brought her despair and loneliness, which is agony to her. What am I to do, in the face of her suffering? She and I have touched; her despondency is immediate to me, and undeniable, and I will miss her as I would an arm. I know I cannot compel her to live our life in wretchedness, nor would I want to if it were in my power. But the thought of her loss transfixes me with sorrow as much as the loss of Hadrianus sank you into grief, not quite a century ago: his True Death was not of his choosing, but your mourning was not lessened because he was beheaded by the order of Shapur II rather than through his own volition.

Nicoris has told me that she wishes to return to her native earth, near Serdica, where her father was garrisoned with other Hunnic mercenaries, and where she and her brothers and sisters were born. Her mother and father are dead and she has no knowledge of what became of the rest of her family, yet she feels the pull of her native earth as all of us do who come to this life, and it is her desire to Truly Die there. Rogerian, or if you prefer, Rugierus has offered to escort her home, for there is a great deal of fighting between this city and Serdica, and a woman alone is at great risk. So far, Nicoris has declined his generous tender of service, and has flatly told me that she does not want to have to refuse a similar proposal from me, so prefers that I not make one, sparing us both the mortification of her declination.

In spite of Huns and their relentless forays through Greek, Gothic, Eastern and Western Roman territories, I find that I, too, long for my native earth. Rogerian and I will sell my house in Constantinople and hire an escort to get us across the Danuvius, then we will continue on our own into that part of the mountains beyond the forests, and to the region my father ruled so long ago.

Your invitation to join you and Niklos Aulirios in Arae Flaviae, or any of your other estates, is truly magnanimous of you, and were things otherwise, I would accept with grateful alacrity, but for now, I believe I must withdraw for a time, to reconcile myself to the loss of Nicoris, and to resign myself to the calamitous turn that has blighted the world around us. Whatever good I may gain from my seclusion, know that your compassion will be a large factor in it, and your on-going undead life will bring me consolation. You may rest assured that wherever I go, you will learn of it as quickly as my couriers can find you. And until that time when we once again see each other, remember that my love continues and deepens.

> *Ragoczy Sanct' Germain Franciscus*
> *(his sigil, the eclipse)*

by my own hand on the Ides of September in the 449ᵗʰ Christian year.